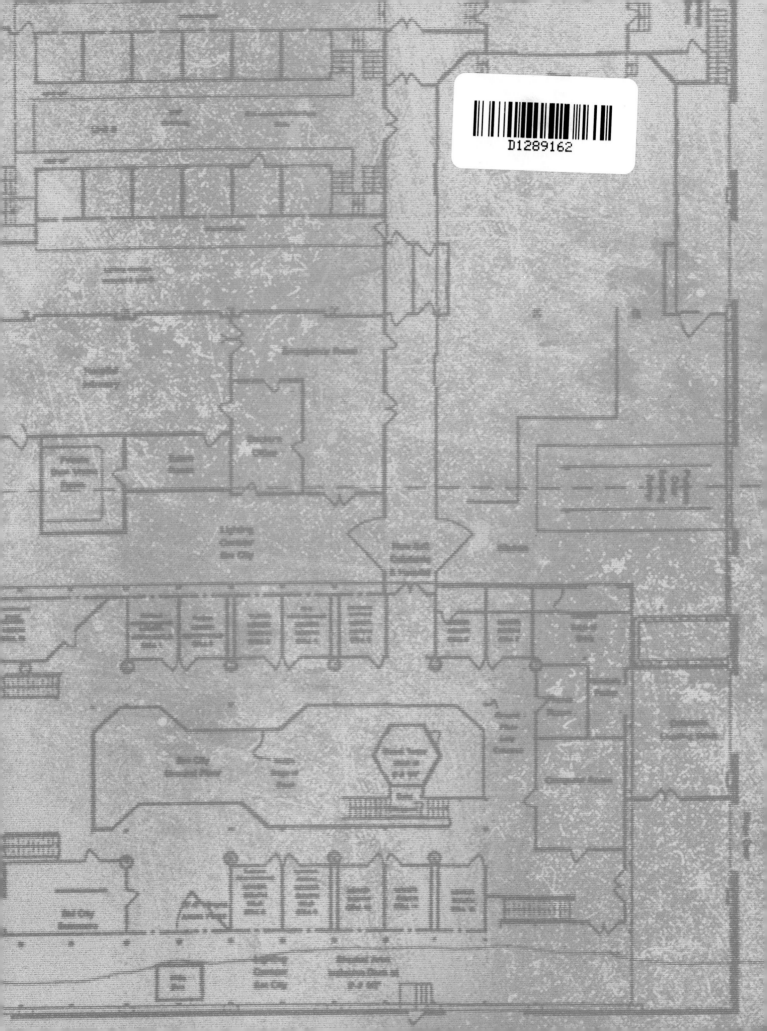

BEHIND THESE WALLS
The Journal of Augustus Hill

OZ.

BEHIND THESE WALLS
The Journal of Augustus Hill

HarperEntertainment
An Imprint of HarperCollins*Publishers*

Photograph on p. iii courtesy of Chris Cozzone/HBO.

Photographs on the following pages are courtesy of Eric Liebowitz/HBO: xiv, 3, 5, 9, 11, 14 (top and bottom), 15, 17, 19, 27, 32, 35, 38, 41, 47, 49, 56, 57, 61, 63, 64, 68, 71, 74, 76, 83, 86, 87, 88, 89, 90 (top and bottom), 93, 95, 97, 98, 99, 102, 103, 107, 109, 112, 115, 116, 119, 120 (top and bottom), 121, 122, 123, 124, 125, 127, 129, 143, 145, 148, 150, 154, 172, 174, 176, 185, 187, 195, 200, 205, 208, 234–235.

Photographs on the following pages are courtesy of Larry Riley/HBO: 35, 148, 162, 169, 172, 221.

Photographs on the following pages are courtesy of Paul Schiraldi/HBO: 164, 174, 176, 185, 187.

HarperCollins books may be purchased for educational, business, or sales promotional use. For information please write: Special Markets Department, HarperCollins Publishers Inc., 10 East 53rd Street, New York, NY 10022.

FIRST EDITION

Designed by Adrian Leichter

Printed on acid-free paper

Library of Congress Cataloging-in-Publication Data has been applied for.

ISBN 0-06-052133-3

03 04 05 06 07 ❖/RRD 10 9 8 7 6 5 4 3 2 1

This book is dedicated
to the
actors
of Oz.
They have balls
for days.

— TOM FONTANA

Contents

Epilogue by Tom Fontana

Behind the Walls of Oz:
A Year-by-Year Account

Cast List

Acknowledgments

Many thanks to Kirk Acevedo, Adewale Akinnuoye-Agbaje, Chris Albrecht, Mark Baker, Josh Behar, Irene Burns, Howard Cohn, Bree Conover, Martin Felli, Jim Finnerty, Alexa Fogel, Cara Grabowski, Miranda Heller, Ernie Hudson, Sean Jablonski, Rob Kenneally, Terry Kinney, Barry Levinson, Shannon Logan-Torres, Peter Megler, Rita Moreno, muMs, Sunil Nayar, Richard Oren, Harold Perrineau, Jeffrey Peters, Bridget Potter, Candace Ross, Debbie Sarjeant, J. K. Simmons, Russell Schwartz, Carolyn Strauss, Lee Tergesen, Lena Tymczyna, Claire Wachtel, Eamonn Walker, Sean Whitesell, Brad Winters, and Dean Winters.

BEHIND THESE WALLS
The Journal of Augustus Hill

PROPERTY OF OSWALD PENITENTIARY

Behind These Walls:

THE JOURNAL OF AUGUSTUS HILL

Entries from 1997

Monday 3.24.97

Freedom—to come and go as I please—is exactly what I don't have, what I'll probably never have again. I know I'll never get out of this fucking wheelchair, beyond hoisting myself into bed or onto the toilet, and I don't think I'll make it out of prison. I won't even be eligible for parole until 2015; that's another eighteen years. Will I still be alive then? I doubt it, though you know, it's funny, being paralyzed is probably the best insurance policy I could have. In Oz, it's all about power, who controls who and who controls what—drugs, sex, whatever—and when the hacks or the inmates (don't matter which) look down on me, stuck in this chair, it's almost like they don't see me at all, like I'm no threat to them. Even guys who knew me when I was on the street dealing drugs, guys who know I'm in for life for killing a cop, often don't bother me. Don't bother *with* me, either.

Do I want to keep living like this, long enough to make it to my parole hearing? Shit, by the time that day arrives, I'll be pushing fifty, still paralyzed from the hips down. The doctors said that I won't get any worse, but I don't trust those prison doctors any more than I trust the cop who cuffed my hands behind my back and threw me off the roof.

Lucky to have survived, people said. Maybe so, but they don't know what it's like to be living in two prisons at the same time—Oz and this wheelchair. If I *am* lucky, it's because of a few people on the outside who haven't turned their backs on me: Annabella, who still loves me; my mom; and Burr Redding. If it wasn't for Burr maybe I wouldn't be here at all; after all, he's the one who got me into dealing drugs, convinced me there weren't any other options in the projects. He was my dad's pal, they went to Nam

Opposite: Augustus faces hard times in Oz.

Burr Redding, lifelong friend of Augustus's father and mentor to Augustus after his father's death in Vietnam, is reunited with Augustus in Oz in 2001, following his conviction for first-degree murder and attempted murder. As boys, Redding and the elder Hill were inseparable friends, sharing good times and bad on the hardscrabble streets of the inner city. Even after both boys fell in love with Eugenia, who later became Augustus's mother, their friendship survived, even deepened. In 1966, Burr and his buddy were drafted and went to Vietnam together. There Augustus's father was killed in a firefight as Burr watched helplessly.

Burr returned from Vietnam in 1970, despondent, embittered, and hopelessly addicted to heroin, a drug as accessible in Southeast Asia as on the streets of American cities. He worked his way up the chain of drug distribution in the ghetto, from runner to supplier, growing into a force to reckon with—fearless, authoritarian, and dangerous to cross.

At the same time, Burr did his best to play the part of father to Augustus, whose real father had never seen him (Augustus was born while the two friends were in Vietnam), and helped look after the boy's mother. He also married, but he and his wife, Delia, had no children of their own. When Augustus was a teenager, Burr drew him into the world of drugs as dealer and user. It was the only world either of them knew.

together, in the same unit, and when my dad didn't make it back, Burr stepped in as guardian angel for my mom and me. But for Burr, life was a struggle for survival, and survival, to Burr, meant dealing. And using.

A minute ago I wrote that Annabella still loves me, and I believe she does, but I know the odds are those feelings won't last until I get out of here, if I ever do. She has stuck by me through the surgery, the rehab, my trial, and the almost two years I've done so far. She's always gotten along with my mom, who, since I got sent to Oz, has really kept an eye on her. But my wife's a foxy woman, young, and one day she's going to wake up and realize that there's more to life than a phone call once a week and an overnight conjugal every few months.

I don't want to turn bitter and blame everybody but myself for my problems. I can't afford to; I need the few folks I can depend on, inside Oz and on the outside, too much. Even Burr, who damn sure made himself scarce after I got busted—'course, that was to make sure he didn't follow me into prison. Since then, he hasn't contacted me, not directly, but I know he helps Mom out with money—one of the many things I can't do now.

I've got to deal with not being in control. Other guys in Oz can't accept not being able to pick up the phone or knock on somebody's door and take care of business. So if something happens to a guy's family or friends, he goes ballistic. And since he can't do anything about it, he shanks another inmate—somebody who's got nothing to do with his problems—or he provokes a fight and gets himself killed. Some guys just lose hope and give up. Like I said earlier, in here people don't see me as a player in the struggle for power, so as long as I don't provoke them, they don't confront me. But I don't want to give up on myself, start acting like I'm as invisible as they think I am.

At least I don't have to worry too much about whether my family's okay—paying their bills, making the rent, shit like that. Moms has always worked, insisted on keeping her job even when I tried to get her to quit, told her I'd take care of her. Said she liked having her independence, didn't want to interfere too much with Annabella and me, and working in the church office gave her the chance to be with her friends and feel like she was being useful. Annabella's got a job now, too, at one of the big department stores in the city. She's always loved clothes, and when I was still on the outside she'd sometimes talk about going to the Fashion Institute to become a designer. With me in Oz, she says she can't do that, but she's got plans to work her way up, get into management.

It's a good thing we didn't have kids before I got arrested. We'd been talking about it, and Moms wanted a grandchild worse than anything. I'd like children, too, but now it's too late. Besides, even with Burr's help, I'm not sure Annabella and Moms could manage.

Oz is the worst place I've ever been. Not because 1,400 inmates are crowded into a gloomy, sprawling place that should've been torn down before I was born. I grew up in projects and tenements as ratty as this place, but in Oz it's like life on the streets has been thrown into a pressure cooker with the flame turned up to high. Whatever it was that got you into prison in the first place is probably inside, too, only in Oz there ain't no women (unless you count a handful of female hacks), or families, or—for the most part—friends. And the worst is, there's no relief from the deadly routine.

Burr Redding joined Augustus in Oz in 2001.

Experimental Prisons

ALEXANDER MACONOCHIE (1787–1860), geographer and penal reformer, was superintendent of the penal settlement at Norfolk Island, New South Wales, Australia, from 1840 to 1844. He introduced a "Marks System," under which each prisoner's conduct was evaluated daily and by means of which "a record will be kept of every man's conduct; he will advance from punishment to probation, and from probation to entire release, as he behaves himself. His fate will be in his own hands." At Norfolk Island, Maconochie introduced the concept of rehabilitation and created the first experimental prison.

All in all, my small country was proving a daunting site for a free settlement as well as for a convict settlement. Nature impeded the former, and the paradox of liberty within punishment hindered the other.

Every scrap of further freedom I allowed the convicts had its cost in increased danger to some of them, though increased opportunities for most. Even the first issue of knives to allow them to eat without tearing the meat ration with their hands increased the number of murderous and injurious attacks. It was not that previously they had lacked weapons—any prison which has a lumber yard and any metal work also produces contraband arms—but what they had as weapons were less freely available, less easily to hand, less concealable, and the number of attacks of convict on convict thereby increased in gravity if not in number. As I wandered my small suzerainty, I had no doubt that all in all the changes I had made were for the better, but their costs weighed on me. The scattered humpies built by the Island ticket-of-leave men, with their few cattle and occasional crops, were vastly to be preferred to the crowded prisons they previously inhabited, and I was convinced these improved conditions had no tendency whatsoever to make men in Ireland or England or Van Diemen's Land or New South Wales more inclined to be transported to them. That was not the cost. The cost lay in the nature and heritage of these men and the women who had accompanied them, both the convicts and the soldiers. Generally speaking, they had been raised in poverty and adversity and hostility by parents (if they had them) who also endured those conditions, and that they had not been weaned from their aggressions by condign punishments for crime was not at all surprising. I knew my way of treating my subjects was to be preferred to that which preceded me on this island, but I could well see how some men and women of goodwill might disagree.

Source: Norval Morris, Maconochie's Gentlemen: The Story of Norfolk Island and the Roots of Modern Prison Reform (New York: Oxford University Press, 2002).

Instead, we got alliances, lots of them, especially when it comes to smuggling drugs in from the outside and selling them to inmates who are using. And there are plenty of those. In the language of Oz, heroin is "tit," I guess because for so many guys it's like mother's milk. We're supposed to be in here to keep us away from whatever it was that landed us in prison, but it's probably even easier to score drugs in Oz than in the middle of the projects where I grew up. For that we have the hacks to thank; they may be on the state payroll, but plenty of them also work for Nino Schibetta, head of the Wise Guys, who seems to control everything but the front gate. Between the drugs, the violence, and the fact that it's impossible to learn how to do anything that isn't a crime, Oz is a trap, a maze that usually leads right back to a cell. Guess that's what they call a "vicious circle."

So these days the buzz is all about Cell Block 5, the new "experimental" wing. It's scheduled to open in a few days, and Tim McManus has been picking the "lucky few" who'll be the lab rats in his experiment. The idea, they're telling us, is that we accept more responsibility for our own lives, and in exchange, we'll get more privileges—they're calling them "freedoms"—than inmates do in gen pop: we can wear our own clothes, move around the cell block more freely, have easier access to books and education, and shit like that.

Tim McManus "runs" Em City, but Leo Glynn runs Oz.

The inmates have started referring to the place as Em City, like in the movie *The Wiz*. We're told there'll be about sixty inmates lucky enough to be part of it. McManus is doing all the interviews himself, handpicking the people he wants. All he talks about is the three "r"s: responsibility, rehabilitation, and redemption. Maybe he thinks he can save everyone, but can you "save" people just by changing a few of the rules and swapping bars for glass walls? Em City doesn't sound much like summer camp to me, or even the Fresh Air Fund, but

he's picked me and I'll go. I hear they're building access ramps and elevators for the handicapped. Yeah, right.

I wonder what the warden thinks about the so-called experiment hatching in his domain. Leo Glynn's a tough law-and-order motherfucker who started out as a hack at Oz maybe twenty years ago and worked his way up through the ranks. I'm told he's got a soft side in the right circumstances, but from what I've seen of Glynn, retribution's more his style than any of the other "r" words.

PRISON VIOLENCE

According to [Alfonso's] sources and the ten years he spent on and off Rikers Island, "the Rock was a violent and crazy place" until the late 1990s. "Most of the fights were along racial lines. Blacks and Hispanics fought constantly. Gangs ran the dorms and controlled the phones." Of the two phones in each dorm, one belonged to the Bloods, a black gang, and the other to the Latin Kings, a Hispanic gang. "If you weren't part of a gang, you had to split a motherfucker's face open to get on the phone," he wrote. "Extortion, stealing, rape . . . I'd need an encyclopedia to complete the list." Jailhouse thugs "would extort punks for their commissary [goods purchased from the jail store] or try to make you their wife." Predatory inmates known as "booty bandits" forced weaker inmates into becoming their personal sex slaves and sometimes traded their sexual services for cigarettes and food from other prisoners.

"Inmates organized into gangs for security," he wrote. "Even today, anyone who goes to a C.O. for help is a 'rat' and the consequences are severe. Back then, death was not out of the question.

"All the officers would do for you after the inmates done fucked you up was move you to another dorm. And when the inmates in that dorm found out you snitched, you were dead meat."

Source: Jennifer Wynn, *Inside Rikers: Stories from the World's Largest Penal Colony* (New York: St. Martin's, 2001).

middle of Glynn's playground and gave Tim McManus the green light to make it happen. Maybe Glynn also sees an opportunity here; they say he's got political ambitions of his own, wants to be the next corrections commissioner himself, or even governor someday. Wouldn't that be fucking news, the first former corrections officer to be elected governor, not to mention the first black man? Maybe he's doing it all for his people, but I'll believe that when he starts making changes that aren't just window dressing.

And what about me? Am I agreeing to be a subject in McManus's great experiment just because I thought I'd have a little more freedom to wheel my paralyzed black ass around the prison? I'm not sure why I signed on. I sure as hell don't believe the Em City hype about redemption, and by the time I come up for parole—if I ever do—I doubt that Em City's still going to be around. A safer environment? Maybe, but if somebody's got it in for you, you can get shanked anywhere in less time than it takes to spit out your toothpaste, and that's not going to change in Em City. If anything, the atmosphere might be more explosive than anywhere else in Oz. McManus plans to choose a cross-section of Oz inmates—lifers and short-termers, guys with histories of violence and low-risk prisoners, blacks and whites and browns and everything in between—so the Em City population will reflect gen pop

People say that he didn't have much choice, that it was Martin Douglas, the corrections commissioner, who agreed to drop Em City right in the

and life on the outside. It's like he thinks he's Noah filling up the ark or something. I bet he's hoping that by throwing everyone together in one rec room they'll fight over who gets the remote for the TV instead of who controls the tit trade. The players in the drug business—the Homeboys and Latinos, who handle most of the retail dealing to their black and Hispanic brothers, and the Wise Guys, who control the flow of drugs into Oz and the wholesale trade inside—will be in each other's faces all the time. Then there's the Aryan Brotherhood—white supremacists preaching racist bullshit—and the Bikers, who don't believe in much of anything but try to keep on the Aryans' good side, in case the people of color gang up on them. The Bikers also try to keep the peace with the Wise Guys, because they love their tits as much as their tattoos.

I wonder if McManus will find some other people in wheelchairs for the "mobility-challenged" group in Em City and we'll train to compete in wheelchair basketball in the Special Olympics. (How I used to love that game! Still do, watching the NBA on TV and in my dreams.) Yeah, right. At least a move to Em City will be a change in the routine, at least for a while, and will help me fight the boredom. Because in here, it's the fucking routine, day after dull ass day, that takes the life out of you, more than anything else.

TRIBES IN OZ

As in many other maximum security prisons, gangs (or tribes) are important to the lives of inmates in Oz, and even, to a degree, in running the prison itself. With rare exceptions, prisoners who are members of a tribe are more able to defend themselves and to survive than those who try to go it alone.

Tribes often exist primarily to make money, especially from smuggling and selling drugs on the inside. This is certainly the case in Oz, where several of the most powerful tribes—Wise Guys, Homeboys, and Latinos—also control most of the drug traffic in the prison. One smaller group, the Irish, also participates in gambling and drug dealing outside the three-tribe cartel, often with the connivance of corrupt C.O.s who smuggle drugs and other contraband into Oz for their own profit. Other tribes, especially the Aryan Brotherhood and the Bikers, don't directly control either drug traffic or gambling (the other important economic activity in prisons); they exist primarily to protect their own members and intimidate outsiders.

The other important tribes in Oz include the gays as well as religious groups, notably Muslims and Christians.

Source: Jeffrey Ian Ross and Stephen C. Richards, *Behind Bars: Surviving Prison* (Indianapolis, Ind.: Alpha Books, 2002).

Wednesday 4.9.97

Moving Day tomorrow! By itself, moving's no big deal, but with just a few of us headed to Em City, you can feel the tension in the air. In prison, just like on the street, everybody's always looking for an edge, and guys have swallowed the hype that Em City'll have it all over gen pop. Inmates who've been selected for Timmy Boy's great experiment are excited, but they're also worried, and some of the guys who were passed over are resentful or jealous.

Inmates are used to getting shuffled around every couple of months—your cell gets switched, or your cell block, or you get a new cellmate. The reason? The hacks claim it's to flush out contraband—drugs and weapons, mostly—hidden in our cells, but I think it's the Law's way of reminding us who's in charge. Even the eight-by-ten-foot patch of real estate where we spend fourteen hours a day every day doesn't belong to us, it belongs to the state. Who we share our cells with, who our neighbors are, the state decides about that, too, to remind us—is there any fucking possibility we'd forget?—that we surrendered our freedom of association, along with the rest of our freedoms, when we were locked up. The inmates may be doing the time, but even our time is stamped "Property of Oswald State Penitentiary."

So when the word got out about Em City, it seemed as if everyone wanted in on the experiment. Tomorrow I'll be moving out of my cell and into a new glass-walled pod somewhere in Cell Block 5, along with the other lucky few who made the cut. I hope it's on the ground floor, so when the frigging elevator breaks down—if there is an elevator—I can still get around. Wherever it is, I'm fucking glad to be getting away from William Giles, my cellmate in gen pop, a bastard who doesn't know anything about black people except that he hates them. Every other word out of his mouth is "dirty nigger" this or that, for no fucking reason.

Thursday 4.10.97

Home sweet home? Not quite, but about sixty of us moved into Em City right after breakfast, and it's the quietest I can remember a cell block being since I was brought to Oz. Maybe it's because everything seems new: fresh paint on the walls, new furniture in the cells, and the public space looks like the waiting room of a bus station, or anyway some fucking place on the outside, instead of a prison. TV monitors built into the walls, and over in the corner near the entrance, a little laundry that's so close to the spitting image of a Laundromat that I wouldn't be surprised to see a goddamned Coke machine next to the dryers. What I didn't notice at first was that the bars are missing—except for the gate at the entrance to Em City, there aren't any! In gen pop the bars are everywhere, and it gets so that you look right through the door of your cell without seeing them. But today, when they're suddenly gone, I keep blinking my eyes, as if the bars' disappearance was some sort of magician's trick. Maybe it is, with Tim McManus playing Houdini, trying to fool us into thinking that we're

Opposite: Em City, with inmates in their pods.

somewhere else—not in prison any longer. Yeah, right! To convince me, Timmy Boy'll have to do a lot more than fill a rec room with a few TV sets and checkerboards.

What I see when I look around Em City doesn't whisper responsibility and rehabilitation to me, it says surveillance and control. Right in the center of Em City, up on a platform halfway between the first and second floors, there's a monitoring station, where twenty-four hours a day the guards will be watching every move we make. Through the glass walls of our cells and on their TV monitors they'll see us getting in and out of bed, drinking water, pissing, and for all I know they'll hear every word we say, even if we're talking in our sleep. We're stripped of our last freedom—privacy. Like being inside a fishbowl, except in Em City the spectators will be in the hollow center of a round fish tank, and the fish trapped behind glass walls all around them.

And those fish are sharks and piranhas and barracuda. Word is, the tribes that control the drugs are taking advantage of Timmy Boy's dreams of proving he can rehabilitate anybody to get their head honchos into Em City. Since I got inside, I've stayed as far away as I could from drugs—dealing, smoking, or snorting—but on the street I was a Homeboy

myself, so I know the brothers, Jefferson Keane and Simon Adebisi, Keane at the top of the pyramid of powder, and Adebisi trying to claw his way up to kick his "brother" off. They've got a lot in common, those two, dangerous to anybody who tries to fuck them over. But as of today, Keane's got the inside track, because he grew up in the city and worked the streets. Adebisi's Nigerian, so when he came into Oz he wasn't as connected to the local brothers. Schibetta tries to keep things calm and orderly—better for business that way—and Glynn seems to treat him almost with respect, instead of like any other inmate. It's weird, but sometimes you could almost think that Schibetta's a member of the prison staff—he's in charge of the kitchen (and probably smuggles drugs in with the deliveries) and always has a cell to himself—as if Glynn owed him something. But McManus's line is always "nobody gets special treatment." He got ideas about how to make prisons work in some university, not on the streets or inside a penitentiary, so maybe he doesn't realize how quick things can turn nasty without guys like Schibetta who know how to keep a lid on the violence.

So we're still in prison, and the hacks are still counting our asses—our mostly black asses, since four out of the five motherfuckers in here are black or Latino. And we're still locked in our cells from five P.M. until seven the next morning. Four-teen hours sealed inside a glass cell. Even if they're calling them "pods" in Em City—maybe because the place reminds somebody of that sci-fi movie where pods take over people's bodies—they're still fucking cells, and lights-out is still ten P.M. It's a few minutes after ten right now, on this first night in Em City, and it's so quiet it's creepy. Funny the things you get used to, but in gen pop you'd always hear guys talking after lights-out through the open bars of their cells: guys talking to their cellmates, their neighbors, and even—pretty common in prison—to themselves. Sometimes a C.O. would pay a visit to a prisoner he thought was making too much noise, tell him to shut the fuck up or rap on the cell bars with his nightstick, but most of the time the hacks left us alone at night. In Em City, we're cooped up behind plate-glass walls, so we can look across to the pods opposite our own, but we can't hear anything. It's like staring at a bunch of TV sets at once, with a different program on each one, and all of them have the sound turned off.

Making things worse—or better—I'm alone in this cell, at least for the time being. I guess because of my being in a wheelchair, they've given me a "private room" on the first tier. In the rest of Oz, there's no way that'll happen—unless, of course, you're in Solitary or in the Hole or in protective custody or some other part of ad seg. Everybody else even-

Separate but equal, even in the Oz cafeteria.

tually gets a cellmate—otherwise, I guess, the governor, the legislature, and half the newspapers and TV stations in the state would be yelling that the warden's running a country club, not a fucking maximum-security prison. Everybody, that is, but Nino Schibetta, who I'm told was a major player in the rackets on the outside. That's funny, me and him the only inmates in Em City with rooms of our own, though I'll bet when space gets tight I'll get a cellmate before Schibetta does. But as long as it lasts, I'll do my best to enjoy it—be grateful there won't be any arguments over space or dirt or the other petty shit that's always flaring up, and that I don't have to watch my ass 24/7, just in case my cellmate takes it into his head to flip out and shank

me or strangle me—but on this first night the quiet, the infernal fucking silence, is keeping me awake. Could be home is just another four-letter word.

Thursday 4.17.97

We've been in Em City since last Thursday, and the honeymoon, if there ever was one, is already over. People can get used to anything—good or bad—except maybe other people. Or maybe too many inmates swallowed Timmy Boy's line that they'd have more "freedom" in Em City than in gen pop. Free! Yeah, right. There's been so much talk about rules and responsi-

In Oz Can't Nobody Hear You Scream

I could've sworn I seen a muthafucka in my cell going

    through my personal effects

His fingers fingering my cigarettes

He came out like nothing was happening

Whistling his tune

So I mushed his ass like,

"Move motherfucka make room . . .

    Hey ain't that my cigarette hanging off the tip of your lip?"

I ain't even give him a chance for his confession

Just leveled his ass with all this aggression

Lefts, rights to the dolex

Boots to the grill

I'm like kill

He's like chill!!!!

Take that for me even being in this place

Take that for the C.O.'s baton across my face

Feel that for the lawyer who ain't give a fuck about me

Feel this for me even being enslaved by poverty fucka

Gimme my damn cigarettes!

"Oh these is Marlboros, I don't smoke these . . ."

Poem by muMs

bility and privileges and freedoms that I guess some of these guys have forgotten where they are—in fucking prison!—and the whacked-out system that put us on ice in the first place. The hacks beat Paul Markstrom the other day when he got into a shoving match with a white inmate, just to remind us we're still in Oz. Or worse,

they sent Jefferson Keane to the Hole for some bullshit reason that never happened, just to intimidate him. And the rest of us.

Meanwhile, Em City's starting to get crowded. The same place that a few days ago seemed like a mansion with more rooms than you could count is feeling like what it is: a dormitory for characters you don't want to live next door to. These inmates are getting in each other's faces over every little thing: Adebisi's got his favorite spot when he's watching TV (the shows are so fucking dumb, who gives a shit where he sits?), Joey chases a couple checkers players away from the table where Nino Schibetta likes to play pinochle (pinochle, for chrissakes!), not to mention the shit inmates fight about all over Oz: turf, and race, or sometimes it's just that somebody ripped off a guy's skin mag. Seems like the less you own, the worse you want it.

There were only a few bunks open after they moved us in last week, and now most of those are occupied by newbies who were processed in this morning. From the looks of it, McManus's philosophy is to handpick new candidates for Em City the minute they walk in the door, before they learn the ropes and get corrupted by the bad elements in gen pop. But you don't get sent to Oz from the Boy Scouts; before a guy is sentenced to a maximum-security joint like Oz, he's usually spent years getting educated on the street and he's probably done some hard time in juvie or the minor leagues. Wherever they've been, whatever they know, they're still in for a shock when they land in Oz. And I'm told that one of the newbies McManus tapped for Em City—Miguel Alvarez, a Latino drug dealer—must've left his street smarts behind when he was sentenced. One of the guys he was chained to when they brought the new crop in this morning shanked him in the chest. He's in the hospital, but I guess he's going to survive, because they're holding his bunk for him.

Two pods to stay out of—Adebisi's and Schillinger's (the leader of the Aryans)—are probably where a couple of the newbies are going to end up. All of McManus's talk about how this experimental block is going to teach us to redeem ourselves is gonna be put to the test when both those guys get a couple of green inmates, still punchy from their sentencing, in their clutches. With those two bastards, nothing is safe—not your money, not your threads, and not your ass.

Wednesday 4.23.97

Some guys have no luck! One of the new guys, Beecher, landed in the vacant bunk in Adebisi's pod. Adebisi must've scared the shit out of him pretty quick, because the next day he got permission to move in with Schillinger. Talk about out of the frying pan and into the fire! Beecher's as white as any member of Schillinger's Aryan Brotherhood, but that won't keep Schillinger from fucking him in the ass. The only difference between Schillinger and Adebisi on that score is that Adebisi prefers his prags young, but he's not particular about the color. Schillinger detests everything that's not just like him: white, masculine, heroic, American. I'm not sure what he's in Oz for, but he's probably in for attacking somebody who threatened his freedoms as an American white man. I wonder how Beecher ever ended up in Oz, though, and he's probably wondering the same damn thing! At work in the clothing factory yesterday, as soon as Rebadow started explaining to him how to do the job, he came back with shit like, "I'm not used to doing menial work. Not that I think it's demeaning or anything." Right! Turns out the bastard was a lawyer. Can't be much of a lawyer if he couldn't even keep his own ass out of a maximum-security joint like this.

It's nothing personal, but I got a funny feeling about Beecher. Whatever he did to get sent to Oz, it's a sure thing he never spent a night locked in a cell with anybody like Adebisi or Schillinger before. If he had, he'd have thought twice before

Beecher faces the calm before the storm.

Beecher transforms into Schillinger's prag.

falling for Schillinger's "friendly" suggestion to ask McManus to switch him from Adebisi's pod.

Adebisi's no choirboy; he'll take anything he wants, if he thinks he can get away with it, and he wants whatever he can hold in his fist: drugs, money, flesh. Power, property, and pleasure, that's what it comes down to in Oz, but Adebisi, at least, stops there. Schillinger's another story; he doesn't care so much about your stuff, he wants to humiliate you, to break your spirit. It makes you wonder what the state is thinking when they sentence a man like Beecher to a place like Oz. I'm told there's some sort of "get-tough" policy that aims to show that if you commit a crime, you'll be punished, rich or poor, black or white.

But does anybody believe that stripping a man of his identity and isolating him from his family is going to rehabilitate him, no matter what he was convicted of? For the state, Oz is nothing but a work camp, where the inmates toil in factories at slave wages. We're supposed to be learning to be good citizens, but I've never talked to anybody who believes that for a minute. For the inmates, it's the gladiator's ring, with a difference—sometimes instead of killing the loser, they fuck him.

I heard that Schillinger and Adebisi got a little nasty when Beecher came back to switch pods, and that if Diane Whittlesey, a guard, hadn't gotten between them things might've gone beyond words. Clueless Beecher probably still doesn't understand what prize prag material he is: doesn't know a thing about prisons or weapons, so he's defenseless against predators.

You want to laugh at Schillinger's Aryan Brotherhood in Oz, the one place where blacks and Latinos probably aren't treated any worse than the white inmates. But maybe that's one more reason for those racists to stick together. They're not used to being outnumbered by all of us black- and brown-skinned brothers, and since there's no love affair between them and tribes like the Wise Guys, they tend to hang out with themselves and the Bikers. Most of the other tribes—the Wise Guys, Homeboys, and Latinos, even the handful of Irish—exist more to do business, because they can trust each other more than they can members of the other tribes. And for protection, though they probably wouldn't have as much to protect themselves from if they weren't ripping each other off over drugs. But the Aryans, it's like racial superiority is their religion. Maybe that's it; they rally round their claim of white supremacy the way the Muslims rally round Allah and the Koran. Of course, the Muslims have Kareem Said, who's some talker even if you don't believe what he preaches.

Schillinger and other Aryans watch the action in Em City.

Love might make the world go round on the outside. Inside Oz, though, there isn't much love, but there's plenty of sex. Today, though, all the talk's been about death, Dino Ortolani's. Ortolani, a Wise Guy with a bad case of machismo, put Jefferson Keane's brother Billy in the hospital after Billy'd made a pass at him in the shower, so McManus had the inspired idea of teaching Ortolani tolerance by assigning him to work with AIDS patients in the infirmary. I guess the experiment worked, sort of, because Ortolani developed so much empathy for a junkie AIDS patient named Sanchez that he suffocated the bastard to help him end his suffering. When the alarm went out, the hacks beat Ortolani almost to a pulp, but I heard he was still so violent that even though they threw him in the Hole, Dr. Nathan had to sedate him. And while he was unconscious, somebody got into the Hole and torched him. Nobody's talking, but everybody suspects that Jefferson Keane was behind it, to avenge Ortolani's beating of his brother, who's still in the prison ward of Benchley Memorial Hospital.

Was that brotherly love talking, then, when Ortolani got torched, or was Keane just settling some old score from the drug wars or resentment over having to take Ortolani's shit in the kitchen, where they both worked? Keane's always been tight-lipped, and he sure as hell doesn't seem sentimental, but family's family. And maybe there's another side to the guy, a side with heart. A day or so ago I heard that he's asked for permission to marry his girlfriend, just when the governor announces that he's putting an end to conjugal visits. You got to admit the guy's got balls, or a great sense of irony: he's up for parole in seventy years or something, and he doesn't know when conjugals will be back, if ever, and what does he do? Starts hearing goddamned wedding bells!

For the rest of us, the governor's threat to pull the plug on conjugals (and what's to stop him?) is no laughing matter! Devlin dropped his bombshell on the afternoon news, and as soon as he did, there was a stampede to Sister Pete's office. Every married bastard in Oz (and some who thought they could pass their girlfriends off as wives) pushing to the front of the line to fill out the form for a conjugal while we can still get them. The sex is a big fucking deal, of course, but for me, at least, there's much more to conjugals than the sex. They're the only times when Annabella and I can feel like we're still a couple, still together. Out in the visiting room, we're always surrounded by inmates and families and hacks and shit, but

Jefferson Keane, settling a score . . .

when we're inside that little room by ourselves, we can almost forget about the walls surrounding Oz that separate us. When Annabella wakes up to the fact that we'll never live as husband and wife again—not even playing house overnight in a suite at "Hotel Oswald"—where will that leave us? And where will it leave me? So far, love has been good to us, in spite of my paralysis and this prison, but how much longer will we be able to hang on to it?

Devlin ran for governor on a promise to get tough on crime, and since he got elected he's been making good on his promise: bringing back the death penalty and getting rid of so-called luxuries for prisoners, like

smoking. Even with talk about rehabilitating prisoners and returning them to society as useful citizens, the public prefers to believe that prison's a one-way street and inmates don't have the right to stay connected to the lives they left behind. John Q doesn't understand— or doesn't want to—that often the only thing keeping an inmate human is the family that's waiting for him on visiting days.

The best thing that happened to me in all those years I was dealing was Annabella. She wasn't no angel sitting at home in the suburbs and turning a blind eye to where all that cash was coming from. She enjoyed the life we were living—the cash, the clothes, the highs, even the celebrity. People on the street recognized us, and we got off on feeling important. I was The Man, and Annabella never said, "Honey, let's get out of this life." If she had, I wouldn't have listened, but she was as sucked in by the glamour as I was. The glamour's long gone now, and it won't be coming back, even if I didn't have another eighteen years until my first parole hearing, even if I were released tomorrow. I don't think I'd want the fast life again, though maybe everything would look different if I were out on the street. Deep inside, I don't believe I'll ever get released, so I don't spend too much time thinking about how I'd live afterward, or about the fact that I don't have skills or education or anything else to fall back on except for dealing drugs. The only ways out of poverty for a black man when I was coming up were music, hoops, and drugs, and I didn't have the tunes or the moves.

Monday 5.12.97

There are so many people playing God in prison that it's hard to avoid at least suspecting that heaven and hell really do exist, and that Oz is part of hell. Of course, it's anybody's guess whose justice is being dealt, but there's an old-fashioned "eye-for-an-eye" ring to what's been going down lately: Ortolani gets torched, and not long afterward Johnny Post's mutilated corpse turns up in a closet. It's retribution all right, but how divine is it? Religion? People like to hang out with their own kind, and that's as true in Oz as it is anyplace else. That's one reason half the inmates try to join one of the tribes; they're hoping to be saved—more from their enemies than from their sins. And maybe they're looking to deal with burdens like fear and loneliness, burdens that nobody higher up is offering to help them with.

So the gangs serve a purpose. On the street or in Oz, the other members of your tribe are watching your back, and you're watching theirs. Now if my brothers are watching my back, I'd rather they have Mach 10s in their fists than hymnbooks, but for a lot of guys, it was a Mach 10 that got them into trouble in the first place. Come to think of it, I'm one of them, and maybe if I hadn't had a weapon when the cops broke down my door, I'd still be walking. Unless they'd shot me dead on the spot. But even when I was on the street, dealing, it wasn't the gang that made me feel important, it was the money. Of course, dealing means you're part of a network of sources, distribution, and protection, so there's always camaraderie and competition. Speaking for myself, I always preferred hanging with a woman to hanging with my buddies, and would rather be shooting hoop than snorting coke.

Would I feel the seductive pull of religion if Annabella, Mom, and Burr hadn't stuck by me? I hope I never have to find out, but I don't think so. In the short time since Kareem Said's been in Oz, you can feel the power shift—slightly, but still, you can feel it—in the contest for the hearts and minds of the brothers here between the Muslims and the Homeboys. I don't have a problem with his message—that we have to seize control of our destinies, even while we're in prison, from the white institutions that try to limit black identity. I just don't see the need to hang that message on the hook of Islam or any other religion.

Tuesday 5.20.97

We haven't had an execution in the state for the last thirty-five years, but everyone in Oz is still a walking dead man, even if we don't always know it. Of course, some of us will come up for parole hearings while we still have at least some of our hair and a few of our marbles left, but will we ever really return to the world, even if we do get released? There's one guy in Sister Pete's drug counseling group, Whitney Munson. He's a fucking

World War II vet, came back from the Pacific with a Purple Heart and an opium habit. Killed a hooker while he was high, and has been in prison since 1945. He'll finally be eligible for parole in 2005. If he's released, what chance will he have of finding a home in a world he hasn't set foot in since the bombing of Hiroshima? It'd be more like taking a walk on the moon.

Is there any difference between

Sister Pete's drug counseling session, blending humor and self-realization.

Capital Punishment in the United States

In 2000, eighty-five inmates were executed. In 2001, sixty-six death sentences were carried out. Since the U.S. Supreme Court reinstated the death penalty in 1976, the number of prisoners on death row has risen steadily. At the end of 2000, 3,593 prisoners were under death sentences in the thirty-eight states that permit executions and in the federal correctional system. All have been convicted of murder.

Of the eighty-three men and two women executed in 2000, forty were in Texas, eleven in Oklahoma, eight in Virginia, six in Florida, five in Missouri, four in Alabama, three in Arizona, two in Arkansas, and one each in Delaware, Louisiana, North Carolina, South Carolina, Tennessee, and California. Forty-nine were white, thirty-five black, and one was American Indian. All but five of the executions were carried out by lethal injection.

White inmates make up the majority of those under sentence of death. In 2000, 1,990 death row prisoners were white, 1,535 black, 29 American Indian, 27 Asian, and 12 of unknown race. Fifty-four were women. Almost two-thirds had previously been convicted of a felony, but just one in twelve had prior homicide convictions. The youngest inmate under sentence of death was eighteen; the oldest was eighty-five.

Source: U.S. Department of Justice, Bureau of Justice Statistics, www.ojp.usdoj.gov/bjs/.

somebody like Whitney, who's up for parole when he's eighty-five, and an inmate serving a life sentence with no possibility of getting out? Not that I can see. To a lot of guys, the promise of a parole hearing is like the fake rabbit the greyhounds chase at the dog track. No way they'll ever catch up to it, but the sight of their quarry just out of reach is enough to keep the suckers running till they drop. To me, holding out that false hope is torture, a form of punishment the state claims it doesn't do any longer. But punishment is what prison's all about, and anybody who pretends that Oz is rehabilitation, preparing people to "reenter society," is just blowing smoke. Shit, half these guys were never "in" society in the first place.

Nobody's going anywhere, but maybe dreaming is better medicine than facing the facts day after day. Because the facts aren't pleasant, and trying to wait out a long sentence can be a fucking killer. Literally. When it sinks into a guy's mind that "life sentence" is really just another word for "death sentence," if he's got no way to dream, he may just give up, and he's ready to die. Some guys don't do anything to speed up the process; they just don't do anything to slow it down. Some people say that Dino Ortolani cracked after seeing his kids the last time they visited, that he couldn't deal with never being with them again as they were growing up, so he committed suicide. Of course, he couldn't just hang himself or slit his wrists—that wouldn't be manly enough for a stud like Ortolani—so he pounded the shit out of Billy Keane and snuffed Sanchez, one of the AIDS patients, knowing that sooner or later somebody out of the dozens of people who wished him dead would do the deed for him. It didn't take long. Maybe Johnny Post, who set him on fire, was looking for his own ticket to nowhere.

After thirty-five years without capital punishment, the state's getting back into the execution business big time. Governor Devlin's convinced the legislature that the constituents sleep better at night if from time to time a convict gets executed. When a reporter asked Devlin what purpose capital punishment served, given the fact that it doesn't deter crime, he answered that since criminal acts are irrational, the punishment should be just as irrational.

Is murder the most irrational of crimes? Maybe, maybe not, but capital punishment—killing in the name of justice—may be the most irrational form of punishment. If it's about evening the score—an eye for an eye, a life for a life—then why not punish other crimes the same way? Like if a guy rips off a pair of sneakers, he doesn't go to prison, he just replaces the sneakers. But who's the victim when the state—which claims to repre-

sent the victim—is also the perp? When the hacks beat the shit out of a prisoner to terrify him into keeping quiet, say, about their own role in the drug traffic? When in exchange for a few bucks a hack lets a prisoner into the Hole long enough to set another inmate on fire? When inmates kill one another? It's not the state that's the victim, but the poor bastard who feels the pain or loses his life.

A sentence with no end in sight, where all you can hope for is to stay alive from one day to the next, that's my idea of cruel and unusual punishment. So maybe when the state decides to assert its ultimate right over us—the right of life and death—it's actually showing more mercy than a sentence of life without parole. Sister Pete, one of the few kind souls in Oz, wouldn't agree that execution is a more merciful punishment than a lifetime in prison. She lost her job as the house shrink when she joined the protests against the death penalty. The word is that Glynn wouldn't permit a staff member to oppose the legislation, not even if she's a goddamned nun! Now isn't that fucked up? Do they expect Sister Pete to be against abortion and in favor of capital punishment? Of course, abortion's not an issue in Oz, but drugs are. And if Sister Pete doesn't come back soon, that's what I'm worried about. There's not much that works in this

APPEALS OF DEATH SENTENCES

A lawyer for a condemned prisoner hoped above all to have the prisoner's death sentence invalidated, but the second choice was to make the litigation last as long as possible. Every day the case dragged on was another day the client stayed alive. Lawyers thus brought up repeated claims of constitutional error before the courts, right up to the moment of execution. Knowing that they could not win with a frontal attack, abolitionist lawyers fought a guerilla war, seeking to sabotage the machinery of capital punishment by tying it up in litigation. These efforts, combined with the difficulty of finding lawyers for the growing number of condemned prisoners, caused the average length of time between sentencing and execution to increase. From 51 months in 1977-1983, the average delay grew to 95 months by 1990 and 134 months by 1995. And even after all those years, judges found themselves making hurried life-or-death decisions the night before most scheduled executions, ruling on constitutional claims in lengthy briefs faxed by lawyers hoping to have the execution put off to another day. The defense lawyers could not be faulted. They were working within an adversary system in which their ethical obligation was to do the best for their clients. It was the constitutionalization of capital punishment that created the paradoxical twin problems of delay and last-minute time pressure.

Those problems exasperated many, not least the judges. "In the most recent case," Lewis Powell [U. S. Supreme Court Justice, 1972-87] complained in 1984, "at least the equivalent of two full days of my time was devoted to the repetitive petitions that clearly were an abuse of habeas corpus. I know Byron [White, U. S. Supreme Court Justice, 1962-93] spent all night here on one occasion." In another case, "there were perhaps a dozen people here until 1:30 A.M. prior to the morning hour set for execution." The problem of last-minute filings only grew worse as scheduled executions became more frequent. All through the 1980s and 1990s Congress debated limiting the scope of the writ of habeas corpus, the procedural vehicle that allowed state prisoners to ask federal courts to review the constitutionality of their convictions and sentences. Finally, in the Antiterrorism and Effective Death Penalty Act of 1996, Congress set strict time limits for condemned prisoners, much stricter than for other prisoners. By then a Supreme Court impatient for congressional action had already done much of the work itself in a series of opinions overruling precedent in order to make it harder for condemned prisoners to have their constitutional claims heard by a federal court.

One brighter note: In the summer of 2001, the Supreme Court ruled that judges may not decide whether the circumstances of a capital crime warrant the death penalty; only juries may make that decision. By a 7-2 vote, the Court declared that an Arizona law permitting judges to decide on death sentences violates the Sixth Amendment right to a jury trial.

Source: Stuart Banner, *The Death Penalty: An American History* (Cambridge, Mass.: Harvard University Press, 2002).

place, but Sister Pete's drug counseling sessions are one of the reasons—maybe the main reason—I've been able to stay clean for the last twenty-two months. I'm pessimistic enough about my future, but if I fall back into that life—doing drugs, dealing drugs—I don't think I'll last long. I'm sure that the people who set up Jefferson Keane were looking for revenge for Ortolani's murder, but the Latinos who tried to murder him in the gym didn't give a shit about Dino Ortolani. They were doing somebody a favor and expected a bigger piece of the drug action in return.

Whatever their motive, one of the Latinos ended up dead, with a broken neck, and now Keane's about to become the first inmate in the state to be executed in thirty-five years. Funny how things work out sometimes. Not long before he was set up, Keane started to fall under the influence of Kareem Said, the informal imam of Oz, after Said helped him get the warden's permission to marry. Then I guess you could say he had a conversion when Said confronted him over bringing Kenny Wangler into the Homeboys. Wangler was a mean kid from the projects—he'd killed another kid over a fucking jacket—but he was only sixteen years old. When Said started talking about how the boy could be saved, Keane broke down. So just as he starts to unlock the chains of the system and starts

thinking about more than having power over other people, the system shuts him down for good.

But maybe Jefferson Keane had the last word after all. While he was on death row and only a few days from his execution date, he got news that his sister was about to die from kidney failure, so Keane offered to donate one of his kidneys for a transplant. At first the governor turned down the request, claiming that Keane was too dangerous to release from prison for any reason. But then the press and the public got behind the humanitarian angle, and Devlin got phone calls from every religious leader in the state—the Cardinal, rabbis, ministers, imams—so he had to cave. Granted a thirty-day stay of execution so Keane could donate a kidney, something that probably wouldn't have happened if the brother wasn't about to die. By dying, Keane was able to help somebody else live, something he hadn't been able to do while staying alive.

Monday 5.26.97

They say that drugs are behind 60 percent of the violence in American prisons. That doesn't leave much for all the other reasons people have for raising hell, but when you're in prison you can't shoot a guy for

Lethal Injection

The idea of executing criminals by poison is at least as old as Socrates. It was briefly considered by the 1888 New York commission that recommended the electric chair. After some of the early botched electrocutions, the use of drugs was proposed as an alternative. But lethal injection was never a serious option in any state before the 1970s. The intravenous administration of medicine had long been familiar, as had the use of lethal injection to kill unwanted animals, so the lack of attention to lethal injection as a means of executing *people* could not have been a function of technology. There must rather have been something abhorrent about the act of injection itself.

Two elements of lethal injection were particularly upsetting. First, an injection of poison required an uncomfortable degree of closeness between the condemned person and the executioner. Even the hangman had been farther away at the moment the trap was sprung, and with the newer methods the executioner had been put at a progressively greater distance. To stand inches away from the condemned person, perhaps to be touching him with one hand while holding the syringe with the other, was to cast oneself too conspicuously in the role of a killer. The ancient tension between support for the death penalty in the abstract and revulsion for the actual act of causing death was as strong as ever, and it made execution by injection difficult to contemplate long after lethal injection had become a simple technical procedure. Second, injecting chemicals into the bloodstream was a task traditionally performed by physicians, many of whom found it troubling that one of their own might be called upon to end life rather than prolong it. Physicians had long presided at executions, but their role had been limited to pronouncing death, not causing it.

By the late 1970s, however, states had not used their electric chairs or gas chambers in more than a decade. In Oklahoma the chair's electric coils were rusted and its wood was rotting. Time had worn down the execution machinery in other states as well. To resume executions would require buying new equipment even if a state retained the method of execution it had used before *Furman*. [In *Furman v. Georgia* (1972), the U. S. Supreme Court abolished the death penalty, but most states quickly rewrote their statutes to address the Court's constitutional qualms.] The decade-long hiatus in capital punishment created by the Supreme Court thus removed much of the ordinary financial disincentive to change. And from the perspective of the state, one great benefit of lethal injection was that it was cheap. Unlike gas or electrocution, it did not require any specialized equipment. All the chemicals, syringes, and intravenous tubing were readily available for purchase. The North Carolina Department of Correction calculated that the total cost of the equipment would be only $346.51 per execution. . . . In the spring of 1977 Oklahoma and Texas became the first states to adopt the new method. Not long after, most of the other states did too. In 1982, Charlie Brooks of Texas became the first person executed in this manner. Lying on a gurney, strapped down to prevent escape, Brooks was injected with three drugs. The first was sodium thiopental, a barbiturate that produced unconsciousness. Next came pancuronium bromide, a muscle relaxant that paralyzed Brooks's lungs. Last was potassium chloride, to stop his heart. The same chemicals, in the same order, were used in most of succeeding lethal injections in other states. "It's extremely sanitary," marvelled Missouri's prison chaplain. "The guy just goes to sleep. That's all there is to it. All of a sudden. And when it's said and done, he breathes a sigh and then he's gone." The American Medical Association barred physicians from taking part in executions, so the tasks were usually performed by prison employees, with physicians providing a sedative ahead of time and an autopsy afterward.

Source: Stuart Banner, *The Death Penalty: An American History* (Cambridge, Mass.: Harvard University Press, 2002)

fucking your wife or messing with your car. In Oz we don't have that much to steal. But rip off a guy's stash—even if it's only cigarettes—and he'll try to kill you for it.

In Oz, sex and violence walk hand-in-hand with drugs close behind. Guys get high to help them forget what's being done to them against their will. Take Beecher. He came inside not knowing shit, and I'll spot you ten points and possession that if he ever used drugs it was pot at a frat party. Unless you count booze, since I hear that Beecher had a serious problem with alcohol and killed a little girl while he was driving drunk. Before he can plead nolo contendere, his ass belongs to Vern, the Great White Dope. Dumb, maybe, but cunning, and definitely dangerous. They sure didn't teach anything about how to be a prag in law school, so Beecher, who's got nobody to protect him, stumbles into somebody who turns him on to drugs, and for the first time since he got to Emerald City, he's got some relief from the fear and the hatred—of what's happening to him, of not having any control over his life, of the system that dumped him into prison, and more than anything else, of himself, for ending up where lawyers think only other people go. In no time Beecher's sucking tit like a homey. Where'd he find the drugs? My guess is Ryan O'Reily, a chameleon who pretends he's everybody's friend but is always scheming. What fucking use O'Reily has for Beecher is anybody's guess, but he never does anything just to help a guy out. I got a suspicion O'Reily's somehow behind the recent rash of deaths in Em City.

What O'Reily's done for Beecher so far has landed him in drug counseling (the guy works for Sister Pete, so there's no way she wouldn't notice how fucked up he gets), but drug counseling doesn't seem to be doing much for Beecher. It doesn't help all that many people, because you got to want to be helped, and Beecher's not ready to admit that he's got a drug problem. Shit, I don't like admitting I'm addicted either, but it's a damn sight better than falling back into the trap of using and dealing. Especially now, with the scene in Em City getting uglier every day. First Schibetta flushes out Paul Markstrom—who did a convincing impersonation of a drug-dealing Homeboy for a few months—as a fucking narc, then Markstrom's found hanging from an overhead pipe. Suicide, they said—Glynn won't admit the local cops planted an informer inside Oz, and a fucking incompetent one at that—but nobody's buying that bullshit. As soon as they cut Markstrom down, Officer Healy gets arrested for passing tits to Ryan O'Reily, who landed in the Hole. There are rumors that O'Reily set Healy up. Why? Who the fuck knows.

DRUGS IN PRISON

How did America's prisons and jails come to be dominated by alcohol and drug abusers and those who deal drugs? Citizen concerns about crime and violence led federal, state, and local officials to step up law enforcement, prosecution, and punishment. As a result of such concern and the heroin epidemic of the 1970s and the crack cocaine explosion in the 1980s, state and federal legislatures enacted more criminal laws, especially with respect to selling drugs and related criminal activities such as money laundering; agents of the Federal Bureau of Investigation and the Drug Enforcement Administration and state and local police made more arrests for all kinds of crime; prosecutors brought more charges and indictments; judges and juries convicted more defendants; and judges imposed more sentences authorized or mandated by law. While in prison, little attempt was made to deal with the underlying inmate drug and alcohol addiction that led to so much criminal activity. Inmates who are alcohol and drug abusers and addicts are the most likely to be reincarcerated—again and again—and sentences usually increase for repeat offenders. The result has been a steady and substantial rise in the nation's prison population over the past generation. Between 1980 and 1996, the number of inmates in federal and state prisons and local jails jumped 239 percent, from 501,886 to 1,700,661. [According to the U.S. Department of Justice, there were 2,027,275 people in prison at the end of 2001, and the prison population continues to rise.]

For 80 percent of inmates, substance abuse and addiction has shaped their lives and criminal histories: they have been regular drug users, have a history of alcohol abuse, committed crimes under the influence of alcohol or drugs, stole to get money to buy drugs, violated drug selling and possession laws, drove drunk, committed assaults, rapes, homicides, and disorderly conduct offenses related to alcohol or drugs—or a combination of the above.

Substance abuse is tightly associated with recidivism. The more prior convictions an individual has, the more likely that individual is a drug abuser: in state prisons, 41 percent of first offenders have used drugs regularly, compared to 63 percent of inmates with two prior convictions and 81 percent of those with five or more convictions. Only 4 percent of first-time offenders have used heroin regularly, compared to 12 percent of those with two prior convictions and 27 percent of those with five or more. Sixteen percent of first offenders have used cocaine regularly, compared to 26 percent of those with two prior convictions and 40 percent of those with five or more convictions. State prison inmates with five or more prior convictions are three times likelier than first-time offenders to be regular crack users.

Source: National Center on Addiction and Substance Abuse at Columbia University, *Behind Bars: Substance Abuse and America's Prison Population*, published by the center (January 1998).

O'Reily introduces Beecher to a Jamaican haze.

Bob Rebadow's in the hospital. Kenny Wangler put him there, started punching him in the middle of the rec area, because he wanted the box of fudge the old man got in the mail. Rebadow wasn't hurt too bad, but he's bruised all over and he took some blows to the head. He's probably the oldest inmate in Em City, so who knows what his health is like? Not only because

prison adds years to a guy's age, but because Rebadow's actually been "executed" once—and survived! In 1965, while Rebadow was sitting in the electric chair, the power failed in five states, with him still alive—half-baked, you might say. The court ruled that he couldn't be executed again, so he's still here. At least he seems to be most of the time, but he claims that ever since his near-death experience God speaks to him once in a while. I guess he was convicted of murdering someone, though it's hard to picture that quiet little guy wasting anybody. I've never caught Rebadow surrounded in light in the middle of one of his revelations, but from time to time he does know some amazing things about other inmates. Inspiration or intuition? And maybe Rebadow is a little bit crazy, but he's a gentle soul, and Wangler had no business messing him up like he did.

I know the world Wangler grew up in—came out of those same projects myself, where the young and the strong rule, and almost nobody expects to live long enough to get old. Still, it doesn't make sense, what Wangler did. Roughing up Rebadow isn't going to convince anybody, not the crudest Homeboy or anybody else, that Kenny's a man. But he did what he'd learned to do on the street: target the weakest victim, the one who's not going to defend himself. It's not because old ladies carry pocketbooks that they're the ones who get mugged most often; it's because they're not likely to be carrying a shank or a gun, and nobody ever got killed by a lipstick.

Except maybe in Oz, where the Schillinger—Beecher relationship just keeps getting weirder. Schillinger controls Beecher's entire life, so when lawyer boy wanted to have a conjugal visit with his own wife, he had to ask Schillinger's permission (one afternoon everyone in Em City heard Beecher screaming, "Please, sir, may I fuck my wife?"). But it seems that after a while it wasn't enough for Schillinger to be fucking Beecher, he wanted him to look like his fucking girlfriend, so he paid one of the local queens to teach his prag how to doll himself up. Of course, what that Nazi doesn't cop to is that the more he humiliates Beecher, the more drugs the poor bastard takes to cope. Then, a few days ago, Beecher did a transvestite act at the annual talent show. Red dress, fishnet stockings, the works. He brought the house down. I was the emcee, so I knew he was so stoned on heroin that it was a miracle he could stand up in those spike heels, much less sing. He managed to do both, but back in their pod, Schillinger got pissed as hell over the drugs (seems to be the only crimes in his book are doing drugs and being black), and threw Beecher out of the cell wearing a T-shirt with the Confederate flag on it. I guess he thought that one of us black prisoners would attack Beecher when we saw the T-shirt. Beecher somehow made it to O'Reily, got high on PCP, then went back and heaved a chair through the glass wall of Schillinger's cell. Then he climbed up on the railing and would've jumped if some hacks hadn't wrestled him down. Meanwhile, Schillinger went to the infirmary with one eye cut up so bad he'll probably never see clearly out of it again—not that he ever did.

LOCKED UP:
THE GRAYING OF AMERICA'S PRISONS

In the past 15 years, the [American] corrections system has been transformed into an industry that warehouses increasing numbers of men until they grow old and die—at times regardless of their danger to society. Across the country, the number of state and federal inmates 55 or older has tripled since 1986, and now stands at more than 50,000. This figure doesn't include elderly inmates scattered among the 700,000 prisoners in local jails.

This graying of America's prisons is forcing dramatic shifts on the penal system's management and economics. As the number of elderly inmates rises, so does the cost of maintaining them. Corrections analysts estimate a geriatric inmate's maintenance costs run as much as 300 percent higher than the average prisoner's. As a result, corrections employees find themselves in a strange, new environment: caring for quadriplegics who can barely move, tending paralyzed stroke victims confined to wheelchairs, and monitoring schizophrenics and Alzheimer's patients who require round-the-clock medication.

The rise in elderly prisoners stems from four converging trends:

- The general aging of the American population, which is reflected inside prisons.
- New sentencing policies such as "three strikes," "truth in sentencing," and "mandatory minimum" laws that send more criminals to prison for longer stretches.
- A massive prison building boom that, since the 1980s, has provided space for more inmates, reducing the need to release prisoners to alleviate overcrowding.
- Dramatic changes in parole philosophies and practices. State and federal authorities are phasing out or canceling parole programs. . . . In many jurisdictions, mandatory 30- and 40-year sentences have replaced similar sentences that might have seen a well-behaved inmate paroled after 10 or 15 years. Now, that inmate stays in.

Inmates over 55 have consistently formed 3 percent of the state inmate population and 12 percent of federal prisoners. So, although the percentages of elderly haven't changed, their total number has more than tripled. In state prisons alone, numbers leaped from 11,260 in 1986 to 40,500 in 1997, according to the Justice Department.

Aging inmates can hang on for quite a while. There were almost 800 prisoners over 75 years old across the country in 1997. Florida alone [in 1998] housed 238 inmates over 70.

It's now not unusual to find prisoners in their 90s. In its nationwide records search, APBnews.com found 13 of them, including 94-year-old Ellef J. Ellefson in Wisconsin, a sex offender. Ellefson isn't scheduled to be released until 2006, when he's 100.

Source: Jim Krane, "Demographic Revolution Rocks U.S. Prisons," APBnews.com, April 12, 1999.

The aim of the hacks is to force inmates to forget about every part of our past lives, good or bad, the better to control us. Even the do-gooders in Oz (there are a few)—who address us by our first names, encourage us to stay in contact with our families, to keep our sights on the next visiting day, the next conjugal visit (until the state took away that "privilege"), the next parole hearing date—are as interested in making sure we "behave" as the hacks. Those bastards treat us like nothing more than punching bags with pulses. The parts of a man's past that survive the passage through these stone walls are the same ones that got him sent to Oz in the first place: drugs, violence, one scam or another. Maybe that's why the state tries to reinvent our identities when we're processed at the Receiving and Discharging Office: we're photographed, fingerprinted, and given our prison numbers. Inside, when a prisoner is called, it's prison number first, name second, as if we didn't really have an identity until after we got our numbers.

But it's really the other way around. Inside Oz, life stops, and counting starts. We're doing time by killing time. We count the years to the end of our sentences or the months to our parole hearings. We count the hours and the days to the next visit from our families. We keep track of how long it's been since the last time we spent the night alone with our wives or girlfriends, until it gets to be so long that we lose track. And more than anything else, some of us count the time since we last used drugs. Detox was easier for me than most. I was in the hospital after my fall, in a haze from morphine and the other drugs they gave me to kill the pain, so I didn't miss the crack, didn't even know I wasn't smoking it. As soon as I recovered, I went to trial and then to Oz. Somewhere in those first months I understood that I had to make a break with the past, at least the crack-smoking, drug-dealing part of my past, if I was going to have a chance of holding on to my life, Annabella especially, and my family, but somehow I knew it was bigger than that, too. So I started thinking about drugs, this time about not using them, and I guess you could say that staying straight has become my new addiction.

Not a bad trade, not always easy, but I stuck to it. That all changed the day I heard that Jackson Vahue was coming to Oz. We knew all about his trial for assault and attempted rape and his conviction from the TV news, so I wasn't surprised they were sending him to Oz. All I wondered was why a guy like Vahue, who had women pursuing him like puppies on a playground, was assaulting a woman. But he was my hero, an NBA All-Star from the projects where I grew up, and I got so excited that instead of cursing the fact that the dumb bastard had probably thrown his career away, I raced over to McManus to ask whether I could be Vahue's sponsor—the person who shows the newbie the ropes, helps him get used to life in Em City—when he arrived.

I was so starstruck at first. All I saw was the superplayer that even the hacks were asking for autographs, not the strongman who wasn't strong enough to control his aggression off the court. Almost the first thing he asked me was whether I had any drugs, and when I told him no, he said, "Then what the fuck good are you?" I know the signs, but this time I didn't bother reading them and kept trying to get buddy-buddy with him. In the gym, a day or two later, I found Vahue in the gym, alone, shooting baskets. Damn, he was pissed! At himself, mostly, though he didn't seem to have a clue what had gone wrong. He narrowed his eyes and stared right through me, as if he was wiping everything else out of his mind to focus on the hoop for a crucial foul shot. Then he said, "The one thing I'm good at don't mean dick in here!" and stormed out of the gym. Later that day I found

him in a corner of Em City with Adebisi and Wangler, snorting tit and reliving one of his moments of past glory. He offered me a hit, and I refused at first—I'd been clean for twenty-two months, and I wanted to stay away from drugs—but he insisted, and, being a bigger fool than I realized, I guess I thought, This is the

TITS

I been fiending for this freedom
I been begging for the be-out
I been jonsing for the jump
    over the wall
But all I keep coming back to is
    them titties
Round and firm for the vein burn
I'm bugging over the reason for
    this shit I yearn
Years in this piece got me
    wanting to block it out
Forget about
Erase it from my think...

Poem by muMs

only road to Jackson Vahue I'm ever going to find, so I took the tit. But even before I started snorting the shit, I knew that I had to get away from there—from him, from the drugs—quicker than he'd find the open man on a fast break.

Partying in Adebisi's pod.

Wednesday

This is Oz, not *Ozzie and Harriet*. What I mean is, just about everybody in Oz is here because something went wrong, not because they did something right. And that's as true for the staff as for the inmates. Take McManus. His master plan for Em City—people from every walk of crime living together and learning to get along—didn't take long to run off the tracks. Sure, everybody's got his reasons, why his life zigged just when

it should've zagged. I got a few of those stories myself, and sometimes there's even a kernel of truth in them. Like Said's argument that it's racism that turns so many people of color into addicts, and the addiction that makes them criminals. He considers himself—and many of the rest of us—political prisoners, not criminals. Maybe so, but I'd like to know what was so fucking political about blowing up a warehouse, even

KIDNAP THE PRESIDENT'S WIFE WITHOUT A PLAN

I got me a plan
It's etched with a knife in the center of my hand
so I keep my fist clenched
walk around DC in the rain
till my wears is drenched
wait for that head of state to take out his garbage
or do a press conference
about the good shape the country's in
about how them welfare cuts gonna begin
when he pat his dog
and kiss his wife good-bye, I move in
put that silly Ho in a headlock
muffle her grill so her screams stop
whisper to her

"Your man ain't here to protect you baby, he's gone"

call up my nigga O north
tell him meet me with the caddy on the white lawn
toss her in the backseat
cover her head with the black sheet
tell her if she don't shut up

"I'm gonna lick two shots off in your domepiece!"

watch her have fits
If she don't understand
give her a quick lesson in Ebonics

"I'm going to shoot you baby!"

take her to my hideout
in the low-income houses down the street
replace her Joan and Davids
with purple Reeboks on her feet
give her four hungry kids
no job
no ambition

no family support
no education
and her last welfare check
give her crappy ass Medicaid
and a ill type of growth growing out the side of her neck
tell her, "fend for yourself
keep you and them shorties in proper health"
then after sufficient time on that hype
I'll introduce her to the glass pipe
let her feel its soothing effects
so she can forget about the absence of them checks
have her sell her jewels for it
make her pay her dues for it
then threaten to take them shorties away
threaten to evict that ass cause of the rent she ain't pay
then whisper sweetlike in her ear

"Everything ain't gonna be all right
you ain't gon be able to go quietly into that good night
your suffering has only just begun and peace ain't gon come
till your life be done"

then I'll lead her up to the roof
show her all the shit she don't own
leave her on the edge all alone
"ain't that a pretty sight? tell your plight, and beware of your dreams 'cause
you ain't never gonna forget what poverty means!"
   These be the words on the note stapled to her neck
as I drop her pale ass back on the white house step
signed, anonymous.

This poem ain't about black and white. It's about those who got
      and those
who ain't got; and the controlling gots is far removed from the ain't
      gots; and
the gap is widening so much so that the finger pointing don't even
      reach no more.

Poem by muMs

Religion in Prison

With the migration of Southern blacks to northern cities in the 1950s and '60s, many northern inmate populations became black for the first time. At about the same time, the rise of the civil rights movement helped to inspire litigation on behalf of prisoners' rights. The first victories of this campaign were in the area of freedom of religion for Black Muslim prisoners. These inmates sought the right to obtain copies of the Koran, read Black Muslim newspapers, observe Islamic dietary laws and hold religious services and meetings. *Cooper vs. Pate* [1964] conferred on this group the right to exist as a recognized religious group. "Thomas Cooper had filed a civil rights complaint alleging that he had been confined in segregation to punish him [for his] religious beliefs and demanding access to Muslim literature and clergy." The lower courts dismissed his complaint, but the U.S. Supreme Court reversed the lower courts' rulings, and as a result Black Muslims in prison were recognized as a separate religious group for the first time.

Source: The Oxford History of the Prison, ed. Norval Morris and David J. Rothman (New York: Oxford University Press, 1998).

one owned by a white man in a black neighborhood.

You got to give Said credit, though, for playing the cards he was dealt. Lots of guys when they first get to Oz are so busy feeling sorry for themselves, complaining about how their lawyer screwed them over or some shit like that, they wouldn't notice if the front door was left open. People like that are almost as trapped by their own thinking as they are behind the bars that cage them in. But Said, the minute he got to Oz, acted like he wasn't a prisoner, even though he was sure as hell in prison, and he got the other Muslims to follow his lead. He didn't rebel or refuse to follow orders, nothing that would give the hacks an excuse for writing the Muslims up or beating them; he just made it clear that nobody in Oz could strip him of his self-respect. Not the Homeboys, who didn't want Said preaching to the brothers against drugs; not Schillinger and the Aryans, who considered him dangerous because he was a man with ideas—about being black and about faith—that threatened their one-note White Is Right doctrine; not even Glynn, who hoped that Said's messages of no drugs and no violence would help him keep a lid on things. Whatever hopes the warden had died when Said stirred up the press over the fact that the report of the investigation about the six recent killings of inmates in Oz had never been released. As soon as that story hit the papers, Glynn showed how pissed he was at Said's maneuver; he sent the hacks into Em City to announce a new rule: no distinctive dress or other shit for any religious group. It was obvious the Muslims were being singled out—shit, we don't have any Hare Krishnas in Oz—and they had to surrender their kufis and their prayer beads and rugs on the spot. Said wouldn't rise to the bait. He just said, "Our faith isn't in our beads," and walked away. But when Glynn came into the cafeteria a few days ago to announce that the report on the killings was in and that it was inmates who were responsible, though some guards may have been involved in "secondary" roles, at first there were just a few guys cursing in the room. Then, at a signal from Said, the Muslims started pounding the tables with their spoons, and in thirty seconds, the whole room had picked up the beat, like the percussion section in a band, and drowned Glynn's voice out completely. He ducked out of there, and you knew that the battle over who controls Oz—the warden or the imam—was on.

In a battle, you'd better know who your friends are. That's not always simple, as Said discovered when Husseini Murshah moved into his pod. Murshah was always pushing to defend Islam against every insult. So Said always seemed to be stepping between him and guys like Scott Ross, a punk with a short fuse who's an old pal of Schillinger's and in tight with the Aryan pooh-bah despite a passion for drugs that pure-white Vern sure doesn't share. You had to wonder whether Murshah wasn't trying to stir up trouble for the Muslims, but mostly he was just trying too hard to impress everybody with his zeal, like a guy who wants you to think he's so cool that Miles Davis was actually copying him! But the morning Said had his heart attack, Murshah was in the pod with him and didn't move a muscle to get help. I guess he didn't think Said was going to pull through, and nobody would suspect that Murshah wanted him dead, but Said doesn't die that easy. He recovered,

came back to Em City, and declared, "This man is not our brother," and that was it: the Muslims cut him off without a word. Wouldn't talk to him, wouldn't sit with him in the cafeteria, wouldn't even look at him. Next thing you knew, he'd gone to the warden and accused the Muslims of stockpiling weapons, so Glynn ordered a shakedown. What could that fucker have been thinking? All of Em City turned against Murshah then, and McManus transferred him to gen pop. A couple days later, Murshah was dead. The official word was that he'd committed suicide, but after the Markstrom busi-

The righteous indignation of Kareem Said.

ness, there were rumors that Murshah was another informer whose mission impossible—to undermine Said's leadership of the Muslims—blew up in his face.

I keep wondering what Murshah thought he was up to. Trying to shove Said aside, or at least stir up conflict within the Muslims, that's obvious. But why? Hunger for power?

Beecher, huh?
I'm guessing
you ain't
Italian.
What are you in for,
shaving strokes off
your golf score?

—Dino Ortolani

Religious fervor? Whatever it was, he had betrayal on his mind, and in Oz betrayal is the worst fucking crime of all. Maybe nobody's ever served a jail term for it, but plenty of guys haven't served out their sentences after they've betrayed somebody. Because if you can't be trusted to watch your brother's back, you're going to have one fucking tough time finding anybody you can trust to watch yours.

As bad as it is to betray somebody else, it's worse—much worse—to betray yourself. One reason is, it can kill you more in different ways than anybody with a shank or a gun can.

It almost killed Said, who maybe could've prevented his fucking heart attack in the first place if he'd started taking his high blood pressure meds when the doctors prescribed them. He didn't like the side effects, he said. Yeah, right! What about the side effects of a heart attack? Does he like them better?

I keep coming back over and over again to the same question: what makes a man with a gift—like Jackson Vahue's for doing things with a basketball you can't believe even after you've seen them, like Said's power to turn people's thinking around—throw it all away for no reason? There's a guy who turned up in Em City sometime in the last few weeks, Eugene Dobbins. He plays the cello, and he must've been some boss musician on the outside, because McManus gave him special permission to practice in the cafeteria every afternoon. The word is, he killed another musician—jealousy or rage or something else was behind it, nobody's sure. One day I heard this sound—sad, simple, but so fucking beautiful—and turned around to see a dude in porkpie hat bowing what looked like a bass, only smaller. Sounded a little like a bass, too, only much sweeter and sadder. I'd never even heard of a cello before, let alone seen one. Dobbins told me all about his cello, its history and stuff. Then he said the damn thing was lonely. When I asked him how that could be, he said it wasn't really meant to be a solo instrument, that he was used to playing in orchestras with maybe ninety to a hundred members. Who knows whether Dobbins is ever going to see a concert hall again, but if he didn't practice every day, pretty soon he'd lose his gift. So McManus—the biggest starfucker in Oz—arranged for a hack to baby-sit while Dobbins played his cello. I couldn't find an entire orchestra for Dobbins—wouldn't that be something, the Oswald Symphony in this dump!—but there is one guy in Em City who plays the trumpet. So I went to McManus and asked him to let the two of them practice together. (I never said I wasn't a starfucker myself, but Timmy Boy's the worst.) So for a while, Dobbins and his cello weren't so lonely. It didn't make all that much difference, except to show that sometimes a person can improve things even inside Oz. I have to admit I felt a little better about myself.

But there was something about Dobbins's cello playing that gnawed at Jackson Vahue. Maybe he saw the two of them as being alike: two guys with amazing gifts that were almost certainly going to shrivel up in Oz. Vahue couldn't deal with that; he could hear the fucking clock ticking on his own career. Dobbins told me about Pablo Casals, a great cellist who lived to be ninety-seven years old and was still performing almost to the day he died. But in the NBA, even an All-Star is starting to get old at thirty, and almost nobody—not even a Michael Jordan—lasts until he's forty in that league. So what did Vahue do? He broke into the chaplain's office, where Dobbins's cello was kept for safe-keeping, and smashed the fucking thing into pieces. That instrument was like a part of Dobbins's own body, except that it was made more than 200 years before he was born. I don't know whether he's going to recover. Maybe Dobbins can get another cello, but it probably won't be the same. And Vahue's got some serious repairs to do on himself, or he's going to self-destruct in this place quicker than a Bryant head fake.

Sunday 6.22.97

The first rule in a place like Oz is, never get attached to anyone. Make a friend and the next thing you know, something bad happens to him and you find yourself grieving for him. Or—an even bigger bitch—he gets lucky, wins a parole or is granted a new trial, and you're grieving for yourself instead. As bad as envy is, self-pity can tie you up in knots so tight you can't move. It's the worst fucking thing a guy can do to himself, because sometimes you've got to react fast just to stay alive. Most of the time Oz is one big snooze, rumors everywhere but nothing happening. Then suddenly, without warning, the place blows.

That's pretty much what happened a few days ago. There's always a shitload of weapons in Oz, mostly home-made shanks made of tools from the factories, pieces of metal or Plexi-glas, instruments from the infirmary, combs, razor blades, or nail files, smuggled into Oz and sharpened until they're deadly instruments. The shakedown Glynn ordered recently turned up hundreds of shanks and other shit, most of which had nothing to do with the Muslims. Nobody was sure they were planning anything. And maybe they weren't. Whatever their intentions were, fate—or chance—took matters into its own grim hands.

What ignited the riot was a couple of white crackheads who started throwing punches over a fucking game of checkers! Before the hacks could break up the fight, the rec area was a free-for-all—inmates rushing in from every direction, swinging at the hacks and at each other. Somebody—I don't know who it was—grabbed my wheelchair and started pushing it away from the violence, and when he finally let go I managed to get myself into one of the pods where some other inmates had taken refuge. Bodies and furniture were everywhere, and I could hear the sound of glass break-ing upstairs, but I couldn't see where the noise was coming from. Then I saw a group of Muslims running down the stairs between the second floor and the control center. They must have been staying out of the fighting on

the first floor, but when they reached the two hacks, who were radioing for help, one of the Muslims grabbed a C.O. and threw him over the railing onto the first floor. The other hack, Diane Whittlesey, they just surrounded, as if they were trying to protect her from the violence below. I noticed Alvarez standing over a mattress in the middle of the rec area that flames were shooting up from. Said stood at the railing with a gun in his hand, fired it once at the ceiling, shouting in a loud voice, "Let's get organized!" And the room grew still.

I could hear Glynn's voice, amplified by a bullhorn, even before I came out of the pod I'd been hiding in, and as I got closer to the center of the common area I saw the gate had been barricaded with tables, chairs, beds, cabinets, and anything else the inmates could shove up against it. The warden was shouting, "I want to speak to someone in authority," and then he started calling for Said. In seconds, the inmates were chanting "Said! Said! Said!" over and over, while Said, wearing his kufi again now that the Muslims got back the right to practice Islam, strode toward the gate. A portion of the barricade was taken down, opening a space just wide enough that Glynn and Said could see each other. When Glynn asked, "What's this about?" Said answered, "If you've got to ask, we've got a long day ahead of us," and the prisoners laughed and cheered. When Said turned back from the gate, I found Dobbins lying on his

face, over in a corner near the TV, conscious but barely moving. One of the Muslims, Zahir Arif, had started moving the wounded inmates into the shower room, and he helped turn Dobbins onto his back and get him to a more protected spot. Dobbins's T-shirt was soaked in blood from a stab wound in his belly. Some asshole had shanked him, either in the confusion of the first minutes of the riot or out of a desire to act the tough motherfucker against a guy who couldn't defend himself. Dobbins may have killed somebody on the outside, but he sure as hell didn't have any idea what was going on during the riot. I know he wasn't taking part or siding with any of the tribes. Yeah, he was white, but he wasn't any more in with the Aryans or the Bikers than Rebadow.

I was on the lookout for Vahue, too, wanted to know whether he was okay and thinking if I found him maybe he could help keep Dobbins safe. That was probably a crazy thought after what Vahue did to the cello, but I knew that at least he wasn't looking to settle any scores with hacks or inmates, or to get in good with the Homeboys. All he wanted from them was drugs, and they were happy to have Jackson Vahue's name on their list of preferred customers.

Dobbins was probably pretty far gone by the time Vahue got to the shower room; but I kept thinking, we got to do something, we can't just let him die. Somehow I got Vahue to agree to try to get Dobbins out of Em City and into the hospital. At first he said Dobbins wasn't his problem, that he hadn't shanked him. Of course he hadn't, but I told him sometimes you just have to stand up and take responsibility. When the big guy looked down at Dobbins on the floor, with me next to him, trying to do something for him, even though I got no legs, I could see I'd finally reached him. Then Vahue lifted Dobbins like he was a bolt of fabric in the clothing factory, talked his way past O'Reily, Adebisi, and Ross at the front gate. And he waited while the crew pulled down enough of the bed frames and other shit that formed the barricade to make it possible to open the gate. Just before he passed through the gate, Vahue turned back toward me, with Dobbins cradled in his arms, and said quietly, "I'll see you." Then he stepped toward the waiting hacks, the gate closed, the barricade went back up, and that's the last I saw of them.

Back in Dobbins's cell, the sheet music he'd used when he was playing the cello—when he still had the cello—was strewn all over the floor. I can't read music, but I picked some of the pages up off the floor. Looking at them, I felt like I could hear Dobbins practicing his cello, but I knew I'd probably never hear him play the cello again, and neither would anybody else. Then I noticed his bow lying under some of the sheets of music. I picked it up and, just in case, took it back to my own cell for safekeeping.

The Muslims may have been planning to engineer the riot, though in the end they didn't start it, but Said was ready to act when the time came. For one thing, he had a gun—the only gun in Em City—that nobody knew about until the moment he fired it, but he also understood what the leaders of the other tribes didn't: to hold on to power, you have to be prepared to share it. In short order a sort of ruling council had formed and divvied up control of Em City among themselves: the Latinos had the hostages, and the Homeboys, Bikers, and Irish controlled the front gate, but what they couldn't control or hide was the destruction. When the riot broke out, all of the guards in Em City, some of them hurt pretty bad, had been taken hostage. Many of the inmates were injured, too, some of them just as bad as the hacks. Nobody was doing anything to get medical help for the wounded and injured.

After the council carved control of Em City up among themselves, the hostages were cuffed and dragged into one room, and the barricade thrown up against the front gate was secured, a sort of edgy calm came over Em City. For us ordinary prisoners, there wasn't much to do but wait, and for the time being the council wasn't saying much. We heard that they'd told Glynn they planned to submit a list of demands,

Whittlesey, Father Mukada, and the other hostages in Oz await their fates.

but I wonder if anybody was working on them besides Said. Somebody must've gotten hungry, though, because on the morning of Day Two the council telephoned Glynn's office to request that some food be sent into Em City. Later that day McManus showed up at the gate with a cart stacked high with sandwiches; the deal was that if he was allowed in to check on the condition of the hostages, we'd get something to eat.

The hostages had all been moved into one of the classrooms, and nobody but the Latinos, who were guarding them, could get near them. But through the glass I could see them, sitting up against the walls, with their hands bound behind their backs. One of the hacks, though, wasn't sitting up, he was lying on his back, breathing but otherwise not moving much. Another hack had blood all over the front of his shirt, and it was obvious those two needed medical attention right away.

The gatekeepers agreed to let McManus in—unaccompanied by any other hacks—with the sandwiches. Once he was inside, McManus negotiated to get the two badly injured hacks—Armstrong and Mineo—released so they could get medical treatment, while he stayed behind in their place. The council agreed, apparently only after McManus told them they'd all be charged with murder if either of the hacks died from his wounds. I heard that when O'Reily was first asked whether he'd vote to release the two hacks, he'd answered, "Let the fuckers die." It was then I realized what kind of reception Vahue and Dobbins must've gotten on the far side of the gate.

But none of the council members would vote to let Whittlesey, the only woman, go as well, when McManus tried to talk them into it. Did they intend to rape her, or did they just want another bargaining chip, or a human shield if the governor sent the S.O.R.T.—what they call the Special Operations Response Team, hacks who get special weapons and training to fuck us over even worse than the regular hacks—or the National Guard in?

Friday 7.4.97

With Em City firmly under the prisoners' control, the council prepared a set of demands and sent them out to Glynn and Devlin when they released the two injured C.O.s. Then there was nothing to do but wait. All the talk of how it's better to die on your feet than live on your knees doesn't mean much when you're sitting on your ass hoping somebody'll hand you a fucking ham sandwich. Even if you supported the riot—or the uprising, as the Muslims and some of the others started

calling it—it didn't take long to figure out that if "they" were locked out of Em City, "we" were sure as hell locked in. It wouldn't take long

They call this the penal system. But it's really the **penis system,** it's about how big, it's about how long, it's about how hard. Life in Oz is all about **the size of your dick,** and anybody who tells you different ain't got one.

—Augustus Hill

before the council unraveled. Some of these so-called allies hated each other as much as they hated the cops, so without the hacks to keep them apart, what was going to stop them from fighting among themselves?

The strangest thing about the riot was that the Aryans hadn't really taken part, and no member of the Aryan Brotherhood—not Schillinger or any of his lackeys—was represented on the council that was running Em City. A couple people said that Schillinger had a parole hearing coming up and hoped to make a good impression on the parole board by refusing to participate in the riot. His decision might actually have strengthened the council; without the Aryans constantly baiting the Muslims, Said didn't have to struggle so hard to hold his people to the Muslim principle of nonviolence. Even with the Aryans keeping a low profile, it didn't look like the alliance would hold together very long, especially after word went around that the heroin in Em City had run out. Without tits, Adebisi, Wangler, or one of the other Homeboys—or maybe even one of the Bikers (some of them are serious users, too)—was sure to crack, and soon. First the Homeboys ransacked every pod in Em City where they thought there might be some heroin hidden. Failing to find any tits, Adebisi went into a rage and seemed about to strangle Wangler, until Said pointed his gun at Adebisi's head. Then Adebisi let go of Wangler's neck and started howling, "Give me some fucking tits," and Said had him tied up to prevent him from going berserk again. Watching what was happening from the sidelines, us little guys weren't sure which was worse: the attack that was sure to come before long from the other side of the gate, or the storm that was just as certain to erupt inside.

Devlin didn't keep us waiting long. He never had any intention of negotiating with prisoners, hostages or no hostages. Letting the council present its list of demands was nothing more than playing for time, a way to get the wounded hostages out, and maybe find out from them where the other hostages were being held. As time went on, Em City grew almost as quiet as a graveyard. Nobody talked much, the council members just hung around the turf their tribes controlled, there was no communication with the outside, nobody went in or out of the cell block. For a while, some of us figured that with McManus inside, either he'd find a way to negotiate with the council, or they'd try to use him as a go-between to Glynn and Devlin. I mean, McManus was the one guy in Oz with the balls to enter Em City after the inmates took control, so it made sense that his presence would change things. But nothing happened, he became just one more hostage, locked away with the others, so we weren't sure whether the governor was trying to wear us down or starve us out. For two long days, we just waited, growing wearier and tenser as the hours mounted up and the food ran out. Once in a while a high-pitched howl from Adebisi or another inmate who was going through heroin

RIP: Victims of the Riot

- Scott Ross, leader of the Bikers, shot by C.O. hostage Diane Whittlesey with a handgun belonging to Richard Heim, a member of the S.O.R.T., during the assault on Em City.

- Eugene Dobbins, stabbed at the outset of the riot by another inmate, died later of his wounds.

- Edward Hunt, C.O., cause of death unknown.

- Anthony Nowakowski, C.O., cause of death unknown.

- Five other inmates, causes of death unknown.

withdrawal would break the silence, but otherwise all you could hear were the sounds of doors opening and closing, guys whispering to each other, moving around and occasionally arguing. Strange, but with no one person in charge, there was less yelling and disturbance in Em City than on an ordinary day.

Then the lights went out. The council's first reaction was to drag the hostages out to the gate and line them up as a first line of defense, in case the S.O.R.T. started shooting. A minute later, it was like the heavens had opened, only the clouds were tear gas and the stars fire from the S.O.R.T.'s rifles. In the dark, you couldn't tell where the shots were coming from, and besides, the tear gas made it almost impossible to see anything. I got as far away from the gate as I could and huddled in a pod whose furniture had been taken when the barricades were thrown up, together with some of the other inmates who were trying to keep out of the line of fire. And in a few minutes, it was all over. The S.O.R.T. took control of Em City, the dead and the wounded were carted away, and the rest of us were in handcuffs and on the way to gen pop.

Except for the leaders, that is. Only one of them, Steve Ross, the head of the Bikers, was killed; the others weren't even badly hurt—I guess the S.O.R.T. had trouble locating them in the dark and commotion—but Devlin and Glynn knew who they were, of course. Their names were on the list of demands the council had sent to the warden, and the four survivors were dropped into Solitary: Said, Adebisi, Alvarez, and O'Reily. I suppose the aim was to punish them for their roles in the riot, but compared to what life in gen pop was like for us, Solitary might've been close to Club Med. The whole prison was in lockdown because of what went down in Em City, and now we were doubling and tripling up in cells that were meant to hold one inmate. I'd rather take Solitary anytime than try to tiptoe around in an eight-by-ten cage with a guy screaming, "This is my fucking cell"; he wants you out or wants you dead and doesn't much care which way he gets rid of you. If that wasn't already bad enough, a couple cells down the block, Robson, an Aryan pal of Schillinger's, woke Beecher, his new cellmate, in the middle of the night, demanding a blow job. What did that bug Beecher do? He bit the end of the cocksucker's dick off.

Sunday 7.13.97

Do I care if Em City ever comes back? I don't know, but I'd sure like to get out of this crowded cell. Who knows whether McManus will ever make it back to Oz. He's in the hospital, shot in the chest by—nobody knows, a prisoner, maybe, or a member of the S.O.R.T. The word is he'll recover, but whether he'll have the stomach to come back to Oz is anybody's guess. His luck was a hell of a lot better than poor Dobbins's, though. I finally passed Jackson Vahue in the corridor today, and he told me that Dobbins didn't make it. Couldn't stop to say anything more, and I don't even know what cell block Vahue's in. The little bit of home we had back there, it's sure gone now.

Maybe Em City and the riot are just history, but a lot of people are competing to own that history. Governor Devlin and Warden Glynn and just about every politician in the state has an opinion about what happened and why it happened and whether having the S.O.R.T. storm the block saved lives. After all, when it was all over there were only eight dead; it could've been a lot worse, say the defenders of using force. I say, why doesn't somebody ask the eight who died?

They can't do that, so the governor's appointed a commission to investigate the riot and figure out who was to blame. And they've been all over Oz like ants over ice cream, especially the head of the commission, Alvah Case, a hotshot law professor who started out asking everybody what caused the riot, but recently switched gears to concentrate on the death of Scott Ross. Seems he suspects Ross wasn't just caught in the crossfire when the S.O.R.T. rushed Em City, but was shot at close range, murdered. Case looks and sounds a little like a high school coach when he asks a question, like he's trying to figure out

whether he's going to move you up to the starting five or leave you on the bench. Whatever Case or the rest of the commission turns up, though, I'm betting the report will spin the truth so hard that when it stops spinning, things will look good for Devlin's reelection next year.

1997 Victims

- **Dino Ortolani:** Hotheaded, homophobic Wise Guy, incinerated by Johnny Post in retaliation for savagely beating Billy Keane, gay brother of Homeboys leader Jefferson Keane.

- **Johnny Post:** Tortured, partially dismembered, and executed on orders from Wise Guy boss Nino Schibetta, to avenge the death of Dino Ortolani.

- **Jefferson Keane:** First prisoner executed at Oz after restoration of death penalty. Convicted of murdering a Latino inmate and killed by lethal injection.

- **Richard L'Italien:** Convicted of murdering Jennifer Miller, his former lover. While on death row he confessed to having killed 39 other women, after having sex with all of them. Executed by lethal injection.

- **Nino Schibetta:** Hemorrhaged after Adebisi and O'Reily mixed ground glass in his food, in a plot to take control of the drug traffic from the Wise Guys.

- **Paul Markstrom:** Undercover narcotics detective who infiltrated the Homeboys and was hanged when they discovered his true identity.

- **Husseini Murshah:** Tried to muscle his way into a position of power among the Muslims, but was rejected by Said for failing to aid him during his heart attack. Banished to gen pop, Murshah cut his own throat in his cell.

- **Donald Groves:** After killing a C.O. in a failed attempt to assassinate Glynn, Groves was executed by firing squad.

Entries from 1998

Monday 5.18.98

After ten gruesome fucking months in gen pop, we're back in Em City, but it doesn't feel like coming home. The place looks the same, and so does McManus, though maybe he's a little less sure of himself after his brush with death. Still, he made a nice speech from the railing of the command station, like he was the captain of a ship addressing his crew before sailing off in search of a new continent. McManus announced that he'd chosen exactly four people from each of the ten groups in Oz—Wise Guys, Homeboys, Latinos, Aryans, Christians, Muslims, Irish, Bikers, Gays, and Others—to form the population of the new Em City. How the fuck "others" got to be a group, and how the fuck I got stuck with them, is something I'd like to know. The other "others" turned out to be Beecher, Rebadow, and a clown I never saw before named Busmalis, who introduced himself, while brushing his teeth at the same time, as "the Mole" ("I dig"). It looks to me like "other" means nut job, and the idea of bunking with those mental cases is giving me nightmares. McManus says I fit in with them because I got a disability, but I'm in a fucking wheelchair, not on a direct line to God, biting guys' dicks off, or tunneling my way out of Oz.

I don't want to get back with the Homeboys, even if I did sell as many drugs as any of them on the outside. But bunking with Beecher is making me as jumpy as hanging with Adebisi would. I'm scared of falling asleep around that bug. McManus's brush with mortality may have made him more human, but there's still too much of the mad scientist in him, something that makes him still see us prisoners as lab rats in Dr. M.'s experiment to prove that we can be turned into useful members of society. This time around, Dr. M.'s forming a council of representatives of all the groups in Em City. To discuss our grievances, he says, but it's really to push his agenda. First meeting: guys are yelling about bringing back conjugals and cigarettes, which were banned by some bullshit rule that was supposed to make Oz a healthier environment, but that's not what's on McManus's mind. He wants to start a fucking high school! Everybody who didn't graduate from high school is going to get his GED. And damned if he doesn't get a new guy named Charles Coushaine, who'd been a schoolteacher on the outside, to agree to teach the class! I wonder if he's asked Said to be one of the

Rebadow and Busmalis plot their escape.

teachers, or is he afraid of what it is Said might teach? He wasn't even at the council meeting, and the word is he's boycotting the whole idea.

Wednesday 6.3.98

Sometimes I've got to like McManus in spite of his fucking "I know what's good for you" attitude. Take Kenny Wangler. He almost took Coushaine's head off in class when Coushaine leaned on him to read out loud. When McManus discovered that Wangler doesn't know how to read and that's

probably why he attacked Coushaine, Timmy Boy really took Wangler under his wing, and now the kid's starting to make real progress. Will reading Booker T. Washington get him away from Adebisi's influence? I doubt it, not as long as he's in Em City, with Adebisi getting Kenny to do his dirty work and probably having sex with him. The kid's been in Oz for almost a year now, and he's still only seventeen. Maybe I'm thinking about Wangler because he's a little bit like I was at that age, looking up to Burr Redding but fearing him, too, more than a little. At least I could read, maybe not well enough to keep me from landing in Oz, or to get me out now that I'm here. But Wangler, who knows? If he keeps

Education in Prison

In the spring of 1997, I taught my last creative writing class in the Washington State prisons. This particular class lasted for three weeks, and ran from 9 A.M. to 3 P.M. every day. It took place at the Washington Corrections Center in Shelton, a medium-security facility, [which] is reputed to be one of the "softer" joints in the system. Still, WCC Shelton is a prison. And after spending eight years driving around the state and teaching classes at prison after prison, I had come to view prisons—whether "soft" or "hard"—as spiritual emergency wards; as repositories of society's poorest, most vilified outcasts; as repositories for men and women who live in settings that are notable for their exceptionally high levels of psychic pain, self-loathing, pent-up frustration, hate, gore, fear of rape, desire to rape, proximity to evil, proximity to grace, the ever-present threat of sudden violence, and—above all—despair.

MAKING STREETS SAFER

As you might expect, teaching in such settings exacted a high emotional toll on me. Nevertheless, no job I've held before or since has made me feel more useful. I felt that through the act of teaching in prisons, I was contributing to crime prevention. I felt this intuitively when I was alone with my students, and I felt it intellectually based on studies I'd read.

One study in particular comes to mind. It was conducted by the National Institute of Justice—the research arm of the federal Justice Department—during the mid-to-late 1980s. The study followed 105,000 state prisoners during the first few years after their release. Among its major findings were these: Sixty-six percent of the entire group were rearrested for a felony or a serious misdemeanor within three years of their release.

- Of those who volunteered to get a high school diploma while in prison, that number dropped to 45 percent.
- Those who received a two-year college degree while in prison were rearrested at a rate of 27.5 percent.
- Those who received a four-year college degree while in prison were rearrested at a rate of 12.5 percent.

This is a dramatic set of statistics, and one that ought to be as meaningful to governors, state legislators, law-enforcement officials, and other policymakers as it is to educators and social workers. These numbers should carry a great deal of weight for anyone who professes a belief in crime prevention.

EDUCATION PROGRAMS DECIMATED

Unfortunately, this is not, apparently, the case. For there has been no clamor for more and better educational programming. On the contrary, the pendulum has swung the other way. In my home state of Washington, for example, as part of a new "no frills" approach to incarceration, the community-college system within our prisons—once a model for the nation—has, by legislative fiat, been dismantled. Even high school degrees are no longer offered to those convicts who want them.

Sadly, Washington State is not alone. Education programs have been or are being eliminated in state after state. . . . A new "lock 'em up and throw away the key" sentiment has swept across the land. Of course, in most cases the key is not really thrown away. Sooner or later most prisoners are released. Indeed, approximately half a million prisoners are released every year. Lacking education, which is to say marketable skills, confidence, and an expanded sense of possibilities, it is inevitable that many of these released prisoners—including the ones who would've acquired an education if it had been offered—will return to what they know best: the life of crime. Thus, the polity's desire for vengeance is being fulfilled at the price of public safety.

Source: Robert Ellis Gordon, "My Life as a Prison Teacher," *Christian Science Monitor,* March 12, 2001. Gordon taught story writing in the Washington State prisons from 1989 to 1997. Portions of this article originally appeared in Mr. Gordon's book, *The Funhouse Mirror: Reflections on Prison* (Pullman, Wash.: Washington State University Press, 2000).

Beecher gets a lesson from the Homeboys.

reading until he comes up for parole in five or six years, maybe he won't exactly become somebody, but he might become somebody else.

If I'm ever going to have a chance of getting out of prison, it won't be because of my own reading, but it might happen because of Kareem Said's. Ever since the riot, he's been studying law, not Islamic *sharī'ah*, but good old American criminal law. He says he's planning to make the law devour itself. I don't know if he'll be able to accomplish that, but if he can find a way to make Oz devour enough of itself to create an opening I can walk—or roll—through to freedom, I'll be satisfied. Freedom is a word I haven't even let myself pronounce since I came through the gate, but now it's flown into my mind and I can't get it out.

A couple weeks ago, we heard on the news that Lawrence Kibler, the judge who heard my case and sentenced me, has been convicted of accepting bribes from defense lawyers in return for lighter sentences for their clients. Said thinks there's a chance of overturning my conviction; he says that Kibler might have been tougher on the defendants he didn't take money from in order to compensate for being lenient when he did accept bribes. Said admits it's no sure thing, and I realize that he's got his own reasons—to expose the rot inside the judicial system—but if there's a chance, I'll fucking go for it. So far we've talked to the lawyer who repre-

sented me at my original trial, who says he heard rumors about bribes but that Kibler never approached him. Then Marilyn Crenshaw, the DA who prosecuted Kibler, came in to discuss the case, or at least I thought that's why she'd come. Throughout the meeting, all she does is give Said shit about how he opposed everything she believed in, and then she tells me that I should get myself a real lawyer, and splits. I just sat there wondering, what'd we ever do to her?

After she left, I found out. I hadn't done anything, but Said had. Before he converted to Islam, he and Crenshaw were engaged, and I guess she's still pissed at him for dumping her after he'd found Allah. He acts like he's annoyed with her for not cooperating in his legal plans, but how the fuck did he expect her to act? One day they're in love, and the next day Said's telling her that her white ass isn't good enough for his black dick. Now he's in prison, and it's her laws that put him there. So how could Said expect Crenshaw to cooperate?

Monday 6.22.98

It's weird, man, weird going back to court, even weirder that the "courtroom" is actually the prison library, and weirdest of all that if the judge orders a new trial for me, I could be out of prison tonight. Home. In my own house, with my own wife, sleeping in my own bed, watching my own TV, drinking a beer—my own beer—Burr and my mom coming over, friends dropping in to congratulate me, or calling on the phone. When I close my eyes I can see the living room, the sofa on one wall, the TV opposite, but I can't find a place for me in my wheelchair. We'll shift some of the furniture around, Annabella and me, to make room. But I'm too excited right now to think about it, too nervous to write. Maybe after the hearing.

Monday 7.13.98

At first it seemed like things were going our way at the hearing, that the judge would agree that if Kibler was taking bribes in exchange for lighter sentences, he couldn't be impartial in cases like mine, where he wasn't on the take. The state's lawyer said no, just because Kibler was a crook on Monday, that didn't prove that he was a crook on Tuesday, too, and besides, I had shot the cop and deserved to be in prison. But then I started to notice that whenever Said made an objection— and he made lots of them—the judge overruled him, and the feeling came over me that maybe I wouldn't be getting a new trial and going home after all.

Back in Em City, when Said started talking about filing an appeal and

being "true to our cause," I'd fucking heard enough. I told him I wasn't interested in any cause, or doing something for "my people"; my only cause was getting out of this dump and trying to get my life back. I said some things I probably shouldn't have, like how he made too many stupid objections at the hearing and probably wasn't as good a lawyer as he thinks he is. Maybe that's true, but maybe what's true is that his dream of making the law devour itself isn't going to happen so easy, that the law just might devour a few of our black asses for lunch instead.

The truth is, I don't give a shit about the law; what I'm having trouble with is hoping and then losing hope. I don't think I can take that roller-coaster ride again. One way or another, the trip is going to bring me back to my pod. I can take the chance that I might get a new trial, but after that trial, where will I be? If the yellow-brick road eventually leads to Em City and no place else, maybe I'm better off admitting that Oz is as much home as I'm ever going to find.

Friday 8.7.98

What was it that I couldn't deal with in that hearing? Was it having to depend on somebody else to make my dream of going free come true? I never thought that I wanted power the way

Jailhouse Lawyers

Charles M. Steele, who is accused of a 1994 rape and kidnapping, asked Hamilton County Common Pleas Judge Norbert Nadel [Ohio] if he could represent himself. Already in prison for an unrelated crime, Mr. Steele cited the Sixth Amendment and a 1975 U.S. Supreme Court ruling affirming a person's right to waive counsel. His handwritten request appeared professional and its arguments plausible.

However, Judge Nadel, as is any judge's discretion, rejected the request because he believed Mr. Steele would not be able to effectively defend himself. If Mr. Steele were found guilty, his conviction could be overturned on appeal because of inadequate representation. The judge, instead, appointed counsel and set a trial for September.

"A lot of inmates get the idea that they can defend themselves because of the jailhouse lawyers," Judge Nadel says, referring to inmates who study law books and advise their fellow prisoners on law. "If those jailhouse lawyers were so smart they wouldn't be in jail themselves."

Despite *Ferrata v. California,* the 25-year-old U.S. Supreme Court decision affirming a person's right to waive counsel, there are no Ohio statutes mandating that court systems teach pro se litigants the nuances of court procedure. [S]ometimes, criminal defendants see a chance to tell their stories, unfettered by a lawyer representing them. In April, one of America's Most Wanted, anti-abortion activist Clayton Lee Waagner, acted as his own attorney during his federal trial on weapons and car theft charges in U.S. District Court in Cincinnati. Though acknowledging his guilt, the 48-year-old Pennsylvania man considered it an opportunity to share his radical ideals with a captive audience.

Nevertheless, self-representation in criminal cases remains rare. In his 5 1/2 years on the bench, Hamilton County Common Pleas Judge Steve Martin says he has yet to have a criminal defendant in his courtroom represent himself. He says most criminal defendants realize their freedom is at stake and aren't willing to gamble. Still, he adds, "Every case is different. You'll have a defendant who wants to handle his own case and in that event I'd probably appoint a lawyer anyway. As a judge, my obligation is to make sure people's rights are protected. But, if someone wants to represent himself and makes a stupid decision, that's their choice."

Source: Marie McCain, "More Defendants Go It Alone: More People Eschewing Lawyers to Defend Themselves," *Cincinnati Enquirer,* Monday, August 26, 2002.

Said, McManus, Glynn, and Governor Devlin do, but maybe power is what I had on the street—everybody recognizing me, talking about me, wanting to talk to me. I didn't realize how far I'd run away from the whole power thing since coming to Oz. I don't want people to recognize me or treat me like a celebrity. I just want them to notice me, like one of their neighbors or a friendly face in the crowd.

Maybe Said's out of his depth in a court of law, but in the court of public opinion he's right at home. He complains that Glynn and McManus turn down his requests for the phones and fax machines he needs to do his work, but he does as good a job as the fucking governor in getting the press to pay attention when he wants them to. Not long ago he decided to help Poet, who writes these amazing poems that he sometimes recites in the cafeteria or in the cell block, get some of his writings published (McManus was the one who suggested it to Said, but it's Said who has the publishing connections), and not only are they coming out in an anthology called *Unheard Americans*, but now writers and journalists from all over have started a campaign to get Poet released. As it happens, Poet's got a parole hearing coming up soon, and if they can keep him going to drug counseling (word is he spent the money the publisher sent him to settle his tit account with Adebisi) and keep him out of trouble, I'll bet he has a shot at getting released. The campaign for Poet has Said written all over it. I wonder if he didn't blow up that warehouse just to get himself incarcerated, so instead of writing about injustice from the outside, he could tear the prison system down from the inside. The riot may have blown up in his face, but there'll be more fireworks from Said before he's done.

Saturday 8.22.98

Poet's going home. Not many guys make parole in Oz; fewer have a home to go to when they get released. I've had home on my mind for the past couple days, ever since the graduation ceremony last Saturday. Less than a dozen inmates got their GED diplomas from what I guess you could call Oz High, but there must've been four times that many of their relatives in the audience. The only place I've seen prisoners' family members is in the visiting room or the infirmary. Suddenly the cafeteria was transformed, for an hour or so everybody in the room—inmates, visitors, even the staff—was just folks.

Poet delivered the valedictory address, a poem. Later, Rebadow, who used to be an architect and turns out to know a lot of stuff that God didn't

tell him, explained that the term "valedictorian" comes from the custom of having a student at every graduation—usually the one with the highest grades—make a farewell speech. Since Poet really was about to leave, it made real sense that he was the class valedictorian. But the absolute fucking shocker was McManus's announcement that the state was about to pull the plug on the prison education program, that this first graduation would be the last. There were a TV reporter and cameraman covering the ceremony, so the story was on the seven o'clock news that night. Devlin, who was on the stage to hand out the diplomas, didn't move a muscle when McManus dropped his bombshell, but Glynn, sitting next to the

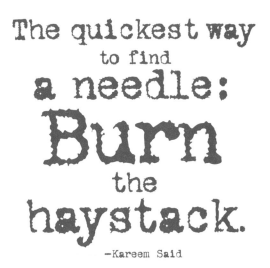

The quickest way to find a needle: Burn the haystack.
—Kareem Said

governor, started twitching in his chair like a duck in a shooting gallery.

The day Poet left Oz, he decided not to take any of his shit with him,

144,000 RHYMES

Too many prisons and not enough schools
too many weapons and not enough tools.
Not enough teachers and too many fools
though
I'm from where fights are born
from where nights are dawned
from true ingredients spit from the sun
I've formed an allegiance with the number one,
the letter a,
the beginning of the day,
the way,
the wisdom
the wish
the will
the river
the tree
the try
the trek
the rub of the neck
the ball of the foot
the back of the thigh
the glimmer in the eye peering at what it's
    intrigued in
tried by what it believes in
I've taken on the likeness of love,
the harbor of hate
the hell of here
and the wonder of the whereafter.
I've discerned the disaster
and drank Dom Pérignon in Armageddon,
I've drank the sacred ambrosia housed in the
    chalice of the rebellious cherubim
disguised as quarter juices
I've died toothless and been reborn
    144,000 times.
I've got 144,000 rhymes for every brain cell.
But I waste away in a cell.

Poem by muMs

said he wanted to leave everything connected to prison behind. I guess he figured that with nothing to tie him to Oz on the outside, nothing would be able to bring him back there. Will he succeed? I hope so, but I don't know, since it's what's in your head that you can't shake, but he's going to try. The rest of us, who are remaining inside, try to figure out ways to keep something of our families with us. We don't see them often, sometimes don't see them at all, so all we can do is keep our memories of them alive. After a while, though, what we remember no longer exists out there, if it ever did. Then maybe it's time to start over. Only when you're in Oz, there might not be much to start over with.

Thursday 9.3.98

When Schillinger's parole hearing went against him, he blamed Beecher and tried to have him killed. That's what the hacks said, anyway—that Schillinger offered Whittlesey two grand to do the deed, that she pretended to go along with the scheme, demanded the money up front, and busted him when she was supposed to show him the body. Schillinger claimed that he'd been set up, and Said agreed to defend him. But even if Schillinger was set up, even if he never offered Whittlesey money to kill Beecher, why would Said defend that racist bastard, especially after what he'd already done to Beecher? I never liked Beecher much myself—when he showed up in Em City he acted like he was a fucking gemstone that had been dropped into the coal bin by mistake—but it was Schillinger's turning him into his prag and humiliating him that pushed Beecher over the edge, into addiction and hating almost everybody around him, especially after his wife divorced him. Beecher swore he'd prevent Schillinger from ever getting paroled, so Ol' Vern had a motive for getting even. Whatever really happened, Said withdrew from the case after he decided that Schillinger was, in fact, guilty, but the damage to Said's reputation had already been done. Said wanted to show that he was prepared to defend all prisoners' rights, not simply the rights of prisoners he liked or agreed with, or who believed in what he believes in. But after talking to Whittlesey, he realized that defending Schillinger wouldn't make him look like somebody dedicated to justice, but like just another jailhouse lawyer. Schillinger accused Said of planning to drop him all along, suckering him in so he wouldn't be able to get another lawyer to prepare his defense in time. I don't think Said would've done anything that low, but as an idea, you've got to admit it's got some appeal.

Who's your best friend in prison? The buddy who's always watching your back? Maybe, but the guy who watches your back might also be checking out your ass. It sounds funny to say this, but my best friend since I got to Oz is my bed. Not because I spend so much time in bed, but because it's where I dream—of being free, back home with Annabella, and sometimes even walking (I'm never in a wheelchair in these dreams) or on the court shooting hoops. You see, I'm lucky; unlike a lot of the cons, in my dreams I'm never still in Oz.

I've just switched beds, but in Em City the beds and the pods are all pretty much the same. What's different are the cellmates, and I've got to say I'm relieved to be putting some distance between myself and Beecher. There's something about the guy that scares me, like he's got a little bomb inside him somewhere that's always about to explode. So when Whittlesey told me to get my stuff together, that I was moving to another pod because McManus doesn't want the inmates getting too comfortable in one situation, I didn't even ask her where I was moving to. I just started packing. The newbie they moved in with Beecher is named Chris Keller, and they seem to be hitting it off. Seems that Beecher jumped in to defend Keller when Mark

Mack, an Aryan punk, tried to shake Keller down when he tried to use the pay phone. Though from the amount of blood pouring out of Mack's nose after Keller'd finished with him, it didn't look like he needed Beecher's help at all. But he probably appreciated the gesture.

Extending a hand in friendship isn't something people do very often in Oz. There are too many reasons not to trust anybody, but every once in a while, a little voice inside you says,

Do it, the way I did with Jackson Vahue. I still miss Vahue sometimes. I don't blame him that I got sucked back into doing drugs for a time, I blame me. He was one angry motherfucker, true enough, and hard to be around most of the time, but I guess that was because he had to face his losses every day. Other guys can sometimes tell themselves, I'll do my time and get on with my life, so they work out and lift weights like they're trying to become contenders. But Vahue was already a

Beecher and Keller come closer together.

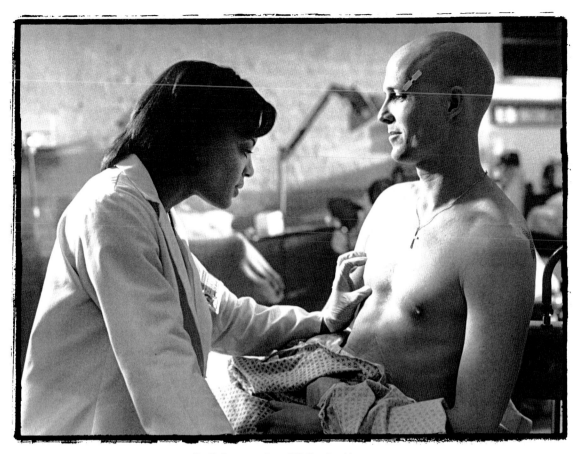

Dr. Nathan examines O'Reily after his surgery.

fucking contender, and he knew that every day he spent inside was cutting his career short.

Ryan O'Reily was just another small-time drug dealer, only his gang was the Irish, and he'd shot a guy or two on the street. Nothing fancy. But in Oz he plays angles that Minnesota Fats never imagined, worming his way into Em City, and even trying to con Nino Schibetta into believing that he didn't have anything to do with Dino Ortolani's death. All this is SOP for Oz, where guys are constantly trying to scam each other, except that O'Reily managed to get over on guys that nobody else could fool, like a basketball player who's got the same moves as everybody else, only when he does them you somehow don't see them coming. So good, in fact, that he may have succeeded in faking himself out. His latest victims include a couple people he probably didn't mean to hurt. What happened was that O'Reily fell in love—not with a cellmate, like Beecher and this newbie, Chris Keller, seem to be doing, but with Gloria Nathan, the doctor who runs the infirmary.

You see O'Reily got a tumor in his chest—basically, breast cancer, in a guy! (apparently, it happens a lot more than we like to think)—and while Dr. Nathan was diagnosing him and arranging for him to have surgery at

Benchley Memorial Hospital, he took her kindness for love. He fell for her, and hard.

All the time O'Reily was dealing with the disease and the fear and the chemo, Dr. Nathan gave him plenty of support. Who knows, maybe she liked the idea of helping a patient recover from a "normal" illness—even if it's rare for a man to have breast cancer. She's got to be tired of patching inmates up after they've been knifed or beaten or raped, or tending to the addicts and gays slowly dying of AIDS. And who knows, she was married, but she's also one hot lady doctor, and maybe she even liked the attention.

Apparently O'Reily decided that what was keeping him and Dr. Nathan apart wasn't him or his murder conviction, but her husband. So he talked his own brother, Cyril, who suffers from some kind of mental retardation and who worships O'Reily as if he were a god, into murdering Dr. Nathan's husband. Now Dr. Nathan's a widow, and Cyril O'Reily's an inmate in gen pop. On the outside, O'Reily's wife had been looking after Cyril, but in here, he's on his own, and gen pop's no kiddie playground. If nobody else takes advantage of Cyril, Schillinger probably will, to fuck with O'Reily's head as well as his brother's. Any way you look at it, it ain't good news for Cyril. I don't know if love conquers all, like they say, but this time it's fucked up a couple of lives.

Who cares about Bob Rebadow? Almost nobody. Most people either ignore him or think he's some kind of freak. It's true he sometimes knows things about people that no human being could have told him, but still—nobody cares. But if the question is who cares about Rebadow's grandson, a kid nobody in here, not even Rebadow, has ever seen, the answer is just about everybody. Why? Because the kid has leukemia, and Rebadow just got a letter saying his dream is to visit Adventure Country. Jaz Hoyt, a biker who works in the post office, where they open every package and read every letter that comes into Oz, brought it up at this week's Em City council meeting. A few days later, people who wouldn't have bothered saying "Fuck you!" to Rebadow were handing him cash—McManus even got the hacks to kick in—and more than three grand for the trip was on its way to the grandson.

Funny how things play out in Oz. A nameless, faceless kid becomes everybody's unseen poster child, while his grandfather—somebody we see every day—remains invisible. Tomorrow, the same men who handed Rebadow fifty or a hundred dollars for his grandson's trip will look right past him in the cafeteria or the cell block. When we acknowledge

SEXUALITY GONE AWRY

Deprived of meaningful outlets for sexual expression, men in prison develop myriad coping techniques. Prison's secondary staple, after cigarettes, is pornography or "paper pussy." Smut books circulate and become a coveted commodity and currency. Some men assign personalities to the porn stars and invent names in order to augment masturbatory fantasies. Severed from relationships with the living, the mind seeks its shadow through projection. It should be no surprise that prison is a hotbed of homosexuality, which, in turn, is intricately linked to a system of dominance among men. Although all prisons have rules that prohibit homosexual sexual contact, it continues unabated, fanned by bans against conjugal visitation and implicit administrative acceptance. At one level, homosexual relations reflect and reproduce pecking orders of dominance and submission among the prisoners themselves. At another level, savvy administrators look the other way on such couplings, because they can utilize those relationships to extend their control. For example, as in any macho subculture, homosexuality is extremely stigmatized. An official may threaten a closeted homosexual with exposure, thus triggering certain violent retribution and potential rape. To avoid such threats, the gay prisoner may inform on other inmates, thus enlarging the web of interprisoner conflict and distrust while solidifying centralized administrative control.

The following two cases show that sexual fantasy sometimes spills over into delusion, complicating relationships among fellow prisoners and between prisoners and professional staff. One prisoner, struck by a nurse's gentle manner, badly misinterpreted a simple smile for genuine affection, and in his mind there arose the belief that she was his wife. He went into a fixation so pointed that, after several suicide attempts, which were probably staged in order to gain her sympathy or access her nursing skills, he was committed to a regional mental facility for several weeks. After his return, he no longer claimed that the female staffer was his wife, but his fingers fidgeted constantly and his tongue perpetually darted in and out of his mouth. These are telltale symptoms of tardive dyskinesia, the permanent side-effects of psychotropic medication that is used to "treat" some psychiatric patients.

Another prisoner, imprisoned for more than a decade, since his midteens, developed a jailhouse reputation for flashing au naturel whenever a female staffer, usually a nurse, came to his cell. Orders and repeated misconduct reports failed to deter his practice. At one point the husband of the female staffer responded by assaulting him. The administration finally assigned a male nurse to attend to his medical needs. The flashings and many of his illnesses ceased.

Both of these cases, though anecdotal, reflect the tortured and maddening lengths that some prisoners go to in order to give some, albeit twisted, expression to their sexuality. Both situations might have been mitigated by a conjugal visitation program. Both men, and tens of thousands like them, spend their twenties, an age of peak sexuality, in shackles—unable to touch and be touched and barely able to dream. Upon their inevitable release, what will be unleashed upon the world?

Source: Mumia Abu-Jamal, "Caged and Celibate," in *Prison Masculinities,* edited by Don Sabo, Terry A. Kupers, and Willie London (Philadelphia: Temple University Press, 2001).

MUMIA ABU-JAMAL (born in 1954 as Wesley Cook) was a Philadelphia radio journalist when he was arrested in 1981 for the shooting death of Daniel Faulkner, a police officer. Convicted in 1982, Abu-Jamal has appealed his conviction and death sentence from prison and continued to publish his writings, including *Live From Death Row* (Avon Books, 1998), a collection of essays. In December 2001, a federal judge overturned his death sentence and ordered a new sentencing hearing for Abu-Jamal, but not a new trial.

somebody in Oz, we're admitting to ourselves that he lives where we do. When you notice the people who are different from you, you're admitting that you're in prison. Maybe that's why it got to me when I was thrown in with the "others" after we returned to Em City. Not because they're crazy—even if they are—but because they are the invisible men of Oz, the guys who don't exist for the others. If you're nobody, you're just somebody to be fucked, or fucked over.

Tuesday 11.3.98

It's hard to think of anybody less likely to escape from a maximum security prison than the guy in the wheelchair, but I can't get the idea out of my mind. Probably it was the Judge Kibler business that planted the idea of freedom in my head, but now that it's there I think about it all the time. If I don't stop thinking about escaping, maybe I'll end up as crazy as Busmalis. He called himself a mole, and he wasn't joking. He's digging a tunnel from his cell to the other side of the prison walls, and Rebadow's helping him. They get rid of the evidence by washing the dirt away when they do their laundry. They admitted what they were up to the other day when I noticed a bag of soil that had

spilled onto the laundry room floor. Busmalis even invited me to escape with them, so I asked him if his tunnel had handicapped access. He laughed, and even Rebadow showed a trace of a smile, so I guess those two aren't completely nuts yet. Of course, they haven't finished their fucking tunnel, either.

It's easy to laugh at Busmalis, who probably sleeps in his Greek fisherman's cap, but people are probably thinking I'm getting strange, too. The other day I even asked Schillinger if he thought I could ship out of Oz in a package. What was I thinking, even asking that racist a question? He acted like he didn't even hear me. Later I talked to Alvarez, who works in the infirmary, if it was possible to get out in a body bag, in place of a patient who died. It turns out the bodies are sent to the morgue, where they get embalmed and shit before they're sent back to the family for the funeral. So maybe a coffin's the way to go!

I'd do almost anything to get out of Oz, but these schemes of mine are too crazy and too stupid to work. Still, there's something unnatural about locking people up—in cells or rooms or pods or whatever else the fuck you want to call them—no matter what it is they've done. There was a *National Geographic* special on TV a few weeks back, all about how some animals are cooperative and some are competitive. The story wasn't all that pleasant;

animals fight and kill—within a single species, between one species and another—pretty much the way human beings do. They even have some pretty nasty ways of killing, though of course they don't have Mach 10s and AK-47s and B-52s, but there's one thing that no other animal species does: only human beings cage up their own kind.

Buried alive. That pretty much sums up how everybody feels in Oz. But Mark Mack and one of his neo-Nazi fraternity brothers whose name I didn't even know just swallowed that concept whole. From their pod on the second

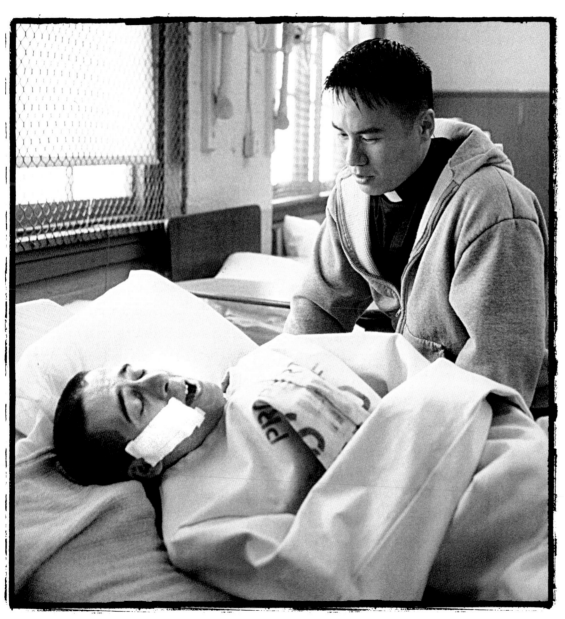

Father Mukada tries to console Alvarez.

floor of Em City, they could see Rebadow and Busmalis at night as they worked on their tunnel. One day Mack threatened to get them both busted unless they agreed to switch pods as soon as Busmalis dug past the outer wall of the prison. Busmalis must've booby-trapped the tunnel, because

I'm living **in the right now.** And what now is telling me, **If we don't get together, we're going down apart.**

-Kenny Wangler

he'd been crawling in and out of it for months without any problems, but when Mack and his pal tried to worm their way to freedom, the fucking tunnel caved in all around them. There was nothing left to do but dig the bastards out just to bury them again.

Every inmate says he wants out, and Mack's not the only one to die trying, but even some inmates who manage to get out can't seem to stay out. Poet's back in Oz. He left everything behind when he was released, but it seems his crack habit followed him into the street, and when a dealer he owed money to came after him, Poet shot him. McManus and

Said are so pissed they won't even talk to the guy, but what did they expect? McManus wanted Poet to prove Devlin wrong, to show that educating inmates transforms them into model citizens. Said thought that Poet would proclaim to the world that the pen is mightier than the crack pipe. Maybe it is, but somehow the world didn't get the message, or Poet needed more than just words to live by on the outside.

If I was suddenly dropped back out on the street, crawling with old friends and old habits, would the same thing happen to me? I don't know, and because I don't, I can't blame Poet for how things turned out. I haven't given up on the idea of escaping, though everybody just laughs at my latest plan—hiding in a coffin that's about to be trucked out to a funeral parlor instead of the corpse it was meant for—so I guess it probably wouldn't work. But neither is trying to wait out these seventeen years. Am I starting to come unglued? Okay, so my plans for escaping are stupid, and telling half the prison about them is even stupider, but maybe doing those things is my way of reminding myself that there's still someplace worth escaping to, that the world hasn't shrunk to the dimensions of Oz. If I can't look forward to getting free in any other way (waiting seventeen years until my parole isn't an idea, it's a bottomless pit my life can't fill up), at least I can dream about being back outside, and those dreams may be all I have to keep me human. I'm starting to see too

Opposite: Alvarez tries to make peace with El Cid.

many guys who say they're going to get out—escape, parole, appeals—digging themselves deeper and deeper into Oz. Even Busmalis, who fucking knew a thing or two about tunnels—burrowing all the way to the outside, shoring the thing up, and then bringing it down all over those two scummy Aryans—what did he think he and Rebadow were going to do once they got to the other side, *if* they ever got there? My guess is they'd be captured before breakfast, facing more time.

One guy who actually got released came back to Oz and asked Sister Pete if he could sleep in one of the cells because no one on the outside would rent a room to him. That was Sippel, a defrocked priest. He'd molested a boy, and it seems the new law requiring sex offenders to register in their communities pretty much made it impossible for him to find a job, and with no job, there weren't any rooms at the inn. Father Mukada, the chaplain, hired him as his assistant, and Sippel spent a couple nights in a cell in gen pop, but Schillinger and some other Aryans trapped him in the gym and crucified the poor bastard—nailed his hands and feet to the fucking floor of the basketball court! I guess molesting children is something else the Aryan Brotherhood disap-

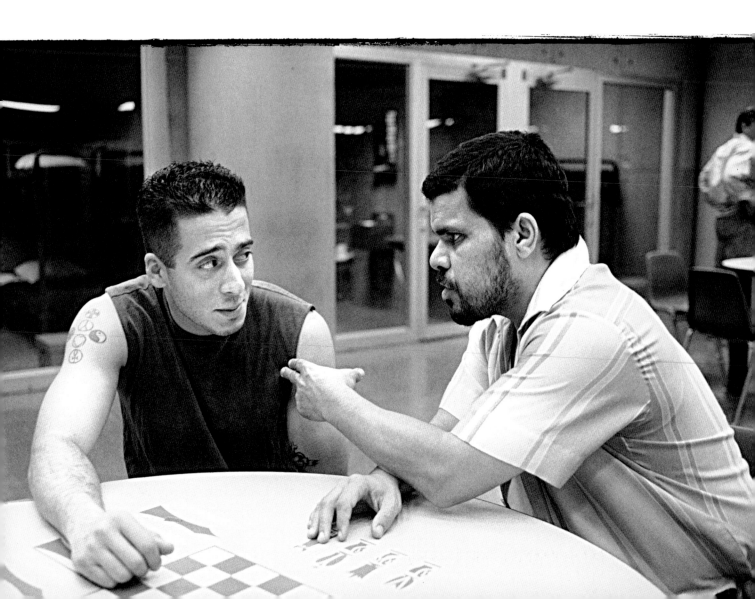

"Sieg Heil! Sieg Heil" Keller and Schillinger prepare to break Beecher's bones.

proves of. Now Sippel's in Benchley Memorial; maybe if he gets out of the hospital he'll finally find someplace besides Oz to call home. The word is that Metzger, the new Em City supervisor, had something to do with getting the Aryans into the gym during off hours. I wonder if Glynn and McManus think there's anything odd about Metzger always happening to be on the scene these days whenever the Aryans decide to fuck somebody up.

Not long after the Aryans taught Sippel about the true meaning of Christian sacrifice, Beecher got twisted up like a pretzel in the same gym. The most twisted thing about it was that the pretzel makers were the guy he'd thought was his friend—his lover, in fact—Keller, and Schillinger, his worst enemy. After Beecher and Keller bonded over the fight with Mark Mack, it seems the two of them got so close that Beecher actually fell in love with his cellmate. For a while, Beecher thought the feelings were mutual, and Keller even got sent to the Hole for getting violent with the hacks when they broke up a heavy petting scene between the two in the laundry, after Keller'd gotten drunk on some prison-made moonshine. When Keller came out of the Hole, though, he wouldn't even talk to Beecher, much less fuck him, and Beecher went to pieces. Next thing he knew he was face-to-face with Keller and Schillinger in the gym, and those two almost literally took Beecher apart. Broke both his arms and his legs. Seems Keller and Schillinger were pals from years back and that Keller was nice to Beecher as a favor to Schillinger. Now Beecher's in the hospital, covered in plaster, and won't be coming back to Em City for a while. The rumor is that Metzger brought Beecher to the gym and watched the whole bone-crunching scene.

Then there's Alvarez, who I guess Sister Pete would call a manic-depressive personality. He got a little depressed when Hernandez—the Latinos address him as El Cid—showed up in Oz, took control of their tribe, and pretty much ignored Alvarez. At the time of the riot, Alvarez had been headman of the Latinos, and he showed what he was made of when he didn't lift a finger to protect Father Mukada, who'd befriended him when he first arrived. Just before the riot started, Mukada'd come into Em City to talk to Alvarez, and when things blew up he just let the padre get beat up along with the hacks. When Hernandez arrived, he dismissed Alvarez as a coward and said he wasn't loyal to the

C.O. Violence

By the early nineties the threat of violence by C.O.s pervaded the Bing [nickname for the Central Punitive Segregation Unit, or CPSU, at Rikers Island]. The inmates knew they'd be beaten with fists or batons for disobeying an order and that no one was watching the shop. "Officials from the Federal Bureau of Prisons did a tour of CPSU," the captain recalled. "As they walked down the cell blocks they said they'd never seen such fear on inmates' faces . . . such absolute terror. The inmates wouldn't talk to them because they knew what we'd do to them if they did."

The captain realized the pendulum had swung too far in the wrong direction when the following incident occurred.

"I was sitting in the captain's office when an officer came in and said, 'Listen, I think you better go to the receiving room, you better go—they're trying to murder this guy.' I went in and they were tossing the inmate around like a rag doll. His whole face was crushed in."

"Did you stop them?"

"I stopped them from murdering him, if that's what you mean."

The inmate, he said, had stabbed a captain in the cheek with a pen. The captain had planned to attend a christening that day, but the ragged gash in his cheek landed him in the hospital instead.

"The officers took the inmate into the receiving room and beat him with batons for fifteen minutes," the captain told me. "They were playing baseball with his face. Every bone in his face was broken. They did everything but make his brains come out of his ears." By the time they were finished, he said, "Everyone was covered with blood. Eight batons were broken. It made Rodney King look like kindergarten."

Source: Jennifer Wynn, *Inside Rikers: Stories from the World's Largest Penal Colony* (New York: St. Martin's, 2001).

Latinos. He told Alvarez he was too white, even calling him "Michael" instead of "Miguel." To prove that he had *cojones*, Alvarez gouged out the eyes of a Latino hack named Rivera, whom El Cid had some sort of grudge against. Now he's back in El Cid's good graces, sure enough, but he's also in fucking Solitary—some say in the same cell his grandfather spent twenty years in. If he's ever released to gen pop or Em City, and not the psych ward, there won't be many hacks who think Alvarez's life is worth much.

When it comes to the ties that bind a man, though—ties of blood, ties of the heart—O'Reily, who likes to have a piece of all sides of the action, may have trumped everybody else. When his brother Cyril was convicted of murdering Dr. Nathan's husband, we all knew who was really responsible, but Cyril wouldn't implicate his brother. He worships O'Reily, but Ryan let Cyril take all the blame for Preston Nathan's murder, even though he probably would've gotten a lesser sentence if Ryan had admitted his own role. McManus wouldn't put Cyril in Em City, where O'Reily might've been able to protect him, so kid brother—who's got the mind of a five-year-old—was left to the not-very-tender mercies of gen pop. Later, when Eugene Rivera was wounded, and lost a lot of blood, O'Reily was the only person in Oz, staff or inmate, who shared Rivera's rare blood type. So O'Reily traded a couple pints of his blood for Cyril's transfer to Em City. While O'Reily gave Rivera the gift of life, he admitted to McManus that he was responsible for Cyril's murdering Preston Nathan. As a result, forty years were added to O'Reily's sentence, so he'll be around, looking after his little brother and adoring the love of his life from a distance. As long as she doesn't quit her job.

The strangest story of someone choosing to stay in Oz when he could be getting out, is Kareem Said's. Every year the governor commutes a couple prisoners' sentences around the time of the major Christian and Muslim holidays, and this year he decided to grant clemency to Said. So shortly before the start of Ramadan, Devlin came to break the news at a

1998 VICTIMS

- **Alexander Vogel:** Murdered in hate-crime fashion—hung by his heels, with the epithet "Jew" scrawled on his chest—by Aryans Vern Schillinger and Mark Mack, who then forced Richie Hanlon to confess to the crime.

- **Ricardo Alvarez:** Patriarch of Alvarez family dies in Oz of Alzheimer's disease.

- **Jara:** Yoruba healer who served briefly as Adebisi's spiritual guide was stabbed by Kenny Wangler on orders from Wise Guy chief Antonio Nappa.

- **Mark Mack:** Aryan thug forced his way into Busmalis's and Rebadow's pod in order to escape through Busmalis's tunnel. Suffocated when the tunnel collapsed during his flight.

press conference in the prison lobby. He praised Said for his efforts to improve the lives of inmates and announced that he was granting the imam an unconditional pardon. So, Said steps in front of the TV cameras, says that any man who'd caused the deaths of eight people in the riot wasn't worthy of granting clemency. Then Said refused Devlin's pardon. Why'd he do it? Because he didn't feel right leaving his brothers behind, the same as O'Reily didn't want to abandon his brother? Or could it have been because Said suspected that Devlin wanted his rabble-rousing ass out of the way, the better to fuck over the brothers who'd remain behind? I don't know, and maybe Said doesn't know, either. But he showed that though you may be able to run away from where you are, you can't escape who you are. And when Said walked back through the gate into Em City, almost every prisoner treated him like he was a god.

Entries from 1999

Sunday 1.31.99

In Oz, changing names isn't much different from changing cells. It happens all the time, and when it's your own name (or your own cell) you think it's a big fucking deal, but when it's somebody else, you may not notice. On the prison records, Poet's probably still listed as Arnold Jackson, but nobody except maybe some hacks ever called him anything but Poet. Kenny Wangler all of a sudden started calling himself Bricks, but I don't think anybody else did, except maybe Poet and Pierce, and whoever was afraid of pissing him off. As for Goodson Truman, he's Kareem Said to everyone from Glynn on down, including people who've got no respect for the Muslims. Raul Hernandez? He's mostly called El Cid, a name that doesn't exactly fit him. I'm told that the name comes from an Arabic word meaning "lord" that's also the source of the name "Said," and the original El Cid was a Spanish general who married the king's niece and spent his life fighting on whichever side—usually Christian, but sometimes Muslim—he thought would hand him the most power if he won. Come to think of it, maybe that's the perfect name for a guy battling for power in Oz.

So the name—of a man or of a prison—is just a part of the hype. When the word came down that the state was changing the official name of Oz from "Oswald State Maximum Security Penitentiary" to "Oswald State Correctional Facility, Level Four," we didn't exactly rush out to buy the new sweatshirt. The sign's in the front lobby, a long way from anywhere most inmates get to see. When it was a penitentiary, there wasn't much penitence, and now that it's a correc-

Poet and Kenny Wangler on a kitchen break.

tional facility, we won't be seeing much correction. What a fucking concept, correction. Especially if they expect the same folks who brought us the riot and the catastrophe that ended it to show us the way to correction. Yeah, right. Except for Sister Pete's drug counseling group, I haven't seen much that's likely to correct anything, and like Sister Pete says, you got to do the correcting yourself, with maybe a little help from your friends. Most of my support has come from my family and from one or two staff members. The other inmates, they're usually too busy taking care of their own business, or trying to sucker you into some scheme

of theirs (whether drugs or other shit), to be much help. William Shakespeare wrote, "That which we call a rose by any other name would smell as sweet," but what happens when the rose smells like a rat?

Since it's the bad motherfuckers who get respect in Oz, sometimes a little rat tries to pretend he's a big rat, or at least a medium-sized one. Not long ago, a trash-talking small-time drug dealer who called himself "Jiggy" Walker (I can't even remember what his real first name is, or if he even had one) and everybody else "niggah" showed up last week and figured he could make a name for himself by claiming that he was Governor

Devlin's personal crack dealer. Said hadn't yet announced his plans for a class-action suit on behalf of the prisoners who were injured in the riot and the families of the victims, but he must've been working on them, so he jumped at the chance to sling some mud at Devlin, who was already busy dodging charges of political corruption and extramarital affairs. Before anybody knew what was happening, Said had Walker—who was so sure of himself I wouldn't've been surprised to hear him greet Glynn with a "Morning, niggah"—repeating his story about selling crack to Devlin to every reporter in the state.

Only one problem: it wasn't true. Devlin called a press conference, brought an army of TV reporters along, produced airline tickets showing that he'd been out of the state on the day Walker claimed to have sold him the crack, and challenged Walker to admit he'd made it all up. We were watching the live report on TV back in Em City, and Jiggy, cool as ever, just grinned and said, "OK, so I lied," and suddenly the show was over. Said was pissed—he doesn't like being the one who's getting jerked around—and I'm sure Glynn was embarrassed, but in Oz you roll with the punches, mop up the blood, and move on. It's not hard to understand what Walker was trying to do: make a quick name for himself, so he wouldn't be seen as just another punk that hard-timers could fuck with or—just as bad—ignore. He probably just figured the news would get around

Alexis de Tocqueville (1805–1859) discovered two approaches to imprisonment during his visit to the United States in 1831–1832. He was impressed by the way American prisons were run, and proposed that French prisons follow their example. In particular, de Tocqueville admired the regimen he saw in Auburn, New York, where prisoners worked in groups during the day (but were not permitted to speak to one another) and were confined to separate cells at night, to give them time to reflect and repent.

We have no doubt, but that the habits of order to which the prisoner is subjected for several years, influence very considerably his moral conduct after his return to society.

The necessity of labor which overcomes his disposition to idleness; the obligation of silence which makes him reflect; the isolation which places him alone in presence of his crime and his suffering; the religious instruction which enlightens and comforts him; the obedience of every moment to inflexible rules; the regularity of a uniform life; in a word, all the circumstances belonging to this severe system, are calculated to produce a deep impression upon his mind. Perhaps, leaving the prison he is not an honest man, but he has contracted honest habits. He was an idler; now he knows how to work. His ignorance prevented him from pursuing a useful occupation; now he knows how to read and to write; and the trade which he has learnt in the prison, furnishes him the means of existence which formerly he had not. Without loving virtue, he may detest the crime of which he has suffered the cruel consequences, and if he is not more virtuous he has become at least more judicious; his morality is not honor, but interest. His religious faith is perhaps neither lively nor deep; but even supposing that religion has not touched his heart, his mind has contracted habits of order, and he possesses rules for his conduct in life; without having a powerful religious conviction, he has acquired a taste for moral principles which religion affords; finally, if he has not become in truth better, he is at least more obedient to the laws, and that is all which society has a right to demand.

If we consider the reformation of convicts under this point of view, it seems to us to be obtained, in many cases, through the system which we are considering; and those Americans who have the least confidence in the radical regeneration of criminals, believe, nonetheless, in the existence of a reformation reduced to these more simple terms.

Source: Gustave de Beaumont and Alexis de Tocqueville, *On the Penitentiary System in the United States and Its Application in France,* translated by Francis Lieber (Philadelphia: Carey, Lea & Blanchard, 1833).

inside the prison, inmates would greet him, "Jiggy, my man, how's the governor?" That way he wouldn't just disappear or become one more faceless face or series of numbers.

Maybe I should've thought of Jiggy Walker when Malcolm Coyle landed in Em City. Here was another guy who seemed like he wanted to get respect by seeming badder than he was, called himself "Snake," and jabbered about how he'd murdered an entire family—the Cianciminos—mother, father, grandmother, a couple kids, including a small baby. Coyle, trying to prove, I guess, that he was as shrewd a niggah as we got in Oz, told Wangler and me that the murders had never been solved and he'd never even been questioned about the case. I wasn't sure he was telling the truth, and even if he was, why the fuck was he telling me about stabbing all those people, raping the mother after he'd cut her throat, and killing a baby in its crib? I'm no angel; I killed a cop, and though I'm not proud of the deed, I'm not ashamed neither. But something sat wrong with me in the way Coyle was talking. Maybe because of those two little kids. I couldn't get them out of my mind; I kept thinking, If they were my kids, I'd want somebody to speak for them. So I went to Said.

At first Said was suspicious of Coyle's story, and maybe he was suspicious of me after the way I mouthed off when my appeal tanked. He reminded me of the Jiggy Walker story—Said didn't want to get burned twice—and said Coyle probably just wanted to build his cred. The only way to know for sure was to get him to reveal something that would implicate him. I don't know why—my way of staying alive in Oz has always been to try to stay clear of other guys' shit, no matter what it was—but the next thing I knew I was back egging Coyle on to talk about the Ciancimino murders some more, hoping he'd say something juicy. When he said a friend of his had videotaped the whole thing, I flashed back to the videotape the hacks supposedly made of Jefferson Keane killing the one Latino inmate, a tape that didn't save Keane's ass. I wondered whether this one would convict Coyle, or cost me my ass instead.

But I had the story, and I had the name of the friend who Coyle said had shot the video of the murders, and before I had a chance to figure out what was going to happen to me, I was in the warden's office with Said, telling Glynn and McManus what Coyle had told me. From there I went into protective custody, waiting to testify to the grand jury and hoping to stay out of the line of fire.

Testifying before the grand jury wasn't anything special. I felt a little like somebody who'd been traded from the Lakers to the Bulls one day and found himself playing against his old team the same night. I'm no rat, but Coyle didn't mean nothing like what I imagine Kobe or Shaq would've meant to me, and what he'd done to complete strangers—and especially to those kids—was way outside any code I could ever respect. In fact, what was special about the experience had nothing to do with testifying; it had to do with the feeling of being out of harm's way for a few hours, not having to worry about what the guy on my left was plotting or who was coming up behind me. Just driving through the city, looking through the windows of the van (who cares if they had fucking mesh all over them), checking out the street life, watching the women, feeling the energy, man, looking at the outside of the buildings for a change, instead of staring at the same depressing interior walls, that made the whole thing worth the risk. I thought, "I'll agree to testify to a grand jury anytime they asked me, even if I got nothing to tell them, just to feel the excitement of being back in the city pulsing in my head."

Turns out maybe I didn't have all that much to tell this grand jury, either. Within a couple of days, Coyle was on his way out, in a body bag. Before I left the prison to give my testimony, I admitted to McManus how scared I was. Then he said, "We'll take care of you," like he was the fucking godfather himself. From what Said told me later, Timmy Boy wasn't so far off the mark, only he was imagining himself in the role that Antonio Nappa actually played. Said somehow got Nappa, Guerra, and Schillinger together, and convinced them all to

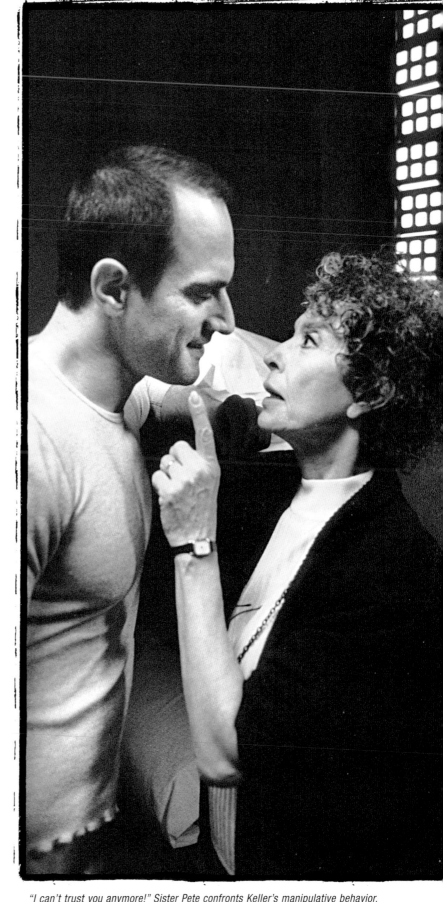

"I can't trust you anymore!" Sister Pete confronts Keller's manipulative behavior.

agree that I should be protected and Coyle should be brought to justice for what he'd done to the Cianciminos. Said stressed how Coyle had committed the murders just for the thrill and had made an innocent family his victims. Nappa and Guerra bought in right away, and when Schillinger heard that Ciancimino had served in Vietnam, he joined them in promising to make sure nobody tried to take me down. Then Nappa said that he knew the Ciancimino family slightly, and told Said, "I'll do you one better." Next day, Coyle was found dead in his cell, his wrists bound to the bars and the blood still pouring from a severed artery in his neck. I was on my way back to Em City, and if Coyle has any friends in Oz, it won't take them long to do the math. McManus's promise that he'd keep me safe just made me laugh.

Thursday 2.18.99

One difference between Oz and places on the outside is that in here, you can't run *and* you can't hide, either. At least not for long. On the street things're different, whether you're a cop or one of the brothers, like me. I always had a sixth sense about when it was safe to take care of business and act like we owned the streets, and when it was time to be cool, stay out of sight, even take a brief vacation. In Oz, though, nobody has that option, not the hacks, not the inmates. Take Metzger. Besides the occasional acts of random brutality all the hacks use to remind us who's in charge, it seemed, from his first day as Em City supervisor, like life just got a little bit too easy for the Aryans. First, when Mark Mack discovered Busmalis's tunnel, he didn't have any problem getting Metzger to switch their pods just when the digging was completed; second, when Schillinger's mortal enemy Beecher got his arms and legs broken during some unscheduled rec time in the gym; third, when Robert Sippel got nailed to the floor of the basketball court; Metzger always seemed to be around, even though in his reports, he claimed that he hadn't seen or heard anything. Not long ago, Busmalis landed in the infirmary after he'd been strangled and fallen down a flight of stairs. Rebadow's not saying much, but he's hinted that Metzger held Busmalis responsible for Mark Mack's death when the tunnel collapsed. Everybody, except the Nazi fucks, hate Metzger, so nobody gets too upset when Metzger turned up dead, slashed to ribbons in a hallway deep inside the old part of the prison. No one knows who did the deed and, unlike Coyle, that person probably won't take credit for it, even if he'd be a goddamn hero. When hacks like Metzger break the rules, there's usually not much the inmates can do to defend themselves. If they complain, the C.O. probably won't get fired, or even disciplined, but the inmates may as well be wearing signs that say FUCK WITH ME. Sometimes it may be smarter just to take a brutal hack out altogether, but when that happens that usually starts open season on all inmates for a while.

Prisoners never know which direction trouble's going to come from. Could be from the staff, from another prisoner, or even from family or friends. And if you're a high-profile critic of the legal and penal systems like Kareem Said, you're bound to end up in everybody's cross-hairs. When Said announced his plans to bring a class-action suit against the state on behalf of the prisoners killed in the riot, he said he wanted to use the system against itself, "to use their laws to reveal our truths." I'm not sure what truths Said had in mind, and the guy must've known that he'd be opposed from every direction, but he probably wasn't expecting the kind of challenge he's gotten from within his own Muslim brothers.

One of the truths Said often repeats to his brothers is this: "We are men, rooted in Africa and living in America." But does he mean that Islam—his brand of Islam, at least—is intended for black people only, or at least for people of color? I'm not personally familiar with the Prophet's writings, but Said's fellow Muslims seem to think that things go better when they're kept within the

family. Schillinger started making comments about Said's meeting in the visiting room with Patricia Ross, Steve Ross's sister, after she came to talk about joining the class-action

Said's Maiden

. . . I figured you easy,

all you wanna do is get your palm greasy.

Capitalize.

See, trying to fuck America has been in your eye

     for 450 years now

you wanna hide your tears in your so-called ALLah-

     giving mission to help your brothers

well, Allah gave me vision and I'ma tell all the others.

Talking about revolution, what I saw is revelation.

You frolicking with the devil's maiden

now you happy 'cause you can manipulate her think

well let me put you onto something while we up

     here in this clink.

While trying to get us all to the heaven above

When she forgets about your contradicting ass

make sure you hide the dirty gloves!

Poem by muMs

suit. When the other Muslims got wind of her visit, some of them started grumbling that Said was betraying the faith. Of course, he told them the meeting was strictly business, that Schillinger—an old pal of Ross's—

Burnt offering: Said resists temptation.

was trying to set the brothers against each other. What else was he going to tell them? But did Said have something else in mind besides just taking care of business? A few months back, when Said was trying to get my conviction overturned, I'd seen the sparks flying between him and Marilyn Crenshaw, so I knew something about Said's attraction to white women that Schillinger and the Muslims didn't, something that maybe Said

wasn't admitting even to himself.

I don't love Annabella because of her color, and I don't see anything wrong with black men and women taking white lovers. Especially not in a place like Oz, where the closest thing to a woman most men have is a copy of *Hustler*. All my energy goes into trying to keep things going with Annabella, especially since conjugals were canceled, but at least we've got our history to keep us clear. What's it like, though, for someone like Said, with no woman on the outside, when he and a woman are attracted to each other, and why does their skin color matter or whether they share the same faith? Isn't love a kind of faith, too, that men and women can share?

Luckily, Ramadan arrived, and for a while everybody forgot about Patricia Ross and the lawsuit, or seemed to. Said wanted to observe Ramadan's daily dawn-to-sunset fasts, which isn't easy to do in Oz, where we're locked in our cells every day from 5 P.M., usually before sunset, until 7 A.M., well after the day's period of fasting begins. McManus made the usual noises about never making exceptions for anyone (never unless he wants to, that is) and turned down Said's request to eat his meals in his cell—unless, that is, Said agreed to withdraw the class-action lawsuit. Said didn't even pretend to consider McManus's offer of a deal; instead, he went on a hunger strike, taking nothing but liquids. For the first few days, Glynn and McManus acted like they hadn't noticed what Said was up to, but then Said played his trump card. He sent Arnold Zelman, the attorney in the class-action suit, to tell Glynn that Said was planning to expand his hunger strike, first to the Muslims in Em City, then throughout Oz, and finally to every Muslim prisoner in every prison in the state. So Glynn caved, and once again, Said,

who's better at manipulating public perception than the fucking governor, was a hero of sorts. For the moment, Said may have used his head and Ramadan to save his ass with the Muslims, but when Ramadan ends, his heart and his dick'll probably screw him up all over again. Said is three things: a man, a Muslim, and a prisoner. Sometimes these three parts work in opposition to one another. Said's too proud to bend to anyone, so he makes enemies, and one of them—maybe an Aryan, maybe a hack, maybe even a Muslim—will jump on this Patricia Ross business to try to cut him down to size.

Monday 3.15.99

Your tribe is supposed to be what helps you stay alive, and when I was out on the street dealing, Burr Redding and the rest of the crew looked out for one another. We had our differences and defectors, for sure, but life was a hell of a lot safer with them than without them. The Latinos in Oz seem to be a little different. El Norte is what they call their tribe, but most of the time you can't be sure which direction they're facing. They're in the thick of the drug traffic, and they even deal moonshine, but I don't think they're heavy users of tits or booze. Still, it's like most of them almost always act like they're hopped up on something, they're unpredictable, turning on each other as often as on their enemies. Especially Miguel Alvarez and Carlos Ricardo. I don't know much about Ricardo, but Alvarez was one of the first Latinos in Em City, and for a while he was El Norte's top man. Since then he's been pushed aside by Raul Hernandez—El Cid—and right now, he's cooped up in Solitary, where he's been off and on for months. First, he went in after he blinded one of the hacks, a Latino named Eugene Rivera, with a scalpel he boosted from the infirmary. He was trying to prove to El Cid, a stone-faced bastard with nerves to match, that he had *cojones*.

Fucking up a hack is usually not a smart move, since when you're in Soli-

"Who raped my daughter?" Glynn pressures Alvarez for information.

tary or the Hole the hacks can do pretty much what they want with you—beat you, starve you, forget about you altogether—and usually nobody'll be the wiser. Somebody up there must like Alvarez, because when Sister Pete introduced her new "interaction program" where victims and aggressors in violent incidents meet to talk about what happened—Miguelito was the first inmate chosen to participate. As part of the deal, he got released from Solitary and was allowed back in Em City. Lucky for him, because from the look of Alvarez when he returned, and from stories going around, the hacks had been starving him in Solitary, not giving him anything to eat or drink more than once or twice a week. I even heard the poor fuck was drinking his own piss, just to stay alive.

So the program starts: Alvarez and Rivera actually met face-to-face a couple times, but I don't think they got to where they could forgive, forget, and move on with their lives, which is what Sister Pete was hoping would come out of the encounters. I guess the Riveras (the wife was involved in the sessions, too) decided not to continue, and before you knew it, Alvarez is back in Solitary. I don't think that has anything to do with Rivera, 'cause around the time the meetings hit a dead end, something odd happened in Em City. The other three members of El Norte—El Cid, Guerra, and Ricardo—were busted for possession, but Alvarez didn't even get searched. It sure as hell looked like Alvarez had set them up, so maybe Glynn put him back in Solitary to make sure the Latinos didn't slice him in two for betraying them.

Glynn's got his own issues with Alvarez. A while back, Glynn's daughter, Ardeth, got raped in the city and the word got around that Alvarez knew who the rapist was but wouldn't name the perp. So like I said, somebody up there must like Miguel, and maybe somebody down here, too—probably Father Mukada, who got Alvarez into the parenting program when his girlfriend was pregnant, or Sister Pete, or Dr. Nathan, who had him working as an orderly in the infirmary. Weird, when the best anyone can do for you is to put you in Solitary and isolate you from the entire world.

Thursday 4.1.99

After getting thrown off the roof, I spent months in the hospital, but knock on wood, not a day in all the time I've been in Oz. Lots of inmates haven't been that lucky, but the ones who've gotten sick or shanked or beaten are lucky Dr. Nathan's still working in the infirmary. A few months ago, when Governor Devlin announced that he was bringing in an HMO to operate the medical services in all the state's prisons, it looked like she

HEALTH CARE/DEPRESSION/SUICIDE

In many prisons a suicide attempt is treated as a disciplinary infraction and punished. Clearly, the policy of charging a prisoner who attempts to take his life with a rule violation is entirely contrary to everything we know from clinical research and practice about the assessment and treatment of suicidality. I have found in quite a few deceased inmates' security files a posthumous citation for violating the prison rule against attempting suicide. How eerie! But this is not a rare aberration. Convicts who attempt suicide and survive must face a hearing on the charge of attempting to take their own lives, and they are likely to be sentenced to a term in solitary confinement. In addition, because the sentence is likely to include the surrendering of "good time" for days worked or for good behavior, the sentence also involves the lengthening of a prisoner's overall prison term. As a clinician, I am appalled by this widespread correctional practice. For example:

Mr. N.M., a Mexican-American prisoner in a high-security facility in California, sent his attorney a letter on September 25, 1991, describing his suicide attempt on July 30 of that year. He had been transferred to a new, higher-security-level prison a few days prior to his suicide attempt. He had been taking relatively strong doses of antipsychotic and antidepressant medications for several years, but the psychiatrist who saw him for a brief assessment interview when he entered the new prison decided he did not need the medications and discontinued them. He complained to an MTA (medical technical assistant), who told him there was nothing he could do. Mr. N.M. was unable to sleep without his medications, and no one listened to his complaints that he was hearing voices telling him to kill himself. A few days later, he sliced his wrist with a razor, severing a vein and narrowly missing the artery.

After the laceration was sutured in the prison hospital, he was placed on suicide watch. The medications he had been on prior to the transfer were reinstated. A few days later, he was transferred to the Administrative Segregation unit, where he was sentenced to remain for thirty days as punishment for the suicide attempt. Thirty days were also added to his prison sentence. He wrote that he felt even more suicidal after hearing the news about the lengthy sentence in solitary confinement.

Source: Terry A. Kupers, M.D., *Prison Madness: The Mental Health Crisis Behind Bars and What We Must Do About It* (San Francisco: Jossey-Bass Publishers, 1999).

might not be around much longer. On TV, Devlin talked about how the Weigert Corporation, which had the contract, would save taxpayers $28 million. What he didn't say was that the head of Med Mor, the conglomerate that owns Weigert, is Ross Davoli, one of Devlin's close "friends" and, more importantly, political supporters.

Dr. Nathan must be some kind of saint, because otherwise you got to wonder why she keeps working here, even after Ryan O'Reily had her husband murdered and after Weigert put this clown Garvey, a so-called doctor, in charge. To keep costs down, Garvey started rejecting treatments and prescription drugs that were too expensive. The whole thing blew up when Alvarez, whom Dr. Nathan and Sister Pete had put on antidepressants even before he was sent to Solitary, tried to hang himself in his cell. Garvey had Alvarez taken off the meds—"too expensive for somebody who was rotting in Solitary." Dr. Nathan managed to revive Alvarez, but one of the orderlies who was in the ward when he regained consciousness said that Alvarez's first words to Nathan were, "Shit, you should've let me die."

But she didn't, and I don't believe she'd let anybody die if she could save them—not Alvarez and not any inmate, no matter what he'd done. But how can she save an inmate who somebody's tried to kill when he's back to his cell block? Will he just be attacked again? Or a depressed inmate in Solitary, who'll probably try to commit suicide again? Or what about the fact that the drugs used in executions by lethal injection are prescribed by the prison doctor? I guess there's nothing Dr. Nathan can do about the system. She's working hard to keep us alive just so we can die some other way.

Dr. Nathan decided to go public about what was going on with Garvey, and called *Channel 2 News*. When Garvey, who'd already given Dr. Nathan notice, tried to get the governor's friends to intervene, his plan backfired, and the next thing we knew, Devlin had asked Dr. Nathan to stay and not to talk to the press. In return, he agreed to feed Garvey to the lions. Turns out the quack'd lost his license for running an illegal abortion clinic in the 1970s, and the story was leaked to the press. As usual, Devlin manages to come out with clean hands, his pals are still getting rich off the state, but at least Dr. Nathan's back in charge of the infirmary and Alvarez is back on Zoloft. And back in Solitary. What do they call it? Bitter medicine.

Tuesday 5.4.99

Tim McManus sure as hell likes to play the little dictator in Em City, even if he makes a big show of listening to everybody's point of view in the unit council meetings. One thing that was on everybody's mind after Metzger's mysterious murder was who'd replace him, but McManus wasn't asking the council for nominations. Not that we weren't worrying about who the next Em City supervisor would be, especially since we suspected—no, knew—that many of the hacks are Aryan Brotherhood members and sympathizers. So when McManus introduced Sean Murphy as the replacement, lots of us in Em City started to breathe a little easier. Murphy wasn't just new to Em City, he was new to Oz, and that meant that he probably didn't have any ties to any of the other hacks or have any issues left over from the riot. Probably, that is, because it turns out Murphy is an old pal of McManus's, so who knows what he's been told about what's gone down here? A couple things I'll bet McManus hasn't told him: why he transferred his old lover Diane Whittlesey out of Em City, or why Claire Howell got her job back after claiming that she was sexually harassed by Timmy boy.

As hacks go, Murphy doesn't seem like a bad sort. The word is that he used to be a Golden Gloves fighter, and maybe that has something to do with McManus's latest bright idea: a prisonwide boxing tournament with one contestant from each of the tribes. Lots of prisons try to keep a lid on violence between inmates by organizing sports competitions of one kind or another. A boxing tournament isn't an especially original idea—nobody ever said Tim McManus is a genius—but the inmates got excited as soon as the word spread. Maybe people started thinking it would catch on and get to be as famous as the Angola Rodeo, with crowds coming in from the outside to watch the fights. Except for the Christians, who objected on the grounds that boxing is just sanctioned violence, every group has entered a fighter. A huge crowd of inmates and staff showed up for the first match, between the Bikers and the Wise Guys. It wasn't much of a fight: the Wise Guys's Chucky Pancamo knocked Steve Pasquin out with one punch in the first round, so quickly that I barely had time to catch Pasquin's name before he'd caught Pancamo's punch. But if there wasn't much action in the ring, there was plenty of betting action all over the joint. Gambling's big in Oz, most of it controlled by the Wise Guys, so the betting wasn't anything new, but this was probably the first time the prison brass thought up an event for guys to gamble on. Seems like McManus thinks that as long as he controls things, they're okay. Maybe so, but I wonder if when Napoleon said, "It's just a small step from the sublime to the ridiculous," he was thinking of ol' Timmy.

ANGOLA RODEO

The bull riding came second to last. Here was an event that replicated the pro tour. The rider had to stay on for eight seconds to score points; the better his form, the more points he would receive. Here was the chance for Johnny Brooks to prove himself, to rise above the helplessness and degradation of contests like the Bust-Out and Convict Poker, where pure luck and sheer craziness played such overwhelming roles, the chance for this forty-year-old man, who would most likely never leave Angola, to prevail on skill and reveal his grace. He could show himself no different from J. W. Hart and Tuff Hedeman and Ted Nuce, the stars of the pro circuit, whose rides were hailed weekly by the ESPN announcer not only as demonstrations of talent but as testaments to integrity and good values. He could be those figures. And he could be, in front of the public, what he was at least part of the time in his job at Angola, a cowboy.

From a railing above the chute, he moved to climb onto the animal. With a cord tied against its belly and near its balls to add hostility, the bull tried to hurdle the wall. It braced its forelegs over the top. Quickly, before he fell backward inside the chute that was just big enough for the bull, Brooks levered himself off. "Get down there," someone prodded at the animal. Brooks tried again, set himself. The bull jostled, slammed its head into the wooden slats, drove Brooks's knees into the boards. The hide of the back was loose, sliding, and Brooks struggled to get his balance. Under the excess skin the bull's muscles contracted and rose—a fast series of giant ripples shuddering along its spine.

A convict pulled the bull rope tight as Brooks had dreamed. His palm faced upward, and the pressure of the rope across it dug the back of his hand inches into the hide. "Ready?" the inmate manning the gate called. "Ready?" The answer was the most minimal nod, the brim of the studded hat moving almost imperceptibly. The gate was tugged open, the man who'd helped with the rope cried, "Outside!"

And so Brooks was. Outside. The bull thrashed and spun out of the chute, and Brooks was out under the gaze of the crowd, his mind shut down and Angola gone from it. Three seconds later he was on his knees in the mud.

A parade of failed rides came after: one first-time contestant sent airborne immediately; a gray-haired sixty-two-year-old bank robber launched into a twisting, Olympic-style dive. Finally a convict named Carey Lasseigne, who went by Buckkey and whose bushy blond mustache and weathered skin made him look like he would do well—made him look, at least, like a typical cowboy—decided to grab the bull rope with two hands. This would have disqualified him in professional rodeo, but here, because not one other man had lasted the required time, a mere completed ride would earn him points. Which was all he wanted. He wasn't after quite the same kind of glory as Johnny Brooks.

Lately his son, Chris, refused to visit him more than once or twice each year. The boy was almost seventeen. He had been two when Buckkey began his life sentence for murder, for killing an acquaintance just one year older than his son was now, shooting him in the back of the head while he pleaded for his life. If Buckkey could win the all-around prize, that silver-plated buckle reading "All-Around Cowboy," if he could send it to Chris for his seventeenth birthday at the end of the month, he felt that Chris, his only child, might come soon. The first time Buckkey had tried for this present, the bull had rammed and pinned him repeatedly against one of the wooden gates. He received 142 stitches to his scalp and later went into seizure on the shower floor. Two years ago he had broken his left hand; before the following weekend he had cracked open the cast and taken it off so he could ride.

Today was the day, this was the year. He needed those points. He didn't care about style. He just clung to the bull. And when the whistle blew announcing eight seconds, he was three Sundays away from that gift.

Source: Daniel Bergner, *God of the Rodeo: The Search for Hope, Faith, and a Six-Second Ride in Louisiana's Angola Prison* (New York: Crown Publishers, 1998).

Sometimes seeing's not believing; your mind just can't absorb what your eyes take in. Example: Schillinger's son Andrew trailing around after Beecher like a faithful sheepdog and even moving into Beecher's pod. Beecher's a strange character, but this one really doesn't add up. The kid's father screwed up Beecher's life—if you can say a guy's life can get screwed up after he's sent to Oz—and from all appearances little Andy's cut from the same mold as his Aryan supremacist father: chained a black man to the back of a pickup truck and dragged the brother to his death. Not only that, but Andrew goes his father one better: he's addicted to heroin. Drugs can do a brutal number on a young man. I know plenty about that from my own crack habit. I was lucky, but for many addicts crack was as brutal a prison as Oz. But at least I wasn't alone; I had Mom and Annabella, even when I was using heavy, while all Andrew's got is a mother who's dead and a fascist of a father in prison.

Beecher and the boy bonded after Beecher stood up for him in a drug rehab meeting, and right afterward, Beecher asked McManus to switch Andrew to his pod. Claims he's trying to save him, and maybe he is, unless he's setting up the kid in some twisted scheme to get revenge on old Vern. The guys Beecher hangs with in Em City are usually Keller, who was probably shanked by Schillinger or one of his Brotherhood flunkies for "betraying" Schillinger and befriending Beecher, and O'Reily. O'Reily's been swearing he'll get even with Schillinger ever since he raped O'Reily's brother Cyril, so it's unlikely that his pal Beecher's decided all of a sudden that he wants to try to save Schillinger's family.

O'Reily's another guy who's impossible to figure out. If you didn't know his story, you'd swear, when you saw him with his brother Cyril, that they were tighter than a pair of handcuffs. Then you remember that Ryan O'Reily is the reason Cyril's squatting in Oz, and the word is that Cyril suffered his brain damage trying to back up his punk of a brother in a fight with some Wise Guys. So what does loving brother Ryan do? Signs Cyril up to do battle for the honor of Ireland in the prison boxing tournament. Maybe Ryan thinks it'll help Cyril work out his aggressions.

Now one of the unusual features of the competition is that they've eliminated weight classes, so you got lightweights fighting heavyweights. Cyril O'Reily's not the smallest fighter in the competition, but he'd have to struggle to make welterweight soaking wet. He's a good boxer, though, with real quick hands. Round one: Jim Robson is hitting Cyril with

Ryan and Cyril O'Reily doing kitchen duty.

one punch after the other. Cyril hits back, but he doesn't seem to be doing much damage. Round two: It's like Robson's a different fighter—slow, unable to land punches. Round three: It's Cyril who's landing blows whenever he wants to. He knocks Robson out! The smart money had been on Robson, so now a lot of people are wondering what turned that fight around, and some of them suspect Ryan O'Reily, who'd bet heavy on his brother—but it was his

brother, for Christ's sake, so of course he was going to back him.

The next match has Alvarez, just released from Solitary, opposing Cramer, the gay contender. This time it's Alvarez who is figured to win easily—he's quick and crazy ("Crazy is good," El Cid is supposed to have said)—and maybe the bettors thought that a gay boxer couldn't be very tough. Well, Alvarez fell apart in the second round and got knocked out. People started to wonder where the real Alvarez had disappeared to; but nobody believed the Latinos would have fixed a fucking fight involving one of their own. Especially not with bragging rights on the line. And people are asking how come O'Reily is on the winning side of every bet.

Nobody had any doubts about the outcome of the next fight, and I don't think the bookies did much business, either. This one was Hamid Khan versus Kenny Wangler, and for all of Wangler's "Call me 'Bricks'" swagger, he's an eighteen-year-old lightweight and Khan's a tough 200 pounds. When the word went around Em City that Wangler, who probably sucks as much tit as he sells, was planning to party on the day of the fight, a Wangler backer was harder to find than a "RE-ELECT GOVERNOR DEVLIN" poster on one of the cell walls. The fight didn't last long, either. In round one, Wangler did a brief imitation of Ali's dancing in the first Liston fight, but as soon as Khan reached him with a punch, he showed what his new nickname was all about: he hit the canvas like a brick and didn't bounce.

There was more excitement the day after the fight, when McManus rushed into Em City to tell Wangler that his wife had been murdered execution-style—together with her new boyfriend. Wangler acted like he was broken up about it, but I've heard some rumors that he was the one who ordered the hit—to get even with her for letting somebody else play daddy to his "prince"—and had made sure his infant son was safe at Wangler's mother's place the night of the killing. Whether those stories are true or not, McManus promised to let him out for the funeral, and afterward it'll be business as usual for him, Pierce, and Poet, who's started writing again but still spends more time mixed up in the Homeboys' tit traffic than penning poetry. Speaking for myself, I don't think I could be writing this journal if I were still using, but Poet's also a performer. For me, writing is private and personal, more a way of keeping myself together than getting across to others. I wouldn't want other people to even know this notebook exists.

Thursday 7.22.99

When I decided to testify against Coyle, it was because I couldn't get the thought of the two little kids he'd murdered out of my head. In Oz, the way to survive is often to forget what you've seen, pretend you don't know things even when they're staring you in the face. Like in this boxing tournament, where almost none of the fights turn out the way you'd expect. It's not like I'm pulling for one fighter—I haven't bet a penny on these fights and I don't care which tribe wins—but when a little guy like Cyril O'Reily doesn't just outbox a brute like Pancamo but knocks him out, you got to wonder what's the opposite of a miracle?

Like I said, I'm not rooting for any fighter in particular, but I will say that I like the way Cyril O'Reily handles himself in the ring. He moves like an athlete, dances and floats a little bit like Ali in his prime, so once in a while, watching him, I'm reminded of what it was like to move without the ball on the basketball court, or to soar—up, up, up—toward the basket on a dunk. But boxing isn't b-ball, and I'm stuck in this chair, not floating, so it's never long before I'm back to earth.

The preliminaries to the match were more like something out of pro wrestling than a Don King extravaganza: Pancamo tossing his headgear away and then Ryan O'Reily doing the same thing with his brother's. Fucking Pancamo had already knocked an opponent out with a single punch, so what was O'Reily thinking, that his brother was already so brain damaged more punches wouldn't matter? He'd bet heavily on Cyril, so he sure as hell wasn't trying to lose the fight, but in the first round it looked like Ireland wasn't going to see any green after this one was over. From the bell, Cyril did such a good job of staying away from Pancamo that Chucky yelled, "You wanna dance or you wanna fight?" And even when Cyril managed to land a punch or two, Pancamo just mocked him, like a horse flicking his tail to get the flies off his ass.

Everything changed in Rounds two and three. Pancamo stopped stalking Cyril, and the fly started landing punches—first one or two, and then flurries of them. When Pancamo finally went down and stayed down, he was hurt. From where I'd been sitting, it really did look like he'd been knocked out. It was only later that we heard that maybe he'd nodded out on heroin, so it was more like Cyril'd pushed him than punched him.

Almost before the ring was folded up, the rumors started. First, someone had spiked Pancamo's spritzer with heroin, then it was the Russians who'd done it, but when Pancamo demanded a rematch, McManus supposedly called him a sore loser and refused to have him tested for drugs.

Saturday 8.7.99

I never knew my own father—I was born while he was in Vietnam, and he didn't make it back—but I don't remember ever feeling as lost as Andrew Schillinger looked the first time he showed up at the drug counseling group. Small, boyish-looking, with brown eyes that never seemed to focus (maybe that was the fault of all the heroin he snorted), he'd been in Oz for a couple weeks, not doing much except drugs. Maybe Andrew wasn't all that interested in staying alive— he sure didn't act like he was— and maybe he would have died if his last name wasn't Schillinger. But it was, so folks assumed that if anything happened to the kid, Vern Schillinger wouldn't rest until he'd taken revenge.

When Andrew moved into Beecher's

Andrew gets his nose candy ready.

pod, everyone suspected it was part of a plot to fuck with Schillinger. But that didn't seem to be happening. Andrew started attending Sister Pete's drug counseling sessions, and it wasn't long before he started acting like he didn't have a chip on his shoulder and he wasn't shoving tits up his nose, either. More surprising was that Beecher wasn't fucking Andrew up the ass, which you'd think he'd do just to get even for being turned into Schillinger's prag when he was fresh meat in Em City.

When Schillinger realized that Andrew had gone drug-free, he was actually happy about it. The two of them met in the cafeteria one day and Schillinger smiled at the boy. I realized I'd never seen him do anything but sneer before—but that smile didn't last long. Schillinger couldn't face the fact that Andrew quit drugs because of Beecher, Keller, and O'Reily. And when he couldn't get the boy away from his new pals, Schillinger got pissed, started an argument, landing Andrew in the Hole. What happened next surprised a lot of people, including me. I've been going to drug counseling ever since I got to Oz, and I can tell the difference between an addict who's clean and someone who's just trying to bullshit the hacks—or himself. Andrew was clean, and besides, when they throw you into the Hole in your birthday suit there's not a lot of places you can be carrying drugs, even if you want to. So somebody

Surrounded but alone, Said puts his faith in Allah.

must've smuggled tits into Andrew's cell, somebody who's on friendly terms with the hacks. The next day Andrew was dead from an overdose. Could it have been O'Reily, who we thought had lost his "in" with the hacks when he set up Healy for smuggling drugs or did Andy beg for them as a way to die, or was it Schillinger, using one of the C.O. members of the Aryan Brotherhood to deliver the goods? Would a father murder his own son, even if the son had betrayed the father, even in a place like Oz? If there's one father who could, it's Vern Schillinger.

Something's going on with the Muslims. After Said invited Beecher to attend one of the Muslims' study groups, Hamid Khan told Said that the faithful needed a leader who was "above reproach" and marched his troops away. Said remains a great scholar, orator, and author, but suddenly he doesn't have any followers. Except Beecher. They'd never had much to say to each other before, but perhaps because Andrew Schillinger's death was tor-

Who's the rat? Adebisi and Peter Schibetta face off.

menting Beecher, he decided that Said could help him find a way out. The next thing anybody knew, the two of them were sharing Beecher's pod, praying together. Who was watching their backs? Hopefully Allah. Has Said been letting his dick lead his head around since he met Patricia Ross? Does he truly believe that Islam is color-blind, as I'm told the Koran states? They might be, but the people in Oz sure as hell aren't. The Muslims won't have anything to do with Said as long as he "fraternizes" with nonbelievers, especially if the nonbelievers have white skin. What's worse, Said can't protect Beecher any more than Beecher can protect him.

There's something pretty fucking terrifying going on in Oz, something that goes beyond the Muslims' political infighting. There's a line being drawn between black and white. Wangler, who works in the kitchen, usu-

Don't beat Cramer because he likes boys, beat him because he's white.

—Simon Adebisi

ally looks right past me. Today, he says hello to me when he hands me my tray, and when I ask him what was going on, he says, "If we don't get together, we're going down apart." A week ago I'd have sworn he didn't give a shit about anybody but his handful of Homeboys.

Adebisi never paid any attention to the Muslims. Just before Hamid Khan's match against Jason Cramer in the boxing tournament, I hear he told Khan, "Don't beat Cramer because he likes boys, beat him because he's white!"

An awful lot of people suffered in the riot two years ago, which was mostly a fucking huge, chaotic free-for-all. Still, there was a feeling that it was us—the inmates—against them—the hacks, and it was confined to Em City. This time it feels like the

Tribal warfare—the Latinos threaten O'Reily.

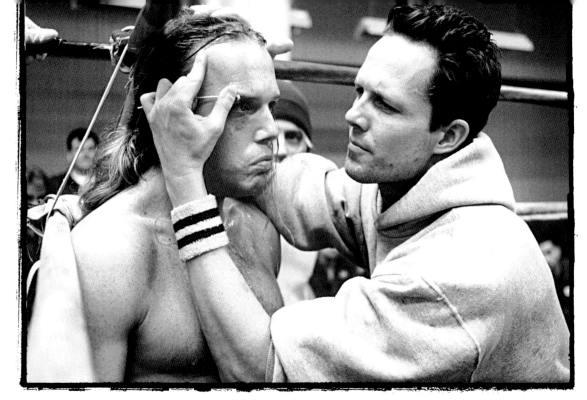

Ryan O'Reily seconding Cyril in the ring.

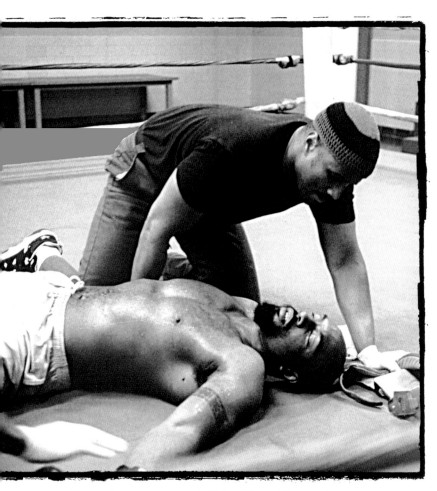

Khan ends up brain-dead, but still breathing on life support.

us against them is black versus white, even among the staff. This time if the place blows, it'll engulf the entire prison. There's always been plenty of racial tension in Oz, but now it seems like all that matters is race. Like I said, terrifying.

Monday 9.20.99

Adebisi's got balls, that's for damn sure, and you got to admire the guy even if what he's doing may cause another riot. For weeks now he's been seizing every opportunity to increase hostility between black and white in Oz. When Wangler went out of his way to be friendly to me in the cafeteria, it was Adebisi who put the words in his mouth. And now Adebisi's using Wangler in a new campaign to get Tim McManus fired and I guess force Glynn to replace him with a black unit manager. Adebisi claimed that McManus "fondled" Wangler and demanded that Glynn charge him with sexual harassment. Everybody knows that McManus has been in and out of bed with just about every woman in Oz except Sister Pete; the guy's a sex addict, but as far as who he fucks, McManus might as well be wearing a "WOMEN ONLY" sign. He already lost one sexual harassment battle when Howell charged that he'd assaulted her in his office and fired her because she refused to fuck him. The blinds were up in McManus's office during that scene, so half of Em City had front-row seats. But nobody's ever whispered a single word about McManus having sex with inmates, though plenty of the hacks do, and with his power he's had plenty of chances. Adebisi, on the other hand, would fuck just about anyone—men, women, black, white, young, old—though these days he seems to have a preference for young black men. In fact, Wangler fits Adebisi's profile better than McManus's. That's why you got to admit: Adebisi's got balls.

Besides going after McManus, Adebisi's busy rounding up as much support as he can among the black inmates, even from Said. I guess Adebisi recognizes Said's brilliance as a leader and speaker, so even if he's been shunted aside for the moment, Adebisi

would rather have Said's blessing, rather than resistance. Said doesn't seem to want any part of the Utopia Adebisi envisions. After their last conversation, Said prostrated himself in the middle of the Em City Common Room and proclaimed his faith—"My life and my death are all for Allah"—as if he was preparing to die. Maybe Adebisi told Said what was about to happen, and now the holy man figures the end is near.

1999 Victims

- **Karl Metzger:** Oz C.O., member of Aryan Brotherhood, bled to death after being slashed by Beecher, in retaliation for Metzger's role in breaking Beecher's arms and legs.

- **Richie Hanlon:** Forced to admit to killing Alexander Vogel, Hanlon had his throat slashed by Stanislofsky, who mistakenly believed that Hanlon had murdered Vogel, a friend of his.

- **Malcolm "Snake" Coyle:** Executed on orders of Antonio Nappa, after revealing to Wangler and Hill that he'd murdered the entire Ciancimino family.

- **William Cudney:** Ryan O'Reily hired Leonid Kosygin to assassinate Cudney, after the Christian fundamentalist threatened to expose O'Reily's role in fixing boxing matches.

- **Antonio Nappa:** Suffocated in AIDS block by cellmate Nat Ginzburg, on orders from Chucky Pancamo, to prevent the publication of Nappa's memoirs revealing years of Wise Guy wrongdoing.

- **Carlo Ricardo:** Unstable Latino shanked by Miguel Alvarez during an attempt on Alvarez's life, on orders of Raul Hernandez.

C.O. Perspective/Newjack

Inmates were allowed to have music. Each cell had two jacks in the wall for the headphones its occupant was issued upon arrival. Through one jack was transmitted a Spanish-language radio station; through the other, a rhythm-and-blues station, except during sporting events, when the games were transmitted instead. Inmates could have their own radios, too, but the big steel cellblock made reception very difficult. Telescoping antennas were forbidden, because they might be turned into "zip guns." By inserting a bullet into the base of an extended antenna and then quickly compressing it, an inmate could fire the inaccurate but still potentially deadly gun. The approved wire dipole antennas were supposed to be placed within a two-by-four-foot area of the wall—where, apparently, they did no good.

To improve their chances of tuning in to a good station, inmates draped wires over their bars and across the gallery floor. Some even tied objects to the end of a bare strand of copper wire and flung it toward the outside wall, hoping that it would snag on a window and that they would win the reception jackpot. (When you looked up from the flats on a sunny day, you could sometimes see ten or twenty thin wires spanning the space between the gallery and the exterior wall, like the glimmering work of giant spiders.)

Antennas strewn across the gallery floor could cause someone to trip, and if they seemed likely to do so, I'd have the inmates pull them in. But the inmate in question on my first day as a regular officer in A-block—a short, white-haired man in his sixties—had gotten his off the floor by threading wire through a cardboard tube, the kind you find inside wrapping paper. One end of the tube was threaded through the bars at stomach level, and the other protruded halfway into the narrow gallery space between cell bars and fence, like a miniature bazooka.

"You're gonna have to take this down," I advised him the first time I brushed against it.

"Why's that?"

"Because it's in my space."

"But I can't hear if it's in my cell."

"Sorry. Try stringing it up higher on your bars."

"Sorry? You ain't sorry. Why say you sorry if you ain't sorry? And where'd you get to be an authority on antennas? They teach you that in the Academy?"

"Look, you know the rule. No antenna at all outside the cell. I could just take it if I wanted. I'm not taking it. I'm just telling you to bring it in."

"You didn't tell that guy down there to bring his in, did you? The white guy?"

I looked in the direction he indicated. There were no other antennas in tubes, and I said so.

"You're just picking on the black man, aren't you? Well, have a good time at your Klan meeting tonight."

Source: Ted Conover, *Newjack* (New York: Random House, 2000).

Entries from 2000-2001

Saturday 1.15.00

The air is so thick with black—white tension that when some old-fashioned violence occurs it's almost reassuring. And you can count on the Latinos to show as much respect for tradition as the Sicilians do. Hernandez, Guerra, and Ricardo were pissed at Alvarez for just walking away when the trio was busted for possession and sent to Solitary, so when they got out the temperature got hot. Funny, but Alvarez himself was on the way back to Solitary himself. Ricardo and Guerra paid him a visit in his pod while he was packing his stuff, but somehow Alvarez managed to shank Ricardo and then held Guerra off until the hacks pulled them apart.

So as the millennium winds down, there are still a few people who are doing business as usual. Like I said, it's reassuring. Though maybe not to Ricardo, who's dead. Am I getting used to killings? Or is it just a comfort to have age-old motives like betrayal and revenge—especially when a major storm between the races seems about to break?

Glynn almost postponed the finals of the boxing tournament, because a black man, Hamid Khan, is fighting Cyril O'Reily, who's white. Finally, the warden agreed to allow the match to go forward, but without spectators. Only the fighters, their seconds, the referee, and the judges would be permitted in the room. The outcome of the fight seemed like it might ignite a riot all by itself. This time there was no talk of Ryan O'Reily meddling with his brother's opponent, but Khan, a powerful guy who outweighed Cyril by a good thirty pounds, ended up brain-dead, breathing with the help of the life-support machines. Back in Em City, almost all the inmates were sitting around the rec area, separated like the black and

Going nowhere—Shirley Bellinger on Death Row.

white pieces at the start of a game of chess or checkers, except for Said and Beecher, who're too stubborn to stay on their sides of the racial divide. As if things weren't tense enough already, right after mail call Officer Murphy started yelling about how we'd turned Em City into a pigsty and he was confiscating all skin mags until we cleaned the place up. I went back to my pod, minus my new copy of *Hustler*. A minute later Adebisi followed me in, talking his "us against them" shit like he's been for weeks. Somehow he'd also managed to rescue my *Hustler,* but when I told him I thought he was fucking crazy, he snarled at me, "You're either one of us or one of them," and left. I thought Murphy's ban on skin mags was so stupid that when I left my pod I didn't even bother to hide the *Hustler.* So of course he saw it, and of course he seized it again, and of course I told him he was an asshole. A couple minutes later, I was in the Hole, naked, without my wheelchair and barely able to drag myself to the can I was supposed to piss and shit in. That's where I spent the eve of the third fucking millennium.

Wednesday 1.19.00

Two fucking weeks in the Hole, all because Officer Murphy caught me with a contraband skin mag. No wheelchair, no toilet or running water, nothing in the cell but a bucket to piss and shit in. Most of the time, that bucket might as well have been on a mountaintop, since with no way to support myself I usually couldn't use it. Instead, I tried to eat and drink as little as I could of the daily slop they shoved into the cell. Even so, by the time a hack finally unlocked the door and shoved my clothes and wheelchair inside, I'd gotten used to lying in a pool of my own piss.

What I couldn't get used to was the fact that the reason I was thrown into the Hole was no damn reason at all. Murphy wanted to prove that he was in charge, so he busted me without thinking about what it would be like for me in the Hole, without the use of my legs, or how long I'd be left there. That didn't surprise me. In Oz, cruel punishment is the usual punishment, not the exception. What did surprise me was how I felt when I finally got back to Em City. Of course, it was a relief to be sitting in my wheelchair, to take a shower and shit in a toilet, sleep in a bed, and eat three meals a day with other people around. But all the movement made me jumpy. I was constantly looking around, watching what everyone else was doing, and I realized that during those two weeks in the Hole at least I didn't have to worry about whether the guy next to me or behind me was going to shank me or shake me down.

Back in Em City, the gulf between black and white inmates was wider than ever. Rebadow told me that a few min-

Opposite: Zahir Arif takes his turn as leader.

utes after Murphy wheeled me off to the Hole, Adebisi convinced some of the blacks in Em City that I'd been singled out because of my color, and he started them chanting "Set Hill free!" The cry caught on with the whites in the cell block, too, and it spread from there through the entire prison. Behind the thick steel door of my cell, I didn't hear anything, and when I returned, Em City didn't look any more like the Rainbow Coalition than it had before. If anything, blacks and whites were closer to civil war than ever, with the Latinos occupying a kind of no-man's-land between the two sides. Besides, I know Adebisi didn't really give a shit about the injustice done to me, he was just jumping on the event to convince the blacks that all the whites—inmates *and* hacks—were oppressing the black inmates. The glue that used to keep things from deteriorating into violence—the tit trade that the Wise Guys, Homeboys, and Latinos shared—is starting to crack, and it looks like Adebisi's trying to shove the other guys aside and take control on his own. He's already talked Glynn into transferring Wangler, Poet, and Pierce back to Em City, so almost everybody suspects something's about to crack. It's hard to believe that Adebisi's not cutting Glynn in on the tits, or why else would he be giving Adebisi's lieutenants back to him at a time like this? It sure as hell wasn't McManus's idea, not after Adebisi and Wangler cooked up the fake sexual harassment charge against him that led to Wangler's being shipped out to Unit B in the first place.

The Muslims, the one tribe in Oz that might have been strong enough to rally support among black prisoners, are coming apart at the seams. For one thing, they've got no leader. Hamid Khan elbowed Said aside when Said started getting too cozy with white folks, but Khan's been brain-dead ever since Cyril O'Reily knocked him out in the boxing final. Khan's family has finally gotten a court ruling to allow them to pull the plug on the life-support system that's been keeping him breathing. They've asked Said to say a prayer for Khan before he comes off life support, but Said won't be back as leader. That job's gone to Zahir Arif, but he doesn't have the charisma to rally the brothers, much less inspire new followers.

Tuesday 2.1.00

If I can't be sharing a bed with Anna-bella, I think I prefer living alone, but that's not a long-term option in Oz except for ad-seg inmates like the guys in Solitary, protective custody, or on Death Row. Of course, there's always the Hole, but my two weeks there felt like a lifetime. So today I got me a new cellmate, one of today's three newbies in Em City. Desmond Mobay is the man I'll be trying to get along with, a Jamaican with an accent so thick it's hard to believe he's been off the island long enough to get

arrested. Just to be friendly, I asked him a few harmless questions as he was settling in—like where he was from and how long he'd been in the States. At first he answered, in one or two syllables, but then he turned a mean stare on me and said, "Are you planning to write my life story?" Maybe he'd seen me scribbling in my notebook, but I just thought, Fuck this. I hope one of us gets transferred, and soon. It's not always easy getting used to Oz, especially if you've never been in prison before, but it's usually a good idea to try to get along with the guy you're going to spend fourteen hours a day locked in a very small room with. Mobay's lucky he didn't get somebody like Jaz Hoyt as his sponsor. I've already seen Hoyt shaking down his newbie, a French guy named Guillaume Tarrant, for cash, and I know it's just going to get worse for Frenchie from here on.

Thursday 2.10.00

Mobay's a mystery. He's been sent to work in the warden's office, supposedly because he knows typing and computer stuff, but right after work today he started talking to me about scoring drugs. The day before he acted like he didn't want to tell me his name, and today he's my buddy. At least until I told him I didn't have anything to do with tits. Next thing I knew, he was asking what he had to do to find drugs in Em City, so I told him, he didn't have to do anything, just stand still, and the drugs would come to him. And it didn't take more than a few minutes before he'd found his way to Wangler, Pierce, and Poet, so I guess he's happy now. I've got my suspicions, though, about Mobay. One day he's shut up tight as a clam, but after just a few hours in Glynn's office, he's talking tits to anyone who'll listen.

Of course, drugs are hardly a secret in Oz, and half the time it doesn't seem like the hacks are doing anything to shut down the traffic. Every once in a while, they'll bust somebody for dealing or possession and send him to the Hole, or shake down the block and bust every inmate with drugs in his cell. But that's just the cost of doing business; it seems like nobody ever gets charged with dealing or possession, even though those are crimes inside as much as they are on the street. Maybe that's because Glynn and McManus can't agree on whether to concentrate on eliminating the traffic or curing the addictions. I don't see how they'd be able to do either one. Sister Pete's drug coun-

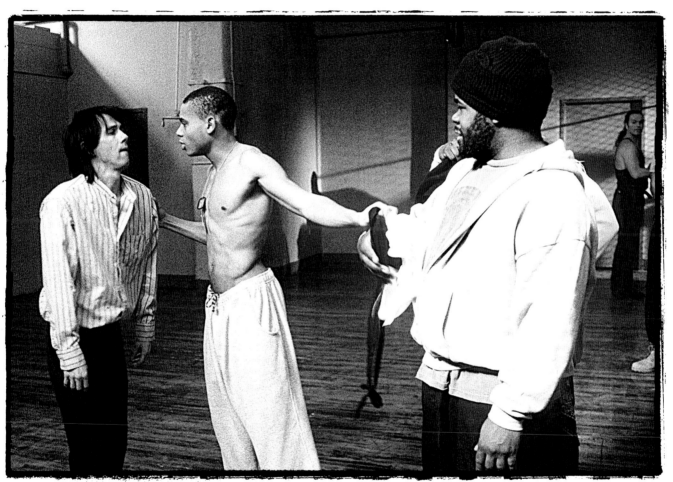

Wangler pushes Tarrant too far.

seling sessions are helping me stay clean, but that's the only program, and there's just a handful of guys in it, out of hundreds in Oz who are using and dealing shit.

Thursday 2.24.00

For weeks there've been rumors that somebody had a gun in Em City, and the whisper was that Adebisi had it. Where it came from nobody knows, or nobody's saying, and I've never heard anybody say he'd actually seen the fucking thing. There was already so much tension, mostly between the white and black inmates, that the threat of a shooting didn't add much to what was already in the air. So when Wangler and his buddies started hassling Tarrant, nobody paid much attention. First Wangler took Frenchie's shoes, tan moccasins that Wangler decided were phat, and the poor guy had to walk around in a pair of slippers from the hospital while he waited for his family to send him a new pair. Then Wangler roughed Tarrant up on the basketball court—he came back from the gym looking like he'd been boxing, not shooting hoops. When Frenchie's new shoes arrived, Wangler tried to cop them, too, right in the middle of the Common Room, and when Tarrant told him to fuck off, folks kind of wondered, What's gotten into Frenchie? A couple seconds later, we knew: Tarrant was pointing a gun at

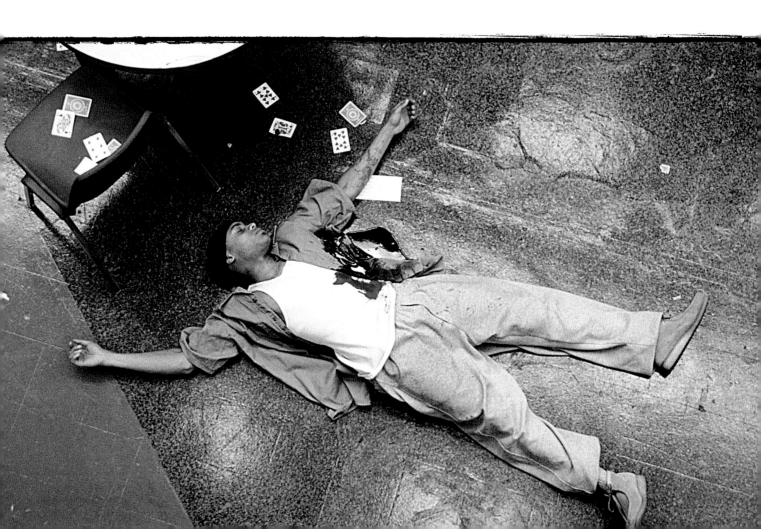

Beecher rescues Keller, who has been shot in the chest by Tarrant.

Wangler, and he started shooting, first at Wangler and Pierce and then all over the place. People threw themselves on the floor, hiding behind anything they could find—tables, poles, staircases. I rolled my ass out of the way as fast as I could. Before it was over, four men were dead—Wangler, Pierce, Lou Rath, and one of the hacks, Officer Howard—and some other inmates were wounded. When the S.O.R.T. finally arrived and closed in on Tarrant, he put the gun barrel in his mouth and blew his brains all over the wall outside Adebisi's pod. Who the fuck had smuggled that gun into Em City? Even more interesting, how did Tarrant, a guy who couldn't even keep his shoes on his own feet, manage to get his hands on it? For a couple days it seemed like a real mystery, but then we heard that a group of black inmates,

led by Adebisi and Arif, had gone to Glynn to complain that McManus had lost control of the block. They wanted him replaced with a black unit manager. Whatever Glynn said to Adebisi and Arif, McManus solved the problem by self-destructing. At Officer Howard's memorial service, he sang "De Camptown Races," an old dialect song that ridicules blacks, and Glynn didn't have much choice but to fire him. So McManus is gone.

Glynn may not have connected Tarrant's shooting spree with the plot to get rid of McManus, but maybe Adebisi figured the best way to get rid of him was to arrange for a "tragic accident." Instead of starting another riot or shooting somebody himself, he took advantage of Tarrant's desperation, planted the gun in his pod, and sat back while nature

Opposite: Tarrant shoots Wangler dead.

Stephen Foster's "Gwine to Run All Night, or De Camptown Races" (1850)

De Camptown ladies sing dis song—[Chorus] Doo-dah! doo-dah!

De Camptown racetrack five miles long—[Chorus] Oh! doo-dah-day!

I come down dah wid my hat caved in—[Chorus] Doo-dah! doo-dah!

I go back home wid a pocket full of tin—[Chorus] Oh! doo-dah-day!

Gwine to run all night!

Gwine to run all day!

I'll bet my money on de bobtail nag—

Somebody bet on de bay.

De long-tail filly and de big black hoss—[Chorus] Doo-dah! doo-dah!

Dey fly de track and dey both cut across—[Chorus] Oh! doo-dah-day!

De blind hoss sticken in a big mud hole—[Chorus] Doo-dah! doo-dah!

Can't touch bottom wid a ten-foot pole—[Chorus] Oh! doo-dah-day!

Gwine to run all night!

Gwine to run all day!

I'll bet my money on de bobtail nag—

Somebody bet on de bay.

Old muley cow come onto de track—[Chorus] Doo-dah! doo-dah!

De bobtail fling her ober his back—[Chorus] Oh! doo-dah-day!

Den fly along like a railroad car—[Chorus] Doo-dah! doo-dah!

Runnin' a race wid a shootin' star—[Chorus] Oh! doo-dah-day!

Gwine to run all night!

Gwine to run all day!

I'll bet my money on de bobtail nag—

Somebody bet on de bay.

See dem flyin' on a ten-mile heat—[Chorus] Doo-dah! doo-dah!

Round de racetrack, den repeat—[Chorus] Oh! doo-dah-day!

I win my money on de bobtail nag—[Chorus] Doo-dah! doo-dah!

I keep my money in an old tow-bag—[Chorus] Oh! doo-dah-day!

Gwine to run all night!

Gwine to run all day!

I'll bet my money on de bobtail nag—

Somebody bet on de bay.

Source: Foster's Plantation Melodies as Sung by the Christy & Campbell Minstrels and New Orleans Serenaders, written, composed, and arranged by Stephen C. Foster (Baltimore: F. D. Benteen; New Orleans: W. T. Mayo, 1850).

took its course. Of course, when Tarrant started shooting, Adebisi had no way of knowing that the victims would be black—much less that one of them would be a hack—but he knew a white prisoner's finger on the trigger would help his case. When Officer Howard got shot, well, Adebisi sort of hit the jackpot.

Saturday 3.4.00

Em City's more or less back to normal. McManus is gone, and Sean Murphy, who's been the unit C.O. supervisor, is in charge—temporarily, we're told. How long things'll stay calm is anybody's guess, but right now I'm almost more concerned about my cellie, Mobay, than about the rest of Em City. I mean, I know some of those fucking Jamaicans love their drugs, but this Mobay hardly talks about anything else, and I know he's snorting every pair of tits he can get his hands on. In Oz you learn real quick not to give a shit what anybody else is up to, and right now I'm not too worried about staying clean myself. Still, I don't want to be around somebody who's using the way Mobay does, and I don't want the Homeboys hanging 'round my door day after day, either. Almost from the first day he was here, Mobay was trying to get buddy-buddy with the Homeboys, and with Wangler and Pierce gone, he's acting like he wants to step in to replace them in moving tits.

Still, there's something about Mobay that doesn't add up. Last visiting day, while Annabella and I were talking, I noticed that Mobay had a visitor, too, a pretty woman who looked damned familiar. When we passed in the corridor outside the visiting room, Mobay said she was his girlfriend, and later he told me she'd come to the city from Washington, D.C., about six months ago. I've been in Oz for more than three years now, but I couldn't shake the feeling that I'd seen that woman somewhere before. And something in my gut said "cop." I started wondering, Could Mobay be undercover? Cops aren't allowed to do drugs, though, and they sure as hell aren't permitted to sell them, so either this Mobay is one fucked-up cop, or I've been inside so long I'm starting to imagine things.

Wednesday 3.15.00

There's at least one thing I'm not imagining: The mole has struck again! Fucking Busmalis dug another tunnel, and this time he crawled his way out of Oz and took Alvarez with him. Busmalis had been mopping floors in the hospital for the last couple months, and he somehow found the time to dig a tunnel under one of the supply closets without anybody noticing what he was up to. Alvarez, who

was in the ward recovering from being stabbed by William Giles, escaped with him. The hacks discovered that Busmalis was missing during this morning's count, and when Murphy went to check the

We're in Oz, and like I said, other rules apply.
—Chris Keller

infirmary area he found the tunnel and Alvarez's empty bed. Afterward nobody said much to us inmates, but the escape made the evening news big time, so by tonight we—and everybody else in the state—knew the whole story. Will they get caught? Probably, and before too long, I'll bet, but I always get a rush when someone manages to sneak out of Oz, even for a short time. It hardly ever happens, but when it does you have the feeling that maybe you'll be next, and, even better, the hacks look bad.

Tuesday 3.28.00

Things are starting to unravel in Em City, and as usual tits are in the middle of it all. A few days ago, Hernandez ratted out Adebisi to the hacks about where Tarrant got the gun he used to turn Em City into the O.K. Corral. Hernandez also told Glynn that the guy who gave the gun to Adebisi was Clayton Hughes, the C.O. Glynn fired a few months back. The day Glynn fired him, Hughes wandered back to the unit and quietly dropped the gun off in Adebisi's pod. Apparently Adebisi didn't deny getting the gun from Hughes, but he claimed that he hadn't given the gun to Tarrant, that Frenchie had stolen the weapon from his pod. As a matter of fact, Clayton Hughes is somewhere in Oz, too. The word is that Glynn fired Hughes in the first place because he'd

who'd planted the gun in Em City, he put the question to him. Hughes admitted giving the gun to Adebisi, and Glynn arrested his best friend's son on the spot.

Hernandez must've figured that his revelation about the gun would mean that Adebisi's ass would get shipped out of Em City for good—to Solitary or even Death Row—but it didn't quite work out that way. Instead, Hernandez got his ass shipped out of Oz, in a fucking body bag. The rumor is that Adebisi had been looking to move up the tits ladder even before Hernandez turned on him. So when Enrique Morales, a cool street-smart drug dealer, turned up in Oz on a second-degree murder conviction, Pancamo, the Mafioso who took over after Antonio Nappon died, and Adebisi offered him Hernandez's share of the tit trade. All he had to do was get Hernandez out of the way.

Depending on who you ask, Morales is either a cunning bastard or a damned lucky one. If he's responsible for Hernandez's murder, he did a good job of covering his tracks. A couple days after Morales arrived, Bob Rebadow moved into Hernandez's pod. It doesn't figure that either one of them requested the switch; Rebadow's a quiet guy who almost never gets close to people, and Hernandez hung with no one but other Latinos from the day he came into Em City. So somebody must've arranged it. A couple of people have said that Morales convinced Murphy that Hernandez had gotten jumpy

Hernandez prepares for a dead sleep.

been acting strange, talking about how Glynn ought to be defending the black inmates, not punishing them. So as soon as Glynn heard it was Hughes

lately and that being around somebody like Rebadow would calm him. Yeah, right. It had the opposite effect. Just after lights-out on the first night: Either Hernandez attacked Rebadow and the old guy shanked him in self-defense, or Rebadow stabbed Hernandez in his sleep and claimed he'd acted in self-defense. I couldn't see anything from my own cell, and all I could hear was terrible howling coming from their pod. Later, we could see the form of Hernandez's body being hauled out of Em City, but the next morning the only trace of the killing was the fact that Hernandez wasn't around for the count. Now why would Hernandez want to hurt Rebadow, and why would Rebadow try to kill Hernandez? My suggestion, if you want to know, you'd have to ask Morales, not Rebadow. 'Course I'm not planning to.

Undercover cop Mobay scouts out Oz.

Sunday 4.9.00

These days my problems with the local drug trade are right in my own pod. My cellmate, Mobay, is quiet enough, but I still don't trust him. Not that you really trust anybody, though occasionally there's someone you know who will watch your back, so you try to keep an eye on his. With Mobay, though, there's something fucked up going on. I'm not talking about the little things which he does because he's not paying attention, like moving my wheelchair so I can't get from bed into my chair in the morning. They piss me off, but I could overlook them if I didn't suspect that he's trouble. He's been trying to get in good with the drug dealers ever since he got to Oz, but most of the time he is more a user than a dealer. Yesterday he stumbled into the cell so fucked up on heroin he could barely stand, and the next thing I knew he was throwing up all over the floor and the wall. I started to say, "Man, I been there, I can help you," but before he could answer, the hacks shook down the unit and found some more tits in Mobay's mattress. To his credit, when they questioned me about them, he stood up and admitted that the drugs were his, instead of sitting back and hoping I'd take the rap. So he's been dragged off to the Hole, and I've got a few days to think about whether to take some responsibility—talk to Mobay about seeing Sister Pete or something—or keep my distance.

Saturday 4.22.00

It's not often there's much really good news in Oz, but today Said announced that the judge in the class-action lawsuit about the riot had ruled in our favor: He declared that the hacks had used excessive force even after they'd retaken control of Em City, and were responsible for the inmates' deaths as well as for many of the injuries to other inmates. The prisoners who were in Em City during the riot started high-fiving each other and talking all at once about how they were going to spend their share of the $45 million, but they quieted down pretty quick when Said explained that the state would certainly appeal the verdict, meaning it would be a long time before anybody saw any money. A few of them even walked out of the room when they heard that. With or without the money, the ruling bought Said some cred. For a while it seemed like maybe he didn't really want us to win the suit, so that he could continue to claim that the

judicial system was corrupt and would never blame the state for any of the violence connected with the riot. In fact, when Said refused to testify at the trial because some new regulation requires all prisoners to wear a bright orange jumpsuit when they travel outside the prison, it did seem that he preferred to lose than to swallow his pride. He claimed that if the jury saw him wearing the jumpsuit, they'd perceive him as a common criminal. I still remember how proud he acted when he represented me in my motion for a new trial. He's still proud, even arrogant, but I got to admit Said's come a long way since my hearing, and this time he has a top lawyer—Arnold Zelman, a social activist who knows how to handle the press—working on the case.

Monday 5.1.00

If there's good news in Oz once in a while, most of the time there's no news at all, or if there is, it's bad. The thing that every inmate fears most is that someone will hurt his family to get revenge on him, and the word is that Beecher's two young children, a boy and a girl, have been kidnapped. The FBI investigator assigned to the case thinks that it's probably a ransom situation, because Beecher's family's wealthy, and the only thing to

A bad system run by blacks is as bad as a bad system run by whites.

—Kareem Said

do is wait for the kidnappers to make contact with the family. Inside Oz, though, people are betting that Schillinger is behind it all, seeking revenge for his son Andrew's death. I guess it doesn't matter to Schillinger that he's the one who killed Andrew, by bribing a hack to smuggle the tits the boy OD'd on into the Hole. In his mind what really killed Andrew was Beecher and Keller turning the son against his loving father. Yeah, right.

Today's mail solved the mystery of who was behind the kidnapping for just about everybody, even if there's no hard proof yet. A package arrived, addressed to Beecher, containing a child's hand. It's been identified as the hand of his son, Gary, and everyone's sure that the boy's dead, though his body hasn't been found. Since the news got out, Beecher's been in his pod, moaning now and then, but mostly keeping quiet, not talking to anyone and hardly moving. What it's like for him, I don't know, but losing a kid must be the worst thing that can happen to a person. And knowing that something you've done is part of the reason your kid has died, I can't imagine a worse feeling than that. Meanwhile, his daughter's still missing, maybe she's dead, too. There's nothing Beecher can do now but hope the FBI finds her before it's too late.

This morning, we could see Beecher through the glass, in his bed, not moving. One of the hacks started yelling at him to come out of his pod. Beecher stayed where he was, but before the asshole could drag him out, Rebadow started yelling, "You can see he's in pain, leave him alone! What does he have to line up for?" The hack said, "Rules is rules," but when Rebadow came back at him with "Fuck your rules!" every inmate in the block started cheering him, and Murphy signaled to the hack to drop it. Ever since his run-in with Hernandez, Rebadow's been like a different guy. He used to walk around hunched over and never making eye contact, but now he looks people in the eye, as if he's no longer afraid. Of course, he's still no match for the younger guys physically, but maybe he figures that if he could hold his own with El Cid, he's got no reason to take shit from anyone.

Maybe bad news comes in pairs. Today the TV brought the report of another legal victory for Said, but one that Said—and almost everybody else—isn't happy about. Months ago,

Said agreed to represent Jason Cramer, who'd been convicted of murdering his male lover, in an effort to get Cramer's original conviction overturned. Nobody doubted that Cramer had killed the guy—he also beheaded him, packed the head in a box, and tried to ship it somewhere via Airborne Express—but one day Cramer got a visit from a woman who'd been on the jury that convicted him. The woman told him that one juror made anti-gay slurs from the day the trial started, and whenever anyone expressed doubt about Cramer's guilt, this juror accused that person of being homosexual as well. Said was sure that Cramer was guilty, but he wanted him to be convicted for what he'd done, not for who he was, so he agreed to represent him.

The hearing didn't last long. As soon as the judge heard the testimony of the anti-gay juror, he threw out Cramer's original conviction and granted him a new trial. But then things started to unravel. First the homicide detective who worked on the case came to talk to Cramer and Said. He told them he was dying of emphysema or some such disease and wanted to clear his conscience. He admitted that he'd tampered with the evidence from the murder scene and gotten a friend in forensics to back him up. Said also discovered that the only eyewitness to the crime had died after Cramer's first trial. As soon as Said saw what might happen—that Cramer might get not just a new trial but an acquittal—he withdrew from the case, but by then it was too late. Cramer got himself another lawyer, and at his new trial there was no evidence and no witnesses to testify against him. He's on his way out of Oz now.

Tuesday 5.16.00

I'm less worried about who's leaving Oz than who's coming in. The newest arrival isn't a prisoner, he's the new Em City unit manager, Martin Querns, and from what I've seen, he figures to be more bad news than ten of the baddest motherfuckers all rolled into one. When Glynn introduced him a couple days ago, Querns made a bullshit speech about how he knows the streets as well as any of us, and announced the cardinal rule of Em City: "Don't fuck with Querns." It's clear, though, that he's got plans to fuck with us, and he's already started. Now McManus sure wasn't any genius when it came to keeping the peace, but setting up the council of representatives of all the groups in Em City was at least a step in the right direction. He usually didn't pay much attention to what we said, but at least he listened. Well, Querns has replaced the council with a group of three "trustees" whose job it is to keep order. And who are the trustees? Pancamo, Adebisi, and Morales, the motherfuckers who just happen to run the tit trade. Is Querns

The philosophy of Querns: Have sex, do drugs, but don't cross me.

their new partner? I don't know, but it wouldn't surprise me.

Glynn is considering Devlin's invitation to run for lieutenant governor in the election this fall. Glynn wasn't on the ticket yet, he was waiting to be nominated. I wonder if he thinks hiring Querns to run Em City will help him and Devlin get elected. Make everybody, white and black, happy by keeping a lid on the unrest in Oz, and having blacks in the two most high-profile positions, so it looks like the state is doing the socially responsible thing.

If Em City turns into Tit Town under our new leader, one guy who'll be happy is my cellmate, Mobay. He's out of the Hole, and in less time than it took him to shower, he was back in the cell snorting heroin he'd scored from Poet.

When I asked him what the hell he was doing, he laughed and said, "Breakfast of champions, man." I'm sure he'll be pushing harder than ever to get into Adebisi's organization, and with Querns in charge around here, the tit trade looks like it's going to become one fucking healthy growth industry.

Friday 5.26.00

McManus is back in Oz, and so's Dr. Nathan, and I'm glad. Yeah, McManus, and yeah, he's back, but now he's running Unit B. Would I like to see him take over Em City again, even though he fucked up royally all the time he was unit manager? Maybe, since my gut tells me Querns is serious bad news for us, even if Em City's quieter now than it used to be. There's less violence, but underneath, the place is out of control—drugs, mostly—and one day it's going to blow.

Do Not Fear Love

Fear not love as it loosens its
    hooks from its gruesome sheath
and capture you in its painfully
    seductive grasp.

Fear not the blood that will ooze
    from your wounds and hold your
    patience to task.

Fear not the tearing sounds of
    passion as they rip apart your
    feelings at the start.

Fear not the fainting pulse of
    your heartbeat for THAT is the
    very best part.

Poem by muMs

Dr. Nathan just returned to work in the infirmary. She'd been out for a few weeks, after she got raped in front of her apartment. I haven't seen her yet—I'm lucky, I never get sick—but guys who've been there say she's still pretty badly bruised. There's a rumor going around that Ryan O'Reily was behind the attack, that he wanted to punish her for rejecting him. After all, how can a woman refuse a man who's so in love with her that he gets his own brain-damaged brother to murder her husband, so she'll be free to be his woman? O'Reily would use anybody to get what he wants, and he doesn't give a shit who gets hurt, but getting someone to rape the woman you love sounds a little sick even for our Irish Iago.

Shirley Bellinger, the only woman in the state on Death Row, is finally gone, too. I never saw her, either. She was convicted of drowning her daughter and brought to Oz because it's got the only Death Row in the system. She got more than her share of press—first woman in the state on Death Row this century—so we kind of followed her appeals on the TV news. Finally, after her execution date was set, she turned out to be pregnant, and Governor Devlin granted her a delay until after her baby was born. Instead of being relieved, Bellinger, who had been pursuing every possible avenue of appeal, insisted that she had to be executed. She told Sister Pete that the baby she was carrying was the child of "Satan in the form of a man." Instead of helping the execution to proceed, Sister Pete arranged to have Bellinger declared insane and committed to the Connolly Institute, where Devlin commuted her death sentence to life. I don't know if Bellinger was really insane, but when the governor ordered her returned to Death Row after she'd had a miscarriage, she stopped ranting that it was Satan who'd gotten her pregnant and that she "had" to die. The rumor going around Oz about her execution is that when she saw the scaffold, she begged the warden not to go through with the hanging, struggling with the hacks and crying, "Please, Sweet Jesus, not yet," or something like that. I wonder which is crazier, the woman who drowns her own daughter or the state that puts her to death for doing it?

Saturday 6.3.00

Mobay's got me more worried than ever. First I thought he might be undercover, until I saw how much tit he was snorting. Then his addiction bothered me, but now it's just his weirdness. Today when I came into the cell he was talking to a white newbie, someone I'd never seen before. I don't even know his name, but he acted like he was looking for a fight, and he was huge, like a linebacker who was cut from his team years ago but still snarls at everybody as if they stood between him and his Super Bowl ring. I must've interrupted their conversation, because Mobay turned the volume up on his Jamaican accent and said, "I would be glad to help you any way I can," and

Bellinger's last walk—on the way to the gallows.

the guy left, saying to me, "So long, Butch" as he exited. I'm thinking, What is this Butch shit. And who is this asshole? And what the hell is Mobay talking to him for?

Before I could figure that one out,

EXECUTION OF WOMEN IN THE UNITED STATES

A poster in 1847 announced the execution of a young girl, 16 years of age, as a "Grand Moral Spectacle." The same announcement went on to say she was to be "publicly strangled," attended by a Minister of the Church of England and the hangman, The Great Moral Teacher. The hangman, it explained, after "fastening her arms to her side and putting a rope round her neck would strike the scaffold from under her." And if her neck didn't break after that he would "pull the legs of the miserable girl until by his weight and strength united he strangled her." The 1786 execution of Phoebe Harris, who was hanged for the crime of coining silver, was witnessed by a crowd of some 20 thousand people. An account of her execution revealed that she was led to a wooden stake, where she stood on a stool with the noose of a rope attached to an iron bolt driven into the top of the stake around her neck. The stool was then removed and as her body convulsed, she "noisily" choked to death for several minutes. About half an hour later her body was chained to the stake and the executioner placed two cartloads of branches and twigs around it and set them on fire. Her body then burned for over two hours. Although, by all accounts, everybody loved a hanging, two years after Phoebe's hanging, when Margaret Sullivan was hanged and burned, an article in the paper noted, "There is something inhuman in burning a woman."

Nevertheless, some people defended the practice of burning women's bodies, saying that although it was a horrible practice, there was no pain involved since the woman was already dead.

Source: Kathleen A. O'Shea, *Women and the Death Penalty in the United States, 1900–1998* (Westport, Conn.: Praeger, 1999).

Mobay started telling me how he wanted my help in committing a murder. I wondered, "Is he serious, or is he testing me somehow?" Anyway, if he really wanted to kill somebody, why would he ask me to help him? In this wheelchair, I'm hardly the most agile accomplice you could find. So I turned him down and shut him down, saying I didn't want to hear any of his bullshit, that I didn't get mixed up in other people's business, criminal or not. He smiled and said that was okay, I should just forget all about it, and afterward he was a little more talkative and friendlier, so I figured maybe Goergen—Mobay told me his name and said they'd met the day Goergen arrived in Em City—had spooked him or something.

I did my best to put it all out of my mind. Later, Mobay asked me to meet him out back in one of the work areas, said he wanted to talk to me about something in private, and I thought, Maybe he's coming around, wants to put some distance between himself and the Homeboys. So I went to the spot he'd proposed, over near one of the freight elevators. He was waiting for me when I got there. Suddenly, Goergen rushed up out of nowhere and grabbed my wheelchair, like he was going to shove me over the edge of the elevator shaft. Man, I was scared shitless! I thought, This is it, Augustus, you survived being thrown off that roof, but you're not going to come out of this one alive. Suddenly Mobay grabbed my chair and said to Goergen,

"Let me do it," and in one motion pushed me away from the opening and elbowed Goergen over the edge. He started pushing my chair back in the direction of Em City in a big hurry, saying, "You should've let me tell you the whole plan!" All I was thinking was fuck his "whole plan," all I want to do is get away from this madman! Though I'm not going anywhere until the hacks stop asking questions about the body that mysteriously turned up at the bottom of that elevator shaft.

Sunday 6.11.00

Things are changing in Em City since Martin Querns arrived, or maybe I should say that Querns is changing things. Now he's started moving white inmates out and bringing black prisoners in. The first groups to go were the Aryans and the Bikers. Nobody believes Querns's claim that he chose the men because they were responsible for violent incidents in the past. I mean, they were, but if you shipped out every inmate who'd started a fight since he got to Oz, Em City would be a ghost town, with me and Busmalis and maybe one or two other guys rattling around the empty cell block.

No, I think Querns has something else in mind, and he's using the drug dealers—and Adebisi in particular—

to make it happen. What is it? I've got no fucking idea, unless to set the Muslims and the Homeboys against each other. They've been pretty much staying out of one another's business ever since Jefferson Keane's conversion a couple of years ago, but now Adebisi seems to have cut a special deal with Querns, who might be planning to cut everybody else out, black and white. After Hamid Khan died, Zahir Arif took over as leader of the Muslims, and Said pretty much stayed out of everything except the lawsuit and other legal matters. Maybe it would've been better if he hadn't, because Adebisi seems to respect him. Yesterday I overheard Arif and Adebisi arguing. "We had a deal, Adebisi," Arif said, and Adebisi answered, "That's true, we did, but now we don't." I can't say what that deal was, but I guess it had something to do with live and let live between the Muslims and Adebisi's crew.

If Arif didn't already have enough trouble with Adebisi, someone who just arrived in Em City will probably add to his problems. Supreme Allah is his name. He's somebody I knew out on the street, where he started life as Kevin Ketchum, a drug dealer and small-time hustler. Somewhere along the way he became a member of the Five Percenter offshoot of the Muslim movement and changed his name. The Nation of Islam doesn't recognize Five Percenters as true Muslims for a lot of reasons, and one of them is that the Five Percenters are often

Supreme Allah.

picious of what Querns is plotting. Murphy, the C.O. supervisor McManus brought in, just transferred out of Em City. He's going to join his old pal, McManus, who's back in Oz running Unit B. Murphy isn't the sharpest guy working at Oz, but on the whole, he's fair, and I say that even though I'm still pissed at him for throwing me into the Hole for holding one fucking contraband copy of *Hustler*.

Tuesday

Adebisi and Querns seem to have an understanding: Adebisi can do anything he likes in Em City as long as there's no violence. The Wise Guys, even if they still control the drug pipeline from the outside, have to go through Adebisi, and the Latinos are reduced to being minor players. Meanwhile, up in Adebisi's pod they're partying all the time. He's on the second floor, so I haven't seen what goes on for myself. Besides, Querns has let him put fucking curtains on the wall of his pod, so nobody can see inside. But we can hear music playing, and I'm told that there's drugs and booze and sex, and that Adebisi's got one of his prags, a slim, young, light-skinned brother wearing high heels, short skirts, and a wig, shaking his ass for their amusement. Glynn's got to know what's going on, so why doesn't he do something about

involved in drugs. I wouldn't be surprised if he tried to muscle in on the Muslims and the Homeboys at the same time. He sure as hell believes he can do both; the name he chose for himself says it all, as far as I'm concerned.

It's not just inmates who are sus-

Five Percenters

Just like Hollywood [DJ Hollywood, early hip-hop luminary] has not been given his due in the history of hip-hop, I feel another smaller but important influence has been overlooked—the Five Percent Nation of Gods and Earths. The Five Percenters are members of a religion that developed in jail among black inmates from the New York area. In fact, let me put it this way—if the Nation of Islam is a religion that finds converts in prison, Five Percenters find their converts under the prison. That's how street it is. It began as an offshoot of the Nation of Islam, but it never had the discipline or the strong organizational structure of the NOI. Based around the idea that the black man was God and that only 5 percent of us had true knowledge of self, it's been very influential over the years in the young black community because it was very much a religion about talking. Slick, smooth-talking crafty niggas gravitated to it because the Five Percent religion's membership was built on the ability of its members to articulate their devotion to a strict set of beliefs with as much flair as possible. A true Five Percenter could sit on a stoop or stand on a street corner and explain the tenets of the sect for hours on end—and be totally entertaining! The Five Percent religion elevates black men, telling them they're all gods here on earth but only 5 percent are true believers. A Five Percenter will say some fly shit like "I've got seven moons, three suns, and two earths." It sounds mystical, but he's really talking about all his women, with his two earths being his closest girls. Not only was their rap hot, but phrases like "knowledge me," "true mathematics," "360 degrees of knowledge," and "dropping science" are just some of the linguistic contributions the Five Percent religion made to hip-hop. Street names like True God, U-God, Wise Allah, and Divine Intelligence emerged because of how Five Percenters labeled themselves. . . . The Nation of Islam is more visible and respectable in terms of its presentation, and is clearly more powerful than the Five Percenters as an organization. However, in the period when the gangs I hung with in the '70s gave way to '80s hip-hop culture, it was the street language, style, and consciousness of the Five Percent Nation that served as a bridge.

Source: Russell Simmons with Nelson George, *Life and Def: Sex, Drugs, Money, and God* (New York: Crown Publishers, 2001).

it? I guess as long as Querns keeps the violence down, Glynn's giving him a free rein.

Who Adebisi's friends aren't is getting interesting. They aren't Pancamo and Morales, who used to be equal partners with Adebisi in the tit trade. They're still partners, but are they still equal? And they aren't Said or Arif, either. Adebisi used to act like he wanted Said's respect, but these days he doesn't seem to give a fuck about that, and he doesn't seem worried about whether the Muslims line up as his allies, either. He's been spending a lot of his time talking to Supreme Allah, though, so maybe Adebisi's figuring Allah will emerge as the new leader of the Muslims, even though Said and Arif think he's a fraud.

Mobay, my cellmate, is having his own problems with the Homeboys. The more he tries to get in good with them, the more tits he snorts, but they still don't seem to trust him. I'm not sure whether he wants to start dealing just to support his own habit, but he's got himself one fucking impressive addiction. I don't trust him, either. I keep wondering, Who is Desmond Mobay? A couple days ago he said that a homicide detective named McGorey had asked him some questions about Goergen's murder, so he may be worried that they suspect him. Maybe that's one reason he's been using like a fish lately. Or maybe he's hiding something else. Last night he must've been talking in his sleep or something, loud enough that he woke me up. I called out to him and, when he answered, he suddenly didn't sound Jamaican.

Meanwhile, Querns is continuing to reinvent Em City in his own image. This time it's the white hacks who are being transferred out and replaced by black C.O.s—plus Claire Howell, the woman who accused Tim McManus of sexual harassment and sued the state after he decided he didn't want to fuck her any longer *and* fired her. Now that's different—sexual harassment because somebody *refuses* to fuck you—but Timmy Boy always could find ways to shoot himself in the foot better than anybody else. This time he's done something decent, though; he's offered jobs in Unit B to all the hacks Querns dumped.

Friday 7.7.00

A little bit of good news goes a long way, and today there was more than a little bit: Father Mukada rushed into Em City to tell Beecher that his daughter, Holly, had been released, unharmed, by the kidnappers. "Beecher's kid's alive," the words went around Em City like a headline, and even people who barely knew Beecher—or were indifferent to him—felt relief. Kids shouldn't have to suffer, no matter

Beecher and his children before the kidnapping.

what their parents do. There's still no clue who the kidnapper was. At first Beecher suspected Schillinger, but then he paid Eli Zabitz, an inmate with links to professional kidnappers, to ask around, and Zabitz came back with a name that was supposedly tied to Chris Keller. That seemed weird—Keller's a killer, but he and Beecher have been tight—and the FBI, which hasn't been much help, tracked down the people Zabitz named and found they had nothing to do with the kidnapping or the killing. So they're questioning Schillinger again. Meanwhile, Querns

has confined Beecher to Em City, to keep him out of harm's way and far from whoever might have been responsible for kidnapping his kids.

For some inmates, though, like Ryan O'Reily, it's always business as usual. An inmate named Nikolai Stanislofsky talked a poor slob, Ralph Gulino, out of his cell phone (the jerk didn't even know they were illegal in Oz, and when Stanislofsky generously offered to make the phone disappear, he gave it right up). When O'Reily caught wind of it, he started scheming to get his hands on the phone himself.

We've got pay phones in Oz, of course, but the hacks monitor our calls, so a cell phone gives you a way of doing business that would otherwise be nearly fucking impossible. Other inmates

"Cell" mates O'Reily and Stanislofsky before they get their wires crossed.

heard about the phone, too, and one day Hoyt, a Biker who just might be the reason Gulino's not around any longer, ganged up on Stanislofsky to try to take ownership. But somehow O'Reily came out of the scuffle with possession of the phone, like a point guard picking off a poor pass, and Stanislofsky ended up in ad seg to protect him from both O'Reily and Hoyt. Meanwhile, for days nobody knew where the phone was, and then, just as we

were lining up for the count the other night, it started ringing. The hacks didn't have any trouble locating its hiding place then, taped to the bottom of a chair in the Common Room. I guess that was Stanislofsky's way of getting even.

Of course, Hoyt and O'Reily both denied knowing anything about the cell phone, just as O'Reily said he had no idea how a new inmate named Patrick Keenan—who'd been convicted of raping Dr. Nathan—got bludgeoned to death in the weight room. So far, nobody's come forward with any clues about who killed Keenan, and I don't think anybody's going to. But the death must've brought the horror of getting raped right back into Dr. Nathan's mind. She's taken another leave of absence from the hospital, and this time, who knows if she'll ever make it back to Oz? And does that mean O'Reily didn't set up the rape after all?

Thursday 7.20.00

Yesterday Schillinger made some comment about Dr. Nathan to O'Reily across the food counter in the cafeteria, and suddenly the two of them are mud-wrestling in the mashed potatoes. Of course, there's been a short fuse between those two, especially after Schillinger fucked Cyril O'Reily. There's always a small army of hacks in the cafeteria, and they broke up the fight pretty fast, but then I noticed that Officer Howell suddenly stepped in after O'Reily'd been cuffed and dragged him away. O'Reily didn't make it back to Em City until sometime after the rest of us returned from lunch. When he finally showed, he didn't look any the worse for wear, the way he should've if one of the hacks had taken him out for batting practice. Could something be going on between Ryan O'Reily and Claire Howell? There's not too many women offering sex to inmates. O'Reily's probably just getting it while he can. But what'll happen if— fuck *if*, when—Howell decides to turn on him? When McManus dumped her, she shook up the whole prison with her sexual harassment suit, so what's an inmate—even a scheming bastard like O'Reily—going to do when she decides to take him down?

The word got around that Stanislofsky was due to return to Em City from protective custody, where he'd been ever since the fight over Ron Gulino's cell phone. Querns is proud of shutting down the violence in the cell block, so he must've warned O'Reily not to touch Stanislofsky. Well, O'Reily was in Em City, so he sure didn't get anywhere near the Russian, but we heard that Stanislofsky had died suddenly, just before coming back to violence-free Em City. And a little while later, Howell walked through the block, and I swear I caught a glimpse of her and O'Reily winking at each other.

Today we got some news that sickened just about everybody who heard it. Schillinger's son Hank beat the homicide charge in the murder of Beecher's kid, got off on some technicality, even though everyone from the judge on down knew he was guilty. I don't know what Beecher plans to do now, but I think the bad blood between him and Schillinger isn't going to end until one of them kills the other. Or somebody else kills them both.

Bad blood can be hard to turn into good, even when there's a history of friendship between two people. Rebadow was released from the Hole today for trying to stab Busmalis. First thing Rebadow did when he walked into his pod was apologize to Busmalis and offer to shake hands with him, but Busmalis refused. All of a sudden Rebadow collapsed on the floor of the cell, crying out in pain and clutching his head. In the infirmary, the doc-

I take a shit in this world, I see **reality,** and I make **the best** of it.
—Burr Redding

tors discovered he's got a brain tumor, so Busmalis begged Querns to let him visit his friend before he's shipped out to Benchley Memorial for surgery—wanted to shake Rebadow's hand, to let him know he's accepted his apology. What did Querns do? Refused, of course. He's still pissed at Rebadow for spoiling his perfect record of no violence. Maybe he's pissed at Busmalis, too, for getting himself stabbed.

Thursday 8.10.00

I still don't have a clue why Mobay wanted to kill Bruno Goergen, but that murder just won't go away. I just spent a few hairy minutes trying to avoid tough questions from Detective McGorey, who's been in and out of Oz interrogating inmates about Bruno Goergen's death for weeks. She's sure he was murdered, which he was, and that I know something about it, which I do, so it's a good thing I've had a lot of practice playing dumb. When I got back to the pod, Mobay was there, acting cool and indifferent as he usually does when he's not drugged out on tits. He wanted to know where I'd been, and when I told him I'd been avoiding McGorey's questions, he just said, "Like she don't know nothing." So I told him we were both cop killers, but that I regretted what I'd done every day, while he didn't give a shit about

taking a life. All Mobay answered was, "Goergen was a monster," so I said, "I guess it takes a monster to kill one." I feel like Mobay'd do anything to worm his way in with the Homeboys. If they made killing me the next hoop to jump through, he'd take me down like he done Goergen, no questions asked.

Meanwhile, the drug dealers literally own Em City. Not all of them, only the ones who line up behind Adebisi. This afternoon, Pancamo and Morales, who used to be Adebisi's partners, got shipped out to Unit B. Replacing them as trustees, Querns announced, would be Poet and Supreme Allah, two of Adebisi's loyal lieutenants, so it looks like he's finally climbed to the top of the pyramid of powder. Every time Querns moves white or Latino inmates out to gen pop, the guys who replace them are black. Considering that four out of five prisoners in Oz are black, it's not surprising. But it's also no coincidence that they all turn out to be followers of Adebisi and his crowd. The biggest surprise, though, occurred this afternoon, when Kareem Said approached Adebisi as he sat surrounded by flunkies in front of the TV and declared, "Simon, you truly have transformed this cell block into a paradise. A utopia. And I'm going to say it for everybody to hear: I want to join you and serve you in whatever way you choose." Adebisi told Said to swear in the name of Allah that he was serious, and Said said, "I do so swear." Then Adebisi said, "I've

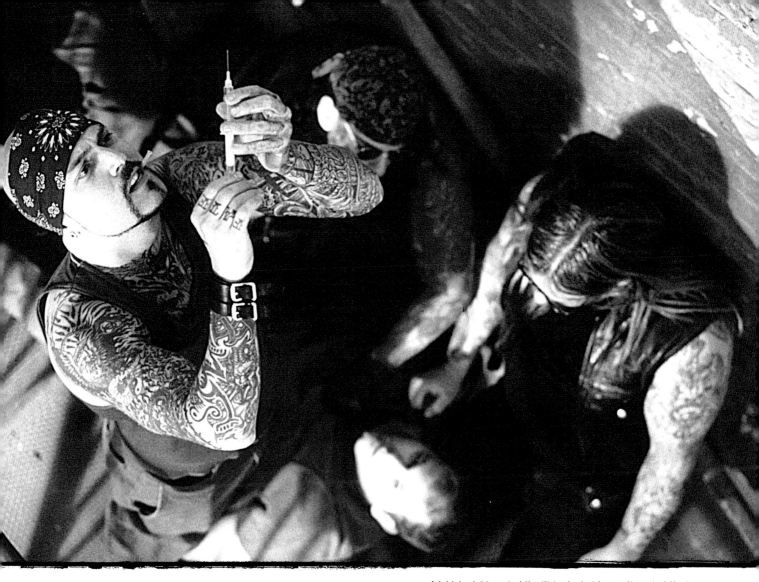

Adebisi might control the tit trade, but he can't control Hoyt.

waited for this moment. Now I can raise you as my equal. Together, there is nothing we cannot do. Nothing. Nothing." By this time, his voice was like a drumbeat, and the crowd around them took up the chant, shouting "Nothing! Nothing! Nothing!" as if nothing was something to be celebrated. If you ask me, Keller and O'Reily, two of the white inmates still left in Em City, were closer to getting it right. They were watching the scene from the gallery above where Adebisi, Said, and their followers had gathered, and when they saw what was happening, Keller said, "Adebisi and Said, hand in hand," and O'Reily replied, "That's the end of the fucking universe."

Tuesday 8.22.00

Oz isn't the whole fucking universe, and Em City's not the capital, but for us suckers who are stuck here, it might as well be. Today Governor Devlin came to the auditorium to announce on live

Devlin introduces the shank-proof vest.

"The governor is down!"—Devlin shot by Clayton Hughes.

TV that C.O.s throughout the state would be wearing new stab-proof vests to protect them from shankings. While Devlin was hyping the vests, Clayton Hughes, the ex-C.O. who's waiting to be tried for planting the gun that Tarrant used to kill four people and himself in Em City, approached through a side entrance and shot the governor. The whole state—including everybody in Em City—watched the whole thing live on the news. We couldn't see Hughes—he was off to the side—but we watched the governor get hit and heard Glynn yell, "The governor is down!"

Even if Devlin doesn't die of his wounds, Hughes will probably be back in Oz. He'll do long, hard time in the prison where his father died, stabbed by an inmate in the same room where Hughes shot the governor. Hughes was convinced that it was a white inmate who'd stabbed his dad, and he started to believe that whites in power were responsible for his personal loss and for the oppression of all blacks. Now it looks like he may end up discovering that his own worst enemy was a black man: himself.

Wednesday 9.6.00

As soon as the TV news announced that it was Hughes who'd shot Devlin, inmates all over Oz started chanting Clayton Hughes's name. Only the black prisoners were chanting, "Clayton, Clayton," over and over, while the whites yelled, "Kill Hughes!" I wasn't chanting anything, because it seemed to me that wounding or killing the governor would only make things worse for prisoners all over the state. At least it got Glynn's attention, though. He'd been standing at Devlin's side when he was shot, and the next day he held his own press conference to announce that he was dropping out as a candidate for lieutenant governor. The attack—by his former buddy's son, no less—must've clued him in to the fact that for too fucking long he hadn't been keeping his eye on what was going on inside his own prison. If he hadn't been spending so much of his time on the campaign trail, maybe he'd've stopped Querns from turning Em City into a free-trade zone for tits. When I heard Glynn's statement,

I thought maybe he'd pay more attention to what was happening in Em City and assert more control—after all, he is the fucking warden—but I also wondered whether it wasn't too late to do much good.

Speaking for myself, I'd be willing to settle for a little improvement in my own pod. Mobay isn't snorting tits like he used to, but he's sure as shit selling plenty, and he's usually hanging with Poet or Tidd or Browne or one of the others from Adebisi's crew. Just before lights-out last night, I'm

C.O. Clayton Hughes: lost soul.

not sure what got into me, but I told him I suspected he was undercover not long after he moved into my pod, that is, until I saw the amount of tits he was snorting himself and selling to other inmates. Then I figured he couldn't possibly be a cop, not until "that night you were so cranked up on tits that your accent disappeared, and I was like, 'What the fuck is that?' "

Mobay just looked at me, without

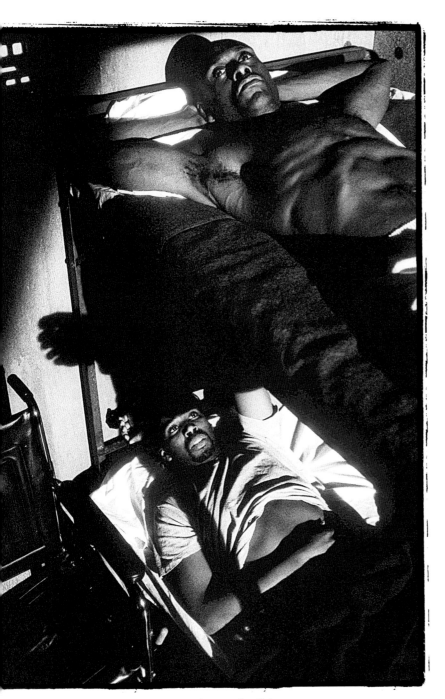

Under suspicion: Hill ponders the secretive Mobay.

saying a word. So I went on to talk about his woman, who looked so familiar to me when I saw her in the visitors' room. "Tore my brain out trying to remember, trying to remember where. Then I had a flash: When they threw me off the roof, I was laying on the cold pavement, and this woman police came over to see if I was still alive. That woman police, she's a dead ringer for your Tina."

Still, Mobay didn't say anything, hardly moved, in fact. Then one of the hacks on the gallery called, "Lights out!" and as we were starting to get ready to turn in, I just said, "Well, good night, Mobay, or Officer whoever-the-fuck-you-are." A second later he had me by the throat and whispered, "You talk that shit to anyone, you're next in the elevator shaft."

Mobay's a slender guy, but I could tell from the force of his grip how strong the bastard was. I knew he could've killed me easily, even if I wasn't in this wheelchair, but I just had to tell him what I thought of him. For my own self-respect. I said, "I ain't going to tell nobody nothing. I'm telling nobody that you're a cop, a cop who breaks the law in the name of the law. I just want you to know that I know you're a fraud, and I don't mean that you're undercover. As a person, you're a fraud."

As soon as I'd gotten the words out, he was swinging at me, knocking my wheelchair flat on the floor and kept punching. I don't remember anything else until I woke up in the infirmary, with the worst fucking headache of my life. It wasn't until I got back to Em City several days later that I discovered that Mobay wasn't there. After the hacks peeled him off me, it seems he went straight to Glynn and confessed to Goergen's murder. Who knows, maybe he'll be back in Oz before long, this time under his real name. And maybe he wasn't such a fraud after all, he just wanted to bust the drug dealers so bad that he lost sight of the line between being a man and something else.

Sunday 9.17.00

We had an unusual visitor at the drug counseling session yesterday afternoon, Chris Keller. He used to be a regular in the group, but after Sister Pete accused him of trying to manipulate her in order to get back into Beecher's good graces, he dropped out. Today he showed up halfway through the session, announced that he was starting to have cravings, and asked Sister Pete—to tell the truth, he fucking begged her—to let him back in. She flat-out refused and told the hack who'd brought Keller to take him back to Em City. It must've been tough for someone like Keller, who doesn't like to admit that anything can touch him, to bare his soul like he did, especially in front of Beecher and Sister Pete. I've never seen her turn

Three ex-wives, and no future: Keller stands alone.

away somebody who'd asked her for help before, no matter what he'd done, so Keller must've betrayed her where she lives in order to rate getting cut off like that. This afternoon, though, Sister Pete paid a visit to Em City, something she doesn't do very often, and one of the people she spoke to was Keller. They were talking in the computer room, so I don't know what they said to each other, but I guess it didn't end well, because after a few minutes I noticed Keller get up, brush past Sister Pete, and walk out of the room as if nobody else was there.

Life in Oz may be tough these days

Busmalis gets bitten by the love bug.

for just about everybody, but for Agamemnon Busmalis, things seem to be looking brighter. If I didn't believe in the story of the holy fool before hearing the latest chapter in Busmalis's life, I'm thinking about believing it now. First, his pal Rebadow survived his brain-tumor surgery and is back in Oz. He's still in the infirmary, but he'll be released to Em City in the next couple days. Busmalis was so happy to see

Rebadow again that when his pal complained about the scar from his operation, Busmalis handed him his own lucky hat to cover it up with. Then he heard that "Miss Sally," the actress who's the star of a puppet show on TV that half of Em City watches only because Miss Sally's got such an enormous pair of tits, was coming to visit him. Busmalis must be Miss Sally's biggest fan, and not because of her tits; he thinks she's an angel. After he escaped he was captured standing outside Miss Sally's apartment building, hoping to get a glimpse of his idol.

As it turned out, Busmalis's visitor wasn't really Miss Sally, but Norma Clark, a secretary whose job it is to read Miss Sally's fan mail and Norma was moved by Busmalis's letters. Apparently she liked him pretty well, too, since Busmalis said from now on he's going to write to Norma instead of Miss Sally.

Saturday 9.30.00

Life may be coming up roses for Busmalis, but most of the rest of us are getting stuck with the thorns. I don't know what's going on, but the body count is starting to climb in Em City for the first time since Querns took over, and that's got just about everybody on edge. First an inmate named

Nate Shamin turned up in the laundry covered in blood. Nobody had a clue as to who might've murdered the guy; he was almost invisible in Em City, with no friends, no enemies. Querns was pissed, though, because even if the guy was a nobody, by getting killed he'd suddenly turned into somebody: the first murder victim in the cell block under Querns's watch. So he told Adebisi he'd better find the killer. The only thing anyone remembered about Shamin was that he and Beecher had fucked, so Adebisi beat up on Beecher for a while. Before anyone solved Shamin's murder, Mondo Browne turned up dead in the kitchen, shanked, and again there were no witnesses. This time the murder hadn't been committed in Em City, but the victim was one of Adebisi's own people, and there was a clue. A necklace was found at the scene of the murder, a necklace that belonged to Supreme Allah. To an outsider, it wasn't easy to guess whether Adebisi's hold on Em City was unraveling or somebody was just trying to make it look that way, but circumstances certainly seemed to indicate that the demonic drugs-for-peace pact between

Querns and Adebisi couldn't last much longer. The one player I can't figure out in all this is Said. He's got to detest everything about the "paradise" Adebisi's created for himself and his followers: the drugs, the alcohol, the sex. But ever since he took that oath of allegiance to Adebisi a couple weeks back, the two of them have been spending more and more time together, talking. Of course, Said doesn't take part in the drinking and orgies that go on every day behind the curtains of Adebisi's pod, but when you see them it's like they're planning something—together. What the fuck it could be nobody on the outside has any idea, and I think both of them are too smart to think they can convert the other.

I've noticed that Said's also been spending time talking to Poet, another member of Adebisi's inner circle, but only when Adebisi's not around. As soon as he pokes his head out the door of his pod, Said and Poet act like they're strangers, and even when the leader's out of sight they never exchange more than a few words, like they're passing secrets or something. I wonder what they've got to hide from Adebisi. But the biggest surprise of all is that Said's going to move into Adebisi's pod! How can he expect to study and pray with Adebisi partying, doing drugs, and playing his trumpet all through to lights-out? Unless

Adebisi's promised to quit that shit, but I haven't seen any sign of his changing, and he hasn't started turning up at Sister Pete's drug counseling sessions.

Monday 10.9.00

Said did move in with Adebisi, and for a day things were quiet in the block, no parties, but no conversions, either. Just quiet behind those white curtains. On the afternoon following Said's move, with no warning Querns was gone and McManus was standing at the microphone on the gallery, announcing, "I'm back!" Then Said returned to his pod and a minute later, Adebisi followed him in. We could hear arguing and scuffling inside, though I couldn't make out anything that was being said from my spot down on the first floor. A minute or two passed, and then a circle of blood appeared on the curtain to the right of the door. At first it was about the size of a fist, but it quickly spread and grew larger. Then the door of the pod opened and Adebisi stepped out onto the walkway, swaying a little but erect. He took a step or two forward, and he seemed to laugh. His knees buckled, blood sputtered out of his mouth, and he pitched forward onto his face, the back of his

Opposite: Said and Adebisi: their fatal showdown.

shirt drenched in blood. A second later Said emerged from behind the curtains, staggering, bleeding from a gash in his neck and gripping a shank in his right hand. Adebisi was dead.

Thursday 1.4.01

With Querns banished from Em City and Adebisi slain, life in the cell block has returned to something like normal. For a change, McManus didn't insist on trying to solve every problem at once; maybe all those months in the trenches in Unit B had given him a dose of humility. But he did restore the balance that had existed between both the inmate and staff populations before Querns came along. He even brought Pancamo, Morales, and some of their crews back, as if he was admitting that the drugs weren't going to disappear overnight, but at least people stopped worrying that the tits were about to fuel a major race war. In other words, the inmates were still scamming and scheming against one another, the drugs were still flowing, there were fistfights, and there was butt-fucking, but from one day to the next, we felt like we could deal with things as they were.

That is, until a TV crew from some "hard-hitting investigative news magazine" showed up to do a segment about Oz: the staff, the inmates, gen

pop, Em City, daily life, and—where would TV be without it?—the dirty underbelly of the place. I don't suppose Glynn was too happy about any of it, but the show's producers had cleared the idea with the commissioner and the governor, so Glynn was, like they say, fucked. The show's star, Jack Eldridge, wasn't actually around for the first couple days. The segment producer, Lisa Logan, and the camera crew roamed through the prison, interviewing inmates and trying to suss out where the juicy stories were. After they found the dirt, I guess Eldridge would come in for the kill, the way the native beaters would go through the bush on safari, to flush out the animals so all the white hunters had to do was take aim and shoot them. They ignored me—I guess they'd already done a report on paraplegics behind bars—and from what I'm told they focused on the usual suspects: Beecher, Schillinger, Keller, Said, O'Reily. What I heard was that they were looking for a story behind Adebisi's death, although there'd already been an investigation into the killing that found that Said had killed Adebisi in self-defense, using the knife that Adebisi had shanked him in the neck with.

One thing the report planned to do was to follow a new inmate around, from the time he was processed in until he settled into the routine a few days later. The guy they chose, Omar White, turned out to be my new cellmate, replacing Johnny Basil (the real name of the undercover cop who called himself Mobay). White's a hopped-up heroin addict who's always on the prowl for more tits, but he's in for murder, not for dealing. First thing he asked me was, "You a cripple or something?" like maybe I was sitting in this wheelchair to make a fashion statement or some shit like that, and then he wanted to know if I had any tits. I told him I didn't do drugs now, and then he wanted to know if I was a fag. What's his problem? Is he just worried about his manhood, or is he not quite right in the head? He's no narc, that's for sure, but the way he was acting, I get the feeling he is going to be more trouble than fucking Mobay ever was.

Wednesday 1.10.01

Jack Eldridge arrived in Oz, his weapons the TV camera and the reporter's instinct for the jugular, to tape the interviews that would later be broadcast. Eldridge had also decided that to capture the real sense of prison life, he'd spend a night locked in a cell, with a small camera recording everything that happened from the hours before lights-out to the moment when the inmates are released from their cells for the morning count. He'd chosen Omar White as his roommate, probably because he'd be familiar to viewers as the prisoner whose orientation was being taped as well. I laughed when I heard that White and Eldridge would be spending the night together; that "veteran" reporter didn't know that he'd be confined with a certified nut for fourteen hours or longer. Well, at least I'd have a night off from Omar's yapping.

But something happened before the media star and the murderer could settle into their pod. O'Reily, who'd been supplying White with tits since he got to Em City, must've planted the idea in White's head that Eldridge believed he was gay. Why go to the trouble? Years ago Eldridge televised a damning report on the Irish gang that the O'Reily brothers belonged to, and O'Reily saw a chance to settle an old score. But he figured that White would wait until he and Eldridge were locked in for the night and then beat or maybe even kill the reporter. Instead, White went after Eldridge on the walkway outside their pod, where the hacks had no trouble subduing him.

After White was dragged off to Solitary, Eldridge decided that brain-damaged Cyril O'Reily would make a peaceful overnight companion, so he asked to have Cyril substituted for White. Ryan O'Reily tried to convince McManus not to allow Cyril to spend the night in Eldridge's company, but McManus ignored him. I didn't have a view of their pod on the second floor, but a couple of the guys who could see what was going on said that at first Cyril seemed calm enough and

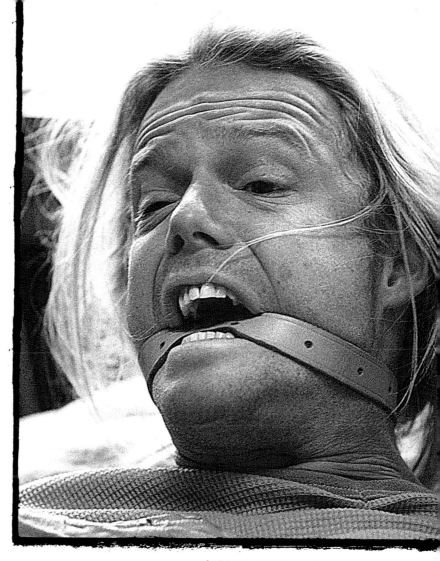

Cyril loses control and gets restrained.

was talking to Eldridge, though he acted puzzled whenever Eldridge looked in the direction of the TV camera and talked to it. Suddenly, though, Cyril must've recognized Eldridge as the same person who'd reported on the O'Reilys in the past. He screamed "You gave my mama cancer!" over and over, all the while punching Eldridge in the face. The beating didn't last long, since the hacks had their eyes on Eldridge, rushed in, and dragged Cyril off him. The network killed the story, but the report of Eldridge's encounter with Cyril was all over the TV news.

McManus's cooked up some schemes to "educate" and "improve" the population of Em City. Today he announced that from now on we'd all be required to watch a weekly instructional video that would be played over the TV screens in the Common Room, and he unveiled a cage—a cube about eight feet square—sitting on a pedestal in the center of the room. Instead of sending troublemakers to the Hole, McManus said, they'd be put into the cage, in full view of the rest of Em City. As soon as McManus stopped talking, Keller called up to him at the control center, "Mr. McManus, sir, how big is your penis?" That got a big laugh from the crowd, but of course it also earned Keller the honor of being the first inmate shoved inside the cage. Sometimes I think that maybe McManus really does want to save us, but if he does, he also wants us to admit that he's our savior, that we couldn't have done it without him. What better way to advertise his power to punish as well, right in the middle of Em City's Main Street?

Salvation's in the air these days, with Timmy Boy leading the parade. The inmate he seems determined to save is Omar White, my hopped-up roommate (when he's not rotting in Solitary). McManus had brought him back to Em City and was pressuring him to go into drug rehab. White got released from Solitary just in time to make room for Alvarez, who was finally captured a few days ago near the Arizona-Mexico border. White didn't hang around Em City long enough to make it to a drug rehab meeting. Before Sister Pete's next session, he was back in Solitary, after cutting Chico Guerra in the cafeteria with a kitchen knife. As far as I know, White and Guerra don't know each other and there's no history between them, so it's anybody's guess what was behind that shit. Maybe nothing, except that White's a bug.

Burr Redding turned up in Em City yesterday. Took me by surprise. I didn't even know he'd been arrested—either my mom hadn't heard or (more likely) she didn't want to talk about it—but he told me that he was convicted of killing six or seven guys in a shootout, so he'll spend the rest of his life in prison. Burr seems even more bitter than he ever did on the street, probably more because his wife, Delia, just died of ovarian cancer than because he ran into some bad luck with the law. Burr's been inside plenty of penitentiaries, and from what he's told me, Vietnam was worse than any of them.

Burr doesn't make much small talk; he never did. Almost the first thing he wanted to know was, "Who's the brothers who need talking to around here?" meaning he's planning to make a play for a piece of the tit traffic. That's no surprise, especially with Adebisi out of the picture, but I hope he doesn't plan to drag me along. As great as it is to see Burr again, to know he's around, I don't want back in that game in the worst fucking way. I pointed Poet out to him, and I know he's already found his way to Pancamo and Morales, too. I guess he's come to an understanding with Poet, because a little while ago, in the Common Room, Poet jerked his head in Morales and Pancamo's direction and said, "You

I live in Oz,
I live in
this chair,
and I wouldn't be here
if you'd let me have the
goddamned
motherfucking
paper route.

—Augustus Hill

know those motherfuckers are planning to kill you, don't you?" All Burr said was, "Good, that's what I want 'em to do." So I asked him, "You want 'em to kill you?" and he said, "I

want 'em to try." I hope he's got more than just me and Poet watching his back if those two come after him. I'll bet they're looking for a way to get their honor back after losing face when Adebisi shut them out of the operation.

Thursday 2.1.01

I sure as hell don't find anything comical about being in prison but once in a while, funny things do happen even in Oz, stuff you find yourself laughing at for days. That secretary from Miss Sally's staff, Norma Clark, who pretended to be Miss Sally the first time she visited Busmalis, has been coming back to see him every week. Now he's asked her to marry him, and she said yes! It's touching, sure, but it's crazy, too, though not as crazy as the story I just heard about Officer Howell and Ryan O'Reily. The two of them have been getting it on for a while— Howell busts O'Reily for something and then takes him into the women's bathroom and they fuck—but when O'Reily told her they were through, she told him it wasn't over until she said so. She had him thrown into the Hole and then forced him to have sex with her in there. I don't know which is funnier, that an inmate would shut down his regular squeeze, or picturing O'Reily submitting to a blow job from Howell while cuffed to a stall in the ladies' room. And she's the woman who claimed that McManus forced himself on her? These jokes are tame compared with the news we heard today: A ship carrying Chinese refugees ran aground off the coast. They don't have visas, of course, so while their applications for asylum are being considered they're going to be housed in state prisons. A bunch of them are supposed to start sleeping in the Common Room in Em City any day now. Are the authorities trying to get them to change their minds about wanting to come to America? Maybe the government just doesn't give a shit about them because they're a political powder keg.

Monday 2.5.01

Nobody's laughing about the Chinese refugees anymore, not since their leader and interpreter, Bian Yixhue, was found dead in a storeroom yesterday. Burr's being blamed for the killing. McManus claims that Bian Yixhue had come to him because he'd been told that Burr had sworn to kill the refugees, that after his experience in Vietnam he hates Asians. Burr denies threatening the Chinese and insists he has nothing against them, that's all bullshit, and I believe him. He's no racist, and I've never heard him say a word against Chinese or Asians or any group, for that matter. He's capable of killing, that's for sure, and he can be heartless about it, but he only goes after his enemies, and he's got nothing against these unfortunate people.

I was still a baby when Burr came back from Vietnam, but when I was old enough he talked plenty to me about his time there, about my dad, about drugs, about what Vietnam did to him. He was angry, all right, but not at the Vietnamese; his anger was directed against the people responsible for sending young men and women into a war they couldn't win and maybe shouldn't have been fighting in the first place, a war where some of them, like my dad, lost their lives, and where others died inside because of what they'd done there. Burr sometimes said that what soldiering had taught him had nothing to do with becoming a brave warrior, that all he'd learned was how to kill women and children.

Who was the dumb fuck who thought those poor refugees would be safe inside Oz? They sure didn't ask any of us inmates.

You'd think that Devlin, after he almost got killed by Clayton Hughes, would realize that nobody's safe, at least not in this prison, but sometimes I think the Governor imagines he's some kind of superman, that the bullets just bounce off his body. Maybe so, but when I saw him on TV in a wheelchair at his inauguration, he didn't look immortal. Neither was Bian Yixhue, and because of Devlin's blindness, he paid with his life.

The first couple days Burr was in Em

City, I thought I really was safe, that there was finally somebody in here I could trust to protect me, but now I realize all I felt was a little less alone. I'm fucking glad that Burr's in Em City, if he's got to be in prison, but I'm not kidding myself. Now that he's making his move to get a piece of the tit traffic, people are going to see me as part of his operation whether I'm involved or not, so when something goes wrong—and something's got to go wrong sometime—I'll be in the line of fire, too. No, the only thing that could save me is getting out of prison, and that doesn't figure to happen. After all, I'm in Oz for killing a cop, so how's that going to sound to the Parole Board, no matter how good a record I have while I'm in prison? If I even make it to my first parole hearing fourteen years from now.

Of course, if you're serving a short sentence and have a clear shot at parole, you might just walk out of prison and get your life back. That's what Jackson Vahue thought he was going to do. I hadn't seen him for a while, but a few days ago we crossed paths in the gym, where I was working out with weights and he was shooting baskets. After serving four years, he told me, he had a parole hearing coming up, and "While you're rotting in here, I'll be back on the court."

I remembered seeing on the news what he'd done to the woman he assaulted, and I thought, Vahue shouldn't be allowed to go free. I looked up the old newspaper stories on the case on the Internet, and when I found the woman's name—Beverly Reed—I called her. Didn't tell her my name, but I told her what was happening with Vahue. Victims have the right to tell their stories to the Board when parole cases are considered, but nobody has to tell them when a hearing's been scheduled, and usually the prisoner's lawyers try to keep the proceedings under wraps. Beverly Reed had something to say to the Parole Board, and after she'd said it, they didn't look kindly on Jackson Vahue's application. I saw him in the cafeteria a day later, and when I asked him how his parole hearing had gone, he exploded. Threw his lunch tray across the room, punched a hack who just happened to be standing nearby, and seemed like he might take the entire place apart. It took three hacks to wrestle him down, and when it was over, Vahue was on a trip to the Hole, not back to the NBA. Before the hacks dragged him away, I took a good look at him pinned down on the floor, moaning like a wounded animal and with his face twisted in pain, and I wondered for the first time, had I done the right thing?

Sunday 2.7.01

Since Adebisi's death, there's been a tense truce between the Muslims and the Homeboys. Supreme Allah's been in Solitary, so he hasn't been pitching his Five Percenter brand of Islam. And even Poet, who owes Said for helping to get Poet's writing published, has been keeping his distance. Once Burr arrived, it looked like the Homeboys finally had a leader they could rally around. One of them, Leroy Tidd, has been pushing to join the Muslims. For days, Said kept chasing him off, saying he didn't believe Tidd's conversion was sincere, but the brother kept showing up at the Muslims' study groups and exercise sessions. None of that made any impression on Said, until one day on the basketball court, when Robson and some of the other Aryans attacked the Muslims. Said wasn't around at the time, but Tidd was, and he jumped into the fight on the Muslims' side. Got thrown into the Hole, too, and Arif must've told Said what had happened. Said pulled some strings to get Tidd released and back in Em City, and when he walked through the gates, Said was there, his arms wide in greeting. He apologized to Tidd and embraced him. Some people still wonder out loud whether Tidd's conversion is sincere, but this time it seems that Said's a true believer. And Leroy Tidd's now Salah Udeen.

Sunday 2.11.01

Inside Oz, God's love is easier to come by than the love of another human being. A new inmate, the Reverend Cloutier, an evangelical TV preacher—

he was bigger than Falwell, Rebadow said—who embezzled hundreds of thousands of dollars mailed in by the faithful, has started saving souls in Oz. I heard that even Vern Schillinger's been nibbling at the bait of salvation, though that's a conversion I'd have to fucking see before I'd believe it. Meanwhile, Busmalis, who finally found true love with Norma, Miss Sally's secretary, got Glynn's permission to marry her, but only if he promised never to dig another tunnel. Busmalis swore he was through digging tunnels, and he's got such a cheerful, innocent look when he smiles that Glynn must've forgiven him for the bad publicity he caused when he helped Alvarez to escape. The only problem was, Busmalis had been working on a tunnel in his cell for weeks, and when he started filling it in, he ruptured a water pipe and practically flooded Em City. So for the time being, instead of cuddling with Norma in the visiting room, Busmalis is enjoying the cold embrace of a cell in Solitary.

Some guys aren't so lucky. Beecher got himself a new cellmate a couple days ago, a pretty boy named Ronnie Barlog, and it looked like the two of them were playmates, too. When Barlog walked into the Common Room in Em City, he and Keller greeted each other like long-lost buddies, so they must've hung out on the street or in another joint. But Barlog didn't last more than a few days; turned up dead from a broken neck.

Nobody's talking about who might've done the deed, but it suddenly hit me that every one of Beecher's last few sex partners—Nate Shamin, Mondo Browne, and now Ronnie Barlog—has been murdered. Could it be rough sex, or foul play?

I was in the laundry with Burr and Poet when Alvarez came in with a bizarre proposal; he wanted to team up with Redding to take Morales out. It made sense for Alvarez, who's been trying to muscle his way back into power in El Norte ever since Raul Hernandez pushed him aside, but what was in it for Burr? Not much. He told Alvarez, "You're playing a dangerous game, son, betraying your own skin," and said, "The trouble with getting in bed with a traitor is you never know when he may betray you." I guess when Alvarez walked out of the laundry he figured his number was up with El Norte, because a minute later, Jorge Vasquez, one of Morales's boys, was lying on the floor next to the cage with his throat slit, and Alvarez was holding off three or four hacks with the shank he'd just used on Vasquez. By the time another hack came down from the control center to flatten Alvarez from behind, Vasquez was dead. Maybe Alvarez figured the only place he'd be safe was in Solitary and did what he had to do to get himself back there pronto. Alvarez goes in and out of Solitary so often they ought to put in a revolving door.

Which is better, struggling to get what you want or waiting patiently? I don't know, but Omar White can never wait. Maybe he hasn't learned that it's easier to survive in Oz by not being too visible than by making a name for yourself. A few of the Homeboys were sitting in the library a couple days ago when Jackson Vahue walked in. White got so excited I thought he might start bouncing like a basketball, but he settled for getting Poet to introduce him to Vahue. All Vahue was after was some tits, so once he got what he came for, he just nodded at White and went on his way. It didn't mean anything, but for some reason it bothered White, and he got so edgy not even tits could calm him down.

Later in the day, he started running on about why Burr was waiting so long before making his move on Pancamo and Morales. He said, "I don't know why we don't go up there and ice those motherfuckers right now." I told him, "Relax, Redding knows the score, he'll tell us when the time is right." But White couldn't sit still, started walking back and forth and finally standing right in front of where Pancamo was watching TV in the Common Room. At first I thought, White's history, but when Pancamo told him to get the fuck out of the way, he just slunk off, and I figured the drama was over for the time being. But it wasn't. He raced up the stairs to the control center, where McManus was talking to the hacks on duty, and shanked Timmy Boy in the gut. In the struggle, White actually got thrown off the mezzanine, scooped up by the hacks, and hauled off to the Hole.

White's certainly made a name for himself shanking McManus, but it's probably not the name he was after. He seemed a little crazy when he first turned up in my pod, but from now on whenever anybody looks at him it'll be like he's wearing a shirt with BUG in big letters on the back. That is, if anybody does see him. After this last performance, White just might do the rest of his time in Solitary.

When I started hanging with the Homeboys after Burr arrived, I experienced the rush you get from being close to the power for the first time since my arrest. I'm not really after the rush or the power now—I'm there out of loyalty to Burr—but when something happens like Alvarez coming to Burr for help in greasing Morales, the tension just creeps right up your spine, and if you lived the way I used to live on the streets, the feeling is a little like being home again, out of this chair, back on my feet. I'm not using and I'm not dealing, either, and I won't start again, but being in the middle of the action is almost as exciting as it used to be. Almost.

Monday 2.19.01

Landed back in the infirmary for the second time a few days ago, this time courtesy of Supreme Allah. I've never had any trouble with him before, not on the streets and not in Oz. It didn't bother me that he was playing on the Muslims' turf at the same time as he was in tight with Adebisi moving tits. Of course, the Muslims called him a fraud, and maybe he was, where the faith was concerned. When Burr arrived, Supreme Allah was in Solitary, accused of murdering two other inmates, one of them Mondo Browne, a Homeboy who'd been close to Adebisi, but I figured when he got out—*if* he got out—he and Burr would get along as well as they had when I was still out on the street. Which as far as I knew was okay. When Supreme saw Burr sitting with me in the Common Room after he got out of Solitary, the first thing he did was come over to say hello. He sounded friendly enough, but when Burr replied, "Get the fuck away from me, Ketchum," Supreme Allah just mumbled something and backed off.

"What was that about?" I asked, and Burr told me how it was the night I was arrested, about how the cops knew where to look for me. I'd always thought they'd had me under surveillance, but Burr said that the cops had arrested Supreme Allah and were squeezing him for information, so the motherfucker gave me up. "If it wasn't for Supreme Allah," Burr said, "you wouldn't be in that wheelchair. You wouldn't be in Oz." I didn't know what to say to that news. I just wheeled myself back to my pod, to be by myself and think, while the truth sank in. The next time I saw Supreme Allah was in the shower. He started jabbering about how I should tell Burr that the spics and wops were plotting to kill him, that he'd tell Burr himself but he couldn't get near the guy. Supreme Allah said he didn't understand Burr's attitude, that he'd never done anything to backhand him. I asked, "What about me?" He acted like he didn't understand, so I told him, "You put me in here. Burr found out that you was the one ratted me out." All Supreme Allah said to that was "Bullshit!" Something in me snapped, and I went after him, wheelchair and all. He shoved the chair away and it tipped over. I fell onto my side and lay on the floor while he punched and kicked me, and then I must've blacked out.

I was banged up pretty bad, but Dr. Nathan, who came back after Keenan was killed, didn't think I'd gotten any internal injuries, and the X rays were negative. She decided to keep me in the infirmary for a couple days, and the next afternoon, who turned up in the bed next to mine? Why, Supreme Allah, looking a lot worse than I felt, with an oxygen mask over his nose and mouth. I didn't know what had happened, and I didn't find out until I got back to Em City a couple days later. Burr had asked Tug Daniels, brother of Craig Daniels, the fellow Supreme Allah had shot in an argument on the street, to pay a visit to Poet at the same time as Supreme Allah's girlfriend was seeing him. It didn't take much to convince Tug to come up to take a shot at Supreme Allah, in revenge for his killing Tug's brother, even though he knew his chances of walking out through the front door after shanking Supreme Allah were about zero. The shanking wasn't fatal, but it'll be a while before Supreme Allah takes another shower.

Saturday 2.24.01

The Beecher–Schillinger wars took a few more bizarre twists over the past few days. A month or so ago Schillinger fell under the Reverend Cloutier's spell and decided he wanted to make peace with Beecher. His son Hank has disappeared, but his daughter-in-law's expecting a baby soon, and from what I'm told Schillinger's taken over the role of granddad like he was born to play it. Even more surprising, he asked Sister Pete to set up a victim-perpetrator interaction with Beecher. After everything that's gone down, deciding which one of them is the victim and which one the perp might be tough. But I guess what matters is that the two of them have already met a couple times, and from what I heard they both want to continue. When Hank Schillinger was found murdered, the fragile peace seemed likely to unravel in a hurry. So, too, when Schillinger's cellmate Robson stabbed Beecher's brother Angus outside the kids' playroom where Beecher and his daughter Holly were visiting. Everybody who knew anything about the Beecher–Schillinger history of violence and revenge suspected that Beecher was behind Hank's death and that the cycle wouldn't end there. When the word came down from the FBI that Keller had arranged for Hank to be murdered, not Beecher, Schillinger had an out, and he took it, promising not to harm Beecher's family in the future. Meanwhile, Keller was being shipped out of Oz to stand trial in Massachusetts for arranging the hit, so who knows, one deadly triangle might finally be broken. I heard that Beecher and Keller had a tearful good-bye in Receiving and Discharge.

There's a blizzard brewing, and it takes something like that to remind us inmates that there's a world out there. Of course, we know that there are trucks bringing food and other supplies to the prison just about every day, the staff drive to work and then go home at the end of their shifts, and every week busloads of new prisoners arrive. For some of us, there are even visits from friends, relatives, and lawyers now and then, but after being here a few years it gets harder and harder to keep in mind all those activities that continue somewhere else, just like the people outside little by little forget about us. Until a storm blows up to remind us.

The snow's been falling for about three days now, but until today the traffic kept moving, so the hacks made it in for their shifts, and there was plenty of food in the cafeteria and hot water in the showers. But today Norma Clark didn't show up for her wedding to Busmalis. Glynn had given permission for Father Mukada to perform the ceremony in the chapel, Busmalis was dressed up in his best godawful sports jacket, Sister Pete had gotten special permission for them to spend the night in one of the old hospitality suites where inmates and their wives used to spend their conjugals, and even Rebadow looked a little like the architect he used to be. Rebadow said later that they waited for several hours, that Sister Pete tried to track Norma down at work (she'd taken the day off) and home (no answer), and finally they gave up the wait. Was it the snow that rained on Busmalis's parade, or did Norma get cold feet from something else? It wouldn't have been much of a marriage, to be sure, but after I heard that Busmalis had never even had a woman, I was rooting for him and Norma to have their honeymoon.

Sunday 3.11.01

For most of us, one day in Oz is like the others. So even a couple new members in the drug counseling group make headlines. We've got a newbie, Edward Gallson, a Marine colonel who raped a female officer at a convention, and Jackson Vahue. Vahue must've gotten clean when he was trying to make a good impression on the Parole Board, but after the decision went against him, he went back to using, heavier than ever. Either he's starting to worry about his heroin addiction, or Sister Pete got wind of his problems and leaned on him to come to counseling. Gallson's a different case, an alcoholic who won't admit he's got a drinking problem, just that he lost control once, and now he's paying the price.

When Vahue talked about himself in drug counseling, he didn't say anything about using drugs or whether they had anything to do with the assault that got him incarcerated; he talked about his legs. Said they were what made it possible for him to get out of the projects and into the NBA, gave him the chance to become somebody, and that he didn't want to forget that. I don't know how anybody else reacted to what Vahue said, but his words really got to me. I guess that's because Vahue's legs transformed him into somebody special, and mine, while I had the use of them, carried me exactly nowhere. Now I'm stuck—in this place and in this chair. In another few years, Vahue's legs are going to start to go, too, slowly, but they won't be coming back, either, and nobody will remember that game against the Bulls in 1995 any longer. All the time Vahue was talking, Poet and I knew something that Sister Pete and all the others at the meeting didn't: that the previous day Burr handed Vahue a set of works when he complained snorting tits wasn't getting him high anymore. And I know what drove Vahue back to the tits, because it was me who helped make sure the Parole Board wouldn't open the front door.

Sunday 3.25.01

Burr's decided to make his move to take control of the tit traffic. He's ordered Tug Daniels, who's now doing time for trying to murder Supreme

Allah, to take out Pancamo, and he's sent word to Omar White in the infirmary to finish off Supreme Allah. Supreme Allah's still there recovering from his stab wounds, so maybe Burr wants to get everything over with before Supreme Allah gets out and the opposition is back at full strength. Jia Kenmin, the Chinese gangster who tried to smuggle the illegals from mainland China into the U.S., asked to be the one to kill Morales, because he wants to avenge Bian Yixhue's death.

Of course, I've known this was coming. Burr's never been big on sharing the power, and he is well aware that Pancamo and Morales have been plotting against him since his first day in Em City. I've got no love for any of them, especially not for Supreme Allah, but what's the good of eliminating those three? Supreme Allah doesn't carry much weight with the Homeboys anymore, and as for Pancamo and Morales, if they get killed, another Wise Guy will step up like they always do, and somebody else will move in to take over El Norte. I've gone along with Burr all my life, and if he was in trouble, I'd do whatever I could to protect him, but this business just doesn't make sense.

I tried talking to Burr in the cafeteria today, but it didn't do any good. I told him a string of killings like these, obviously connected to the drug traffic, would result in a lockdown so tight there'd be no way to move tits for a long time. But he just said they couldn't keep the prison locked down forever. I'm afraid that to Burr, surviving the projects and Vietnam and losing Delia, life's just one ugly struggle after another. When I tried talking to him about the dreams I had for a better life, of doing something besides selling heroin, he just laughed, saying that all I'd ever wanted was to deliver newspapers. Then he said, "I take a shit in this world, I see reality, and I make the best of it." Then I got pissed off, telling him that I didn't need his lectures about reality. "I live in Oz, I live in this chair, and I wouldn't be here if you'd let me have the goddamned, motherfucking paper route."

I hadn't been close to Said for a long while, ever since he failed to get my conviction overturned, but I felt like I didn't have anybody else to talk to about this business, so later that day, when just the two of us were in the shower room, I told him what Burr was plotting. Said encouraged me not to think I was betraying Burr, especially since I was convinced that killing Pancamo, Morales, and Supreme Allah wouldn't help him anyway. Said told me that he'd always admired me for preserving a sense of "decency and honor," even in Oz. I guess he was thinking about my decision to testify to the grand jury about Coyle. I told him I didn't see it that way, and besides, I asked, what good did "decency and honor" do me? He simply said, "You get to sleep through the night." And it's true, I do.

Thursday 3.29.01

Even though I knew Burr's plan to grease his rivals was wrong, still I felt like a rat talking to the hacks. I knew there was no other way, though, so this morning I asked Murphy if we could talk in private. I told him what I knew, that the plan was to take down all three of them, Pancamo, Morales, and Supreme Allah, at the same time that afternoon. Murphy quietly sent the word up the line to Glynn, and just when Daniels, Kenmin, and White were about to strike, the S.O.R.T. moved in. After the word got back to the Common Room, Burr shot me a look—halfway between sorrow and hatred—that I'd never seen from him before. I know I did the right thing, but I don't expect that Burr's ever going to come around to thank me for doing it. I wonder if he'll still be talking to me. The three men who were supposed to take our rivals out aren't going to thank me, either, especially not after they get done stewing in Solitary or the Hole.

Monday 4.23.01

Once in a while you get a pleasant shock, sometimes even from the last place you'd expect it to be coming from. Like Death Row, where my weird old cellmate William Giles has been ever since he was convicted of the knife killing of Louis Bevilacqua. One of the bizarre features of this state's capital punishment law is that the condemned man's allowed to choose his own means of execution. Since execution's come back, most people have just gone along with the hacks' drug of choice, lethal injection, but if someone wants to die some other way, the state's got to accommodate him. Or her. Shirley Bellinger asked to be hanged, and she was, and Donald Groves got executed by firing squad. Well, Giles decided he wants to be stoned to death, and the state refuses to allow it. Some of the anti-death penalty groups have decided to sue on Giles's behalf, arguing that if the state wasn't willing to execute him by the means he'd requested, they couldn't legally kill him any other way. Who knows, maybe the courts will outlaw the death penalty all over again, or at least the lawyers will keep the case in the courts long enough to grant Giles what he'd really like, to die of natural causes. Moses Deyell's another Death Row inmate with his own ideas about dying. He heard about how Jefferson Keane donated a kidney to his sister before he was executed, and decided he'd like to do some good for people by donating his organs. That sounds simple enough, but Deyell wants to meet the people who'll be receiving his organs before he dies, and that's not so easy to do. Deyell talked to Said and asked him to help make it happen. And when Said's involved, you never know, he just might find a way to make it work.

Friday 5.11.01

In Oz, good and evil can be so mixed up together that you don't know where to start in trying to get to the heart of things. Maybe the only place to begin today is with this one stark fact: Salah Udeen is dead. He died today protecting Said from an Aryan wannabe, Carl Jenkins, who tried to shank him in the cafeteria. Udeen caught sight of Jenkins as he was pulling a shank out of his pocket and threw himself in the attacker's path an instant before he reached Said. It was an act of sacrifice, that much is sure, and it would seem to remove the last shred of doubt that Leroy Tidd's conversion to Islam was genuine. I think it was, but not in the way most people thought. The details are still murky, but the rumors going around are that not long ago Tidd was involved in a plan with Schillinger and Robson—Robson was the point man on this one—to assassinate Said.

According to the stories I've heard, after Adebisi's death Tidd approached the Aryans with an offer to kill Said. They wanted Said dead, and he wanted revenge for Adebisi. At first Schillinger refused even to talk to him—the usual bullshit, he didn't do business with niggers, didn't need their help, the whole nine racist yards—but finally Tidd convinced Schillinger that he could get close to Said, gain his confidence, in ways his old adversaries like the Aryans never could. He got his chance during the fight between the Aryans and Muslims on the basketball court, when Tidd came to the Muslims' defense. It turned out, though, that the fight in the gym had been staged, set up by Robson to make Tidd look like the Muslims' friend. When Said helped get Tidd out of the Hole and gave him the name Salah Udeen, Tidd had the Muslim brothers' trust and was finally in a position to carry out his pledge—to kill Said. He could've done it, too, the afternoon he offered to stand guard over Said while he was taking a nap. No one but Udeen knew exactly what his intentions were; all those of us in the Common Room that afternoon saw was Tidd/Udeen rushing to the second-floor railing outside Said's pod, leaning over, and throwing up his lunch onto the tables and inmates playing cards below him. At the time, we figured he'd caught a bug from the disgusting conditions in the Hole and hadn't recovered yet, but it seems that getting so close to taking Said's life is what had made him sick. The stream of puke that sailed over the railing was actually the sign of Salah Udeen's true conversion.

Said didn't know all the facts, but

somehow he understood what had happened. So did the Aryans. They sent that punk Jenkins after Said instead, promising to make him a member of the Aryan Brotherhood if he succeeded in killing Said. Instead, Udeen died protecting Said, and when Said pieced the story together he was inconsolable.

Tuesday 5.22.01

McManus made it back to Em City today, after a few weeks in the hospital. Maybe he was lucky it was Omar White who shanked him; everything that mental case does is half-assed. McManus's first move the morning he returned was to keep everybody in Em City locked in their cells while he called Burr and Morales out to meet with him in the middle of the Common Room, in full sight of all of us. Since we couldn't hear anything, we were straining to figure out what was going on from whatever we could see. Which wasn't much. McManus talked for about a minute, and Burr and Morales looked around, trying to make eye contact with their people inside the pods. Morales and Burr each said something, and finally the two of them shook hands briefly. As soon as the powwow ended, the hacks opened the doors of our pods, and in a few minutes just about everyone in Em City had his own version of what had gone down. The way I heard the story, McManus told

Burr and Morales that if the S.O.R.T. hadn't busted up the attempts to kill Pancamo, Morales, and Supreme Allah, a major war would've broken out, with casualties on all sides. And he said that if they didn't declare a truce that morning, he'd let them choose between being locked up together in the cage until just one of them was still alive or transferring to different units in gen pop, where they'd keep trying to kill each other, only it wouldn't be his problem any longer. Morales and Burr made up their minds fast when they heard what the options were, and McManus insisted on their sealing the truce by shaking hands on the spot, "where everybody can see you."

In Oz, if the justice system doesn't get you, someone else will.

How long will it last? I don't know, but Burr didn't act too mellow when I tried to talk to him. I know in my heart that I hadn't acted against him when I went to the hacks. I want to tell him that even if you succeed in slaughtering your way to power, you have to keep on killing in order to hold on to the power, and that's a cycle that never ends. It's better to share the power, even if that means cutting a deal with low fucking bastards, than to turn into a lower bastard yourself in the struggle to come out on top. But Burr lives by the rules of his own narrow, cruel justice, where killing comes with the territory, loyalty is the only virtue, and the greatest crime is betrayal.

Burr won't talk to me. When I tried to get near him, he turned toward me and said, "Keep away from me. I know it was you who tipped off them hacks. You betrayed me, me who raised you like you was my own. I'm going to let you live, live with the shame of what you done. But you and me are through."

When Burr was finished talking he walked away. He was going to leave me alone, but it was clear that there wasn't going to be a truce in the drug wars anytime soon. A minute later, Jia Kenmin and Morales exchanged some words. I wasn't close enough to hear what they were saying, but when Guerra came at Jenmin and the two of them wrestled each other to the ground, I knew it wasn't "Let's be friends." Nobody got hurt, at least not right then, but Murphy threw Jia into the cage for starting the trouble. He's a cool customer, Jia; walked into the cage like he was climbing the steps to his front porch.

Tuesday 6.5.01

I don't know why Burr can't see that killing Morales, Pancamo, and Supreme Allah won't secure his control of the tit trade. There's already a high enough body count of guys who tried: Schibetta and Nappa, Ricardo and Hernandez, Keane and Adebisi, every one of them a casualty of the struggle to climb to the top of the drug heap. Plus there are the undercover cops who came in thinking they'd wipe out the drug traffic and ended up getting wiped out instead. First Paul Markstrom, executed when his cover was blown, and today I heard that John Basil, who called himself Desmond Mobay while he was undercover, was stabbed in the segregated unit for ex-cops by Clayton Hughes, the hack who cracked so bad he believes everybody's his enemy, from governors all the way down to black narcotics detectives. One inmate, Jeb Horash, said he saw Basil and his wife together in the visiting room a few days ago. He'd finally asked her to visit him for the first time since he confessed to Bruno Goergen's murder. But it looks like

Morales, leader of the Latinos, plots with Adebisi.

instead of getting their life back together, all they've got is his death. I'll bet Glynn's beating himself up about Basil. It's not his idea to bring these narcs into Oz, but he'd probably like to be able to keep them alive while they're inside, and he sure as hell doesn't want them dying at the hands of his friend's son Clayton Hughes.

The first rule in Oz: Never get personally involved. The only times I came close to breaking that rule were when Jackson Vahue arrived and when I testified against Malcolm Coyle in the Ciancimino murder case. Even so, there was a part of me that was always standing outside the situation. I was bending the rule but stopped before I broke it. With Burr, it was different. The man's been like family all my life. When we met again in Em City, it wasn't a question of getting involved, the involvement was there already. There was no way I could turn my back, even though I knew things might get complicated down the road. As they did. I know I did the right thing, but I didn't know how fucking painful the shit was going to be afterward. I'm not ashamed of spilling the plot to the hacks, but I keep hearing Burr's words in my mind—"live with the shame of what you done"—and I feel as bad as I did when I woke up in the hospital and realized that I wasn't ever going to take another step.

In Oz, I've always spent most of my time alone, but once Burr got here I felt right at home as a part of his group. Being back on my own again hasn't been easy, but even so I wasn't prepared for the shock I felt when Supreme Allah started talking to me in the cafeteria today. Here was the guy who put me in the hospital not once but twice, so when he asked me, "Why aren't you eating with your old pal Redding?" I got pissed. I told him to take a fucking walk, but he didn't budge. Instead he said, "Now that you're on the outs with old Burr, you need a friend." "Well, that ain't you, nigger," I told him, but he just kept on. "Look," he said, "I want to make right what I done to you, putting you in that chair, putting you in

Oz. So remember, from now on I got your back covered." Yeah, right, I thought, and I told him, "Keep away from me."

As soon as he walked away, I started wondering, What game is that motherfucker playing? But at the same time I realized Supreme Allah was right, in a way. All the time I was hanging with Burr I was part of everything the Homeboys were plotting, even if I wasn't dealing or using drugs. Now there wasn't anybody to back me up. The Wise Guys and El Norte didn't feel grateful to me for saving their asses, and I wasn't sure Supreme Allah did, either. Maybe he thought I could help him find Burr's weak spot, but I wasn't about to play that game, not for him, not for anybody.

Wednesday 7.4.01

Schillinger's been keeping a low profile for a while, since he found out that his son Hank's wife, Kerry, was pregnant, and especially after he had to tell her that Hank had gotten whacked. Kerry went into labor right in the Visiting Room, and the baby was born in the infirmary. I'll bet that was a first for Oz! Schillinger was in the delivery room when Dr. Nathan delivered the baby, and from that day on, I've heard, his attention's been focused on nothing but his granddaughter's welfare. I'd still see him presiding over the Aryans in the cafeteria, but people were saying that he spent more time reading the Bible and talking to Reverend Cloutier than defending the rights of the Master Race. Until yesterday, that is, when Curtis Bennett, a new inmate who pimped a string of girls in the city, told Vern that he used to see Kerry turning tricks on the street. Well, that started Schillinger wondering whether his grandchild was really his grandchild. At just about the same time, Said got Reverend Cloutier to talk to Carl Jenkins in Solitary. Cloutier persuaded Jenkins to finger Robson for the attack on Said. Jenkins killed Udeen instead of Said, and he was awaiting trial for the murder, but somebody—maybe Robson but probably Schillinger—persuaded him that he was a dead man no matter which way the trial went. The next time the hacks checked on Jenkins in his cell, they found him hanging by his neck. I heard that Schillinger also put the fear of God into Cloutier for meddling in the affairs of the Brotherhood, so it looks like the old Vern Schillinger hasn't really gone away after all; he just took a brief vacation.

Saturday 7.21.01

Just when you think you'll never find anything funny enough to laugh at again, Timmy Boy comes up with something you never could've imagined. He ran into Vahue in the gym a few days ago and started ragging on the pro about not being much of a shooter. Now it's true that Vahue always scored a lot of his points in close, but when you're as strong as he is, and have the height, the moves, and the spring that he does, you're going to find—no, *make*—an awful lot of opportunities close to the basket. Maybe his jump shot never quite compared to Jordan's, but does McManus think his own does?

Somehow—nobody else was in the gym at the time, so there are a dozen versions of exactly what happened—the war of words escalated to where either McManus or Vahue challenged the other to a two-on-two matchup, best of three games. McManus promised to bring Vahue back to Em City if he agreed to the series. The deal is that McManus can draft the best C.O. ballplayer he can find as his teammate and—this is the part that really cracks me up—choose the worst inmate player to be second man on Vahue's team.

McManus selected Agamemnon Busmalis—overweight, overaged, and he'd never played basketball or even heard of Jackson Vahue—as Vahue's teammate. For his side, McManus found Dave Brass, a C.O. who played college ball. Brass was good, and Busmalis was worse than bad, but it didn't matter. Vahue ran every play himself, dominated the boards at both ends of the court, and the score at the end of the single twenty-minute time period was Inmates 56, Staff 30.

The inmates who saw the game laughed

McManus off the court, but he insists he'll be back for Game 2, even though Busmalis can only get better (he even scored two points, on an alley-oop pass to Vahue that dropped through the basket instead). Unlike the boxing tournament that ended with Hamid Khan's tragic death, the Inmate-Staff basketball series promises to supply nothing but comedy. A good thing, too, since Cyril O'Reily, who punched Khan into a coma in the boxing finals, slugged Jia Kenmin in the gym yesterday, after Jia and Ryan O'Reily started scuffling about something, and now Jia's in a coma himself. He was rushed to Bench-

ley Memorial, and the word is the doctors there aren't sure he'll ever regain consciousness. So these days Oz needs all the humor it can find.

Sunday 8.5.01

Moses Deyell, the Death Row prisoner who decided he wanted to donate his organs after his execution, leaped out of the van transporting him to Benchley Memorial, where he was scheduled for some tests, and was shot trying to

escape. Deyell had said he wanted to meet the people who'd be getting his organs. One of them, a blind man named Jiffy Karas who was selected to receive Deyell's corneas, did come to Oz to meet him, but he won't be meeting any of the others. Maybe being outside the prison after so long on Death Row, he couldn't face going back, or he found he couldn't look his own death in the eye, one organ recipient after the other. Or maybe the whole organ thing was a run to try to escape.

Tuesday 8.21.01

Drug rehab is fucking dull dull dull, a handful of guys talking shit about their addictions, half of them can't even stand the others and hardly listen to what's been said. As often as not, they're still using. Sister Pete's the glue that somehow keeps the group together and makes it work. When I say "work," all I mean is that clowns who want to stay clean do stay clean. Could I do it without rehab after three years not touching crack or tits? Maybe, but I don't want to find out.

Some inmates who attend rehab aren't even trying to stay clean, but some of them—like Vahue—are finally making an honest effort. Omar White is there only because McManus'll kick his ass out of Em City if he doesn't

show. A lot of the time you can't tell whether he's hopped up because he's on something or because he needs to get high. Today White just about took the place apart. Beecher was talking about how you've got to want to get clean in order to stop taking drugs, and he was simply talking, about himself maybe, but he happened to be sitting across from White. All of a sudden White started accusing Beecher of criticizing him, of feeling superior because he'd beaten his addiction and White couldn't, because he's white, and who knows what other shit. Then he accused Beecher of not sucking tits because he was busy sucking dick, unzipped his fly, and invited Beecher to blow him right there. Next thing I knew, just about everybody except me and Sister Pete was throwing punches and pushing, and the hacks jumped up on the stage swinging their clubs. The whole incident was over in a minute or two, but half of us ended up in the infirmary needing first aid for bruises and shit. Funny thing is, White, who started it all, didn't have a scratch on him, and I heard McManus, who came over to the infirmary when he got wind of the mayhem, talking to White in a low, passionate voice: "I don't know why, Omar, but I'm not giving up on you, I'm not giving up."

Was it just coincidence that this last fight in drug rehab was started by a black man who thought a white man was dissing him? Every person White has attacked since he got to Oz has

In the library, gym, or anywhere in Oz, Schillinger always spells TROUBLE.

been white, except for when he tried to shank Supreme Allah, but he did that just to increase his line of credit for tits with Burr. Even if White's just nuts, there's a powerful tension running through Oz these days, and just about all of it is along the color line. The Muslims, especially Said, are still raging over the killing of Salah Udeen; probably Said feels more than a little bit responsible, since that shank was meant for him. The news went around today that Glynn had told Said that he had to release Robson from Solitary, since now that Carl Jenkins is dead there isn't anybody to testify against the Nazi prick. Almost as soon as Robson gets back in circulation, he and Schillinger run into a few of the Muslims in the library. Robson loses no time ridiculing Udeen's name and his race. Which was too much for Said. He beat Robson into unconsciousness, and at the same time Arif knocked Schillinger out. Then the hacks rushed in and dragged Said off Robson.

You could always see that Said was an angry man, but he used to be able to divert his anger into his writing, lawsuits, and efforts to influence people's thinking and actions. I'll never forget the way Said responded to Jefferson Keane's threats on Said's first day in Em City. Instead of warning the Homeboys that the Muslims were capable of violence, too, Said decided to demonstrate his commitment to nonviolence in an unusual way. He ordered one of his followers to hit him. The man hesitated at first, but Said insisted, and the man hit him several times until Said was bleeding.

Keane got the message, but nowadays Said's a different man, a violent one. Since his fight to the death with Adebisi, it's like his anger's come to the surface and taken over. Even when I see him at prayer, he doesn't look like a man of peace and calm any longer, but more like a coiled spring.

Monday 8.27.01

In the cafeteria this afternoon, not long before the second game in the McManus–Vahue grudge match was scheduled to start, a couple of hacks—one black, one white—were standing by when Vahue finished lunch. The white hack, Robinson, ordered Vahue to bus his lunch tray. Poet, who'd brought some extra food and a bottle of Gatorade over to the table for Vahue, volunteered to do cleanup for him, but Robinson wouldn't go along. "He buses his own tray," he said, and when Vahue replied, "Fuck that," Robinson clipped him behind the knee with his nightstick and Vahue went down, writhing in pain.

That hack was obviously pissed that Vahue had humiliated McManus and Brass in Game 1 and would've liked to put him on the disabled list. My money would've been on Vahue, though, even if he'd had to play sitting in my wheelchair. I don't know what happened in the infirmary, where Vahue went to get Dr. Nathan to look at his knee. I'm told that McManus offered to postpone the game, but when Dr. Nathan said the injury was just a badly swollen knee, Vahue insisted on playing. I guess he didn't want to admit that even injured there was any way that he could lose to McManus and Brass. But lose he did, 58–46. It's surprising the game was as close as it was, since Vahue could hardly put any weight on the injured leg, couldn't jump, had trouble reversing direction, and looked ready to collapse long before the final buzzer. Some guys at the game were saying that a scout for the Sacramento Kings, a friend of McManus's, was at the game to look Brass over, and that after the game he invited Brass to try out at the Kings' summer camp. Back in Em City nobody cared about Brass's tryout;

he's a solid player, but he's no Vahue. It was Vahue they were pissed at, because they'd been betting heavily on the pro to sweep the series and had lost big.

Saturday 9.22.01

Tug Daniels threatened my life yesterday and today he's dead. I was in the Common Room minding my own business when he came over to where I was sitting and said, "When he die, you die." Not long ago, "he" (that is, Burr) could order Daniels to take Pancamo out, and now Daniels is talking like he expects Burr to predecease all of us. Supreme Allah rushed over to back me up, but I wondered if he and Daniels weren't just playacting for my benefit.

Whatever was going on between Supreme Allah and Daniels, Burr must've gotten wind of it, because today O'Reily found Tug Daniels's body in a Dumpster in the back of the cafeteria. Of course, the hacks rushed us all out of there as fast as they could. But as we were leaving, Supreme Allah came over to me and said, "Our days are numbered, brother. If you and me aren't careful, we're going to end up like Tug Daniels." If I'm not careful, I think Supreme Allah might try to kill me and then try to convince me that Burr was responsible.

Friday 9.28.01

While it seems that almost everybody in Oz is busy dying, one inmate is doing a good job of staying alive: William Giles. By requesting stoning as his chosen method of execution and getting turned down by the governor, he threw the state's death penalty law into the courts. The State Supreme Court has just ruled that the death penalty law as it's written is unconstitutional. I heard that Devlin wanted to solve his William Giles problem by having the old guy declared insane and sending him off to the Connolly Institute for the rest of his life, but I wonder if a man who chooses stoning to fuck with the death penalty applecart isn't really as sane as I am. Devlin announced on the news that he's appointing a nonpartisan commission to rewrite the law so it'll be legal to execute condemned men in the state again. In the meantime, Giles keeps getting closer to what he's hoping for, a chance to die peacefully, of natural causes, maybe even in his sleep. In Oz, that's a lot to ask for—and a lot more than the Giles's victims got, even if they were, as Giles insisted, bad men.

Maybe blood is thicker than water, but in Oz it seems like it's not thicker than tits. I'd been thinking—or maybe just hoping—that when Burr started to realize that things were pretty much back to normal—that he was still moving drugs and not sitting on Death Row for the deaths of his rivals or, worse, trying to avoid getting shanked every day—he'd come around. So far, that hasn't happened, and I don't see it happening anytime soon. Whenever I try to get in to talk to Burr, I get the same treatment from Poet, who's usually playing gatekeeper outside Burr's pod. "He's busy," Poet says, "and as far as you're concerned, he's always going to be busy."

Meanwhile, somebody's trying to set me up. The hacks found a vial of heroin when they shook down my pod this morning. I told them it wasn't mine, and they know—this whole fucking prison knows—that I've been off drugs completely for more than three years now. Don't sell them, either. Sister Pete stood up for me, but that asshole McManus wouldn't believe the drugs weren't mine. He insisted I was either using or dealing. I wanted him to put me in the Hole; as much as I hated it there, putting in my time was better than yo-yoing back to Em City where it would look like I ratted

somebody out. But McManus refused to send me to the Hole, so I went to my pod smelling like a rat.

Who was it who planted that shit? I think I found out as soon as I had a conversation with my new "friend" Supreme Allah in the cafeteria. The more he tried to convince me that it was Burr who'd stashed the tits in my pod, the surer I got that Supreme Allah was the culprit. Meanwhile, Supreme Allah was trying to talk me into taking Burr out. Of course, he couldn't get close enough to Burr to spit on his shoes, much less shank him in the heart, but for the time being, neither could I. And I wasn't acting like I was in any hurry to do favors for Supreme Allah, either. But I suppose Supreme Allah figured those things would change in time, and if I made it possible for him to take over the Homeboys' share of the drug traffic, he promised he wouldn't forget what I'd done for him. The Homeboys were laughing—maybe they thought it was funny seeing two outsiders talking together—and when I told Supreme Allah to leave me the fuck alone, he got pissed. "You know, I'm getting tired of trying to please you, Augustus," he said. "I'm going to take care of business myself."

Supreme Allah started to move in the direction of where Burr was sit-

Sister Pete: the moral voice of Oz.

I remembered from the 'hood that Supreme Allah was allergic to something. I couldn't recall what it was. I paid an inmate working in the infirmary to get me a copy of Supreme Allah's medical records. That told me what I needed: Supreme Allah was dangerously allergic to eggs. That part was easy; getting to somebody who could help me was much harder. When I caught up with Poet in the laundry, he just snarled at me: "Don't you be talking to me, snitch. As far as we're concerned you're a dead man. A ghost. A ghost on wheels." He seemed pleased with that last phrase, like maybe the poet in him woke up for a second. But when I told him, "I'm trying to save Burr's life," that got his attention. Then I was able to tell him about Supreme Allah's allergy. Poet works in the kitchen, and he says, "Yeah, when we be preppin' his meals, we got to fix them real special." "Not today," I said, and Poet smiled.

At lunchtime, Supreme Allah put his tray down opposite mine, and as soon as he sat down, he started in: "Burr's still alive, Augustus, what's up with that?" I watched him start to eat his lunch and said, "I got to get close to him, don't I? Got to get back in his good graces, and that's going to take some time." He stared at me

ting, and when I saw he was cuffing a shank, I grabbed his arm and told him, "I'll kill him. If he's going to die, I'd rather he died at my hands. I'll make sure it won't hurt." I had no idea right then what I was going to do, but I'd called his bluff. Supreme Allah preferred to have somebody else do his dirty work, so he'd let me take care of Burr. And I've bought myself a little bit of time, but not much.

across the table, snarled, "You ain't got time," and went back to chewing his food and looking like he was considering his next move. I stared back at him, peeling my orange, not saying a word. He took a few bites, then shoved his tray away and stood up, clutched at his throat, and started gagging. I asked him, calmly, "Something wrong?" The motherfucker gasped, "Who did this shit? Did you . . ." and then fell to the cafeteria floor, spitting out his half-chewed food and struggling to breathe. His face ballooned up huge. The allergic reaction must've squeezed his windpipe shut, and in less than a minute he was dead.

Supreme Allah had been responsible for most of my problems, but it gave me no pleasure to watch him die. So when Burr came over after we returned to Em City, I felt relief that he was talking to me again. He said, "Poet told me what you done. I came to thank you and welcome you back into the fold." I told him that I could accept the thanks but not the offer. "I don't want to sell drugs." Burr replied that it was my choice and he respected me for my decision.

I answered, "Respect? I killed a man today. I caused his death to happen. Even though Supreme Allah was going to hurt you, even though the motherfucker screwed me to this chair, I don't feel good about what I done." When he heard that, Burr stood up, put his arms around me, and said,

"Well, then, Augustus, I raised you right." Then he walked back to where the Homeboys were waiting for him, and I felt more alone than I have anytime since I've been inside.

Saturday 11.24.01

The feelings I have for Burr aren't gone, but the old days are never coming back. He's gotten too hardened—from years on the streets, from doing time in a string of prisons, and, I guess, from Delia's dying—to turn the clock back now. Today somebody else paid for Burr's drive for revenge and control. An unlikely guy it was, Edward Gallson, the ex-Marine who was sharing a pod with Burr. He talked Gallson into getting rid of Morales, but that crafty Latino didn't get to the top of El Norte by marching in formation. When Gallson made his move on Morales, he ended up getting crushed by the elevator they were supposed to be repairing together. A horrible accident? I don't think so, and even if it was, how many more horrible accidents are there going to be before these drug wars end?

Of course, if you don't die one way in Oz, you might just die in another. The word reached Em City today that Clayton Hughes finally got the death he'd been looking for. Hughes had been in Solitary for weeks, ever since he stabbed John Basil. When a guy's in Solitary, he usually doesn't have much chance to hurt anybody but himself. Somehow Hughes overpowered a guard, took his keys and radio, locked him in the cell, and declared himself Gamba Khufu, president of the Republic of Huru. Over the hack's radio, he could talk to the staff throughout the prison, so he contacted Glynn, his old protector, who tried to talk Hughes out of his delusion. Glynn ordered the S.O.R.T. to stay just outside the door to Solitary and entered the cell block alone. Nobody seems to know just what happened while Glynn was inside, but in the version of the story I heard from Igor Barkowacs, Hughes had a knife and tried to stab the warden. He was stopped by an inmate from a nearby cell, Greg Penders, who shoved him away from Glynn. As they struggled over the shank, Hughes was stabbed in the chest. He died in Glynn's arms, just like his dad.

Tuesday 12.4.01

Sometimes a guy will go into a slump, and these days Tim McManus seems to be in a serious tailspin. After winning Game 2 of his basketball challenge against Vahue, because Vahue had only one leg to stand on, and getting his teammate Brass a tryout with Sacra-

mento, McManus ran into one disaster after another, some just ridiculous but some tragic, too. First, somebody didn't like the way the second game had gone, so to make sure the final wouldn't turn into an upset, they arranged for Brass to have a little accident at work. They staged a fight in Unit B where Brass worked, and while the fists were flying, an inmate took a slice out of the jamoke's Achilles tendon. He'll walk again, but his tryout with the Sacramento Kings is never going to happen.

After Brass was injured, McManus's pal Murphy offered to play the third game against Vahue and Busmalis. Murphy's not bad as a pickup player, but without Brass the staff was really out of their league, and the game turned into a joke. Final score: Inmates 62–28, and that was only because Vahue was laughing too hard most of the time to run up the margin.

Next thing McManus did was to appear as a contestant on *Up Your Ante*, a quiz show lots of the inmates watch. For a guy who thinks he knows everything, he's an ignorant bastard, and he lost in the first round—insisted a "tittle" was a breast implant. When the Latinos started making jokes about McManus, Omar White decided to defend his mentor's honor and shanked Pedro Calderon, who was dead before the credits finished rolling on the quiz show. As if he was trying to prove that he always comes up with the wrong answer, when McManus heard the news, he insisted that he wanted to keep White in Em City! Nobody knows what he's thinking, but I sure as hell pray McManus doesn't go on any more quiz shows as long as Omar is his number one fan.

Saturday 12.11.01

Beecher's coming up for parole, and the word going around is that his lawyer thinks he's got a chance of going free. I was told that instead of trying to keep the parole hearing secret, Beecher insisted that the parents of Kathy Rockwell, the little girl he ran over, be told about the hearing, so that they could give their views to the Parole Board if they wanted to. That was a ballsy move (remember Vahue?), but to improve Beecher's odds Sister Pete arranged for the Rockwells to meet with Beecher before the hearing. What I heard was the Rockwells didn't forgive Beecher, but Mrs. Rockwell had convinced her husband that the Christian course to take would be not to interfere with his chances for parole. A miracle?

Of course, Beecher's problems aren't just outside Oz, they're inside, too, and when Schillinger heard that the man who had a hand in his sons' deaths—and who also screwed up Schillinger's own attempt to win parole—might be going free, he went

ballistic. Beecher lucked out there, too. Said and Cloutier—an unorthodox alliance—managed to convince Schillinger that he'd be better off not to start trouble before Beecher's hearing, and Schillinger agreed. Another miracle?

As usually happens in Oz, there wasn't enough forgiveness to do Beecher much good. The Parole Board decided that the things Beecher had done years ago meant he still wasn't ready to reenter society, in spite of everything he'd been through and the steps he's taken since. But they agreed to consider his case again in a year.

That wasn't the end of Beecher's troubles, though. Schillinger decided to call off the truce, and he and Robson attacked Beecher in the library. Lucky for him, Said was there and managed to shank the two Aryan fucks before they could hurt Beecher. Said didn't get a medal for his heroics, but a trip to the Hole.

Tuesday 12.25.01

Beecher's parole hearing wasn't the only dud in Em City recently. It turns out that Padraic Connolly, the Irish political radical who'd lost his fight to avoid getting deported to face murder charges in England, decided to set off a bomb in Em City. O'Reily agreed to assist him, though O'Reily's political sympathies don't extend past his own family. Maybe he was depressed because Cyril may be sent off to a mental hospital after putting two guys in comas. Whatever it was, O'Reily helped Connolly obtain the makings of his bomb. Then, after a little soul-searching, Ryan decided the whole thing was a bad idea. So he told the hacks, but in the meantime, Connolly had snuck back to Em City during lunch hour and set the timer on the bomb. McManus tried to talk Connolly down, but the Irishman just kept counting down—two minutes, one minute, forty seconds—until the hacks had no option but to unlock the gate and let every inmate and staff member run for cover. Which, of course, we all did. And then we waited, with the S.O.R.T. huddling with us behind the stone walls that we all hoped were going to protect us. But the bomb didn't go off, and after a few seconds, we heard Connolly cursing, kicking the thing across the floor of the Common Area, and then waiting passively until the S.O.R.T. finally worked up its courage and rushed in to tackle him.

We thought Em City was safe, and it was, but a couple minutes after the crisis had ended, we heard a huge explosion from somewhere else in the prison. A little while later, we learned that somebody had left the gas on on one of the stoves in the kitchen. A hack must've gone in there for a cigarette break, and when he struck the match for his smoke, the whole place blew. Lunch had been over for a while, so all the inmates and staff had left.

At first they thought that the hack was the only casualty, but when the firemen went to extinguish the blaze and search through the ruins, they found Reverend Cloutier, badly burned but still alive. He must've gotten on the wrong side of somebody, because he'd been walled up in a tiny space behind the refrigerators. If it hadn't been for the explosion, he'd've starved to death, or suffocated. Would hellfire have been worse than what Cloutier did suffer? He may never be able to tell us.

Entries from 2002

Monday 1.14.02

Oz is Oz, but going back to Em City after all those months in Unit B is a little like coming home. In the five years since Em City opened, we've moved out once before, after the riot. Back then, some of us still believed that it was better in Em City than anywhere else in the prison, not just physically but in other ways, too. Em City was cleaner, more comfortable, with its own computer room, laundry, and classroom, but it also seemed like an inmate might have more of a chance of getting his life together. That could mean staying off drugs, keeping clear of violence, or even preserving connections with family

2000-2001 VICTIMS

- **Simon Adebisi:** Stabbed by Kareem Said in the pod they shared, after Adebisi attacked Said for giving evidence of Adebisi's crimes to Warden Glynn.

- **Supreme Allah (former name Kevin Ketchum):** Died of an allergic reaction to eggs in food served to him by Poet, to prevent Allah from carrying out his plan to assassinate Burr Redding.

- **Ronnie Barlog:** Former protégé of Keller had neck broken while giving his ex-mentor a blow job after bragging that he'd had sex with Beecher.

- **Johnny Basil (undercover name Desmond Mobay):** Shanked by Clayton Hughes in a fight in the cell block reserved for former police officers.

- **Shirley Bellinger:** Executed by hanging, for the drowning death of her daughter, after a delay due to pregnancy ended in miscarriage.

- **Louis Bevilacqua:** Stabbed in the neck by William Giles, during exercise period for inmates from Solitary.

- **Mondo Browne:** Homeboy and onetime sexual partner of Beecher, killed by Beecher's jealous lover Keller.

- **Carlton "Tug" Daniels:** Strangled to death by Redding after attempting to double-cross Homeboys in drug wars against alliance of Supreme Allah and the Latinos.

- **Moses Deyell:** Death Row prisoner who volunteered to donate his organs after execution. Leaped to his death from the van transporting him to the hospital for evaluation.

- **Edward Gallson:** Former Marine officer enlisted by Redding to kill Morales, who turned the tables on Gallson and crushed him under elevator cab they were repairing.

- **Nat Ginzburg:** Murderer of Antonio Nappa, Ginzburg died in his sleep of AIDS on the night before his scheduled execution.

- **Bruno Goergen:** Rogue cop pushed down elevator shaft by undercover narc Desmond Mobay/Johnny Basil, who was trying to get accepted by the drug traffickers.

- **Ralph Gulino:** Died of a heroin overdose forcibly administered by Jaz Hoyt, in struggle for control of Gulino's cell phone.

- **Raoul Hernandez:** Stabbed by Bob Rebadow under orders from Enrique Morales, who wanted to take control of El Norte from Hernandez.

- **Officer Joseph Howard:** C.O. killed by stray gunfire from Guillaume Tarrant.

- **Clayton Hughes:** Stabbed with his own shank during a scuffle with Greg Penders, who intervened when Hughes attempted to kill Warden Glynn.

- **Karl Jenkins:** Would-be Aryan committed suicide by hanging himself in his cell in Solitary after receiving a death threat from the Brotherhood for ratting on them.

- **Patrick Keenan:** Rapist of Gloria Nathan, had skull crushed in gym by Ryan O'Reilly.

- **Hamid Khan:** Died after being taken off life support, of brain damage suffered in boxing match against Cyril O'Reily.

- **Mark Miles:** Death Row convict strangled and beaten to death by fellow inmate Moses Deyell, through a hole in the wall between their cells.

- **Junior Pierce:** Wangler's sidekick, shot by Tarrant.

- **Lou Rath:** Third inmate shot by Tarrant, firing at random in the Em City Common Room.

- **Hank Schillinger:** Execution-style slaying arranged by Chucky Pancamo as a murder for hire paid for by Beecher, in retaliation for Hank's killing of Beecher's son, Gary.

- **Nate Shamin:** Bleeding body turned up in the Em City laundry. Possibly murdered by Keller after Shamin had sex with Beecher.

- **Nikolai Stanislofsky:** Electrocuted in bathtub by C.O. Howell as a service to her lover, Ryan O'Reily.

- **Guillaume Tarrant:** After killing three inmates and a C.O. in a shooting rampage, turned the gun on himself as the S.O.R.T. closed in.

- **Leroy Tidd (Muslim name Salah Yudeen):** Shanked by an Aryan when he threw himself into the assassin's path during an attempt on Said's life.

- **Jorge Vasquez:** Latino lieutenant had throat slashed by Alvarez during a fight.

- **Kenny Wangler:** Shot by Guillaume Tarrant, after robbing and tormenting him, with the gun Adebisi placed in Tarrant's pod.

- **Fred Wick:** Biker who died suddenly from effects of experiemental aging drugs being tested by Oz inmates.

- **Bian Yixhue:** Used by Morales in a plot to discredit Burr Redding with the prison authorities, Yixhue bled to death after Morales attacked him with a stapler.

- **Eli Zabitz:** Coerced by Schillinger into feeding misinformation to Beecher about his children's kidnapping, Zabitz died of a heart attack when Keller and Robson simultaneously arrived to kill him.

and friends on the outside. This time, the place looks the same, and moving back into one of the pods is a damn sight better than sharing a cell in gen pop with three other inmates. Still, it feels different coming back, like we're just traveling in circles, or shuttling back and forth between gen pop and Em City, with an occasional detour to Solitary or the Hole.

This trip, some of the long-term inmates from Solitary are on the merry-go-round with us, while the air ducts in that part of the building get cleaned out. A couple of them even used to be in Em City, White and Alvarez. But after months of being alone inside their cells, all of them are too used to being cooped up by themselves, and they've brought that baggage with them. Now there's an ad-seg edginess to the cell block, of guys who are over-eager to stay out of Solitary—if they can—but also afraid they won't be able to cut it surrounded by so many people.

Alvarez has a long history with the Latinos, especially with Chico Guerra. Almost before Alvarez had a chance to stow his shit in a pod, the two of them were fighting again. Alvarez threw the first punch, but it was Guerra and two of his amigos who'd tried to ambush Alvarez in the shower room. The hacks found a shank on Guerra, while Alvarez was holding nothing but his towel, so it was Guerra who ended up in the cage. From what I hear, though, it's only a matter of time before Alvarez ends up back in Solitary or in a body bag. He can't stand it any longer when somebody gets too close to him, and he's been threatening everyone he thinks ever did anything to him. In the gym the other day, he had a pair of ugly scenes with Morales and Giles. Morales just backed off, but Giles butted Alvarez in the balls and then floored him with one punch. Not bad for a loon who looks like he could be your grandfather. Before Em City opened, Giles was my cellmate, but for the past five years he's spent just about every fucking day in Solitary. I wouldn't want to tangle with him if I didn't have to.

After Alvarez, it was Omar White's turn. That guy's always been like a lighted firecracker, nervous as hell when he's looking for tits, and just as nervous when he's high. While Guerra was in the cage, White started calling him a gorilla, picking up where he left off when he shanked one of Guerra's buddies, which is what landed him in Solitary in the first place. Locked in the cage, there wasn't much Guerra could do. But later, in the cafeteria, Carlos Martinez started ragging on White, saying, "Guerra's not the gorilla, you are," and shit like that. White leaped at him, fists flying. He didn't do any harm—the hacks peeled him off Carlos toot sweet—but a few minutes later White was in the cage instead of Guerra.

Things aren't much better for some of the inmates who've been spared long sieges in Solitary but have been out of circulation. Take Said. He spent a good piece of time stewing in the Hole for defending Beecher by shanking

Schillinger. Ever since Adebisi's death, you can almost see the steam rising off Said, and it doesn't take much for him to boil over. Of course, with Schillinger and Robson around, there's always some reason to be provoked. Right after Said was released from the Hole, Robson, who delivers the mail, handed Said a package from his family. Only Robson or one of the other Aryans who work the post office had fucked with the contents, so when Said opened the box it was full of turds. The second Said saw it, he flew over that mail cart and tackled Robson. Envelopes and parcels were flying everywhere, and Said might've strangled Robson if they hadn't been in the middle of the Common Room. There were a couple hacks not five feet

Here in Oz,
you will always be known as one of
Adebisi's
bitches.
No matter what you do,
you can't
erase that.

—Kareem Said
to Peter Schibetta

from where the two of them got into their wrestling match, and they pulled Said and Robson apart. Now that Sister Pete's talked Beecher into trying to

broker a peace agreement between the Muslims and Aryans, the three of them— Schillinger, Said, and Beecher— are meeting face-to-face every day.

Sister Pete's got the patience of a saint, and she can be persuasive, but she's going to need a minor miracle to bring about real peace between these guys.

Tuesday 1.23.02

When an inmate who didn't call anybody a spic or a nigger, didn't stiff anybody for drugs, and didn't demand a blow job from the wrong pair of lips turns up dead, it seems like the laws of nature have been violated. That's what happened about a year ago, when Patrick Keenan was found dead in the gym, his skull split open by weights that his attacker had used like a sledgehammer. Keenan's name was probably familiar to just about every inmate in Oz—he was convicted of raping Dr. Nathan.

Glynn did what he usually does when he stumbles over a crime he can't solve: acted tough and then forgot all about what happened. I guess he hoped that everybody else would forget, too. That way, there'd be no further recriminations inside the prison and nobody on the outside demanding an investigation or yelling that Glynn should be fired. Usually his tactics work.

Sister Pete's impossible dream: peace between the Muslims and the Aryans.

About a week ago, the Keenan murder case suddenly came back to life. We started to hear rumors that someone had real information about the crime, and that maybe there was even an eyewitness to the murder. Nobody mentioned any names, though. No sooner had we heard about the first witness than a second one turned up. Mark Montgomery, an inmate out in gen pop, supposedly told the warden that he'd heard Henry Stanton—another guy we'd never heard of—threaten to kill Keenan. Of course, Stanton denied the accusation. The witness was hardly a Sunday School teacher; if every

inmate who shouted, "I'm going to kill you, you motherfucker!" actually did it, Oz would be abandoned; and besides, it wasn't certain that Stanton had ever met Keenan, or even laid eyes on him.

Glynn decided to see whether Stanton's memory would improve if he had some time to think without being disturbed, so he threw him into the Hole. Meanwhile, he had the hacks search Stanton's cell, where they found a newspaper clipping about Dr. Nathan's rape. People started saying maybe Stanton had a thing for Dr. Nathan or a hatred of rapists. If so, he might've had a motive for killing Keenan after all. Or maybe somebody else obsessed with Nathan had planted that article in Stanton's cell. So is Stanton just a schmuck who happened to be in the wrong place at the wrong time and couldn't get out of the way? And, ultimately, do any of us care who whacked the scumbag who raped Dr. Nathan, one of the few good souls in Oz?

Friday
2.15.02

Sometimes the news that's most shocking is the news you somehow knew was coming. At mail call today, I got that kind of news: a letter from some lawyers in the city that Annabella was divorcing me. I was sitting with Burr and Poet in the Common Room when I read the letter, and Poet asked me if I was surprised. I said I wasn't, and it's true, but at the same time I was shocked. I don't really know why. All the signs that something was wrong had been obvious for months: Annabella hadn't been visiting me as often as she used to, and when she did, she acted distant, like she was thinking about something else—or somebody else. Even Moms, whenever I talked to her, tried to duck my questions whenever Annabella's name came up. She'd always say Annabella was fine, but I could tell that she was in a hurry to move on to something else. Today's the first visiting day since

the gas explosion, and Moms is on her way up from the city to see me. She's been talking about how bad she wanted to come up for weeks, and I sure as hell miss her, too. Now that Burr's in Oz, Moms is all I have left on the outside. I wonder whether she'll have anything new to tell me about what happened with Annabella when she gets here.

Burr tried to console me, in his gruff way, of course, like he's always done, but today there seemed to be more of a bitter edge than I remembered from years past. He said, "What do you expect? You been cooped up in Oz for the last seven years. That's a long time for a young gal to keep a candle lit." Of course, I knew things couldn't last between us until I finally got released, which won't be before 2015, if it ever happens at all, but I told Burr that even if my marriage was finished, Annabella and I had loved each other, and the least she could've done was to come up here to say good-bye in person, instead of paying some fucking lawyer to send me a goddamned letter the Aryans would open and read in the mailroom before I ever got to see it.

Burr told me, "You'll survive, son. You've survived this shithole, you'll survive a divorce." I'm not sure it's that simple. Sure, I'd been surviving in this shithole, but that was because I had Moms and Annabella on the outside. "Losing her is like giving up my last piece of hope," I told him. "It's like admitting to myself that every-

Augustus in mourning after his mother is suddenly killed.

than I knew. My second shock of the day came when Burr told me, "Delia and I was fixing to divorce, too, just before she got sick. Of course, after she got sick, I couldn't just leave her there." When I told him that he and Delia had always seemed happy, he said she was always smiling because she was constantly tanked up on vodka, that from the time he returned from Vietnam the haze of alcohol had separated them. "No," Burr said, "you and your Moms was the only real family I ever knew."

I looked over at Burr, and it was like I was seeing the man he really was for the first time. Here was the friend who'd done his best to keep me from being lonely after my dad died, who'd been almost a father to me, only he was more alone than I'd ever been. I felt like I could see behind his anger, his toughness, to something sadder. And then I thought, Moms is going to be in the Visiting Room in just a little while, so I said to Burr, "Maybe you and me could visit Moms together." "You know, I'd like that," he told me. "I'd like to see Eugenia. She always had the sweetest pair of eyes." Then he smiled for a moment and, reaching out, took the lawyers' letter out of my hand and crumpled it into a ball. I watched as his hand tightened into a fist and his smile faded. Back on Burr's face was the angry, vaguely threatening mask he always wore.

Neither one of us got to see Moms. About an hour later, Burr and I and the other inmates who were expecting

thing I had out there is gone, gone forever."

At that moment I felt like I wasn't anywhere near as tough as Burr was, still in control after everything that had happened to him, especially Delia's dying. What I didn't know was that there was more to Burr's story

visitors were called out to the cafeteria. Glynn met us there, holding a piece of paper in his hand. The bus carrying Moms and a couple dozen others to Oz for visiting day had gone off the road and turned over. A few passengers had survived and were in the hospital, but most had been killed. When Glynn read the names of the dead I was barely conscious of the others; I was just listening for the name I knew I'd hear: Eugenia Hill. All I could think about was how well Moms knew the pain of not having the chance to say good-bye to someone you love, that Dad died 12,000 miles away from her, and now she and I weren't going to be able to say good-bye to each other, either. The only person left for me to say good-bye to now was locked inside Oz with me: Burr.

Sunday 2.17.02

I don't know what I've been feeling for the last day and a half. Maybe this is what shock is like, only this time it's as if the whole prison's in shock. There must be someone in every cell block who had a wife, or a mother, or a child, or a brother on that bus. In Em City, there's Arif, whose wife, Sonsyrea, was killed, and Morales's sister, and in the cafeteria I remember hearing Glynn tell Schillinger that his granddaughter had survived but not Kerry. I wonder how many of the other inmates are like me, with nobody left to visit them now.

Of course, McManus came over, pulling his usual long face, to tell me I'd be allowed out for the funeral and that he was making all the arrangements. I asked McManus whether Burr couldn't go, too, and McManus said he was sorry, but D.O.C. regs didn't allow friends of the family to attend funerals, just relatives. I hadn't said anything to Burr about asking permission for him to attend the funeral, but I knew he would've wanted to go when I told him that McManus had nixed the idea. He didn't react, at least not directly. Instead, he started talking about the past, something he does a lot these days, about hanging with Dad when the two of them were just thirteen, fourteen years old, and when they first met Moms, around that same time. Then all of a sudden he grabbed my hand, dropped something into the palm, and closed his fist around it. It was his high school ring. Burr asked me to put the ring in the grave with Moms.

Tuesday 2.19.02

First time out of Oz in almost three years, since I testified to the grand jury about Coyle, but now the city felt strange, like someplace that didn't have anything to do with me anymore. And yet I was right back in the neighborhood where I'd grown up, gone to

MUKADA ON THE BUS CRASH

I should've died in that bus crash. I didn't, but I don't know why.
Almost no one else on the bus survived, and how could they have? Our driver had no choice but to swerve off the road when that truck came right at us in the wrong lane, and then the bus pitched down the steep embankment and rolled over. There weren't any seat belts for the passengers, so we were tossed around like marbles in a jar. It lasted just a few seconds, but when the bus came to rest on its side, there were almost no sounds coming from the people in the bus. I could hear a few low moans and Kerry Schillinger's baby, Jewel, crying, but no one called out and I couldn't see anyone else moving. I must've been in shock myself; I could see that there was blood on my hands, but I wasn't sure whether I was badly hurt or not. All I thought was, "If I can get out of the bus, maybe I'll be able to find someone or a way to call for help and get everyone who's still alive to a hospital."

The bus had come to rest on its side, and somehow I managed to climb up on one of the seats and get out through a window. At the time of the accident, we were only ten minutes from the prison, on a completely empty stretch of road. I couldn't see any houses or a telephone, and I had to wait for five or ten minutes before I finally saw a van approaching. The driver, on his way to a delivery, had a cell phone and called 911 to ask for help and tell the police where we were. Then I went back to the bus, to see if I could look for survivors and do anything before the EMTs arrived, but I couldn't crawl back inside. So I waited for help, listening for sounds of life on the inside, but all I heard was Jewel, her cries getting fainter.

The people on the bus were some of the first friends and relatives to visit Oz since a large part of the prison was devastated by the gas explosion, so most of them hadn't been able to see their sons, husbands, and brothers for months, and they were excited but also anxious. Some of the passengers were visiting inmates I knew well, and a few I'd even met on previous visits. Besides Kerry Schillinger, who was taking Jewel to see her grandfather for the first time since Hank Schillinger's body had been found, there were Augustus Hill's mother, Eugenia; Sonsyrea Arif, wife of Zahir; and Annette Osorio, Enrique Morales's sister.

Annette started flirting with me almost immediately, but I saw that she was nervous about something and was trying to cover up her unease. She sat down next to me and started telling me about herself and her brother. When I told her I saw her brother at Mass every Sunday, she laughed and said that Enrique had never attended church on the outside. Of course, I knew that for many of the inmates church services were more a means of breaking the monotony than an opportunity for prayer and Communion. Annette didn't seem especially religious, either, and she let me know that her purpose in visiting was far from holy. She removed her jacket to reveal a long scar on the inside of her forearm. She said that her husband was responsible for the scar, that he abused her, and that she was planning to ask her brother to take revenge. When I suggested that what she had in mind was wrong, she called me a "self-righteous jizzball" and retreated to the back of the bus.

I didn't talk much to Sonsyrea Arif or Eugenia Hill, but I could hear them talking, especially Sonsyrea, who fulminated at length about the injustice of U.S. drug laws and the fact that if the percentage of people sent to prison in this country continues to increase at its current rate, there'll be more people inside prison than out by the middle of the century. When I asked her to lower her voice, because Kerry Schillinger was trying to get Jewel to take a nap, she accused me of trying to prevent her from speaking the truth. I think Eugenia Hill was able to reach her, though. She urged Sonsyrea to talk more about how important it was to her and her children that Arif was no longer using drugs, and she said how grateful she was that her son Augustus wasn't using crack any longer.

Eugenia had other things on her mind, though. She was on her way to Oz to tell her son that his wife, Annabella, wanted to divorce him, and she wanted to cushion the blow by giving him the news in person.

One way or another, all of the women I talked to on the bus were paying the price of their husbands, sons, and brothers being in prison. Kerry Schillinger had a different story, but somehow it was similar: Hank, the father of her daughter, was dead because of the crimes he'd committed at his father's bidding. Kerry was on her way to Oz hoping to cement a connection between Vern Schillinger, the only family she felt she still had, and his granddaughter. Now all those women are gone, because a trucker fell asleep at the wheel.

school, learned to survive on the streets, fallen in love with Annabella, and where I'd been thrown off the roof, which landed me in Oz. The van drove right past the projects where Moms and I lived all those years, just the two of us in her tiny, spotless apartment. Caar's Funeral Home, where she was laid out, was on the corner of Fremont and Douglass, just a couple blocks from where I went to high school. I wheeled past the front door, with its long white canopy stretching over the sidewalk, every day when I was a kid, but I never dreamed I'd be going there to have my last look at Moms's sweet face.

There were two hacks escorting me, one on either side, everywhere I went from the moment we left Receiving and Discharge. I don't think they were expecting me to try to escape—that's just D.O.C. procedure—and at least I wasn't shackled at the wrists and ankles like other inmates are whenever they leave the prison compound. The hacks, a couple guys I'd never seen before named Haber and Fanon, even helped me out of my wheelchair at the funeral home, so I could see Moms in her coffin and bend down to touch her face and kiss her good-bye.

Only I felt like I couldn't really say good-bye to her. Moms was still there, in a way, but I wasn't there myself, not any longer. After the bus crash, Annabella hadn't phoned me, though I was sure she'd heard the news, but I'd half expected to see her at the funeral home—she'd been real close

with my Moms, even before my arrest— and when she didn't even make an appearance it was like that part of my life hadn't ever even happened. A couple of Moms's friends who came by talked about seeing Annabella in the neighborhood—they acted like they didn't know she filed for a divorce— so I knew she was still around. But the more people talked to me as if nothing had changed, almost acting like they'd seen me in the supermarket that morning and would see me in church on Sunday, the more I felt like I wasn't really there. Meanwhile, Burr was in Em City, waiting for me to get back from the burial, and suddenly it seemed like Em City was the one place I truly belonged.

The funeral was at Bethany Baptist Church, where Moms had never missed a Sunday service or a bake sale as long as I can remember. Reverend Clifton kept it short, simple, and not too solemn, just like Moms would have wanted it, I guess. I hardly heard what the minister said—something about the strange twists and turns of life's journey—and I don't remember the hymns the choir sang or what her friends said when they came over to comfort me, touching my arm and whispering a few words about what a good woman she was or how they'd miss her. I just kept staring at the plain pine coffin and thinking, "She can't be in that box, she can't be."

Then we left the church, the hacks who were my escorts and me, got into the prison van for the drive to the cemetery. All around us on the streets, cars and people were passing by the entrance to the church where the hearse was waiting, as if they wanted to remind me that life was still going on. I knew that was true, but it didn't feel true to me. From the van, I could barely see out through the windows. I had to crane my neck to catch the scene on the street, and the last thing I noticed before we drove off was a heavyset brother wearing a T-shirt with a big red tomato on the front, and in the center it said "Tomato Fann."

The scene at the cemetery was strangely quiet and almost peaceful. It must've been around noon when we arrived, and the sun was high in the sky and bright. Living inside the way we do in Oz, never seeing more of the sun than filters in through the narrow, opaque windows of the prison, I'd forgotten what sunlight was like. I remembered how much Moms loved being out of doors in weather like this and tried telling myself that she'd be pleased that the day was sunny, and the leaves were starting to sprout on the trees whose branches reached almost to the gravesite. I knew she liked this spot. She'd brought me here often when I was growing up and told me about how she'd chosen this spot to bury Dad after his body had been shipped home from Vietnam. The trees were smaller then, of course, but now they shaded both of their graves.

When Moms's coffin was lowered into the grave, Reverend Clifton recited some verses from the Book of Isaiah, which she loved: "The righteous man perishes, and no man takes it to heart; And devout men are taken away, while no one understands. For the righteous man is taken away from evil. He enters into peace; They rest in their beds, Each one who walked in his upright way." Then I took Burr's ring out of my pocket and dropped it into the grave with her coffin.

Thursday 2.21.02

Life in Oz is so cheap that these walls absorbed the lives that were lost in the bus crash as fast as a rag soaking up spilled water. By the time I got back from the funeral night before last, Em City had been locked down for the night, but at breakfast a handful of people took the time to tell me they were sorry about my Moms. When Rebadow, Said, Poet, and a few of the others spoke to me, I'd almost forgotten about how many inmates had just gone out to the funerals of their wives, sisters, and children: Arif, Morales, Schillinger, and people whose names I didn't even know but I felt like now I was connected to them. Thank God Schillinger's granddaughter was still alive, but since Kerry's parents are taking her to live in Montana or someplace, who knows whether she'll ever learn about her grandfather.

For most people in Oz, inmates and

staff, it seemed like it was just another day. And why not? Some of them have themselves killed almost as many people as died on that bus, or tried to, and they're still doing business as usual. I even heard that a day or so after the bus crash, Miguel Alvarez offered Chico Guerra an original way to end the feud: Alvarez would let Guerra shank him—wound him, but not fatally—and promised not to retaliate and not to let the hacks know who'd done the deed. That way, Guerra would be able to claim that he'd defended his honor, and the two of them could get on with their lives. The way Poet tells the story, Guerra accepted Alvarez's terms, but when he came at Alvarez in the gym, instead of wounding him in the shoulder, as they'd agreed, he stabbed Alvarez in the chest, missing his heart by a quarter of an inch.

A quarter inch isn't much of a margin of error, not when it's the space between living and dying. From my first day in Oz, I've done my best to make sure my margin of safety is as wide as possible, steering clear of drugs, tribal warfare, and every kind of personal shit. The few times I've

Hangin' on to power: Pancamo runs the Wise Guys from his hospital bed.

dropped my guard, when Jackson Vahue's presence clouded my judgment, when I stuck my neck out by testifying against Coyle, and when I had to tell "Desmond Mobay" that I knew he was a narc and a corrupt one, I was lucky that I didn't get really fucked over as a result.

Sometimes I ask myself why I took those risks, doing things that definitely didn't improve my chances of surviving. Was I trying to get myself killed? I don't think so. I never pulled that kind of shit when I was out on the street. I mean, I did what I had to do to move the drugs, but I tried not to make enemies, didn't want to become an urban legend, never acted any tougher than I had to. But inside Oz, I think I wanted to remind myself that I wasn't really inmate 95H522, that I was still Augustus Hill, still connected to the people I loved, to Moms, to Burr, and to Annabella. Until last week, when I lost the connection to the two people on the outside who mattered most to me, who were more a part of who I was—son, lover, friend—than whoever I was in prison. True, I've never really believed that I'd get back to my life on the outside, though something in me kept hoping that I would, hoping that somehow I'd be able to keep the connection alive, though I didn't know how that could be possible for so many years, especially with Annabella.

When Burr turned up in Oz, I wanted to be close to him—fuck, I was close to him, even when he cut me off because I'd told the hacks he was plotting to kill Pancamo, Morales, and Supreme Allah—but I didn't want to go back to dealing, just to being Burr and Augustus, family. Now he's the only family I've got left, and there's nothing waiting for me on the outside any longer, and my gut tells me that's no fucking good. I don't know how guys like William Giles or Bob Rebadow have made it in Oz for so long, connected to nobody inside or out, because to me, not having a home to dream of is too much like being dead already.

Friday 3.15.02

Some inmates will grab at anything to make it possible to get through another day—maybe that's why there are more drug addicts coming out of prison than going in—but the one guy in Em City who seemed able to get by with almost no contact with anything outside himself—no religion, no drugs, no friends, no visiting days— was Bob Rebadow. He's survived Oz more than thirty-five years now, and on what? A box of fudge his mother sent him every month, until he came down with diabetes and had to give it up; an occasional message from God, who's been talking to Rebadow ever since his electrocution was botched in 1965; and Agamemnon Busmalis, his cellmate, a guy so innocent he watches *Miss Sally's Schoolyard* because he likes the show and not for Whitney Allen's huge tits.

Everything changed for Rebadow when his grandson, Alex—he'd never seen the boy—was diagnosed with leukemia. The kid had one wish: to visit Adventure Country. After the inmates and hacks in every corner of the prison anted up the three grand so Alex could make the trip, Rebadow stopped refusing to see his family, invited his grandson to visit him, and now he lives for the boy. Recently Alex's leukemia went out of remission, and when the family couldn't find a bone marrow donor, Rebadow combed the library and the Internet in search of alternative cancer therapies. He thinks he's found one, the roots or bark of a South American evergreen called *lapacho morado,* and now he's scheming to find the money to find and buy enough of the stuff to cure his grandson. As long as the boy lives, the old man has a reason to stay alive. But if Alex dies, what'll happen to Rebadow? That's the question I've been asking since Moms died—about myself. Except that Rebadow can't control whether Alex lives or dies, but if I hadn't been in Oz, Moms wouldn't have been on the bus to Oz. Instead, she'd've been walking the few blocks between her place and mine to visit her grandkids—the kids I'll never have—and Annabella'd still be with me.

Wednesday 3.20.02

In Oz, everybody acts tough. Forget about shedding tears, if an inmate—or a hack—so much as blinks, in less than half an hour the prison will know the motherfucker's afraid. And once the word is out, there's usually no way to rehabilitate your cred, especially not in a joint like this one. That's why most guys make sure they reply to every insult, retaliate for every blow, and do their best to take the other dink out before he has a chance to move on them. Last week, Taylor, the head of the FBI's investigation into Hank Schillinger's murder, came back to ask some more questions. The way I heard the story, Keller had confessed to putting out the contract on the kid, but the guy who actually did the hit testified that he'd never heard of Keller and pointed at Pancamo instead. Of course, Pancamo didn't admit anything, but as soon as Schillinger heard the story, he took an army of Aryans to the gym and tried to shank Pancamo. Pancamo knocked the knife out of Schillinger's fist, but then his luck ran out. Robson came in behind Pancamo, picked up the shank, and stuck Chucky in the side. Waska Garboric, who was working bedpan, told me that when the hacks were wheeling him into the infirmary, with his shank wound bleeding pretty good, Pancamo was trying to climb down off the gur-

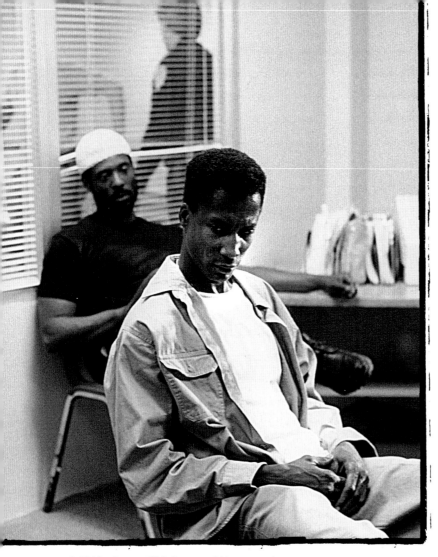

Said tries to save White's ass and his own soul.

ney, yelling, "I'm fine, I'm fine, I'm fine. Just give me a fucking Band-Aid." He's still in the infirmary, but I guess the Aryans got the message that it'll take more than a gang of them and a knife to whack that Wise Guy.

Before the bus crash, I thought I knew what that message was, but I'm not sure anymore. When I look at the other inmates, in Em City or the cafeteria, I see guys acting tough, but to me they don't look like tough guys any longer, they look like lost souls. Behind the swagger, they're choking down their fears—of dying in Oz, one godforsaken way or another, alone,

forgotten by everyone on the outside. The one person who acted like he'd beaten the odds by rejecting violence, Kareem Said, fell apart after stabbing Adebisi. He killed Adebisi in self-defense, but since then it's like the act uncorked a flood of rage he can't control. A couple days ago in the cafeteria, he tore into Ahmad Lalar, a recent convert, for sneaking a bite of his bread while the Muslims were reciting the prayer before eating, practically strangling the kid and banishing him on the spot. Instead of throwing Said into the Hole or, worse, putting him on display in the cage, McManus has assigned him to help Omar White—that bug's like a fly trapped in a bottle—figure out how to stay away from fighting and drugs. The two of them are sharing Said's pod now, and if it works, this brainchild of McManus's might turn out to be his most inspired act. But if it fails, Said and White could end up tearing each other up inside, and maybe even worse.

For some reason, I keep thinking about Clayton Hughes, whose father was shanked in the cafeteria by an inmate about twenty years ago. Hughes must be just a few years younger than me, and it seems he came to work in Oz because he was looking for answers and perhaps to prove himself to Glynn, who'd been his dad's closest friend. Only I'm not sure he knew what the questions were. He wanted to know who'd killed his father, but he also started acting strange, used a stun gun he'd smuggled in on a prisoner and got rough with some of the older inmates, like Rebadow, who wouldn't tell him what he wanted about his father's death. At first it just seemed like he'd lost his cool, but later—there were rumors that Giles had revealed it was Glynn himself who'd killed Hughes's father—he started acting crazy.

For a while, Glynn tried to find a way to keep Hughes—transferred him out of Em City to the library—but finally he decided he had no choice but to fire him. Apparently Hughes had decided that black inmates weren't criminals, but political prisoners, and before he left the compound he made a last stop in Em City and planted a gun in Adebisi's pad. That was the gun Tarrant later used to kill a hack and four prisoners, including himself.

Hughes's story didn't end, though, until after he'd dropped all the way to the bottom circle of Oz's version of Hell: Solitary. Along the way, he got arrested for dropping the gun on Adebisi, and while he was out on bail, he talked his way into the prison during Devlin's press conference and shot the governor. This time there wasn't any bail, and Hughes ended up in Unit J, the cell block for cops-turned-felons, where he killed Basil/Mobay, my old cellmate. That got Hughes a single in Solitary, where he overpowered a hack and declared himself Gamba Khufu, president of the Republic of Huru. Glynn thought he could talk sense to Hughes, so he went into the Solitary block alone, but

Hughes lunged at Glynn with a Don Juan, a shank made out of a bedspring. Another prisoner, Penders, who was the only prisoner Hughes had let out of his cell, grabbed for the shank, and when they struggled the knife found Hughes's own gut instead. He died in Glynn's arms, just like his dad.

Now Hughes is dead, and one way or another he took a lot of other people down with him. I wonder what drew him to Oz in the first place. Was he searching for the father he'd lost there as a child? Did he think Glynn, his dad's friend who'd kept an eye on the son while he was growing up, could help him find what he was looking for? I don't know, but it turned out his death had something to do with Glynn, just like his dad's did.

Thursday 3.28.02

I haven't really been able to sleep since my Moms died. It's not like in the old days back in gen pop, where you always sleep with one eye open because there was so much noise and you feel like you never knew what your cellmate is going to do. These days I'm more afraid of what I'm going to see if I start to dream. It's usually about Moms. In the dream, she's still alive and we're back at her place, together, like nothing's happened, and when I wake up it takes me a moment to remember that I'm locked in here and she's in the ground, and I never did get the chance to tell her, one last time, how much I loved her.

Awake, I sometimes catch myself trying to edge back into the dream, and in Oz that can be dangerous, because if you drop your guard for just a second, you can't be sure it won't be the wrong second.

Tough as it is to stay focused on the present, to resist drifting back into the dream where things are like they used to be, Poet made me snap to attention when he came rushing up to where I was sitting with Burr in the Common Room with news: Schillinger had been released from the Hole, where he'd been ever since Pancamo was shanked in the gym. I saw the trace of a smile flicker in Burr's eyes, quick as a hack shining his flashlight into your cell at night, and then he said: "Good. Now we can sit back and watch the Nazis wipe out the Sicilians."

Poet wasn't so sure. He was betting on Morales and El Norte to back the Wise Guys and thought the two of them might be able to hold off the Aryans. Burr hesitated for a second, like he was about to agree with Poet, but then he said, "Unless Morales sees an

opportunity to move three squares forward, change partners. I want you to tell Enrique that I want a sitdown." Poet sped off in search of Morales like he was a fucking FedEx messenger, and less than half an hour later, Burr and Morales were as tight as a couple of long-lost cousins.

I wasn't at the meeting in the second-floor classroom (besides Burr and Morales, only Poet and Guerra were present). But later, Burr and I were talking, and I could sense that his heart wasn't really in running tits anymore, that he was just used to being top dog and couldn't imagine letting the power go. I was thinking, Shit, he must know he's never going to see the other side of these prison walls again, and neither am I, so what the fuck does he need the power or the money for? His Delia's dead and gone, Moms is, too, there's nobody out there who needs him, so why keep fighting, why not let somebody else run the risks? All Burr wanted to talk about was the past, about how Moms had gotten herself and my dad "riled up" about the civil rights movement in the sixties, how she'd dragged him down to Washington, D.C., to hear Dr. King speak at the march, while Burr stayed behind in the city, drinking and "waiting for something better to come along." I got lost listening to Burr thinking back over things that happened before I was born, but I'm not sure it was doing me any good, because all of a sudden I heard myself say, "I miss Momma so fucking much."

I hadn't called her that in years, and it was true, I did miss her, and I knew there wasn't a thing I could do about it. Neither could Burr. He just said, "I know, I know," and I could hear in his voice how he was mourning her, too.

Sunday 3.31.02

Sister Pete's a good person. I don't really see the point of going to drug rehab sessions anymore, and half the guys there aren't trying to stay clean, they're just trying to stay in Em City or cop a break from the dull routine. But there's something about being around Sister Pete; I feel a little calmer or something, so I'm still showing up. Most of the time we're not even talking about drugs. Like today, Guerra started in about how his girlfriend has sent him a postcard from Maui. He didn't mind that she'd gone to Hawaii without him, but he said it bothered him that he was never going to be able to travel to beautiful places like the islands.

Big fucking deal, I thought, and I told him there were worse things a woman could do to you than go on vacation to Maui. I'd never said a word to any of those bastards about Annabella, except to say, yeah, she was my wife when somebody saw her on visiting day. But today, I couldn't hold in what I was feeling, and I said, "She could

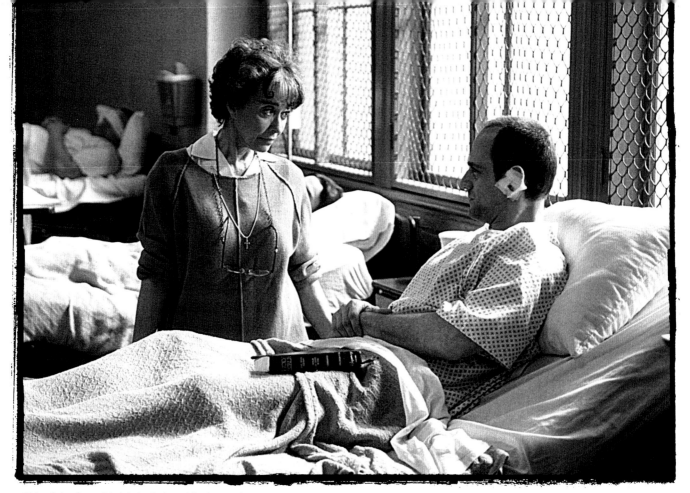

Sister Pete: fixer of twisted minds and broken souls.

leave you. She could send you a letter one day, and say, you know, she'd decided it's time for her to move on with her life." Suddenly everybody in the circle was staring at me, but I kept talking. "I'm saying, I thought the worst thing that could happen to me was losing my legs, losing my freedom. But Annabella, that was like losing my manhood, like a big chunk of who I am."

When I stopped talking, I could sense that the eyes of everyone in that little circle were still on me, but somehow I wasn't really seeing them. Instead, I was seeing Annabella, her eyes were turned toward me, staring at me, but she was also walking away from me, and then she turned and kept walk-

ing, so all I was conscious of was her hair flowing down her back and her legs—those long, beautiful legs—walking faster and faster.

Thursday 4.4.02

I used to dream of escaping from Oz, and a few years ago I was ready to try any kind of scheme to get out. I even thought of stowing away in a coffin in place of the body of some dead inmate that was being shipped off to the funeral home. Now I think the only coffin I'll ever be in will be my own, that there isn't any other way out, at least not for me. One inmate, though, seems to have beat the system somehow, though nobody knows how it happened. A few weeks ago, Reverend Cloutier was sent back to Oz. He'd been so badly burned in the gas explosion that he spent months in Bench-ley Memorial, and when he returned they set up a private room in the infirmary. Almost nobody's seen him, but I heard that he could hardly move and couldn't speak, just make moaning sounds. Sup-posedly he was recovering slowly but getting better, though nobody was sure he'd ever really recover. Then a few days ago one of Hoyt's Biker pals, a gorilla named Gunner, snuck into Cloutier's room while making the rounds with the mail cart and tried to suffo-cate the Reverend, to keep him from ever revealing the facts about how Cloutier got to be bricked up in the kitchen wall in the first place. Dr. Nathan caught the Biker, but it took a couple hacks to drag him off Cloutier. The poor guy was still breathing, I'm told, but the next day, when Father Mukada (barely out of the hospital himself, after the bus crash) went in to pray with Cloutier, as he'd been doing the past few weeks, his bed was empty. Cloutier couldn't move, let alone walk, so there's no way he could've gotten out of the bed on his own, but nobody saw anyone go into the room, and nobody saw anyone come out. It's funny, too; a couple days after Cloutier vanished, it was Easter Sun-day, and I heard Father Mukada's sermon was about the resurrection of Jesus.

DRUG REHAB IN PRISON

Because the largest and most accessible population of addicts is in our prisons and jails, it makes sense to address them where they are. Additionally, as casual drug use drops, there is a large population of serious "hard core" addicts who are more reluctant to volunteer for treatment in community-based programs. In fact, these two populations frequently intersect. While it may be almost impossible to coax members of this group into community-based programs, success may be had in the prison or jail environment where there may be greater motivation, more spare time, and interest piqued by the good reputation of an effective program. A variation on this theme is coerced treatment as a condition of probation or as a part of a pretrial diversion program. In contrast with traditional thought that suggests that a client must display desire and initiative for treatment in order for success to follow, there is some evidence that demonstrates that coerced treatment, whether through community-based services or during incarceration, can be just as effective as voluntary treatment.

Another advantage of TCs [therapeutic communities] stems from evidence that retention in treatment has been demonstrated to be one of the most important variables in predicting positive outcomes. Unfortunately, less than desired retention rates in community-based programs remain a serious obstacle to treatment success. This is true for all major modalities and for TCs in particular. One major advantage of beginning treatment in a correctional institution is that retention is significantly improved. Inmates in prisons and jails do not leave the institutions when they "feel like it." Even those inmates who are removed from treatment for rule infractions can often be recruited back to complete treatment at a later date.

Source: Drug Treatment Behind Bars: Prison-Based Strategies for Change, edited by Kevin E. Early (Westport, Conn.: Praeger, 1996).

Monday 4.15.02

We were sitting around one of the tables in the Common Room, playing cards to pass the time, when I heard McManus's voice, announcing something from the C.O.'s command center. He's always announcing some bullshit or other, so at first I didn't pay much attention, but then I realized he was talking about dogs, about bringing a program for training guide dogs for the blind into Oz, and my ears perked up. Poet heard him, too, and said, "Shit, I don't want no dogs in here, man. Where I grew up, there was this Rott—pit bull mix, a mean motherfucker, I'm sure he had some Schillinger in him. Took a chunk out of my leg, man."

Burr looked over at Poet and just said, "Something tells me you deserved to get bit," but I wasn't paying either one of them any mind. I was thinking, I'd like to have a dog around. "Maybe a dog would take my mind off my problems," I said, half thinking out loud. And I went off to ask McManus how to sign up. It turned out the program, called "Man's Best Friend," was working in a number of other prisons. They were planning to start small in Oz—they were looking for only three volunteers. Not many inmates were interested, but Alicia Hindon, the trainer from Man's Best Friend, made it clear she was only looking for people she thought would do a good job of disciplining and caring for their dogs. She took me, though, maybe because she thought my own disability made me a good bet to understand what it's like for a blind person. The other two volunteers were Alvarez, who convinced Hindon he'd make a good dog trainer because he was looking for a way to make up for blinding Eugene Rivera, and Greg Penders, who's new to Em City.

Tuesday 4.23.02

Hindon didn't lose any time getting started. The day after she chose her volunteers, she came back to Oz with the three dogs we were going to train. Penders immediately went over to one of them, a beautiful dog with a glossy black coat, and started to call it his bitch. Hindon wasn't having any of that. She sent him right back to his side of the cafeteria, where we were doing the training, said these were dogs, not bitches, and that she'd be deciding which of us would handle which dog. Hindon's a no bullshit type and Penders immediately "heeled." Then we got to work, practicing the first lessons in how to train a dog to obey through love and trust. Alvarez was right when he said there wasn't much of either of those things in Oz. When Hindon explained that the dogs would be living right in our pods with us, I knew it wouldn't be easy making room for a third creature in a space that was pretty tight for two. All the same, I thought, I wouldn't mind sharing space with someone I could love and trust for a change, even if it was a pooch.

I knew we'd get shit from everybody else in Em City when we brought the dogs back, and sure enough, there were dumb comments about how we'd brought our dates home with us. The heckling doesn't bother me, though. I am worrying about whether I'll be able to gain the trust of my dog, Layla, with the way I'm feeling. I'd better stop thinking about what the dog is going to do for me and start feeling responsible for it, and for getting it ready to help someone who couldn't see.

At the same time, I'm worrying about other things, too: whether I'll be able to protect Layla from the other inmates. Nobody bothered me, but Guerra got right into Alvarez's face. Alvarez told Guerra to leave his dog, Julie, a gentle golden retriever, alone, and Guerra asked whether Alvarez was afraid he might hurt the dog. Just at that moment, Julie started growling at Guerra, who jumped back, alarmed. Alvarez laughed and said, "No, I'm afraid she might hurt you," and led Julie into his pod.

Through the glass, I could see them playing. With people, Alvarez always seems edgy, tensed up, like he's about to attack, but with the dog he looks like he's completely at ease. I'd like to feel like that with Layla, but I don't, at least not yet.

Wednesday 5.1.02

Beecher's not so busy dealing with his own problems these days that he doesn't have time to give me some advice, too. For days I've been having the same vision, again and again: Moms is on that bus, and she's calling my name, and then everything goes dark. Nothing pulls me away from that scene, not even talking to Burr. Sometimes, like earlier today, I feel like I've got to get off by myself for a while, so I leave the dog in my pod and try to find an empty corner in the Common Room, where there's nothing and nobody to distract me.

That's where Beecher found me earlier today, and he didn't just want to console me, he wanted to give me fucking advice. About how I had to let my mother go, picture her dead, buried, her flesh decaying, so I could move on to "everything good about her." Beecher's had more than his share of grief—his wife killing herself, his son murdered, and the dead boy's hand turning up in a

Inmate Guide Dog Training Programs

Emmy, Walker, Delta, Cans and Pepper are the five newest graduates of the guide dog training program at the Coleman federal correctional complex, the only one of its kind in the federal prison system. The dogs arrived as furry bundles of enthusiasm and disobedience. A year with their inmate handlers, and they are ready for the final step in becoming a working guide dog. "It's just like with real kids," says Julie Aichroth, director of the program. "We are so proud, and now they get to move on."

When similar programs began in a handful of state prisons in the early 1990s, skeptics thought the dogs could be a distraction. Or worse, the inmates would turn out delinquent dogs. The concerns eased as the programs had one success after another. Many prisons see improved behavior by the dogs' handlers and a renewed hope.

In the outside world, it's hard to find people willing to commit the time it takes to raise one of the puppies. Inmates have nothing but time. Southeastern Guide Dogs Inc. provides the dogs and instruction. The inmates work as handlers, training and socializing the dogs every day from the time they are 10 weeks old until about 15 months. After that, the dogs go on to "polishing school" outside the prison for six months of advanced training. The dogs are then placed with the sight-impaired. "Our mission is to put out the best dogs," said Aichroth, who works for Southeastern Guide Dogs. "That all starts with the inmates." The handlers are chosen from among the women at the minimum-security work camp facility at Coleman, 75 miles north of Tampa in Sumter County [Florida]. They must be non-violent offenders eligible to leave the prison grounds for daylong furloughs with the dogs. It's a yearlong commitment with a lot of grunt work, but the competition to be one of the five or six handlers is intense. The dogs live inside the prison and are the inmates' responsibility. Days start early with morning feeding, kennel cleaning and doggy playtime. Inmates teach the basic commands, such as sitting and staying, and make sure the dogs are housebroken. To graduate, the dogs must become well-behaved in a variety of situations. The dogs and their handlers make supervised visits to malls, courthouses and downtown Tampa. Often the dogs accompany the handlers to the prison hairdresser, chapel and gym and go to meals in the cafeteria with all the other inmates. The handlers must wean their dogs from a litany of bad habits. "Ever tried to put a doggy bone in front of a puppy and get them not to eat it?" said 24-year-old Shannon Tindall, who trained Delta. "That's the easy stuff around here."

The choice to become a handler is not always an easy one. Handlers, who work as volunteers, could have paying jobs with food services. For Tindall, who is serving 16 months for bank fraud, the benefits far outweighed any downside. She said she has learned how to cope with problems, set goals and work with others in stressful situations. She has earned a certificate in veterinarian assistance and intends to earn her two-year veterinary technician certificate after she is released this spring. Tindall recalled with a smile the time she put in extra hours when Delta, a yellow Lab, had worms. The bond, she said, was tough to sever as Delta was about to move on. "Wow, this letting-go thing is a bit harder than I thought," Tindall said before the graduation ceremony.

Sheila Hernandez wept as she described her relationship with Cans, the Australian shepherd lying obediently at her feet. Hernandez got Cans last July as a "rehab project," a dog from outside the prison having trouble with training and socialization. "He's come a long way," said Hernandez, who has 2-1/2 years left of a five-year drug conspiracy sentence.

Problem dogs often are given to the prison handlers, a testament to the program's success. The dogs trained in the prison excel in obedience and consistency as they receive constant, hands-on training. The last class graduated four dogs, three of which are now active guides. It's a good average, in line with national numbers, said Aichroth, the program director.

Hernandez, Cans' trainer, has been chosen to stay in the program. Her new puppy is Amy. She is tiny, shy and poorly behaved compared with the new graduates. To Hernandez, the new puppies show how far the other dogs have come and all the work that lies ahead. She also knows that a year from now she'll be crying again. "It's part happiness," she said of Cans' graduation. "But I already miss him."

Source: Graham Brink, "Time to Train," *St. Petersburg Times,* February 25, 2001.

package the murderer sent to him in Oz—but his stupid fucking lessons aren't going to take away the pain of picturing my Moms trapped inside that bus as it rolled down the embankment, of realizing in those last moments that we weren't going to have another chance to meet. Being closed up in small spaces freaked her out, and every time I look around my pod I can't see anything but the inside of that bus.

I told Beecher to get out of my face, to take a fucking walk. Shit, why did that bastard think he knew what I was feeling and what I had to do about it? I wasn't sure myself, I just knew I couldn't get past that one image of the bus with Moms in it swerving off the road and rolling down the embankment. I wasn't sure I'd ever be able to get that image out of my mind, much less get over Moms's death.

The next thing I did, though, was worse than anything Beecher was urging me to do: I hunted down Poet. He was in a pod with a couple of the Homeys, snorting. When I said, "Give me something," Poet looked surprised and asked, "Some of this?" I said, "Yeah, I need a consolation prize," and he tossed me a vial, saying, "Welcome back," with a laugh. Poet knew it'd been years since I'd touched drugs, since we'd been sitting side by side in the drug rehab meetings for a long time, and he knew how serious I'd been about staying clean. He'd never quit himself, just paid off

somebody in the infirmary to switch urine samples whenever he had to do a drug test. So he kept on about how surprised he was, but by the time the words were out, I could hardly hear him. I was too high, and it was almost like I wasn't there. But I wasn't any-place better, either. The drugs were working all right, but what they did was make those images—Moms in the bus, then the bus veering off the road and rolling over and over—sharper than ever.

After a few minutes the images faded from my mind, and the room came back into focus. Poet hadn't said anything, and he didn't have to. We both knew we didn't want Burr to walk in and find me snorting tits. Burr himself had never done much heroin or coke himself; in all the time I knew him, his drug was alcohol. But he knew how much trouble I'd gotten into with crack on the streets, and how much depended on my staying clean. So I cleared out, taking some tits back to my pod for insurance. Layla stood up and wagged her tail when she saw me, maybe thinking I'd play with her or take her for a walk. Instead, I patted her back for a minute, scratched her ears and filled up her water bowl, and then I shoved some more tits up my nose. This time the images of Moms and the bus didn't come back, but the room started to spin, so I crawled into bed, thinking maybe things would look a little better if I slept for an hour.

Just woke up. Have I been asleep for hours or weeks? Naw. I can't have slept too long, or the hacks would've pounded on the glass to get me out of bed and into the Common Room for the evening count. I feel dizzy—shit, lines on this page keep going in and out of focus—dizzier than I can ever remember, and I'm sweating like I'm in

> How is love wrong, Kareem? **In whatever form it takes, how is love wrong?** Especially here in Oz, where there's **so little of it.**
>
> —Tobias Beecher

the jungle or someplace like that. I don't know what the fuck's the matter. Could it be the tits I snorted? It's been a while since I did any drugs, but I've never had any problem with them and sure as hell never got sick from them.

I wonder why Burr hasn't come by. He'd've seen something was wrong as soon as he looked at me. I guess he's in the cafeteria supervising the kitchen, since he's in charge there now. Otherwise he'd've checked on me for sure. He always stops by my pod if he doesn't see me, and he'd've realized that something was wrong as soon as he took a look at me.

I don't see anybody out in the Common Room, so they must all be in the cafeteria, eating dinner. I couldn't eat anything, but man, am I thirsty! And there's Layla, sitting in the corner so quietly. I'll bet she's thirsty, too, and hungry. I haven't fed her since—since when? I can't remember. Shit, I'd better give her something to eat right now. I just got to drag myself out of bed and into my chair—

I wasn't back from the hospital for two hours, was still in the infirmary, for Christ's sake, when I had my first visitor. I was still feeling pretty damn sick, and I must've been, because Dr. Nathan put me into the private room (the one where Cloutier'd been when he vanished—was I going to evaporate next?) until my fever came down and all the infection was out of me. At Benchley Memorial, they said I had septicemia, that my fever had shot up to 105, and if the doctors there hadn't caught the infection in time, my kidneys would've failed, and I never would've seen the inside of Oz again. That wouldn't have bothered me one fucking bit, but I don't want to die without having a chance to say good-bye to Burr, at least.

But the face looking down at mine in the hospital bed belonged to McManus, one of the last people in Em City I wanted to see. It's funny, though; the question out of McManus's mouth was the same one I knew Burr would've been asking me: Who gave me the drugs? Of course, McManus approached things from a slightly different angle, with some bullshit about how I was trying to kill myself, even if I wasn't doing it consciously (Yeah, right! Jesus!), by snorting all those tits and letting my catheter get contaminated. But he switched from his social worker hat to his detective hat pretty damn quick. I told him it didn't matter where I got the drugs, that what I did I did, and nobody else was going to suffer for my actions.

The trouble is, according to McManus, somebody else already had suffered. He told me that Salvatore DeSantos, one of the Wise Guys, was brain-dead from an LSD overdose, and he suspects that Burr Redding was getting even with DeSantos for giving me the tits. I knew Burr would be pissed as hell, but I wondered why he thought I'd be buying drugs from the Sicilians, especially now that they were all but cut out of the business by him and Morales.

I told McManus I wanted to talk to Burr, but he wouldn't let Burr come to the infirmary, told me if I had any messages for Burr, he—McManus—was my AT&T. Yeah, right! Give me Sprint anytime, pal.

Saturday 6.22.02

When I got sent to the hospital, that was the end of the Man's Best Friend program for me. They had to take Layla away and look for another inmate to train her in a different prison. Besides getting off drugs and staying off, that's the one thing I wish I'd've been able to see through to the end. Maybe if I'd been thinking about what a trained guide dog would mean to the blind person who'd get her after the training ended, things would've turned out different. Instead, I hoped that having a dog around would help take my mind off my own problems, Moms's dying and Annabella's leaving. Then I wouldn't have needed those tits and I wouldn't have ended up in the hospital, and Layla would be somewhere out in the city right now, helping somebody to live a better life.

Out of the three inmates who started the program—Alvarez, Penders, and me—the only one who stuck it out was Alvarez. From what I heard, he didn't just train Julie, he accomplished a fucking minor miracle.

Alvarez got it into his head that he wanted Eugene Rivera, the hack he blinded a couple years back, to get Julie. When Alicia Hindon first approached the Riveras, they refused. They didn't want anything to do with a dog Alvarez had trained. Alvarez kept working with Julie, but what he didn't know was that McManus (he's fucked up a lot of things and people, but he can be a persistent motherfucker, and I'll give him credit for this one) was working on the Riveras until he finally brought them around.

On the day Alvarez put Julie through her final test, and Hindon said Julie had graduated and was ready to start working as a guide dog, Eugene Rivera came walking into the cafeteria to pick her up. Alvarez must've been surprised, but the real surprise was this. It seems he'd never given up on his hope that Julie would become Rivera's guide dog, so he'd taught the dog to understand commands in Spanish and English. He told Rivera to tell Julie to come in Spanish, the language the Riveras speak at home, and when Rivera said *"Ven aquí,"* the dog trotted right over to her new master. Alvarez has hurt a shitload of people since he's been in Oz, Rivera being one of them. I can't say that training Julie for Rivera even started to make up for blinding the guy, but every time Rivera takes a step with that dog, that'll be a step forward for Alvarez, too. I wish I'd've done something like that for someone, anyone.

Tuesday 7.2.02

All the time I was in the infirmary, I didn't hear much about what was going on back in Em City. Being in that private room was fucking deluxe, but as far as getting the news of what was going on in Oz, it sucked. After that one visit from McManus, I didn't have much company. The doctors and the nurses came in and out, checking my progress and shit, but they weren't telling me about the scene back in Em City. Dr. Nathan examined me pretty often, and whenever she did, she'd lecture me about how I had to look after my health, that somebody with my condition (I guess she didn't want to say "paralyzed") needed to do everything he could to avoid getting infections. She said the risk of complications was greater because I couldn't be as physically active as someone who had the use of his legs.

Every time Dr. Nathan stopped in, she'd say something encouraging to me, trying to keep my spirits up and get me to concentrate on getting better. She never said anything about Moms or Annabella, but I was sure she knew and wanted to steer me away from thinking about them and toward thinking about myself.

Her strategy didn't exactly work—I never stopped thinking about Moms, especially—but it didn't exactly fail, either. On the morning she discharged me from the infirmary, she reminded me, "Just because I'm sending you back to Emerald City doesn't mean you're completely well, or that you can stop taking care of yourself again." And when I just said, "Uh-huh," she came right back at me: "Don't 'uh-huh' me, Augustus, or I'll come and clean your catheter myself." I thought, that sounds like a sweet proposition to me. I didn't forgot about what Dr. Nathan's been through herself, and I know it's got to be

fresh in her mind right now, with Cyril O'Reily, who strangled her husband, on Death Row for murdering Li Chen. His trial for Chen's murder started when I was in Benchley Memorial, and the verdict and sentencing happened while I was still recuperating in the infirmary, so I've only heard a few of the details. But I know that anti–death penalty groups on the outside and some people inside Oz—Sister Pete; Suzanne Fitzgerald, Ryan O'Reily's mother; Father Meehan, a priest who

Sister Pete speaks out against the death penalty with Suzanne Fitzgerald.

LAST CONVERSATION BETWEEN AUGUSTUS HILL AND BURR REDDING

When Augustus got sick from using drugs and ended up in the hospital, I wanted to kill whoever had given those tits to that boy. When he came back to Em City and I thought he'd be OK, I still wanted to punish the bastards that done it. But Augustus didn't blame me or anyone else for using drugs again, only himself. I admitted to him, "I got angry when I heard you was using that shit again. I wanted to lash out in every kind of direction. Then I realized that I was really angry at myself for being so blind that I didn't see that you had been back on that shit again, for getting you strung out on it in the first place."

Augustus tried to stop me but I wouldn't listen. "I set down there at the table, sitting in your daddy's chair, eating your momma's food, and all along Eugenia never knew that I was feeding you that shit, that I had you slinging for me. Why'd I do that? Why, why'd I tell a lie, hurt that sweet girl?"

Then Augustus told me, "It's like you said: Life happens the way it happens."

But I said, "That's a copout. We make life happen. I got you strung out on that shit because I wanted you dependent on me, 'cause I was always afraid that you were going to leave me. And yet I almost lost you altogether forever."

What he said next near to broke my heart. He said, "Burr, you didn't never need no drugs to keep me close to you, man. I always loved you. Always."

I couldn't help crying then. "Look at me," I said, "acting like a weepy old woman."

To break the mood I guess, we went out into the Common Room. We hadn't gone more than ten yards when someone came at me with a knife and Augustus rolled his chair into the son-of-a-bitch's path. He took the shank that was aimed at my heart, and a minute later he was gone. All Augustus said before he died was, "I can feel my legs."

I never wanted to outlive that boy.

was imprisoned for political crimes—are holding protests and creating a media campaign to stop the state from executing Cyril because he's too brain-damaged to understand completely what his violent acts mean or to assist in his defense. I wonder how Dr. Nathan feels. She spends every day keeping low motherfuckers—lots of them guys who've killed people—alive, but what about her husband's murderer, who's got an IQ of 51 and a half brother, Ryan, who put Cyril up to the job because he was in love with Dr. Nathan himself?

Thursday 7.4.02

As soon as I got back to Em City and the second I wheeled myself into my pod, Poet followed me like a heat-seeking missile. He wanted me to hear his story before Burr got out of the Hole. Poet knew that Burr always took revenge for attacks, and he held whoever'd given me the heroin responsible for my septicemia. Making things worse was the fact that Burr recognized that I was that close to dying, and that was hard to take now that Burr and I don't have anybody left except each other.

Poet admitted that because of him, Burr was in the fucking Hole, explaining how he'd misled Burr into thinking Guerra had sold me the tits, "so our little peace treaty with the spics, it kind of fell apart. Burr and

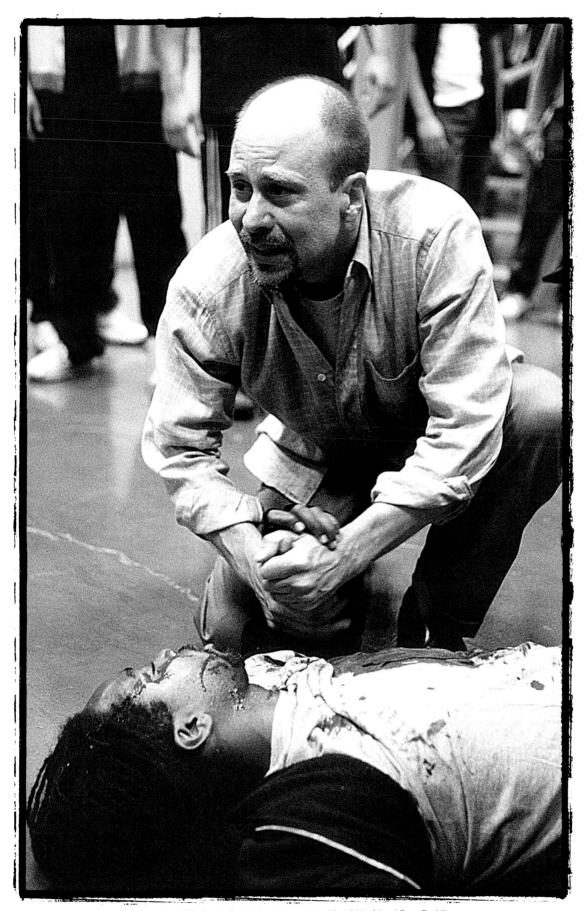

Augustus Hill: dead after trying to save the life of his friend Burr Redding.

2002 Victims

- JIM BYRNES: Killed by Jaz Hoyt after he has a vision in which Reverend Cloutier orders him to kill Hoyt and Tommy Kirk.

- LI CHEN: Stabbed by Cyril O'Reily, who leaped to his brother's defense after Chen tried to stab Ryan.

- SALVATORE DESANTOS: Died of an LSD overdose introduced into his food because Redding mistakenly believed that DeSantos had given heroin to Hill.

- ADAM GUENZEL: Forced by Schillinger to attempt to escape, he is electrocuted when he tries to climb over the perimeter fence.

- AUGUSTUS HILL: Threw himself in the path of a knife intended to kill Burr Redding, his friend and mentor

- AHMED LALAR: Died of multiple lacerations inflicted by Robson in retaliation for Said and Arif's stabbing of Schillinger and Robson.

- JAIME VELEZ: Killed by Guerra, who fractured Velez's skull against the shower room wall, after Velez tried to murder Guerra to impress Alvarez.

Morales got into a little fandango, and now they both in the Hole."

When I told Poet I wasn't going to rat him out, he was so relieved you'd've thought he'd just received a pardon from Governor Devlin. I said, "I wanted those drugs. Don't matter who gave it to me. I'm going to tell Burr that." Wearing a huge smile underneath his dreadlocks, Poet said, "All right, thanks, man," and before he walked out the door, he added, "If I was a girl, you'd get tongued." I told him, "If you was a girl, son, you'd be butt-ass ugly."

I know Burr. He's going to be hot to know who I got those tits from, and Poet knows what Burr's capable of doing to get revenge. Somehow I've got to get Burr to see that I'm the only person to blame for what I did—not him and not whoever the dealer was. Maybe he won't want to hear it, but I've got to make him listen and get him to believe. I can't afford to lose his love again now.

Epilogue

BY TOM FONTANA

On July 16, 2002, we finished shooting the last scene of the last episode of the last season of *Oz*. When assistant director, Ivan Fonseca, yelled, "That's a wrap!" the moment was filled with a mixture of sadness, sobriety, pride, and laughter.

Many people ask me why we stopped production. The better question may be: Why did we start in the first place?

In 1971, I was twenty years old, attending college, and protesting everything: the war in Vietnam, racial injustice, misogyny. One sunny day in September, a prison, not far from my hometown of Buffalo, exploded into violence. Attica.

Until those riots, I believed that prisons were simply places where bad guys went after being captured by Jack Webb or the Mod Squad or Batman. I never really took the time to think about what it was like inside, day after day.

In order to quell the uprising, New York State Governor Nelson Rockefeller deployed an armed force of National Guardsmen, who swarmed the prison, shooting everyone in sight. As a result thirty-three inmates and eleven guards were dead and eighty-seven people were wounded. The guilty had been punished, but in a most inhuman way.

This shocking action lead to a great national debate about what had caused the riot, about the appropriateness of the state's response, about the benefits of redemption over retribution. Throughout the country, as a result of Attica, positive changes have been made in the penal system.

Like most Americans, I thought that the "problem" was solved.

But over the years, as crime continued to rise, conservative pundits blamed the lawlessness in our streets on the ineffectiveness of prison reform. Drug recovery and educational programs corroded, as revenge once again became our nation's prime agenda.

While I was writing and producing *Homicide: Life on the Street*, we went "on location" to Jessep, the prison outside Baltimore, to film part of an episode. Walking the halls, I was stunned: The place was rife with fear and racism, the men had no privacy and even fewer rights. After several visits, I came to see their struggle to survive as a microcosm of our society in general.

I decided to create a series about life "behind bars." I went to various networks, pitching different versions of the series—juvenile detention, minimal security, a boot camp—all rejected by terrified executives. Television had room for cops, doctors, lawyers, and lifeguards, but not for the stories of the men and women who live each day on the edge of an abyss.

Meanwhile over at HBO, they were having great success with prison documentaries produced by Sheila Nevins, currently EVP of HBO Original Programming, and they were contemplating their first drama series. My friend Rob Kenneally, a man with his finger on the pulse of TV, called to say that HBO was interested in a show set in a prison.

Wow!

I went to meet with Chris Albrecht, the current HBO chairman and CEO; Anne Thomopoulos, currently SVP of HBO Original Programming; and Bridget Potter, President of HBO Original Programming at that time. Chris said the words every television writer longs to hear: "I don't care if the characters are likable as long as they're interesting..."

Wow!

I spent about two years researching and writing drafts of the show—I even did one set "ten minutes" into the future. At first, the project was called *Club Med,* but when I decided that a medium-security penitentiary didn't have enough balls, I called it *The Max.* Unfortunately, MTV announced they'd be programming a new series called *MAXX* (which had nothing to do with prison), so I had to keep thinking.

Suddenly, like a bolt from Olympus, I remembered that the name of the State Commissioner of Corrections during the Attica riots was Russell Oswald. I thought calling the penitentiary "Oswald" would be a back-handed tribute to the old bureaucrat. And just as quickly, the abbreviation ("The name on the street") popped into my head: *Oz*.

What attracted me to the title was its ironic implications and not just because of the obvious L. Frank Baum connection.

There was Frank Oz, the Muppet master, and Amos Oz, the writer. There was Ozzy Osbourne and Ozzie Nelson. There was Oz Beg, the Mongol warlord. Oz is ounces. And the nickname for Australia, which started out as a penal colony.

In six seasons, the TV series *Oz* has examined many social issues while also depicting the struggle to survive in our crazy world. And every once in a while, after a long, hard climb, there are moments of redemption, of spiritual awakening. Moments that are, hopefully, as surprising as the violence.

The trickiest part about writing *Oz*, with more than thirty regular characters, is balancing the stories. In retrospect, I wish I had taken more time with some of the key issues—like the return of the death penalty in the first season—and a little less time on the more bizarre ones (though, in twenty years, people will think I'm prescient when it comes to the aging drug!). Whereas I think I successfully defined and examined the gang culture that percolates in every prison, I'm not sure I spent enough air time exploring the gang mentality of the correctional officers. In any case, I know that in the years to come, as I watch *Oz* in reruns, I'll want to rewrite the whole damn thing.

When we were filming the first season, the actors and I were convinced that no one would care or tune in. We were wrong. One only has to walk down the street with a member of the *Oz* cast to see how popular the show has become. Our audience is large and diverse—young blacks, middle-class housewives, middle-aged gays, doormen, ministers, district attorneys, and at least one eighty-year-old Italian-American woman, my mom. We have received praise from conservative columnist Stanley Crouch, from children's illustrator Maurice Sendak, from Rosie O'Donnell, and from Kid Rock. All without a traditional TV hero in sight.

So, here we are, at the end of our journey. After six seasons, with the unflappable support of Chris Albrecht; Carolyn Strauss, EVP of HBO Original Programming; and Miranda Heller, VP of HBO Original Programming, I decided to pull the plug. I want the show to go out strong, like *M*A*S*H* and *The Mary Tyler Moore Show*.

To answer my own question: "Why did we start *Oz* in the first place?" First, to put a human face on our faceless prison population. Second, to tell a tiny piece of the truth, not just about the people in prison, but our individual selves as well.

Behind the Walls of Oz:

A YEAR-BY-YEAR ACCOUNT

Season One

EPISODE ONE

The Routine

Welcome to "Emerald City," the experimental unit of Oswald State Penitentiary (Oz to the inmates), designed by Tim McManus. The diverse population includes Homeboys, Latinos, and Wise Guys, who compete for control of the drug traffic; Muslims, Aryans, and Christians, who wage a war of beliefs; and others, including Bikers, gays, Irish, and unaffiliated inmates who try to keep breathing by staying out of the line of fire. Among the candidates for overall leadership: Kareem Said, a Muslim author and activist who preaches nonviolence and abstinence; Jefferson Keane, head of the Homeboys, who doesn't; and Mafia don Nino Schibetta, who regards Oz as fertile ground for gambling and drug distribution. Middle-class newbie Tobias Beecher, a lawyer before his imprisonment, is rescued from one predator, Simon Adebisi, by another, Aryan

leader Vern Schillinger. He makes Beecher his prag, an experience that marks Beecher for life. When macho, hot-headed Wise Guy Dino Ortolani puts Jefferson Keane's gay brother Billy in the hospital for cruising him, Keane dispatches Johnny Post to bribe his way into Ortolani's cell and incinerate him.

EPISODE TWO

Visits, Conjugal and Otherwise

Schibetta doesn't take kindly to the murder of his protégé, so he schemes to find out who killed Ortolani before Warden Glynn does (Glynn is unaware that his own staffer Burano is really a member of the "Family," who feeds the results of his investigation to Schibetta and takes orders from him). Meanwhile, the inmates are in an uproar after the governor, James Devlin, declares an end to conjugal visits. They rush to beat the deadline, but a demoralized Beecher is forced to beg Schillinger for permission to have sex with his own wife. Jefferson Keane is serving a life sentence, but he applies to marry his fiancée, Mavis, and with Said's assistance wins Glynn's approval—for a marriage by proxy. Schibetta's quest for revenge gets a boost when Ryan O'Reily is transferred from gen pop to Em City and schemes to trade information about Ortolani's killer for the don's goodwill. Father Ray Mukada, the Roman Catholic chaplain, persuades Ricardo Alvarez, a lifer who is Miguel's grandfather, to talk to his grandson about taking responsibility for the baby he has fathered with his girlfriend, Marisa. Miguel finally agrees and is allowed to assist at the birth. Meanwhile, Johnny Post is fingered as Ortolani's killer, and the Homeboys lose a valued member.

EPISODE THREE

God's Chillin

In a bid to keep violence from spiraling out of control, Glynn threatens to lock Oz down if Schibetta, Said, and Keane fail to keep the Wise Guys, Muslims, and Homeboys in line. A dis-

traught Keane sets fire to his mattress and is sent to the Hole, where Healy, a crooked C.O. who is a confederate of O'Reily, beats him as a warning not to rat on his accomplice. When Keane, already drawn to Said because of his role in convincing Glynn to permit Keane's marriage, is released from the Hole, he considers converting to Islam. Meanwhile, O'Reily pressures Beecher for legal help, but Beecher learns his wife is planning to divorce him. Sister Pete comes to Beecher's aid by hiring him to work in her office. Mavis's betrayal plunges Keane into despair, but Said helps him through his crisis and toward accepting his brother's homosexuality. Keane converts to Islam but ends up on Death Row when the hacks force him to become a "gladiator." Locked in the gym with two Latinos, he breaks the neck of one of them, Martinez, in self-defense.

EPISODE FOUR

Capital P

Governor Devlin lobbies successfully for legislation restoring capital punishment in the state, and Keane, convicted of murdering Martinez, is the first prisoner slated for execution. When Keane discovers that his sister, Grace, will die of renal failure unless she receives a new kidney, he offers to donate one of his own kid-

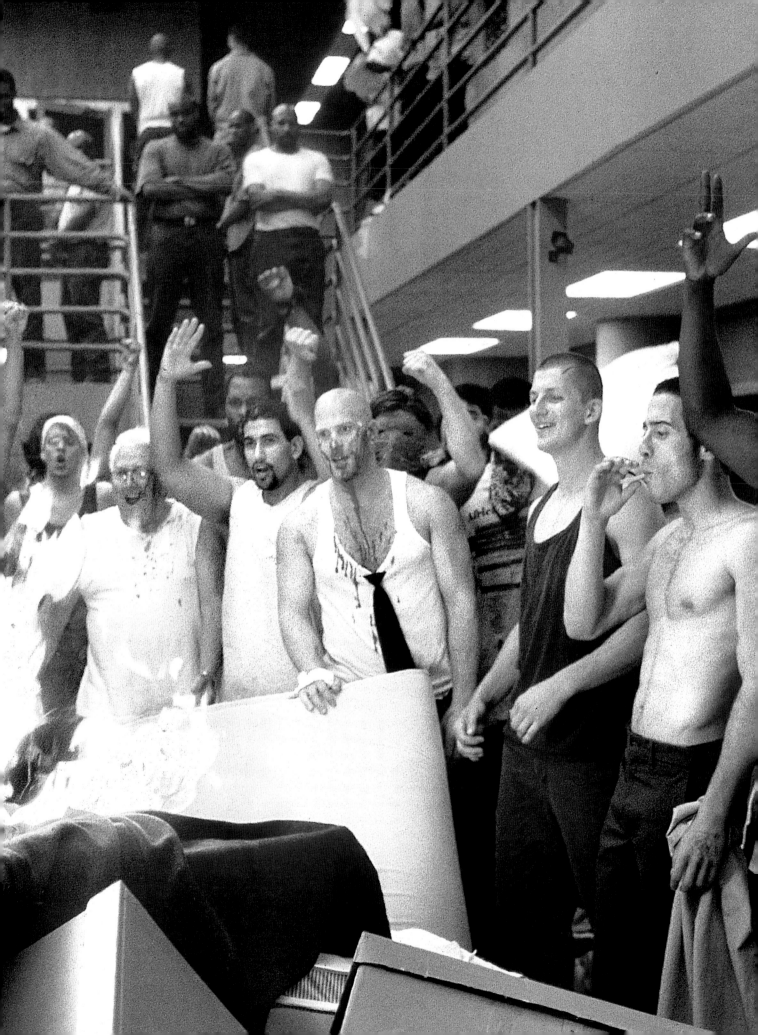

neys and implores McManus to help persuade the authorities to grant permission. The governor agrees to a thirty-day reprieve, and after the operation, Keane urges his grateful father to reconcile with Billy, his other son, who is gay. Keane becomes convinced that to end the cycle of violence among the tribes who control the drug trade in Oz, it's best for him to be executed, even though he acted in self-defense. Beecher, who learns of a videotape featuring Keane's fight with the Latinos (taped by the sadistic C.O.s who forced him into the gym in the first place), is outraged by the injustice and wants to overturn Keane's conviction, but Keane refuses to cooperate and implores Beecher to stop all legal proceedings. After Keane's death, Richard L'Italien—slaughterer of at least thirty-nine women, all former sexual partners—is also executed by lethal injection.

Straight Life

Drugs are big business in Oz, and undercover cop Paul Markstrom's attempt to learn the smugglers' secrets backfires. When Schibetta stages a fake shipment of tits into Oz, Markstrom is found out and hanged. Despite a lockdown in Emerald City, however, drugs continue to trickle in—and the blame shifts from prisoners to corrupt officials. Schemer Ryan O'Reily betrays former partner in contraband Officer Healy, who gets arrested; and Diane Whittlesey, desperate for money, agrees to smuggle cigarettes into Oz for inmate Scott Ross to sell, a move that capsizes her already rocky relationship with Tim McManus. O'Reily also turns Beecher on to marijuana and heroin, when Beecher seeks relief from the escalating humiliation of being Schillinger's prag. Conventional drugs don't fare so well, either; Said refuses to take the medication prescribed to treat his high blood pressure. He fears its side effects and blames the high incidence of hypertension among blacks on the racist society.

To Your Health

When Ricardo Alvarez, who's been in solitary confinement for years, is discovered mumbling to himself in his cell, suffering from Alzheimer's disease, son, grandson, and staff are at a loss about what to do. Sister Peter Marie, the prison psychologist, proposes releasing the elder Alvarez, since he can't possibly do further harm to anyone, and because the prison system can't provide care for elderly, seriously ill inmates. Even relatively healthy older inmates, like Bob Rebadow, who was beaten up by teenaged inmate Kenny Wangler, are at risk. Rebadow contemplates trying to escape, as much from the fear of danger as to enjoy freedom. Meanwhile, Beecher, coerced by Schillinger into cross-dressing and wearing women's makeup, gets deeper and deeper into drugs. High on PCP, he hurls a chair through the glass wall of Schillinger's pod, and the flying shards nearly take out one of Schillinger's eyes. When Augustus Hill's NBA idol Jackson Vahue arrives in Oz, Hill follows his hero's lead and starts snorting heroin after two drug-free years. Kitchen workers O'Reily and Adebisi conspire to murder Schibetta by mixing ground glass into his specially prepared dishes. Said, after refusing medical treatment for high blood pressure, suffers a heart attack.

claim it was suicide, but Said suspects foul play, and the Muslim leader uses the press to demand an investigation of the numerous recent inmate deaths. To pay homage to Said's gutsiness and style, murderer and cannibal Donald Groves plans to kill Glynn, but instead he kills a C.O., Smith, by accident. Condemned to die for the murder, Groves chooses the form of execution he thinks is appropriate for political assassins: the firing squad. Meanwhile, after ingesting the steady diet of ground glass O'Reily and Adebisi have been feeding him, Schibetta hemorrhages and dies. Hill hears concert cellist Eugene Dobbins practicing and resolves to find another musician for Dobbins to practice with. He succeeds, but Vahue, in a jealous rage, seizes Dobbins's priceless cello and destroys it. Beecher, after many degradations, finds a way to get even with Schillinger.

Plan B

Huseni Murshah, who failed to come to Said's aid when the Muslim head man suffered his heart attack, is repudiated by Said when he returns from the infirmary, and is shunned by all of the faithful. Murshah is transferred to gen pop and dies under mysterious circumstances. Prison officials

A Game of Checkers

Beecher's time in the Hole doesn't improve his relations with Schillinger, whose sight might not return to his damaged eye. Meanwhile, the Muslims are planning to start a riot, but two white inmates beat them to it when they get into a fight over a game of checkers. Once the violence begins, just about every inmate in Em City joins in, trying to settle old scores and vent their pent-up frustration. The guilty and the innocent suffer equally, including Dobbins, the cellist Hill admires, who is shanked in the early mayhem of the riot. In an effort to save Dobbins's life, Hill convinces Jackson Vahue to carry the cellist out of Em City to the infirmary, but on the other side of the gate, Dobbins is neglected and Vahue abused by the angry guards. The prisoners make hostages of all staff in Em City, including Father Mukada and a number of C.O.s. Said organizes the Muslims, Homeboys, Latinos, Bikers, and Irish into a loose coalition. McManus succeeds in negotiating a swap—himself for two badly injured C.O.s—but is unable to secure the release of Whittlesey, the only woman. The rioters submit a list of demands, but Governor Devlin opts to answer with the S.O.R.T., armed with tear gas and guns. When the smoke clears, eight people are dead.

* * * * *

Season Two

The Tip

Oz is locked down after six inmates and two officers are killed in the retaking of Em City, with the prisoners transferred either to Solitary or gen pop. A special commission is appointed to investigate how Governor Devlin handled the riot, and why it happened in the first place. Legal scholar Alvah Case, the commission chairman, roams the halls with impunity, questioning both inmates and officers. Case determines that the death of inmate Scott Ross was no accident. Ross, a former Biker who'd blackmailed Whittlesey into continuing the cigarette-smuggling scheme, may have shot McManus during the riot, and someone may have retaliated. The investigation puts a bright spotlight on McManus and Whittlesey, who seem to have something to hide. Meanwhile, inside gen pop a prisoner named James Robson underestimates Beecher when he demands oral sex—and gets a painful surprise in return.

Ancient Tribes

Ten months after the riot, Em City is reopened. Refreshed and reinvigorated, McManus rethinks his vision for the unit. He creates a council representing each group to help keep order, and initiates classes so that inmates can get high school equivalency diplomas. After O'Reily tells Peter Schibetta that Adebisi was responsible for his father's death, the son cashes in a favor from Glynn and takes over the kitchen. As Schillinger's parole hearing gets closer, Beecher taunts him mercilessly—trying to ruin his quest for freedom. When Glynn's daughter is brutally raped by a group of Latinos, the warden takes out his rage on Alvarez. O'Reily learns he may have breast cancer, and Dr. Nathan's bedside manner works like a love potion, impelling O'Reily to try to win her heart in a completely heartless style.

Great Men

Diagnosed with cancer, O'Reily goes to a hospital to get a prison-paid lumpectomy, a cheaper procedure than a mastectomy. Alvarez refuses to tell Warden Glynn who raped his daughter,

even though he knows. Wangler is enjoying school, but his cellmate, Adebisi, forcibly discourages him from learning to read. Said begins studying law, planning to use the legal system against the very people who created it. When Augustus Hill's judge is convicted of accepting bribes, Said tries to get Hill a second trial. Even though the odds are stacked against him, Hill becomes intoxicated with the idea of going free. The Aryans are losing credibility in Oz, so Schillinger arranges to have a tough guy named Vogel killed. Next on his personal hit list: Beecher. In the end, the prison is galvanized by the arrival of Shirley Bellinger, a prisoner convicted of drowning her young daughter; she is placed on Death Row to await execution.

Losing Your Appeal

Despite Said's best efforts, Hill's court appeal is denied. Devastated, when the judge refuses to grant a new trial, Hill turns his anger on Said, accusing him of incompetence and valuing headlines more than results. Elsewhere Said does get results, when he

finds a way to get Poet's poems published. Meanwhile, O'Reily survives his lumpectomy and continues to lay the charm down with Dr. Nathan, sure that he can overcome her resistance. Richie Hanlon is convicted of killing an Aryan inmate and then tries to cut a deal on a murder he didn't commit. Schibetta is desperate to have Adebisi killed, and offers Alvarez a piece of his drug biz to do it. But Adebisi makes Alvarez a counteroffer. The judge who sentenced Beecher appears to have a guilty conscience, and asks to meet with him. Back in his cell, Beecher's new roommate, Chris Keller, seems to hate Aryans as much as Beecher—but as with everything in Oz, nothing is as it seems.

EPISODE FIVE
Family Bizness

Keller continues trying to convince Beecher to trust him, especially after Beecher learns that his wife has committed suicide. But even in his distraught state, Beecher rejects Keller's advances. Meanwhile, O'Reily has become so completely infatuated with Dr. Nathan that he convinces his brother Cyril to kill her husband. With the mutual hate and disgust between Adebisi and Schibetta at a breaking point, Adebisi tries poisoning his arch rival—but not

fatally. Sister Peter Marie figures out that William Giles witnessed her husband's murder, but her efforts to learn who the killer was, or why he murdered Reimondo, remain unsuccessful. Poet, now a happily published author and valedictorian of the graduating class in Oz, gets his parole, but one reformed prisoner is not enough to convince Governor Devlin to further support McManus's high school equivalency program. He discontinues state funding.

EPISODE SIX
Strange Bedfellows

Barely recovered from Adebisi's poison attempt, Schibetta enlists Pancamo to help him enact retribution. But the two are not powerful enough to overpower Adebisi, who ends up raping Schibetta in return. Schillinger wants Said to use his newly minted lawyering skills to help him fight a recent murder charge, but Said backs out when he concludes that Schillinger is guilty. When new arrival Jiggy Walker claims he was Devlin's personal crack dealer for years, Said tries to whip the media into a frenzy to embarrass and discredit the corrupt governor. But the governor, already under suspicion for other wrongdoing, exposes Walker's lie, thereby clearing his good name and

Opposite: Whittlesey and Ross hatch a smuggling scheme.

sending Said into a justifiable rage. Meanwhile, Dr. Nathan confronts O'Reily about her husband's death. Alvarez is bumped out of the Latino power seat by Raoul Hernandez, aka El Cid. Sister Pete finds out that Giles murdered the man who killed her husband, and Schillinger's conspiracy to destroy Beecher moves closer and closer to reality when Beecher falls in love with Keller.

and heavy love letters with Bellinger, but when they finally meet, Bellinger is horrified to discover that her lover is a black man. Robert Sippel, a Catholic priest who spent ten years in Oz for molesting a fourteen-year-old boy, is released. Poet returns after shooting a drug rival who attacked him at a book signing.

Animal Farm

Imprisoned for strangling Dr. Nathan's husband at his brother Ryan's request, mentally challenged Cyril O'Reily is raped by Schillinger before landing in the Hole, despite Ryan's best efforts to get him transferred to Em City. Learning that Bob Rebadow's grandson has leukemia, inmates and staff donate $3,000 to help him fulfill his lifelong dream of going to Adventure Country before he dies. El Cid convinces Alvarez that the only way he can win the respect of the Latinos is to "pluck out" the eyes of prison guard Rivera. New Mafia leader Antonio Nappa wants Adebisi to be punished for raping his godson Peter Schibetta. Adebisi wants Nappa murdered, but Kipkemei Jara, an African fortune-teller, convinces him otherwise. Adebisi exchanges hot

Escape from Oz

Two Aryans try to escape Oz via a tunnel Busmalis and Rebadow have dug, but are killed when the passageway, sabotaged by Busmalis, collapses on them. Hill gets the idea of escaping Oz by hiding in a coffin but never finds the nerve to do more than fantasize about it. Sippel reenters Oz because he can't find acceptance on the outside. Schillinger crucifies him—literally—on the gym floor. Alvarez is put into Solitary after gouging out the eyes of C.O. Eugene Rivera, who is desperately in need of a blood transfusion. When Dr. Nathan finds out that O'Reily is the only prisoner whose blood type matches Rivera's, O'Reily agrees to donate the blood on the condition that his brother Cyril is transferred to Em City. Whittlesey, transferred to gen pop, is replaced by fanatical

Aryan Brotherhood member Karl Metzger. Aided by Metzger, Keller and Schillinger finally reveal their sordid plot to destroy Beecher when they trap him in the gym, mentally break his will, and then physically break his arms and legs. Adebisi loses his mind when his fortune-teller is murdered by Wangler on orders from Antonio Nappa. Said is pardoned by Governor Devlin but makes a speech about hypocrisy, injustice, and corruption; he refuses his own freedom, choosing instead to go back to Em City.

* * * * *

Season Three

The Truth and Nothing But

The name of the prison changes to "Oswald State Correctional Facility." Clayton Hughes, whose father started out as a C.O. with the warden, appeals to Glynn to hire him. New officer Claire Howell develops more than a professional relationship with McManus. To Dr. Nathan's dismay, a managed health care company takes over control of the infirmary, leading to dire consequences for Alvarez. Cyril continues to have nightmares of his rape, and Ryan plots revenge. Said begins a hunger fast when McManus refuses to assist him in observing sunrise-to-sunset fasts. New inmates Coyle, Kahn, and Ricardo develop alliances with various veteran inmates. Keller admits to his role in setting up Beecher, which results in his immediate transfer to protective custody. Beecher finally gets revenge on Metzger for handing him over to Schillinger.

Everyone at Oz is trying to figure out who's responsible for the death of Metzger, particularly Schillinger and Said. Sean Murphy arrives to take over as C.O. administrator of Em City on a recommendation by McManus. During a conversation between Howell, McManus's latest lover, and Whittlesey, McManus comes to tell Whittlesey that her mother has died. After McManus comforts the grieving Wittlesey, Howell throws a jealous tantrum. Despite the warden's hesitation, an inmate boxing program is established and the inmates are anticipating the competition. Coyle reveals the shocking details of his crimes to Hill. He decides that Coyle should pay for what he's done. Keller, who has been in protective custody, returns to Em City, only to find himself in a painful situation. Adebisi gets approval to work in the AIDS ward. Schillinger's son Andy has been arrested. Alvarez's mental health declines because the HMO running the infirmary will not cover his medication.

Dr. Nathan takes action against medical administrator Garvey. Ricardo and Hughes both get reprimanded for a confrontation. Shirley Bellinger finds out why Richie Hanlon is on Death Row. A Russian mobster, Nikolai Stanislofsky, arrives in Em City. As the boxing matches draw nearer, each group in Oz prepares its boxer. Hill testifies against Coyle, despite the inherent dangers. Said requests assistance in protecting Hill against retaliation from the Homeboys. Nappa, Schillinger, and Guerra agree. Additionally, Nappa discovers he has AIDS and relinquishes his control of the Wise Guys to Pancamo.

Upon Andy Schillinger's arrival in Oz, Vern makes a request that he be moved to Unit B. The warden refuses, and Andy ends up in Em City, where he becomes friends with Beecher. After McManus ends his relationship with Howell and fires her, she sues him and the state for sexual harassment. Ryan sneaks drugs into Alvarez's "spritzer" in order to "fix" the boxing match. Wangler finds out that his

Opposite: Beecher finds God.

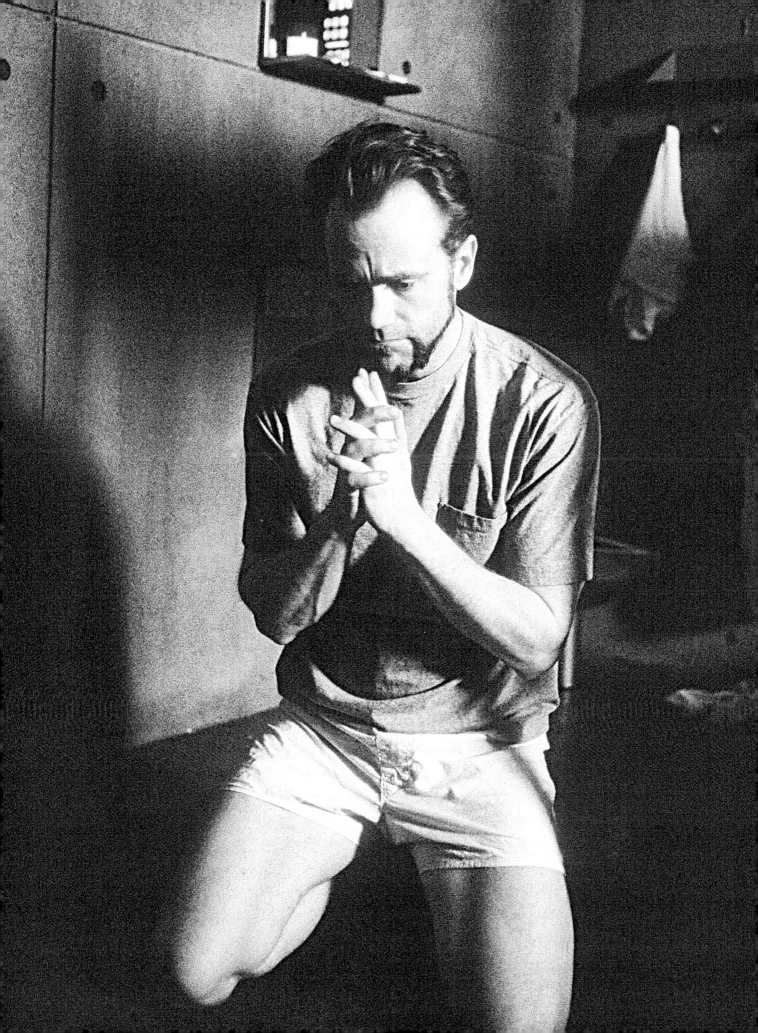

wife is cheating on him, and orchestrates the murder of her and her lover. Said's sister visits him and causes him much distress by bringing up past pain. A court overturns Richie Hanlon's death sentence, but he is subsequently murdered by Stanislofsky.

EPISODE FIVE

U.S. Male

Khan is the victor over Wangler in their boxing match. When news of Wangler's wife's murder reaches Oz, he provides convincing answers to McManus's questions. McManus's sexual harrassment suit is beginning to affect his everyday life as he struggles with his decision to settle or go to court. Beecher and Andrew's new friendship enrages Schillinger. Andrew lands in the Hole, where he dies of a heroin overdose. The newest inmate, Kosygin, an infamous assassin, is mysterious, so the other inmates keep their distance. The Muslims tell Said that his blossoming relationship with Patricia Ross must come to an end. Clayton Hughes asks Glynn for information about the death of his father, Glynn's friend and fellow C.O. in Oz.

EPISODE SIX

Cruel and Unusual Punishments

Ryan requests Kosygin's help in protecting his brother when Cudney threatens to divulge the secret behind Cyril's boxing victories. Afterward, Ryan conspires to have Kosygin and Stanislofsky eliminated, but fails. Finally, he lets the guards in on what Hernandez, Guerra, and Ricardo are doing, and they get busted. Nappa continues to work on his memoirs, dictating them to his cellmate, a gay cross-dresser named Nat ("short for Natalie") Ginzburg. McManus tried to help Wangler establish a relationship with his son by encouraging him to join the parenting program. When Beecher asks for lessons in Islam, Said invites him to join the Muslim study group. Infuriated, the Muslims oust Said as imam, and he moves to Beecher's pod. After continuing sessions with Keller, Sister Pete's questions about her own faith increase.

EPISODE SEVEN

Secret Identities

Adebisi complains to the warden that McManus fondled Wangler. Bellinger asks McManus for help in selecting the right method of execution. Nappa finishes his book. Sister Pete's anger and confusion lead her to confession and finally to question the celibate life she's chosen. Adebisi spreads anger and disorder among black and white inmates, which results in a fight and ends in a lockdown. Said convinces Beecher to forgive Keller and Schillinger for their brutal attack.

Out of Time

Miguel's plea to return to Solitary is ignored, and he ends up killing Ricardo when Guerra and Ricardo attack him. Glynn believes that he has found out who raped his daughter, but his information may be incorrect. The hostilities between whites and blacks is intensifying, but Beecher and Said continue their friendship. The warden allows the boxing finals to take place despite the racial tension. The match ends in tragedy, with Hamid Khan in an irreversible coma from Cyril's final punch. Hill is sent to Solitary for possessing a contraband copy of *Hustler*. Clayton Hughes leaves Oz, and an explosive holiday gift arrives for an inmate.

●   ●   ●   ●   ●

Season Four

A Cock and Bulls Story

At a meeting of the entire prison population, Glynn threatens grave disciplinary steps if there is a recurrence of interracial violence. Then he ends the lockdown. Hamid Khan's family sues for the right to have him removed from life support, and they ask Said to pray at his bedside when the plug is finally pulled. Saying that he has lost the taste for power, Said assures Arif that he will not oppose him as the Muslims' chosen leader now that Khan is dead. Meanwhile, Cyril's guilt at having delivered the death blow to Khan in their boxing match causes him nightmares, and his behavior fluctuates dangerously. When big brother Ryan asks Sister Pete to help, she suggests an interaction among the O'Reilys, Gloria Nathan, and Preston Nathan's parents, but Gloria rejects the idea. When a long-term resident in Solitary commits suicide by eating away at his own flesh, Sean Murphy proposes allowing Solitary inmates out of their cells for an hour's exercise every day, hoping to improve their mental and emotional states. The plan backfires when William Giles reacts to a conversation between Miguel

Alvarez and Louis Bevilacqua by stabbing both men. Bevilacqua dies. Father Mukada counsels Beecher to make peace with Schillinger by performing a secret act of kindness, and Beecher decides it's worth a try. After a miscarriage ends her pregnancy, Shirley Bellinger returns to Death Row facing execution. Hill gets a new podmate, a Jamaican named Desmond Mobay, whom Hill immediately distrusts because of Mobay's edgy manner and eagerness to make connections in the drug trade. Another newbie, Ralph Gulino, lets Stanislofsky con him out of his cell phone, which turns into a sought-after hot potato in Em City. Governor Devlin recruits Glynn as a candidate for lieutenant governor, even though he realizes that Devlin just wants to offset his opponent law professor Alvah Case's appeal to black voters. McManus, who'd bought an engagement ring for Whittlesey, learns from Sister Pete that Diane won't be returning from vacation; she's fallen in love with a Buckingham Palace guard in London. Guillaume Tarrant, distraught after being robbed and roughed up by Wangler and friends, receives drugs from O'Reily and a gun from Adebisi. Accosted by Wangler again, Tarrant starts shooting wildly, and the body count mounts up quickly.

Mobay's efforts to be accepted as a member of the Homeboys are rebuffed by Adebisi, who doesn't trust him. After McManus sings a racially insensitive song at the memorial service for Officer Howard, the Em City C.O. who was killed by one of the bullets from Tarrant's gun, Glynn fires him. Chances of a larger exodus loom as Sister Pete continues to question her vocation as a nun. A private investigator, hired by Beecher's father has located Hank Schillinger. Hank agrees to pay a visit to his father—for a fee that the Beechers pay through Father Mukada. Hill thinks he recognizes a woman visiting Mobay as the cop who found Hill after he was thrown off the roof, and this increases his suspicion that Mobay isn't who he claims to be. Said breaks off with Patricia Ross, but his legal efforts to overturn Jason Cramer's conviction meet with strong opposition from the Muslims. Without his homeys Wangler and Pierce, Poet is distraught, but Adebisi advises him to accept the facts and live in the here and now. O'Reily becomes obsessed with Gulino's cell phone and battles Stanislofsky for possession of it. Bellinger keeps busy in her cell, entertaining a C.O. and perhaps an inmate, too. Busmalis, working in the infirmary, escapes through a new tunnel and takes Alvarez with him.

Opposite: Busmalis and other inmates are entertained by Miss Sally's Schoolyard.

Escapes make the public nervous, so Glynn's potential candidacy is in danger when Busmalis and Alvarez turn up missing and the tunnel is discovered. Closer to home, Hernandez tells Glynn that Tarrant got his gun from Adebisi, but that it was Clayton Hughes who originally gave it to Adebisi. When Hughes admits to planting the gun right after Glynn fired him, the warden arrests him. Adebisi and Pancamo offer Hernandez's share of the drug business to Morales, if he'll eliminate Hernandez. Morales subcontracts the job to Rebadow, who accepts when he realizes that Morales hasn't really left him any other option. His time as Hernandez's podmate is brief, but he's soon reunited with Busmalis, who is recaptured loitering outside Miss Sally's apartment. Rebadow chastises him for not including him in the escape party. Adebisi returns from the Hole, more determined than ever to force Glynn to replace McManus with a black man as Em City unit manager. O'Reily continues his efforts to get control of the cell phone, and as in most of O'Reily's schemes, someone ends up dead—this time Gulino, the phone's original owner, when Hoyt administers an overdose of heroin. Said wins a new trial for Jason Cramer—a victory he regrets when he realizes Cramer will

go free on a technicality—and Shirley Bellinger delivers surprising news to her ex-husband. When Schillinger learns that Beecher was responsible for locating Hank, the Aryan suspects a plot and vows to take the offensive by paying Hank to kidnap Beecher's two young children.

McManus returns to Oz, but since Glynn has hired Martin Querns to run Em City, McManus is forced to take over Unit B. When Beecher's children are reported kidnapped, Beecher grows frantic and frustrated, especially because the FBI insists on treating the case as a ransom situation. Schillinger pretends innocence and ignorance, so Beecher enlists the help of an inmate, Eli Zabitz, who has connections to kidnappers. What Beecher doesn't know is that Schillinger is paying Zabitz to feed Beecher false information. When a package containing the severed hand of his murdered son, Gary, is delivered to Oz, Beecher does a tailspin. Meanwhile, as the date of Bellinger's hanging gets closer, the efforts of the anti—death penalty faction increase. The cardinal visits Oz, determined to dissuade Sister Pete from resigning her orders. Said reports that the court has ruled in the inmates' favor in regards to their lawsuit connected to the riot, but the plaintiffs are disappointed when they learn that the state plans to appeal rather than pay the $45 million award. More legal news reaches Oz: Just as Rebadow had predicted, Jason Cramer has been acquitted; there were no witnesses and no evidence against him in his retrial for his lover's murder. O'Reily's futile search for the cell phone continues, but he gets distracted when Dr. Nathan decides to come back to work sooner than expected. As the morning of Bellinger's execution dawns, the condemned woman hints that it was Vern Schillinger—"Satan in the form of a man"—who'd gotten her pregnant and tells Glynn that a corrupt C.O., Lopresti, had been visiting her Death Row cell for sex at night.

Gray Matter

After Shirley Bellinger is hanged, another Death Row inmate, Mark Miles, uses her hand mirror to help him paint a self-portrait on his cell wall. Across the corridor, Nappa murderer Nat Ginzburg is beginning to show severe symptoms of AIDS, and he asks to have his execution date moved up. The third resident of the block, Moses Deyell, severely injures his hand when he flies into a rage at Miles's racist name-calling. To prove that he's not an undercover narc, Mobay is ordered by the drug lords to commit a murder. A new prisoner, the rogue cop Bruno Goergen, whom Mobay knows from the streets, threatens to blow Mobay's cover. Hill is enlisted as an unwitting—and unwilling—accomplice to Goergen's murder, a ploy that increases his distrust of Mobay. Whittlesey phones McManus from London; she wants to be friends, but he hangs up on her. Supreme Allah, a member of the Five Percent Nation, arrives and immediately challenges the authority of both the Muslims and the Homeboys. Beecher leaves Oz to attend his son's funeral. Rebadow, invigorated after murdering Hernandez, tries to kill Busmalis. Cyril O'Reily's behavior becomes more and more erratic, and when he gets into another fight, Dr. Nathan ups the dosage of his sedatives. Ryan O'Reily finally ends up with the cell phone after Hoyt fumbles it in a struggle with Stanislofsky, and he meets Dr. Nathan's attacker, who's incarcerated in Oz after his conviction for the rape.

A homicide detective, McGorey, begins questioning inmates about Goergen's death, and Mobay's at the top of her list. Meanwhile, Mobay's addiction to tits grows just as the drug cartel increases its pressure on him to prove himself as a dealer. Realizing his own addiction, he turns to Sister Pete for help. The atmosphere in Em City deteriorates, as Querns seems not to notice anything the black inmates do as long as there's no violence. He continues replacing white prisoners and staff with blacks, beefing up the palace guard around him and adding foot soldiers for Adebisi's effort to take full control of the unit. When Arif complains that the Muslims are being ignored and challenges Querns's authority, an arrogant Querns throws him out of his office. Sister Pete convinces Glynn to move up the date of Ginzburg's execution, in order to reduce his suffering from the symptoms of AIDS. Glynn tries to balance his personal and political lives, with uncertain success. Beecher's daughter is returned alive to the home of Beecher's parents by her kidnappers, while the FBI determines that Keller had nothing to do with the abduction. Meanwhile, Keller confesses to Father Mukada that he murdered men he'd picked up in gay bars,

but when Mukada refuses to absolve him, he gets angry. Stanislofsky finally gets revenge in the cell phone fiasco when a well-timed call leads the C.O.s to its hiding place.

Howell starts getting it on with O'Reily and, to prove her devotion, she electrocutes Stanislofsky as he relaxes in the bathtub. After he's released from the Hole, Rebadow tries to make peace with Busmalis. Cyril makes a recovery that surprises everyone, including the doctors and his brother. Homicide detective McGorey starts interrogating Hill about Goergen's murder, and she isn't impressed by his innocent act. Hill confronts Mobay, who attacks him. Adrift, Arif turns to Said for guidance, and Said starts looking for a way to end Querns's and Adebisi's control of Em City. To get closer to the action, Said pledges his loyalty to Adebisi and moves into the head Homeboy's pod. Hank Schillinger beats the kidnapping rap, so Beecher takes out a contract on Hank's life with Pancamo. After Keller threatens to kill

Eli Zabitz, a terrified Zabitz asks Schillinger for protection. Schillinger agrees but instead sends Robson to eliminate Zabitz, who succumbs to a heart attack when confronted with both attackers. Hughes, now raging out of control, nearly succeeds in assassinating Devlin at a press conference. Keller turns to Mukada in his search for the road to Beecher and salvation.

You Bet Your Life

After the governor is shot on Glynn's turf, the warden withdraws from the race for lieutenant governor. A bloody corpse in the laundry room suggests that Querns is losing control of his unit, and Querns orders Adebisi to find the killer. Adebisi's suspicion focuses on Beecher, since the dead man, Nate Shamin, was a former sexual partner of Beecher's. When Mondo Browne's corpse turns up outside Em City, Querns's worries deepen. His investigative efforts point to Supreme Allah as the culprit, but Supreme's really been framed for the two killings by O'Reily and Keller. Mobay, conscience-stricken, comes clean about his involvement in Oz's recent crimes. After Cyril O'Reily remarks, "We don't choose God, God chooses us," Sister Pete finds a rea-

son to remain a nun. On Death Row, Miles goes on another racist tirade, and Deyell throttles him through a hole he's dug in the wall separating their cells. Vern learns his daughter-in-law's pregnant, and the prospect of a grandchild mellows him. Looking for evidence of Adebisi's crimes, Said hears from Poet about the videotapes of Adebisi's in-pod "parties." To test Said's loyalty, Adebisi gives Said a tape, but Said turns the evidence over to McManus. The result? Querns gets fired, and McManus is reinstated and plans to transfer Adebisi and his cronies out of Em City to Unit B. Enraged about these new developments, Adebisi confronts Said and the two struggle behind the drawn curtains of their pod. Both are badly wounded, but it is Adebisi who becomes the last casualty of the unrest in Em City.

Medium Rare

Adebisi's legacy of crime and disorder continues to haunt Em City. A team from an investigative TV news show arrives in Oz to film a report from the front lines of the prison system. When Glynn refuses them access, he learns that the crew already has the blessings of both the commissioner and the governor. Ryan O'Reily remembers Jack

Eldridge, the journalist, as the man who'd done an exposé of the O'Reilys' street gang twenty years earlier, and he immediately starts plotting his revenge. After interviewing a number of inmates—including Poet, who asserts there's been a cover-up and presses the show's producer to hunt for Adebisi's videotapes—the target of the report becomes Adebisi's death. When McManus gets wind of this, he implores Glynn to destroy Adebisi's tapes or risk a scandal that could cost them both their careers. Eldridge plans to spend a night in a pod with newbie Omar White, whose first days in Oz are being recorded by the TV crew, but after White attacks the reporter, Eldridge opts to make Cyril O'Reily his podmate instead. The stunt backfires when Cyril recognizes the reporter as the author of the earlier exposé and beats him viciously, yelling, "You gave my mama cancer!" over and over.

Conversions

McManus introduces a new device for disciplining unruly inmates: a cage in the center of the Common Room. New inmate Burr Redding, surrogate father and mentor to Hill, arrives and starts maneuvering to take control of the drug business. Dr. Nathan returns, after a leave following the murder of Patrick Keenan, the man who raped her. Tidd, distraught about Adebisi's death, proposes a plan to kill Said to Schillinger, hoping for his support. Meanwhile, Reverend Cloutier, evangelical preacher and embezzler, entices Schillinger with promises of inner peace. Several dozen illegal aliens from China are housed in Em City while the government decides their fate, and their leader gets used and then discarded by Morales in his power struggle with Redding. Glynn, who needs a new secretary after a disastrous attempt to have Busmalis do the job, hires an administrative whiz with looks to match. Meanwhile, Busmalis, out of a job, falls in love—with Miss Sally's secretary.

Revenge Is Sweet

After Morales spreads a false story about Redding's hatred of Asians, the Homeboys' honcho is accused of killing Bian Yixhue, the Chinese illegals' spokesman, but Redding asserts his innocence. Alvarez, looking for a way out of Solitary, offers to be Glynn's eyes and ears in Em City, but when he proposes playing double agent to Morales, all Enrique wants Alvarez to do is get Redding out of the way. Robson and Hoyt warn

Reverend Cloutier not to try converting Schillinger. Schillinger, though, is looking for peace of mind, and he opens his first counseling interaction session with Beecher by reading a passage from Scripture. Tidd works his way toward winning Said's trust by defending Arif in a fight with the Aryans, but what the Muslims don't realize is that the Aryans have staged the incident expressly to make Tidd look like a hero in the Muslims' eyes. Arif pleads with Said to recognize Tidd's conversion as sincere. Hill discovers that Jackson Vahue is coming up for parole and decides to warn Vahue's victim, Beverly Reed, so she can have her say to the Parole Board. As a result, Vahue's parole is denied. Busmalis requests permission to marry his true love, Norma Clark. When Glynn runs into Querns, now the warden at Lardner, at the wardens' conference, Querns gives him dire news about Clayton Hughes. Glynn decides to transfer Hughes to Oz, where he thinks he can protect him from physical harm. Hughes ends up in Unit J, for bad cops, which is also where Johnny Basil (aka Desmond Mobay) is locked up. Newbie Ronnie Barlog is an old pal of Keller's, but when Ronnie boasts about Beecher and blow jobs, Keller sees red. The FBI offers Ronnie a sentence reduction in exchange for corroborating evidence of Keller's involvement in some past murders. After Ronnie asks Beecher for his legal opinion, Beecher warns Keller that he's about to be sold out. At first Keller doesn't believe him. When Keller doesn't like Ronnie's answers to his questions about the FBI interrogator, he decides to take matters into his own powerful hands. The Weigert Corporation looks for inmates to test a new drug designed to speed up aging and thereby reduce overcrowding in prisons. Em City inmates flock to participate, in hopes of getting early releases.

EPISODE TWELVE
Cuts Like a Knife

Back in Em City, Alvarez is considered an outcast by both the Homeboys and his own Latino brothers. When one of the Latinos challenges him, he slits the man's throat and is sent back to Solitary. McManus is alone in opposing the drug experiment, even after inmates like Cyril O'Reily start to age rapidly. A Biker named Wick collapses and dies from the drug. Tidd, now Salah Udeen, is welcomed into the Muslim fold. With easy access to Said, he prepares to shank the leader while he sleeps, but at the last moment he experiences a true conversion and becomes a steadfast follower instead. Omar White stabs McManus, thinking the other inmates will now respect him. Johnny Basil gets a visit from his former partner, but only because their lieutenant demanded it. Jia Kenmin, responsible for the Chinese refugees' plight, arrives in Oz for other crimes. Supreme Allah comes back to Em City from Solitary, and Redding spurns him. Hill is puzzled until Redding reveals that it was Supreme Allah who betrayed Hill's whereabouts to the cops the night he was arrested. When Hill confronts Supreme Allah about Redding's accusations, Supreme Allah first denies his role and then beats Hill mercilessly, landing him in the infirmary. Father Mukada meets Reverend Cloutier for the first time, and they argue about Timmy Kirk's "conversion" from Roman Catholicism to born-again Christianity. Schillinger learns that his son Hank is dead. He suspects Beecher and plots his revenge until Keller, in a rare selfless act, convinces Schillinger that he was responsible for Hank's death, thereby sparing Beecher and his family further tragedy. As Keller prepares to leave Oz to stand trial in Massachusetts for Hank's murder, Sister Pete assures him that God has finally chosen him.

A storm brews when the Wick family sues Oz over the death that resulted from the aging-drug tests. Meanwhile, Dr. Nathan's being investigated by the state medical board for her part in the ill-advised tests, and if she's found to be culpable, she could lose her medical license. Ryan O'Reily meets a woman named Suzanne Fitzgerald, who claims to be his real mother, a former member of the Weather Underground who walked out on her abusive husband and infant son more than thirty years earlier. Ryan immediately starts worrying that he's going to lose his mother who has long been on the run. Suzanne has decided to turn herself in to face the charges pending since her activist youth. Sexually speaking, Howell tells Ryan that the thrill is gone and she's thinking about taking Cyril as her next partner. Johnny Basil finally gets the courage to face his wife, after encouragement from Glynn. On the eve of his wedding day, Busmalis confesses to Rebadow that he's a virgin, but the next day he's left at the altar. When Schillinger tells Kerry, his daughter-in-law, that Hank's body has been found, she immediately goes into labor, and Dr. Nathan delivers the baby—a first for the Oz infirmary. Beecher meets a lawyer, Catherine McClain, who tells him his parole chances are decent as long as he stays out of trouble. She takes a personal interest in him as well. Instead of minding his manners, Beecher gets into a fight with his new podmate, Edward Gallson, an ex-Marine officer with a dangerous drinking problem, and lands in the Hole. Vahue convinces himself that he doesn't need Sister Pete's help, even though he really does, and instead takes Redding's advice to upgrade his highs by mainlining heroin instead of snorting it. Redding's plan to kill off his drug-dealing rivals fails when Hill goes behind his back to the hacks. As a result, Hill ends up persona non grata to his lifelong mentor and the Homeboys. Giles throws the future of capital punishment into question when he demands to be stoned to death. Deyell declares his desire to donate his organs after he's executed, but he wants to meet the beneficiaries, a complicated proposition. Salah Udeen proves his devotion to Said the hard way, by throwing himself in the path of a shank meant for his imam, making the supreme sacrifice.

EPISODE FOURTEEN
Orpheus Descending

McManus, recovered from his stab wound, lays down the law to Redding and Morales: Shape up or ship out to gen pop. Supreme Allah goes to Pancamo with a plan to get Hill to kill

Redding. Redding and his new cellmate, "the Colonel," cultivate a delicate alliance. McManus is still determined to help White change, even after White stabbed him. He devises a scheme to make White a special rehab project of Said's. Basil's wife visits, and Basil asks her to bring their son next time; he's ready to face the boy. Unfortunately, Hughes, on a rampage, kills Basil before his new attitude has a chance to bear fruit. Glynn's secretary finds him drinking to excess in his office, despondent over problems in his personal life and his failure to save Clayton Hughes. She offers to drive him home. Sister Pete arranges for Beecher and Keller to talk by phone when she sees how depressed Beecher is without his lover. Schillinger starts to doubt his granddaughter's paternity after a new inmate, a pimp, reveals that he'd seen Kerry turning tricks on the same streets as his girls. Said asks Cloutier to persuade Jenkins to testify about Robson's role in Udeen's death. Jenkins confesses, but Cloutier gets a visit from Schillinger and the Aryans, warning him to keep his nose out of the Brotherhood's business. Jenkins, in Solitary, receives a death threat that convinces him to take his own life. Later, he's discovered hanging in his cell. Cyril O'Reily puts Jia in a coma during a fight in the gym.

Even the Score

When Guerra rats out White to McManus because Omar's still using drugs, McManus orders a shakedown and gives White a stark but simple choice: stay clean and go to counseling or take up permanent residence in Solitary. White complies, but at the first drug rehab session, he starts a fight and gets thrown into the Hole again. On the basketball front, McManus provokes Vahue into challenging him to a two-on-two staff vs. immates series. McManus and C.O. Dave Brass lose game 1, but Brass does so well a Sacramento Kings scout comes to watch him in game 2. Things turn sour when Vahue (victim of a C.O.'s spite because Vahue outclassed the staff in game 1) insists on playing hurt and the inmates lose. The gamblers who lost big on game 2 decide to end Brass's career, and an inmate severs his Achilles tendon during a staged melee in Unit B. When Redding learns that Supreme Allah and Tug Daniels are plotting to kill him, the Homeboys' leader serves as Daniels' judge and executioner. Sister Pete refuses to go along with Governor Devlin's scheme to have Giles declared insane in order to get around the problems created by Giles' unconventional choice of execution. Padraic Connolly, I.R.A. radical and political refugee, forms a dangerous alliance with O'Reily. Together they plot to blow up Em City. Despite his acquittal in Adebisi's death on grounds of self-defense, Said, an advocate of nonviolence, continues to be tormented by what he has done.

Famous Last Words

Hill keeps trying to talk to Redding, but is constantly rebuffed. Well aware of Supreme Allah's plans to murder Redding, Hill gets hold of Supreme Allah's medical records and connives with Poet to bring about Supreme's demise. Redding thanks Hill and offers to bring him back into the fold. Hill welcomes the renewal of their friendship but declines the invitation to peddle tits again. The Colonel's attempt to kill Morales, on assignment from Redding, backfires, and Gallson ends up crushed by the freight elevator. Cloutier's fortunes suffer a reversal when he is stripped of his eminent position in his church and endures the renunciation of his former followers, who wall him up behind a refrigerator in the kitchen and leave him to starve to death. After Hughes overpowers a C.O. to take control of the Solitary block, Glynn goes in alone to calm him down. Hughes tries to kill Glynn but dies himself when another inmate, Greg Penders, wrests the shank from him. In despair, Glynn dictates a letter of resignation to his secretary, but she refuses to type it up. Murphy offers to be McManus's teammate in the final basketball game. McManus is routed in the first round of the popular TV game show *Up Your Ante*. His one-man fan club, Omar White, attacks the inmates who laughed at McManus's ignorance on the quiz show. When McManus confronts him about his loss of control, White snaps again and this time roughs up his hero. Beecher's chances for parole look bright, and this enrages Schillinger. He and Robson attempt to ambush Beecher in the library, but a vigilant, enraged Said shanks them instead. O'Reily's mother persuades him that bombs aren't the answer, so he warns Glynn of Connolly's plans to detonate a bomb in Oz. When Connolly discovers he's been betrayed, he rushes back to retrieve the device from its hiding place in his pod and sets the timer. As the clock ticks off the seconds before detonation, the Common Room is cleared of staff and inmates, who take refuge behind Oz's thick stone walls. When the bomb fails to explode, the S.O.R.T. charges the I.R.A. radical and subdues him. A little while later, a C.O. on a cig-arette break lights a match in the kitchen, unaware that O'Reily had left the gas on. A major explosion destroys sections of the prison but frees the trapped Cloutier from behind the wall.

• • • • •

Season Five

Visitation

Following the destruction wreaked by the gas explosion, the newly rebuilt Oz reopens with a ribbon-cutting ceremony, led by the governor. Though Warden Glynn has changed his mind about resigning, he remains pessimistic. White, Alvarez, Penders, and the other inmates in Solitary are temporarily transferred to Em City while the air ducts in their wing of the prison are cleaned. Back in circulation, Alvarez faces off with Guerra, but the C.O.s intervene and Guerra is sent to the Cage. In the gym, Alvarez threatens Morales, but Giles lands a punch. White ridicules Guerra in the Cage, only to replace him there after getting into another fight. Cloutier is returned to Oz from the Benchley

Memorial Burn Unit, unable to speak and barely able to move. Kirk has taken over Cloutier's congregation, while Hoyt languishes in Solitary. A Catholic priest, Father Meehan, arrives in Em City determined to change Ryan O'Reily's attitude about life. Still recovering from their stab wounds in the infirmary, Schillinger and Robson plan to take revenge on the Muslims. Glynn calls a mass meeting in the cafeteria to warn the Muslims and Aryans against violence. Said, in the Hole for shanking Schillinger and Robson, intends to plead guilty to charges of attempted murder. Sister Pete initiates an interaction involving Beecher, Said, and Schillinger, but Robson keeps things stirred up when he delivers a foul package to Said. Arif reveals to Glynn that he saw O'Reily murder Keenan, but he refuses to testify publicly out of fear of retaliation. Meanwhile, Ryan, busy trying to rekindle the connection to Dr. Nathan, shifts suspicion for Keenan's death to Henry Stanton by planting evidence in his cell. Hill gets a letter from a lawyer informing him that his wife has filed for a divorce. Depressed, he focuses on the impending visit from his mother, who is riding on a bus with other prisoners' family members for the visiting day. The entire population is shocked by news that the bus has crashed, claiming many of the lives of those on board, including Hill's

mother, Eugenia; Sonsyrea, Arif's wife; Morales's sister, Annette; and Schillinger's daughter-in-law, Kerry. Father Mukada, also on the bus, survives, but is badly injured.

Laws of Gravity

Because of his fued with Guerra, Alvarez proposes a novel way to resolve the dispute: Guerra will stab Alvarez in the shoulder without killing him, and Alvarez won't retaliate. When Guerra secretly plans to murder Alvarez, Morales forbids Guerra to do so. Unable to grieve for his sister, who died in the bus crash, Morales wants a moratorium on violence. Guerra and Alvarez keep their appointment in the gym, surrounded by witnesses. Hill prepares to leave Oz to attend his mother's funeral. As a non-relative, Redding isn't allowed to join him, but he gives Augustus a memento—his high school graduation ring—to place in Eugenia's grave. Rebadow defends Busmalis from Poet's ridicule, but then gets more bad news about his grandson's health and starts to search for alternative therapies for leukemia. Montgomery—who'd given false testimony against Henry Stanton regarding Keenan's murder demands more hush money from Ryan, who devises a plan to have Mont-

Opposite: Father Mukada, one of the few survivors of the bus crash.

gomery eliminated instead. A suspicious Glynn confronts O'Reily with the shamrock and chain taken from Keenan's body after he was murdered. Suzanne Fitzgerald arrives in Oz to start an arts program; she's been sentenced to perform community service after confessing to crimes committed during her radical underground past. O'Reily intimidates inmates into signing up, but then tries to convince her to quit. Officer Brass returns to Oz, with limited mobility. He wants to know who attacked him, hoping for revenge on whoever it was who ruined his chances for a career in pro basketball. McManus confesses that he misled Morales into believing that Brass planned to play in Game 3. When Glynn refuses to assign Brass to any area but reception, McManus urges his ex-teammate to sue the prison. Ellie O'Connor, McManus's ex-wife, arrives as the governor's liaison to the state prisons, but memories of their failed marriage prevent McManus and O'Connor from collaborating effectively. Peter Schibetta returns to Em City from the psych unit, after recovering from the trauma of having been raped. Meanwhile, the FBI suspects that Pancamo is responsible for Hank Schillinger's death, and when Agent Taylor shares his suspicion with Vern, Schillinger shanks Pancamo. With Pancamo in the infirmary, Schibetta starts thinking about reclaiming his old position as leader of the Wise Guys. Said's

seething rage causes him to attack a new convert, Ahmed Lalar, over a minor infraction, while McManus makes a bold, desperate proposal to help Said regain self-control and save Omar White. McManus makes Said White's mentor, in hopes of curbing White's erratic and sometimes bizarre behavior. White moves into Said's pod, with orders to obey Said implicitly. Mukada returns to Oz after recovering from his injuries in the bus crash and asks to see Cloutier, in order to pray with him. Kirk tries to convince Mukada to allow him to officiate at an ecumenical service, but Mukada refuses. Kirk decides to have Cloutier killed before he recovers sufficiently to expose Kirk's part in walling him up. When Jim Byrnes has a vision in which Cloutier orders him to kill Hoyt and Kirk, Byrnes dies in the attempt. Hoyt is sent to the Hole, where he begins to receive visions from the Reverend.

Dream a Little Dream of Me

In the infirmary, Alvarez tells Glynn he doesn't know who stabbed him, and the warden observes that the wound was suspiciously close to Alvarez's heart. Back in Em City, Alvarez confronts Guerra, but Morales declares the feud between the two rivals set-tled. Miguel also gains a follower: Jaime Velez, who was impressed by Alvarez's gutsiness in taking the shank. Brass, reassigned to the cafeteria, pressures Morales, but the Latino leader won't reveal the identity of Brass's attacker. Reb-adow asks Brass to buy him a lottery ticket, with the winning numbers God had revealed to him. Busmalis starts a letter writing campaign to get *Miss Sally's Schoolyard* back on the air. Jia Kenmin recovers from his coma and offers to make peace with the O'Reilys. Cyril accepts, but Ryan remains distrustful. When Jia and newbie Li Chen sign up for singing lessons with O'Reily's mom, Ryan worries for his mother's safety. Schillinger, out of the Hole, ral-lies the Aryan Brotherhood to retal-iate against Pancamo. In the infirmary, Peter Schibetta consults with Pancamo about how to deal with Schillinger. Peter Schibetta approaches Said about forming an alliance against Schillinger. Said declines, so Schibetta goes it alone and is raped again, this time by Vern. When Poet informs Redding that Schillinger's back in Unit B, Red-ding seizes the opportunity to make a pact with Morales: They'll shut out the Wise Guys and share the drug trade. Keller returns to Oz, after being cleared of charges in the Hank Schillinger murder case. He refuses to cooperate with the FBI's investi-gation of the murder, but asks Sis-ter Pete to help him make contact with Beecher. Meanwhile, Beecher makes the same request, but Glynn refuses. Robson and Said face off, but Arif intervenes. Beecher, Said, and Schillinger resume their inter-actions, but their progress is short-circuited when they disagree about drugs. At the same time, Said warns White about using drugs, and McManus challenges Said to stick with the struggle of turning White around. When Said discovers that White's interested in singing, a door opens, and White starts taking lessons from Suzanne Fitzgerald. His incessant practicing annoys the neighbors—until McManus finds him a private practice room. Meanwhile, Glynn, O'Connor, and McManus argue about funding for the arts program, but ultimately find a way to continue it. Redding reminisces about Hill's parents' involvement in civil rights, but his words are no consolation to a grieving Augustus. When Guerra talks about his girlfriend visiting places he'll never get to see, Augustus reveals his impending divorce. Kirk sends a Biker to Cloutier's infir-mary room in another attempt to elim-inate the Reverend, but Dr. Nathan thwarts the attempt in the nick of time. When Hoyt is released from the Hole, Cloutier, in a vision, tells him to kill Kirk. He fails in that attempt but confesses to a string of killings he has committed. On

Mukada's next visit to Cloutier in his private room, the chaplain discovers that the Reverend—who still can't walk or speak—has vanished, just before Easter Sunday.

Next Stop, Valhalla

Alvarez tells Velez to kill Guerra, but Chico outsmarts the young Latino and fractures his skull against the shower wall. Guilt-ridden, Alvarez confesses to Father Mukada, who is still searching for the reason he survived the bus crash. A guide dog training program is introduced in Oz, and Alvarez, Hill, and Penders are selected as the first three participants. While looking for his assailant in Unit B, Brass gets a vile shower from Carlos Martinez, an inmate, who is fiercely beaten by the hacks and thrown into Solitary. When Dr. Nathan warns Brass about the risks of HIV infection, he gets enraged. Dr. Nathan tries to treat the badly bruised Martinez in his cell, who starts fondling her. She flashes on her rape and pummels him. At their interaction, Beecher and Said try to force Schillinger to admit to having raped Beecher. When Schillinger denies the charge, Beecher loses control. Later, Schillinger warns Schibetta not to name names when talking about his recent rape. Sister Pete offers to help Keller find a lawyer, and Catherine McClain, Beecher's lawyer and new love interest, agrees to consider representing Keller. When Beecher discovers that Adam Guenzel, the son of a family friend, has been imprisoned for raping a young woman, he seeks a way to protect the newbie from sexual predators. Said declines Beecher's plea to help Guenzel, and McManus refuses to place the young man in protective custody. Beecher convinces Pancamo to dispatch Wise Guy Frank Urbano to save Guenzel from Robson. Nathan suggests that O'Reily tell his mother the full story of his misdeeds. While Ryan is making up his mind, Li Chen attempts to kill him, but Cyril grabs the knife and shanks Chen instead. Chen dies, Cyril is sent to Solitary, and Ryan is placed in the Cage. In mourning for his mother, Hill rejects Beecher's macabre advice and seeks solace in drugs he obtains from Poet. Redding asks Glynn for control of the kitchen and enlists White as a courier for the delivery of drugs to a gen pop dealer. White's singing starts to annoy Said, so the imam redoubles his effort to empathize with his charge which causes the Muslims to complain that he's distracted. Robson decides to attack the Muslims' weakest link, Ahmed Lalar. Together with another Aryan, Robson lacerates Lalar with a box cutter.

EPISODE FIVE
Wheel of Fortune

Said and Arif tell Glynn that Robson has murdered Lalar, but the warden hesitates about taking action. Robson gets White agitated by calling him Said's "slave." Angry and full of rage, Said confronts White about muling drugs. Unsatisfied with White's response, Said beats him severely. McManus gets White to confide in him, but gets nowhere with Said, who prefers to stay in the Hole and face his demons. Chucky Pancamo's condition worsens, and he starts to fear that he is dying. On orders from Schillinger, Franklin Winthrop gets into a fight with Guenzel, part of a plan to make Guenzel suspect Beecher of homosexuality. After Guenzel accuses Beecher of being gay, Schillinger offers Tobias a deal: A job delivering the mail, which will give him access to Keller, in return for having Guenzel transferred to gen pop, where Schillinger can turn him into his prag. Beecher, desperate to see Keller and angered by Guenzel's behavior, agrees. Keller discovers the feds have compelling evidence linking him to a past murder. Meanwhile, Howell makes her move on Keller. Rebadow's lottery ticket wins, but Brass claims the prize for himself, disappearing with the money. Hill, gravely ill from heavy drug use, is hospitalized with septicemia and

drops out of the guide dog training program. The program continues with the two remaining volunteers, Alvarez and Penders. Morales asks Mukada about his sister, who died in the bus crash. Mukada hints at her marital problems, so Morales invited Annette's husband to visit him in Oz. When his brother-in-law arrives, Morales bashes his head in and is sent to the Hole. Kirk seeks to return to Roman Catholicism, but Mukada rejects his entreaty. Catherine McClain urges the O'Reily family to hire a big-name lawyer to save Cyril from the death penalty for killing Chen, but Cyril's father and aunt refuse to help pay the costs, and Ryan fears for his brother's life.

EPISODE SIX
Variety

Said returns from the Hole, contrite, and the Muslims welcome him back to Em City. He apologizes to White, who explains how he was coerced into moving drugs for Redding. Said declares himself cured of his former "addiction to power." The inmate variety show takes shape with Mukada as MC and White the featured performer. Suffering from stage fright, White seeks advice about performing from Poet and comes away with a vial of heroin, just in case he needs false courage. But

Omar swallows his fears and sings on stage—without the need of drugs. Robson's painful teeth force him to the dentist, something he secretly fears—and not simply because the dentist is a person of color. The dentist recommends gum replacement surgery. Alvarez wants to give his dog, Julie, to Rivera, the Oz guard he blinded, at the end of the training program. When the Riveras are told about the proposal, they refuse, angered and suspicious of Alvarez's true intentions. As Cyril's trial looms, Ryan tries to figure out a way to save his brother. Redding continues to search for the culprit who gave Hill the drugs. Poet, in an attempt to hide his involvement from Redding, forces Busmalis to tell Redding that one of the Wise Guys, Salvatore DeSantos, did the deed. This results in Redding putting a megadose of LSD in DeSantos's food, and Salvatore's brain explodes. Schibetta declines Sister Pete's recommendation that he enter therapy to recover from his post-rape trauma, and Glynn refuses to help identify the inmates who raped Peter. A vengeful Kirk hires arsonists to set fire to the rectory where Mukada lives; Mukada suffers smoke-inhalation and minor burns, but several priests lose their lives. Chucky's condition worsens and out of fear, he summons Sister Peter for spiritual help. McClain withdraws as Keller's lawyer when she realizes that he's been dishonest and manipu-lative and is probably guilty. In response to her questions, Beecher admits that he'd misled her about Keller as well, so McClain breaks off her relationship with him, too. Beecher repents his abandonment of Guenzel when he finds Adam naked in the gym, traumatized and weeping after being gang-raped by the Aryans.

EPISODE SEVEN
Good Intentions

Hill returns from the hospital, but is isolated in the private room in the infirmary. McManus visits him, demanding to know who supplied the drugs, but Hill refuses to rat on his source. When Redding discovers that Busmalis lied about DeSantos, his fury leads him to believe Poet's next deception—that the Latinos were responsible. His confrontation with Morales gets the two of them thrown in the Hole. Cyril is convicted of Li Chen's murder and Ryan refuses to agree to appeal for clemency on the grounds of Cyril's mental impairment, thinking that death is preferable to having Cyril spend the rest of his life in Oz. Meanwhile Sister Pete, Father Meehan, and Suzanne Fitzgerald meet to devise another strategy in Cyril's defense. O'Reily colludes with the hacks to lure Jia Kenmin into a situation where they can beat him. When Father Meehan confronts O'Reily about his position on Cyril's fate, Ryan reveals the story of his abusive and unhappy childhood. Penders disobeys C.O. Lopresti's order to clean up dogshit from the floor of the Common Room, so Lopresti beats him, and Penders sics his guide dog (which he's secretly trained to attack) on the hack. Alvarez alone has successfully trained his dog to perform its intended service. Rebadow fumes over not getting the lottery money which he intended to use to get a bone-marrow transplant for his grandson. McManus searches Oz's databases for a suitable donor and finds an inmate named Woodward. When Rebadow meets Woodward to make his request, the man prefers to keep his white ancestry secret rather than give Alex a chance to live. Next, Rebadow seeks a faith healer for his grandson, but he meets with resistance from his family. Clarence, Kirk's arsonist connection, testifies against Timmy, who denies the charges of his involvement in the rectory fire. Peter Schibetta comes back to Sister Pete after talking to Dr. Nathan, better able to deal with his rape. The rumor that Robson's replacement gums were from a black cadaver impels Robson to assault the dentist, who quits his job in a hurry, but not before telling Poet to spread the word that Robson's gum donor was a person of color. Robson lands in the Hole, and Schillinger consults with an Aryan Nation leader, resulting in Robson

being declared impure and getting expelled from the Brotherhood. Said and Beecher discuss Guenzel's quandary. Beecher confesses that he's responsible for abandoning Guenzel to Schillinger. Said counsels Beecher to have nothing further to do with Keller, but McManus rejects Beecher's request to give up his job in the mailroom. Sister Pete questions Guenzel about his rape. He claims to know nothing about his attackers' identities, but curses Beecher. When Sister Pete tries to get information from Beecher, Said, and Schillinger, they clam up and she expresses her disgust with them. Schillinger hatches a plan to force Guenzel to attempt to escape, and he is electrocuted on the prison's perimeter fence.

EPISODE EIGHT

Impotence

Desperate to get back at the Aryan Brotherhood, Robson buys heroin to use as an anesthetic and attempts to cut the grafted gums out of his mouth himself. The operation fails and Robson is moved out of Schillinger's cell. McManus tells Glynn that he's going to support Alvarez's bid for parole, but Miguel's hearing doesn't go well. When a belligerent Parole Board member questions him accusingly about his record, Alvarez loses his composure and physically attacks the man. Dr. Nathan's guilt worsens as Pancamo slips into a coma from the septic infection he contracted in the infirmary. Schillinger tells new inmate Cutler he has to kill a black inmate to qualify for membership in the "Brotherhood," so Cutler selects Said as his victim. White learns of the plan and in his attempt to protect Said, now his close friend and role model, he nearly strangles Cutler. When McManus sends White to Solitary, Said accuses the unit manager of racism, because Omar's motive was to protect a black man's life. Rebadow gets permission to visit his dying grandson, Alex, in the hospital. Busmalis finally gets a letter from Norma. She wants to visit him, and when she does, he discovers she's pregnant—with another man's baby. The night Rebadow returns to Oz, Alex dies. Brass returns, repentant, intending to give his lottery winnings to their rightful owner, but he's too late. Beecher's mother visits with a report on Guenzel's funeral, and Beecher is inspired to offer to help Guenzel's friend Franklin Winthrop, but Winthrop's not interested. At the next interaction session, Beecher decides to tell Sister Pete what he knows about Guenzel and Winthrop, resuling in Schillinger getting convicted of rape. He is transferred to Solitary indefinitely. Keller is found guilty of one of the homosexual murders and is moved to Death Row. Beecher visits Keller,

over Said's objections. Cyril becomes Keller's Death Row neighbor, and gets violent when the hacks try to confine him in his new cell. Father Meehan overcomes Ryan's antagonism, getting him to recall the emotionally wrenching death of his infant sister, Carolyn, as a result of their father's mistreatment. After finally confronting his father with the truth, O'Reily has a change of heart and dedicates himself to saving Cyril's life. Hill, out of the infirmary and back in Em City, assures Poet that he takes full responsibility for his drug use and not to worry about Redding. McManus demands that the Wise Guys and Latinos make peace in their drug wars, and they agree, but Morales and Urbano decide to eliminate Redding. Hill and Redding have a heart-to-heart talk, wherein Redding blames himself for Hill's involvement in drugs and subsequent problems. They return to the Common Room together, just in time for one of the Wise Guys to attempt to assassinate Burr. Hill propels himself into the path of the shank and becomes the latest victim of the prison's violence.

•　•　•　•　•

MIGUEL ALVAREZ

Grandfather: Ricardo
Father: Eduardo
Mother: Carmen
Girlfriend: Maritza
Son

TOBIAS BEECHER

Father: Harrison
Mother: Victoria
Brother: Angus
Grandmother: Cordelia
Wife: Genevieve
Older Son: Gary
Daughter: Holly
Younger Son: Harry
Genevieve's Father: Jonah
Genevieve's Mother: Margaret

AUGUSTUS HILL

Mother: Eugenia
Wife: Annabella

LEO GLYNN

Brother: Mark
Wife: Mary
Oldest Daughter: Ardeth

CHRIS KELLER

Ex-wife: Bonnie
Ex-wife: Kitty
Ex-wife: Angelique

TIMOTHY McMANUS

Ex-wife: Eleanor O'Connor

GLORIA NATHAN

Husband: Preston
Preston's Mother: Patricia
Preston's Father: Lars

RYAN O'REILY

Father: Sheamus
Mother: Suzanne Fitzgerald
Aunt: Brenda
Brother: Cyril
Cyril's Mother: Tess
Cousin: Matthew
Sister: Carolyn
Ex-wife: Shannon

SISTER PETER MARIE REIMONDO

Husband: Leonard

KAREEM SAID

Sister: Harriet Truman

VERN SCHILLINGER

Father: Heinrick
Sister: Greta Schillinger Weinstein
Wife: Martha
Son: Andrew
Son: Hank
Daughter-in-law: Kerry
Granddaughter: Jewel

Cast List

ACTORS	CHARACTERS	ACTORS	CHARACTERS
Kirk Acevedo	*Miguel Alvarez*	Robert Clohessy	*Sean Murphy*
Granville Adams	*Zahir Arif*	Kevin Conway	*Sheamus O'Reily*
Adewale Akinnuoye-Agbaje	*Simon Adebisi*	Will Cote	*William Cudney*
Mary Alice	*Eugenia Hill*	Peter Criss	*Martin Montgomery*
Jamar Allah	*Supreme Allah*	Douglas Crosby	*Vic D'Agnasti*
Whitney Allen	*Miss Sally*	Michael Delmare	*Jia Kenmin*
Dena Atlantic	*Floria Mills*	Jonathan Demme	*PSA Director*
Zuill Bailey	*Eugene Dobbins*	Carl DiMaggio	*Len Lopresti*
Andrew Barchilon	*Hank Schillinger*	John Doman	*Edward Gallson*
Arija Bareikis	*Tricia Ross*	Mike Doyle	*Adam Guenzel*
Brian Bloom	*Ronald Barlog*	Sean Dugan	*Timmy Kirk*
Robert Bogue	*Jason Cramer*	Charles "Roc" Dutton	*Alvah Case*
Tim Brown	*Jason Armstrong*	Kathryn Erbe	*Shirley Bellinger*
Betty Lynn Buckley	*Suzanne Fitzgerald*	Bill Fagerbakke	*Karl Metzger*
Charles Busch	*Nat Ginzburg*	Edie Falco	*Diane Whittlesey*
Philip Casnoff	*Nikolai Stanislofsky*	Cyrus Farmer	*Adrian Johnson*
Reg E. Cathey	*Martin Querns*	Rick Fox	*Jackson Vahue*
Anthony Chisholm	*Burr Redding*	Mtume Gant	*Reggie Rawls*

ACTORS	CHARACTERS	ACTORS	CHARACTERS
Seth Gilliam	*Clayton Hughes*	Tom Ligon	*Alvin Yood*
Mike G. Goodfella	*Joey D'Angelo*	LLCool J	*Jiggy Walker*
Luis Guzman	*Raoul Hernandez*	Domenick Lombardozzi	*Ralph Gulino*
Uta Hagen	*Gwendolyn Rebadow*	John Lurie	*Greg Penders*
Juan Carlos Hernandez	*Carlo Ricardo*	Gavin MacLeod	*Cardinal Abgott*
Edward Herrmann	*Harrison Beecher*	Eddie Malavarca	*Peter Schibetta*
Ernie Hudson	*Leo Glynn*	Tom Mardirosian	*Agamemnon Busmalis*
Ernie Hudson Jr	*Hamid Khan*	Mark Margolis	*Antonio Nappa*
Zeljko Ivanek	*Governor James Devlin*	Malachy McCourt	*Dylan Meehan*
David Johansen	*Eli Zabitz*	Ellen McElduff	*Eleanor O'Connor*
Melina Kanakaredes	*Marilyn Crenshaw*	Anne Meara	*Brenda O'Reily*
Jinn Kim	*Kuang Gongjin*	Chris Meloni	*Chris Keller*
Erik King	*Moses Deyell*	Method Man	*Tug Daniels*
Terry Kinney	*Tim McManus*	Zakes Mokae	*Kipkemi Jara*
Fred Koehler	*Andrew Schillinger*	Rita Moreno	*Sister Peter Marie Reimondo*
Jordan Lage	*Richie Hanlon*	George Morfogen	*Bob Rebadow*
Jenna Lamia	*Carrie Schillinger*	muMs	*Poet*
David Lansbury	*Robert Sippel*	Tony Musante	*Nino Schibetta*
Leon	*Jefferson Keane*	Brian O'Byrne	*Padriac Connolly*
Carlos Leon	*Carlos Martinez*	Harry O'Reilly	*Bruno Goergen*
Toni Lewis	*Alicia Hinden*	Milo O'Shea	*Dr. Frederick Garvey*

ACTORS	CHARACTERS	ACTORS	CHARACTERS
Austin Pendleton	*William Giles*	J.K. Simmons	*Vern Schillinger*
Pepa	*Andrea Phelan*	Jacques Smith	*Leroy Tidd*
Harold Perrineau	*Augustus Hill*	Elaine Stritch	*Grace Lema*
Luke Perry	*Jeremiah Cloutier*	Lee Tergesen	*Tobias Beecher*
Andy Powers	*Franklin Winthrop*	Treach	*Malcolm Coyle*
Sandra Purpuro	*Catherine McClain*	Nelson Vasquez	*Eugene Rivera*
Michael Quill	*Mark Miles*	Lauren Velez	*Gloria Nathan*
Lance Reddick	*Desmond Mobay/John Basil*	Ben Vareen	*A.R. Whitworth*
Roger Rees	*Jack Eldridge*	Thomas G. Waites	*Henry Stanton*
Judy Reyes	*Tina Rivera*	Eamonn Walker	*Kareem Said*
Blake Robbins	*Dave Brass*	Joel West	*Glen Shupe*
Eric Roberts	*Richard L'Italien*	Sean Whitesell	*Donald Groves*
R.E. Rodgers	*James Robson*	Kathleen Widdoes	*Victoria Beecher*
Kristen Rohde	*Claire Howell*	J.D. Williams	*Kenny Wangler*
Steve Ryan	*Michael Healy*	Dean Winters	*Ryan O'Reily*
Otto Sanchez	*Chico Guerra*	Scott William Winters	*Cyril O'Reily*
Michelle Schumacher	*Norma Clark*	B.D. Wong	*Father Ray Mukada*
Phil Scozzarella	*Joe Mineo*	Michael Wright	*Omar White*
Jon Seda	*Dino Ortolani*	Emmanuel Yarbrough	*Clarence Seroy*
Evan Seinfeld	*Jaz Hoyt*	David Zayas	*Enrique Morales*
Ally Sheedy	*Lisa Logan*	Chuck Zito	*Chucky Pancamo*

All poetry included in this book is written by muMs, who portrays Poet on the television series *Oz.*

|||| |||| |||| |||| |||| ||||